Alta Ma
February, 1960
Aunt Helen

Eleanor Childs.
1903.

A. D.

Alice M. Dix,
825 N. Water,
Wichita,
Kans.

Oct. 1912.

In Connection with

The De Willoughby Claim

In Connection with
The De Willoughby Claim

By

Frances Hodgson Burnett

New York
Charles Scribner's Sons
1899

In Connection with The De Willoughby Claim

CHAPTER I

HIGH noon at Talbot's Cross-roads, with the mercury standing at ninety-eight in the shade—though there was not much shade worth mentioning in the immediate vicinity of the Cross-roads post-office, about which, upon the occasion referred to, the few human beings within sight and sound were congregated. There were trees enough a few hundred yards away, but the post-office stood boldly and unflinchingly in the blazing sun. The roads crossing each other stretched themselves as far as the eye could follow them, the red clay transformed into red dust which even an ordinarily lively imagination might have fancied was red hot. The shrill, rattling cry of the grasshoppers, hidden in the long yellow sedge-grass and drouth-smitten corn, pierced the stillness now and then with a suddenness startling each time it broke forth, because the interval between each of the pipings was given by the hearers to drowsiness or heated unconscious naps.

In such napping and drowsiness the present occupants of the post-office were indulging. Upon two empty goods boxes two men in copperas-coloured jean garments reclined in easy attitudes, their hats tilted over their eyes, while sev-

1

eral others balanced their split-seated chairs against the house or the post-porch and dozed.

Inside the store the postmaster and proprietor tilted his chair against the counter and dozed also, though fitfully, and with occasional restless changes of position and smothered maledictions against the heat. He was scarcely the build of man to sleep comfortably at high noon in midsummer. His huge, heavy body was rather too much for him at any time, but during the hot weather he succumbed beneath the weight of his own flesh. Hamlin County knew him as " Big Tom D'Willerby," and, indeed, rather prided itself upon him as a creditable possession. It noted any increase in his weight, repeated his jokes, and bore itself patiently under his satire. His indolence it regarded with leniency not entirely untinged with secret exultation.

" *The* derndest, laziest critter," his acquaintances would remark to each other; " the *derndest* I do reckon that ever the Lord made. Nigh unto three hundred he weighs, and never done a lick o' work in his life. Not one! Lord, no! Tom D'Willerby work? I guess not. He gits on fine without any o' that in his'n. Work ain't his kind. It's a pleasin' sight to see him lyin' round thar to the post-office an' the boys a-waitin' on to him, doin' his tradin' for him, an' sortin' the mail when it comes in. They're ready enough to do it jest to hear him gas."

And so they were. About eight years before the time the present story commences, he had appeared upon the scene apparently having no object in view but to make himself as comfortable as possible. He took up his quarters at one of the farm-houses among the mountains, paid his hostess regularly for the simple accommodations she could afford him, and, before three months passed, had established his reputation and, without making the slightest apparent effort, had gathered about him a large circle of friends and admirers.

"His name's D'Willerby," Mrs. Pike would drawl when questioned about him, "an' he's kin to them D'Willerbys that's sich big bugs down to D'Lileville. I guess they ain't much friendly, though. He don't seem to like to have nothin' much to say about 'em. Seems like he has money a-plenty to carry him along, an' he talks some o' settin' up a store somewhars."

In the course of a month or so he carried out the plan, selecting Talbot's Cross-roads as the site for the store in question. He engaged hands to erect a frame building, collected by the assistance of some mysterious agency a heterogeneous stock consisting of calicoes, tinware, coffee, sugar, tobacco, and various waif and stray commodities, and, having done so, took his seat on the porch one morning and announced the establishment open.

Upon the whole, the enterprise was a success. Barnesville was fifteen miles distant, and the farmers, their wives and daughters, were glad enough to stop at the Cross-roads for their calico dresses and store-coffee. By doing so they were saved a long ride and gained superior conversational advantages. "D'Willerby's mighty easy to trade with," it was said.

There was always a goodly number of "critters" tied to the fence-corners, and consequently to business was added the zest of society and the interchanging of gossip. "D'Willerby's" became a centre of interest and attraction, and D'Willerby himself a county institution.

Big Tom, however, studiously avoided taking a too active part in the duties of the establishment. Having with great forethought provided himself with a stout chair which could be moved from behind the counter to the door, and from the door to the store as the weather demanded, he devoted himself almost exclusively to sitting in it and encouraging a friendly and accommodating spirit in his visitors and admirers. The more youthful of those admirers he found useful in the extreme.

"Boys," he would say, "a man can't do more than a thousand things at once. A man can't talk a steady stream and do himself justice, and settle the heftiest kind of questions, and say the kind of things these ladies ought to have said to 'em, and then measure out molasses and weigh coffee and slash off calico dresses and trade for eggs. Some of you've got to roust out and do some clerking, or I've got to quit. I've not got the constitution to stand it. Jim, you 'tend to Mis' Pike, and Bill, you wait on Mis' Jones. Lord! Lord! half a dozen of you here, and not one doing a thing —not a derned thing! Do you want me to get up and leave Miss Mirandy and do things myself? We've got to settle about the colour of this gown. How'd you feel now, if it wasn't becoming to her complexion? Just help yourself to that plug of tobacco, Hance, and lay your ten cents in the cash drawer, and then you can weigh out that butter of Mis' Simpson's."

When there was a prospect of a post-office at the Crossroads, there was only one opinion as to who was the man best calculated to adorn the position of postmaster.

"The store's right yere, Tom," said his patrons, "an' you're right yere. Ye can write and spell off things 'thout any trouble, an' I reckon ye wouldn't mind the extry two dollars comin' in ev'ry month."

"Lord! Lord!" groaned Tom, who was stretched full length on the floor of the porch when the subject was first

4

broached. " Do you want a man to kill himself out an' out, boys? Work himself into eternal kingdom come? Who'd do the extra work, I'd like to know—empty out the mail-bag and hand out the mail, and do the extra cussin'? That would be worth ten dollars a month. And, like as not, the money would be paid in cheques, and who's goin' to sign 'em? Lord! I believe you think a man's immortal soul could be bought for fifty cents a day. You don't allow for the wear and tear on a fellow's constitution, boys."

But he allowed himself to be placed in receipt of the official salary in question, and the matter of extra labour settled itself. Twice a week a boy on horseback brought the mail-bag from Barnesville, and when this youth drew rein before the porch Big Tom greeted him from indoors with his habitual cordiality.

" 'Light, sonny, 'light! " he would call out in languidly sonorous tones; " come in and let these fellows hear the news. Just throw that mail-bag on the counter and let's hear from you. Plenty of good water down at the spring. Might as well take that bucket and fill it if you want a drink. I've been waiting for just such a man as you to do it. These fellows would sit here all day and let a man die. I can't get anything out of 'em. I've about half a mind to quit sometimes and leave them to engineer the thing themselves. Look here now, is any fellow going to attend to that mail, or is it going to lie there till I have to get up and attend to it myself? I reckon that's what you want. I reckon that 'd just suit you. Jehoshaphat! I guess you'd like me to take charge of the eternal universe."

It was for the mail he waited with his usual complement of friends and assistants on the afternoon referred to at the opening of this chapter. The boy was behind time, and, under the influence of the heat, conversation had at first flagged and then subsided. Big Tom himself had taken the initiative of dropping into a doze, and his companions had one by one followed his example, or at least made an effort at doing so. The only one of the number who remained unmistakably awake was a little man who sat on the floor of the end of the porch, his small legs, encased in large blue jean pantaloons, dangling over the side. This little man, who was gently and continuously ruminating, with brief "asides" of expectoration, kept his eyes fixed watchfully upon the Barnesville Road, and he it was who at last roused the dozers.

"Thar's some un a-comin'," he announced in a meek voice. "'Tain't him."

Big Tom opened his eyes, stretched himself, and gradually rose in his might, proving a very tight fit for the establishment, especially the doorway, towards which he lounged, supporting himself against its side.

"Who is it, Ezra?" he asked, almost extinguishing the latter cognomen with a yawn.

"It's thet thar feller!"

All the other men awakened in a body. Whomsoever the individual might be, he had the power to rouse them to a lively exhibition of interest. One and all braced themselves to look at the horseman approaching along the Barnesville Road.

"He's a kinder curi's-lookin' feller," observed one philosopher.

"Well, at a distance of half a mile, perhaps he is," said Tom. "In a cloud of dust and the sun blazin' down on him like thunderation, I don't know but you're right, Nath."

"Git out!" replied Nath, placidly. "He's a curi's-actin'

feller, anyway. Don't go nowhar nor hev nothin' to say to nobody. Jest sets right down in that thar holler with his wife, as if b'ars an' painters wus all a man or woman wanted round 'em."

" She's a doggoned purty critter," said the little man in large trousers, placidly. He had not appeared to listen to the conversation, but, as this pertinent remark proved, it had not been lost on him.

His observation was greeted with a general laugh, which seemed to imply that the speaker had a character which his speech sustained.

" Whar did ye see her, Stamps? " was asked.

The little man remained unmoved, still dangling his legs over the porch side, still ruminating, still gazing with pale, blinking eyes up the road.

" Went over the mountain to 'tend court to Bakersville, an' took it on my road to go by thar. She was settin' in the door, an' I see her afore she seen me. When she hearn the sound of my mule's feet, she got up an' went into the house. It was a powerful hot mornin', 'n' I wus mighty dry, 'n' I stopped fur a cool drink. She didn't come out when fust I hollered, 'n' when she did come, she looked kinder skeered 'n' wouldn't talk none. Kep' her sunbonnet over her face, like she didn't want to be seen overmuch."

" What does she look like, Ezry? " asked one of the younger men.

Mr. Stamps meditated a few seconds.

" Don't look like none o' the women folk about yere," he replied, finally. " She ain't their kind."

" What d'ye mean by that? "

" Dunno eggsactly. She's mighty white 'n' young-lookin' 'n' delicate—but that ain't all."

7

In Connection with
The De Willoughby Claim

Tom made a restless movement.

"Look here, boys," he broke in, suddenly, "here's a nice business—a lot of fellows asking questions about a woman an' gossiping as if there wasn't a thing better to do. Leave 'em alone, if they want to be left alone—leave 'em alone."

Mr. Stamps expectorated in an entirely unbiassed manner. He seemed as willing to leave his story alone as he had been to begin it.

"He's comin' yere," he said, softly, after a pause. "Thet's whar he's comin'."

The rest of the company straightened themselves in their seats and made an effort to assume the appearance of slightly interested spectators. It became evident that Mr. Stamps was right, and that the rider was about to dismount.

He was a man about thirty years of age, thin, narrow-chested, and stooping. His coarse clothes seemed specially ill-suited to his slender figure, his black hair was long, and his beard neglected; his broad hat was pulled low over his eyes and partially concealed his face.

"He don't look none too sociable when he's nigher than half a mile," remarked Nath in an undertone.

He glanced neither to the right nor to the left as he strode past the group into the store. Strange to relate, Tom had lounged behind the counter and stood ready to attend him. He asked for a few necessary household trifles in a low tone, and, as Tom collected and made them into a clumsy package, he stood and looked on with his back turned towards the door.

Those gathered upon the porch listened eagerly for the sound of conversation, but none reached their ears. Tom moved heavily to and fro for a few minutes, and then the parcel was handed across the counter.

"Hot weather," said the stranger, without raising his eyes.

"Yes," said Tom, "hot weather, sir."

"Good-day," said the stranger.

"Good-day," answered Tom.

And his customer took his departure. He passed out as he had passed in; but while he was indoors little Mr. Stamps had changed his position. He now sat near the wooden steps, his legs dangling as before, his small countenance as non-committal as ever. As the stranger neared him, he raised his pale little eyes, blinked them, indulged in a slight jerk of the head, and uttered a single word of greeting.

"Howdy?"

The stranger started, glanced down at him, and walked on. He made no answer, untied his horse, mounted it, and rode back over the Barnesville Road towards the mountain.

Mr. Stamps remained seated near the steps and blinked after him silently until he was out of sight.

"Ye didn't seem to talk none, D'Willerby," said one of the outsiders when Tom reappeared.

Tom sank into his chair, thrust his hands into his pockets, and stretched his limbs out to their fullest capacity.

"Let a man rest, boys," he said, "let a man rest!"

He was silent for some time afterwards, and even on the arrival of the mail was less discursive than usual. It was Mr. Stamps who finally aroused him from his reverie.

Having obtained his mail—one letter in a legal-looking envelope—and made all other preparations to return to the bosom of his family, Stamps sidled up to the counter, and, leaning over it, spoke in an insinuatingly low tone:

"She was bar'foot," he said, mildly, "'n' she hadn't been raised to it—that was one thing. Her feet wus as soft 'n' tender as a baby's; 'n' fur another thing, her hands wus

9

as white as her face, 'n' whiter. Thet ain't the way we raise 'em in Hamlin County—that's all."

And, having said it, he slipped out of the store, mounted his mule, and jogged homeward on the Barnesville Road also.

CHAPTER II

BEFORE the war there were no people better known or more prominent in their portion of the State than the De Willoughbys of Delisle County, Tennessee. To have been born a De Willoughby was, in general opinion, to have been born with a silver spoon in one's mouth. It was indeed to have been born to social dignity, fortune, courage, and more than the usual allowance of good looks. And though the fortune was lavishly spent, the courage sometimes betrayed into a rather theatrical dare-deviltry, and the good looks prone to deteriorate in style, there was always the social position left, and this was a matter of the deepest importance in Delisleville. The sentiments of Delisleville were purely patrician. It was the county town, and contained six thousand inhabitants, two hotels, and a court-house. It had also two or three business streets and half a dozen churches, all very much at odds with each other and each seriously inclined to disbelieve in the probable salvation of the rest. The " first families " (of which there were eight or ten, with numerous branches) attended the Episcopal Church, the second best the Presbyterian, while the inferior classes, who could scarcely be counted at all, since they had not been born in Delisleville, drifted to the Methodists.

The De Willoughbys attended the Episcopal Church, and, being generally endowed with voices, two or three of them sang in the choir, which was composed entirely of members

11

of the attending families and executed most difficult music in a manner which was the cause after each service of much divided opinion. Opinion was divided because the choir was divided—separated, in fact, into several small, select cliques, each engaged in deadly and bitter feud with the rest. When the moon-eyed soprano arose, with a gentle flutter, and opened her charming mouth in solo, her friends settled themselves in their pews with a general rustle of satisfaction, while the friends of the contralto exchanged civilly significant glances; and on the way home the solo in question was disposed of in a manner at once thorough and final. The same thing occurred when the contralto was prominent, or the tenor, or the baritone, or the basso, each of whom it was confidently asserted by competent Delisleville judges might have rendered him or herself and Delisleville immortal upon the lyric stage if social position had not placed the following of such a profession entirely out of the question. There had indeed been some slight trouble in one or two of the best families, occasioned by the musical fervour of youthful scions who were in danger of being led into indiscretions by their enthusiasm.

The De Willoughbys occupied one of the most prominent pews in the sacred edifice referred to. Judge De Willoughby, a large, commanding figure, with a fine sweep of long hair, mustache and aquiline profile; Mrs. De Willoughby (who had been a Miss Vanuxem of South Carolina), slender, willowy, with faded brunette complexion and still handsome brunette eyes, and three or four little De Willoughbys, all more or less pretty and picturesque. These nearly filled the pew. The grown-up Misses De Willoughby sang with two of their brothers in the choir. There were three sons, Romaine, De Courcy, and Thomas. But Thomas did not sing in the choir. Thomas, alas! did not sing at all. Thomas, it was universally conceded by every De Willoughby of the clan, was a dismal failure. Even from his earliest boyhood, when he had been a huge, overgrown fellow, whose only redeeming qualities were his imperturbable good-humor and his ponderous wit, his family had regarded him with a sense of despair. In the first place, he was too big. His brothers were tall, lithe-limbed youths, who were graceful, dark-eyed, dark-haired, and had a general air of brilliancy. They figured well at college and in their world; they sang and danced in a manner which, combining itself with the name of De Willoughby, gave them quite an ennobled sort of distinction, a touch of patrician bravado added to their picturesqueness in the eyes of the admiring; and their little indiscretions were of a nature to be ignored or treated with gentle consideration as the natural result of their youth, spirit, and Southern blood. But at nineteen Thomas had attained a height of six feet five, with a proportionate breadth and ponderousness. His hands and feet were a disgrace to a De Willoughby, and his voice was a roar when he was influenced by anything like emotion. Displays of emotion, however, were but rare occurrences with him. He was too lazy to be roused to anger or any other violent feeling. He spent his leisure hours in lying upon sofas or chairs and getting very much in everybody's way. He lounged through school and college without the slightest *éclat* attending his progress.

It became the pastime of the household to make rather a butt of him, and for the most part he bore himself under the difficulties of his position peaceably enough, though there had been times when his weighty retorts had caused some sharp wincing.

"You're an ill-natured devil, Tom," his brother De

Courcy said to him, as he stood fingering the ornaments on the mantel after one such encounter. " You're an ill-natured devil."

Tom was stretched on a sofa, with his big hands under his head, and did not condescend to look around.

" I'm not such a thundering fool as you take me for, that's all," he answered. " I've got my eyes open. Keep to your side of the street, and I will keep to mine."

It was true that he had his eyes open and had more wit and feeling than they gave him credit for. No one understood him, not even his mother, who had deplored him from the first hour of his over-weighted babyhood, when she had given him over to the care of his negro nurse in despair.

In the midst of a large family occupied with all the small gaieties attendant upon popularity and social distinction in a provincial town, he lived a lonely life, and one not without its pathetic side if it had been so looked upon. But even he himself had never regarded the matter from a sentimental point of view. He endeavoured to resign himself to his fate and meet it philosophically.

" I wasn't cut out for this sort of thing, boys," he had said to his friends at college, where he had been rather popular. " I wasn't cut out for it. Go ahead and leave me behind. I'm not a bad sort of fellow, but there is too much of me in one way and too little in another. What the Lord made such a man as me for after six thousand years' experience, I haven't found out yet. A man may as well make up his mind about himself first as last. I've made up mine and nobody differs from me so far as I've gone."

When he left college his brothers had already chosen their vocations. Delisle County knew them as promising young lawyers, each having distinguished himself with much fiery eloquence in an occasional case. The cases had not always been gained, but the fervour and poetry of the appeals to the rather muddled and startled agriculturists who formed the juries were remembered with admiration and as being worthy of Delisleville, and were commented upon in the Delisleville *Oriflamme* as the " fit echoings of an eloquence long known in our midst as the birthright of those bearing one of our proudest names, an eloquence spurred to its eagle flights by the warm, chivalric blood of a noble race."

But the " warm, chivalric blood " of the race in question seemed to move but slowly in veins of its most substantial representative. The inertness of his youngest son roused that fine old Southern gentleman and well-known legal dignitary, Judge De Willoughby, to occasional outbursts of the fiery eloquence before referred to which might well have been productive of remarkable results.

" Good God, sir! " he would trumpet forth, " good God, sir! have we led the State for generation after generation to be disgraced and degraded and dragged in the dust by one of our own stock at last? The De Willoughbys have been gentlemen, sir, distinguished at the bar, in politics, and in the highest social circles of the South; and here we have a De Willoughby whose tastes would be no credit to— to his overseer, a De Willoughby who has apparently neither the ambition nor the qualification to shine in the sphere in which he was born! Blow your damned brains out, if you have any; blow your damned brains out, and let's have an end of the whole disgraceful business."

This referred specially to Tom's unwillingness to enter upon the study of medicine, which had been chosen for him.

" I should make a better farmer," he said, bitterly, after

15

a prolonged discussion. " I'm not the build for women's bedrooms and children's bedsides. De Courcy would have suited you better."

" De Courcy is a gentleman—a gentleman, sir! He was born one and would shine in any profession a gentleman may adorn. As for you, this is the only thing left for you, and you shall try it, by G——! "

" Oh," said Tom, " I'll try it. I can only fail, and I've done that before."

He did try it forthwith, applying himself to his studies with a persistence quite creditable. He read lying upon sofas and lounging in the piazzas, and in course of time was sent to attend lectures in Philadelphia.

Whether he could have gained his diploma or not was never decided. Those of the professors who commented on him at all, spoke of him as slow but persevering, and re-garded him rather as a huge receiving machine of orderly habits. The Judge began to congratulate himself upon his determination, and his mother thought it " a good thing poor Tom was disposed of."

But one terrible morning just before the first course of lectures was completed, he suddenly returned, walking into the Judge's office without any previous intimation of his intention.

When he turned in his seat and confronted him, the Judge lost his breath.

" You! " he cried; " you! "

" Yes," said Tom, " I've come back." He was rather pale and nervous, but there was a dogged, resigned look in his eyes. " I've made up my mind," he added, " that I cannot stand it. Turn me loose on one of your plantations to—to boss niggers. You said once I was fit for an overseer.

16

Perhaps you weren't wrong. Say the word and I'll start to-morrow."

The Judge's aquiline countenance turned gray with fury. His fine mustache seemed to curl itself anew.

" You—you accursed scoundrel! " he gasped. " You accursed, underbred hound! Tell me what this means, or I'll strangle you."

" You'll say I'm a fool," said Tom, " and I suppose it's true, and—and——" with a tremour in his voice, " I've no need to be particular about the names you call me. I ought to be used to them by this time."

" Speak out," thundered the Judge, " and tell me the whole disgraceful truth! "

" It won't take long," said Tom; " I told it when I said I'd made up my mind I couldn't stand it. I've been walking the hospitals and attending the clinics for the last three months, and I've had a chance to see what my life would be if I went through. I've seen things to make a man tremble when they came back to him in the dead of night— agony and horror—women and children! Good Lord! I can't tell you. De Courcy could, but I can't. I'd rather be in hell than live such a life day after day. I tried to stand up against it at first. I thought I might get used to it, but I haven't the nerve—or something was wrong. It got worse and worse, until I used to start up out of my sleep in a cold sweat, hearing screams and groans and prayers. That was the worst of all—their prayers to us to help them and not to hurt them. Four days ago a child was brought in—a child four or five years old. There was an operation to be performed, and I was the man chosen to hold it still. Its mother was sent out of the room. My God! how it screamed when it saw her go and knew it was to be left to us. They told me to hold it because I was the strongest, and—and I put my hands on it. I'm a big fellow to look at, and I suppose it knew there was no help for it when I came near. It turned as white as death and looked up at me with the tears streaming down its face. Before the operation was half over it hadn't the strength left to scream or struggle, and it lay and looked at me and moaned. I should have given up the job, but somehow I couldn't make up my mind to—to leave it. When it was all done, I gave it back to its mother and went to my rooms. I turned sick on the way and had to sit down to rest. I swore then I'd let the thing drop, and I bought my ticket and came back. I'm not the man for the work. Better men may do it— perhaps it takes better men. I'm not up to it." And his shaken voice broke as he hung his great head.

A deadly calm settled upon the Judge. He pointed to the door.

" Go home to your mother, sir," he said, " I've done with you. Go and stay with the women. That's the place for you."

" He's a coward as well as a fool," he said afterwards in the bosom of his family; " a white-livered fool who hasn't the nerve to look at a sick child."

It was a terrible day for the household, but at last it was over. Tom went to his room in an apathy. He had been buffeted and scorned and held up to bitter derision until he had ceased to feel anything but a negative, helpless misery.

About a week later Delia Vanuxem appeared upon the scene. Delia Vanuxem was a young cousin of Mrs. De Willoughby's, and had come to pay her relatives a visit. It was the hospitable custom of Delisleville to cultivate its kinsfolk—more especially its kinswomen. There were always in two or three of the principal families young lady guests who were during their stay in the town the sensation of the hour. Novelty established them as temporary belles; they were petted by their hostesses, attended by small cohorts of admirers, and formed the centre for a round of festivities specially arranged to enliven their visits.

Delia Vanuxem bore away the palm from all such visitors past or to come. She was a true Southern beauty, with the largest dark eyes, the prettiest yielding manner, and the very smallest foot Delisleville had ever fallen prostrate before, it being well known among her admirers that one of her numerous male cousins had once measured her little slipper with a cigar—a story in which Delisleville delighted. And she was not only a pretty, but also a lovable and tender-hearted young creature. Her soft eyes and soft voice did not belie her. She was gentle and kindly to all around her. Mrs. De Willoughby and the two older girls fell in love with her at once, and the Judge himself was aroused to an eloquence of compliment and a courtly grandeur of demeanour which rose even beyond his usual efforts in a line in which he had always shone. The very negroes adored her and vied with each other to do her service.

It was quite natural that a nature so sweet and sympathetic should be awakened to pity for the one member of the gay household who seemed cut off from the rest, and who certainly at the time existed under a darker cloud than usual.

From the first she was more considerate of poor Tom than anyone who had ever been before, and more than once, as he sat silent and gloomy at the table, he looked up to find her lovely eyes resting upon his big frame with a questioning, pitying glance.

" He is so much too big, Aunt Jule," she wrote home once. " And he seems somehow to feel as if he was always in the way, and, indeed, he is a little sometimes, poor fellow! and everyone appears to think he is only a joke or a mistake; but I have made up my mind never to laugh at him at all as the other girls do. It seems so unkind, and surely he must feel it."

She never did laugh at him, and sometimes even tried to talk to him, and once drew him out so far in an artful, innocent way, that he told her something of his medical failure and the reasons for it, manifestly ashamed of the story as he related it, and yet telling it so well in a few clumsy, rather disconnected sentences, that when he had finished her eyelashes were wet and she broke into a little shuddering sigh.

" Oh! " she said, " I don't think you are to blame, really. I have often thought that I could never, never bear to do such things, though, of course, if there was no one to do them it would be dreadful; but——"

" Yes," said Tom, " there it is. Someone must do it, and I know I'm a confounded coward and ninny, but—but I couldn't." And he looked overwhelmed with humiliation.

" But after all," she said, in the soft voice which had always the sound of appeal in it, " after all, I'm sure it was because you have a kind heart, and a kind heart is worth a great deal. You will do something else."

" There is nothing else for me to do," he said, mournfully; " nothing that won't disgrace the rest, they tell me."

It was small wonder that this was his final undoing, though neither was to blame. Certainly no fault could be attached to the young creature who meant to be kind to him, as it was her nature to be to all surrounding her; and surely Tom's great and final blunder arose from no presumption on his part. He had never thought of aspiring to the proud position with regard to her which Romaine and De Courcy seemed to occupy by natural right. It was only now and then, when they were unavoidably engaged, that he had the courage to offer his services as messenger or escort, but even those rare pleasures were a little too much for him. He was so unused to such privileges that they intoxicated him and set his mind in a whirl which prevented his thinking clearly, or, indeed, ever thinking at all sometimes.

Even when it was all over, he scarcely knew how he had been betrayed into the weakness he was guilty of. It was not like him to lose sight of his manifold imperfections; but for once they were swept out of his mind by a momentary madness.

It was on the occasion of a ball at the Delisle House. The Delisle House was the principal hotel, and all important festivities were held in its long dining-hall disguised as a ball-room. The ball was given by a gallant Delisleville Club in honour of Miss Delia Vanuxem, and it was a very magnificent affair indeed. The disguise of the dining-room was complete. It was draped with flags and decorated with wreaths of cedar and paper roses. A band of coloured gentlemen, whose ardour concealed any slight musical discrepancies, assisted the festivities, which—to quote the *Oriflamme* of the next morning—" the wealth, beauty, and chivalry of Delisleville combined to render unequalled in their gaiety and elegance, making the evening one of the most successful of the piquant occasions

> When youth and pleasure meet
> To chase the glowing hours with flying feet.

In Connection with
The De Willoughby Claim

Usually Tom's part in such festivities was to sit uncomfortably in dull corners, taking up as little room as possible, or piloting his way carefully through the crowd to the supper-table with an elderly lady or a wall-flower clinging timidly to his huge arm. But during this one evening he lost his equilibrium. Delia had been more than usually kind to him, perhaps because she saw his unhappy awkwardness as he towered above everyone else and tried to avoid treading upon his neighbours. She gave him such a pretty smile across the room that he obeyed the impulse to go to her and stand at her side; then, when she left him to dance with De Courcy, she gave him her fan and bouquet and fleecy white wrap to hold, and somehow it seemed not unnatural that De Courcy should bring her back to him as to a sentinel when the dance was over. Thus it was as she sat, flushed a little and smiling, her face uplifted to his, while she thanked him for taking care of her possessions, that the wild thought which so betrayed him rushed into his brain.

"Delia," he faltered, "will you dance once with me?"

It was so startling a request, that, though she was quick enough to conceal her surprise, she hesitated a second before recovering her breath to give him her answer.

"Yes, Tom, if you like," she said, and glanced down at her programme. "The next is a waltz, and I can let you have it because Dr. Ballentine has been called away. Do you waltz?"

"I have learned," he answered, rather huskily and tremulously. "I do it badly, of course, but I know the steps well enough."

He was so helpless with nervousness that he could scarcely speak, and his hands trembled when they stood up together and he laid his arm reverently about her waist.

She saw his timidity and looked up at him with a kind smile.

"I must be very little," she said, "I never knew before that I was so little."

He had thought he should recover himself when the music and motion began, but he did not. He looked down at the delicate head which reached barely to his beating heart, and a blur came before his sight; the light and the crowd of dancers dazzled and confused him. The whirling movement made him dizzy, and he had not expected to be dizzy. He began suddenly to be conscious of his own immensity, the unusualness of his position, and of the fact that here and there he saw a meaning smile; his heart beat faster still, and he knew he had been led into a mistake. He swung round and round too quickly for the music, missed a step, tried to recover himself, became entangled in his partner's dress, trod on her poor little feet, and fell headlong on the floor, dragging her with him and striking against a passing couple.

It was his brother De Courcy with whom he had come in such violent contact, and it was De Courcy who sprang to Delia's rescue, assisting her to her feet with all possible grace, and covering her innocent confusion with a brilliant speech, but not, however, before he had directed a terrible scowl at the prostrate culprit and sworn furiously at him under his breath. But Delia was very good to him and did not desert him in the hour of his need, giving him only kind looks and managing to arrange that he should lead her to her seat as if he had not been in disgrace at all.

But the shame and pain of his downfall were sharper pangs than he had ever borne, and before the night was half over he slipped away from the dancers and rushed home to his own room, where he lay awake through the long hours, cursing himself for his folly, and tossing in a fever of humiliation and grief.

In the morning when he came down to the breakfast table, the family were already assembled, and the Judge had heard the story from De Courcy, who told it all the more forcibly in the absence of Miss Vanuxem, who had spent the night at the house of another relative.

When Tom entered, his paternal parent was ready to receive him.

"Trod on Miss Vanuxem's dress and tore it off her back in the ball-room, did you?" he burst forth. "Made a fool of yourself and a bear-garden of the Delisle House ball-room! What were you trying to dance for? Leave that to men who can manage their limbs, and don't inflict yourself on women who are too high-bred to refuse to dance with a man who ought to be a gentleman. Stay at home, sir! Stay at home, and don't make a disgraceful spectacle of yourself in public, particularly when there are lovely women present to witness your humiliation."

It was the figurative last straw. Tom's mind had been dark and gloomy enough to begin with, but when during his father's harangue he glanced up and saw De Courcy bending his aquiline face over his paper with a slightly sardonic smile, he could stand no more.

To the utter dumfounding of his mother and sisters, and even the irate Judge himself, he pushed his chair back and sprang to his feet with an actual roar of rage and pain. His great body seemed to swell until its size overwhelmed them; his eyes blazed, he shook his tremendous fist.

"Leave me alone!" he shouted, "leave me alone! Yes,

24

In Connection with
The De Willoughby Claim

I did make a fool of myself! Yes, I did knock a woman down and tear her dress and look like an ass and set the whole room laughing at me, women and all—the best-bred and sweetest of them! It's all true, every word of it, and more too—more too! And that's not enough, but my own father serves it up again, and you fellows sit there and grin over it to make it worse. That's right, pitch in, all of you, and drive me mad and put an end to it."

He upset his chair and a small negro boy with a plate of waffles, and, striding over the scattered ruins, dashed out of the room with tears of fury in his eyes.

It was the turning-point of his existence. He made his bitter resolve as he walked out of the house down the street. Early as it was, he went straight to Delia, and when he found himself alone with her, poured forth all the misery of his sore heart.

"If I had been born a clod-hopper it would have been better for me," he said. "I have no place here among men with decently shaped bodies and clear heads. I'm a great clumsy fool, and there's no help for it. If I'd had more brain, I might have managed the rest; but I'm a dullard too. They may well sneer at me. I think I will go away and bury myself somewhere among the people I ought to have lived among by rights. In some simple country place I might find those who know less than I do, and forget the rest; and perhaps be content enough in time. I shall never marry. I—I suppose you know that, Delia." And he took her little hand and laid it on his own open palm and sat silent a moment looking at it, and at last suddenly a great drop fell upon it which made them both start. He did not look up at her, but took out his big white handkerchief and wiped the drop gently away and then stooped and kissed the spot where it had fallen. Her own lashes were wet when their eyes met afterwards, and she spoke in a subdued voice.

"I have always liked you very much, Cousin Tom," she said; "you mustn't talk of going away. We should miss you much more than you think. I know I should be very sorry."

"You won't be here to miss me, Delia," he answered, sadly.

The hand on his palm trembled slightly and her eyes faltered under his gaze.

"I—think it—is possible I shall live in Delisleville," she whispered.

His heart bounded as if it would burst his side. He knew what she meant in an instant, though he had never suspected it before.

"Oh! Oh!" he groaned. "Oh, Delia! which—which of them is it? It's De Courcy, I could swear. It's De Courcy!"

"Yes," she faltered, "it is De Courcy."

He drew his hand away and covered his face with it.

"I knew it was De Courcy," he cried. "He was always the kind of fellow to win. I suppose he deserves it. The Lord knows I hope he does, for your sake. Of course it's De Courcy. Who else?"

He did not stay long after this, and when he went away he wrung her hand in his in a desperate farewell.

"This is another reason for my going now," he said; "I couldn't stay. This—is—good-bye, Delia."

He went home and had a prolonged interview with his father. It was not an agreeable interview to recur to mentally in after time, but in the end Tom gained his

26

point, and a portion of his future patrimony was handed over to him.

"I shall be no further trouble to you," he said. "You mayn't ever hear of me again. This is the end of me as far as you are concerned."

That night, with a valise in his hand, he took his place in the stage running towards the mountain regions of North Carolina, and from that day forward the place knew him no more. It was as he had known it would be: no one was very sorry to be rid of him, and even Delia's sadness was at length toned down by the excitement of preparation for and the festivities attendant upon her triumphant union with the most dashing De Willoughby of the flock.

When this event occurred, Tom's wanderings had ended temporarily in the farm-house referred to in the first chapter, and his appearance in this remote and usually undisturbed portion of his country had created some sensation. The news of the arrival of a stranger had spread itself abroad and aroused a slow-growing excitement.

They were a kindly, simple people who surrounded him —hospitable, ignorant, and curious beyond measure concerning the ways of the outside world of which they knew so little.

In the course of time, as the first keenness of his misery wore away, Tom began to discover the advantages of the change he had made. He no longer need contrast himself unfavourably with his neighbours. He knew more than they, and they found nothing in him to condemn or jeer at. To them he was a mine of worldly knowledge. He amused them and won their hearts. His natural indolence and lack of active ambition helped the healing of his wounds, perhaps; and then he began to appreciate the humourous side of his position and his old tendency to ponderous joking came back, and assisted him to win a greater popularity than any mere practical quality could have done.

The novelty of his *rôle* was its chief attraction. He began to enjoy and give himself up to it, and make the most of his few gifts. Life was no longer without zest. His natural indolence increased with the size of his great body as the years passed, and his slow whimsical humour became his strongest characteristic. He felt it a fine point in the sarcasm of his destiny that he should at last have become a hero and be regarded with admiration for his conversational abilities, but he bore his honours discreetly, and found both moral and physical comfort in them.

He insensibly adopted the habits of his neighbours; he dressed with their primitive regard for ease; he dropped now and then into their slurring speech, and adopted one by one their arcadian customs.

Whether the change was the better or the worse for him might easily be a matter of opinion, and depend entirely on the standpoint from which it was viewed. At least he lived harmlessly and had no enemy.

And so existence stood with him when the second great change in his life took place.

CHAPTER III

SCARCELY a month before the events described in the opening chapter took place, the stranger and a young woman, who was his companion, had appeared in the community. There was little that seemed mysterious about them at the outset. A long, uninhabited cabin, a score or so of yards from the mountain road, had been roughly patched up and taken possession of by them. There was nothing unusual in the circumstance except that they had appeared suddenly and entirely unheralded; but this in itself would have awakened no special comment. The mystery developed itself from their after reserve and seclusion. They guarded themselves from all advances by keeping out of sight when anyone approached their cabin. The young woman was rarely, if ever, seen. The man never called at the post-office for mail, and upon the few occasions on which a stray human being crossed his path, his manner was such as by no means encouraged the curious. Mr. Stamps was the only individual who had seen the woman face to face. There was an unmoved pertinacity in the character of Mr. Stamps which stood him in good stead upon all occasions. He was not easily abashed or rebuffed, the more especially when he held in view some practical object. Possibly he held some such object in view when he rode up to the tumbled down gateway and asked for the draught of water no woman of the region could refuse without some reasonable excuse.

In Connection with
The De Willoughby Claim

" 'Tain't airs they're puttin' on, Cindy," he said to the partner of his joys and sorrows the evening after his ride over the mountain. " Oh, no, 'tain't airs, it's somethin' more curi's than that! " And he bent over the fire in a comfortable lounging way, rubbing his hands a little, and blinked at the back log thoughtfully.

They were a friendly and sociable people, these mountaineers, all the more so because the opportunities for meeting sociably were limited. The men had their work and the women their always large families to attend to, and with a mile or so of rough road between themselves and their neighbours, there was not much chance for enjoyable gossip. When good fortune threw them together they usually made the best of their time. Consequently, the mystery of two human beings, who had shut themselves off with apparent intent from all intercourse with their kind, was a difficulty not readily disposed of. It was, perhaps, little to be wondered at that Mr. Stamps thought it over and gathered carefully together all the points presenting themselves to his notice. The subject had been frequently discussed at the Cross-roads post-office. The disposition to seclusion was generally spoken of as " curi's-ness," and various theories had been advanced with a view to explaining the " curi'sness " in question. " Airs " had been suggested as a solution of the difficulty, but as time progressed, the theory of " airs " had been abandoned.

" Fur," said Uncle Jake Wooten, who was a patriarch and an authority, " when a man's a-gwine to put on airs, he kinder slicks up more. A man that's airy, he ain't a-gwine to shut hisself up and not show out more. Like as not he'd wear store-clothes an' hang round 'n' kinder blow; 'n' this feller don't do nary one. 'N' as to the woman, Lord!

In Connection with
The De Willoughby Claim

I should think all you'unses knows how womenfolks does that's airy. Ef this yere one wus that way, she'd be a-dressin' in starched calikers 'n' sunbonnets 'n' bress-pins, 'n' mebbe rings 'n' congrist-gaiters. She'd be to the meetin' every time there was meetin' a-showin' out 'n' lettin' on like she didn't know the rest on 'em wus seein'. It don't sound to reason that either on 'em is airy."

It had been suggested by a bold spirit capable of more extended flights of the imagination than the rest, that they were "Northerners" who for some unworthy object had taken up their abode within the bound of civilisation; but this idea was frowned down as being of a wild nature and not to be encouraged.

Finally the general interest in the subject had subsided somewhat, though it was ready to revive at any new comment or incident, which will explain the bodily awakening of the sleepers on the post-office porch when Mr. Stamps made his announcement of the approach of "thet thar feller."

Up to the moment when the impulse seized him which led him to take his place behind the counter as the stranger entered the store, Tom De Willoughby had taken little or no part in numerous discussions held around him. He had listened with impartiality to all sides of the question, his portion of the entertainment being to make comments of an inspiriting nature which should express in a marked manner his sarcastic approval of any special weakness in a line of argument.

Among the many agreeable things said of him in his past, it had never been said that he was curious; he was too indolent to be curious, and it may be simply asserted that he had felt little curiosity concerning the popular

mystery. But when he found himself face to face with his
customer, a new feeling suddenly took possession of him.
The change came when, for one instant, the man, as if in
momentary forgetfulness, looked up and met his eyes in
speaking. Each moved involuntarily, and Tom turned
aside, ostensibly, to pick up a sheet of wrapping paper.
The only words exchanged were those relating to the cour-
tesies and the brief remarks heard by the loungers outside.
After this the stranger rode away and Tom lounged back
to his chair. He made no reply to Stamps's explanatory
aside, and no comment upon the remarks of the company
whose curiosity had naturally received a new impetus which
spurred them on to gossip a little in the usual vague manner. He gave himself up to speculation. The mere tone of
a man's voice had set his mind to work. His past life had
given him experience in which those about him were lack-
ing, and at the instant he heard the stranger speak this
experience revealed to him as by a flash of light, a thing
which had never yet been even remotely guessed at.

"A gentleman, by thunder!" he said to himself.
"That's it! A gentleman!"

He knew he could not be mistaken. Low and purposely
muffled as the voice had been, he recognised in it that
which marked it as the voice of a man trained to modulated
speech. And even this was not all, though it had led him
to look again, and more closely, at the face shadowed by
the broad hat. It was not a handsome face, but it was one
not likely to be readily forgotten. It was worn and haggard, the features strongly aquiline, the eyes somewhat
sunken; it was the face of a man who had lived the life of
an ascetic and who, with a capacity for sharp suffering,
had suffered and was suffering still.

In Connection with
The De Willoughby Claim

"But a gentleman and not a Southerner," Tom persisted to himself. "A Yankee, as I'm a sinner; and what is a Yankee doing hiding himself here for?"

It was such a startling thing under the circumstances, that he could not rid himself of the thought of it. It haunted him through the rest of the day, and when night came and the store being closed, he retired as usual to the back part of the house, he was brooding over it still.

He lived in a simple and primitive style. Three rooms built on to the store were quite enough for him. One was his sitting- and bed-room, another his dining-room and kitchen, the third the private apartment of his household goddess, a stout old mulatto woman who kept his house in order and prepared his meals.

When he opened the door to-night the little boarded rooms were illuminated with two tallow candles and made fragrant with the odour of fried chicken and hoe-cakes, to which Aunt Mornin was devoting all her energies, and for the first time perhaps in his life, he failed to greet these attractions with his usual air of good cheer.

He threw his hat into a chair, and, stretching himself out upon the bedstead, lay there, his hands clasped above his head and his eyes fixed upon the glow of the fire in the adjoining room, where Aunt Mornin was at work.

"A gentleman!" he said, half aloud. "That's it, by Jupiter, a gentleman!"

He remembered it afterwards as a curious coincidence that he should have busied his mind so actively with his subject in a manner so unusual with him.

His imagination not being sufficiently vivid to help him out of his difficulty to his own satisfaction, he laboured with it patiently, recurring to it again and again, and turning it over until it assumed a greater interest than at first. He only relinquished it with an effort when, going to bed later than usual, he made up his mind to compose himself to sleep.

" Good Lord! " he said, turning on his side and addressing some unseen presence representing the vexed question. " Don't keep a man awake: settle it yourself." And finally sank into unconsciousness in the midst of his mental struggle.

.   .   .   .

About the middle of the night he awakened. He felt that something had startled him from his sleep, but could not tell what it was. A few seconds he lay without moving, listening, and as he listened there came to his ear the sound of a horse's feet, treading the earth restlessly outside the door, the animal itself breathing heavily as if it had been ridden hard; and almost as soon as he aroused to recognition of this fact, there came a sharp tap on the door and a man's voice crying " Hallo! "

He knew the voice at once, and unexpected as the summons was, felt he was not altogether unprepared for it, though he could not have offered even the weakest explanation for the feeling.

" He's in trouble," he said, as he sat up quickly in bed. " Something's gone wrong." He rose and in a few seconds opened the door.

He had guessed rightly; it was the stranger. The moonlight fell full upon the side of the house and the road, and the panting horse stood revealed in a bright light which gave the man's face a ghostly look added to his natural pallor. As he leaned forward, Tom saw that he was as much exhausted as was the animal he had ridden.

"I want to find a doctor, or a woman who can give help to another," he said.

"There ain't a doctor within fifteen miles from here," began Tom. He stopped short. What he saw in the man's face checked him.

"Look here," he said, "is it your wife?"

The man made a sharp gesture of despair.

"She's dying, I think," he said, hoarsely, "and there's not a human being near her."

"Good Lord!" cried Tom, "Good Lord!" The sweat started out on his forehead. He remembered what Stamps had said of her youth and her pale face, and he thought of Delia Vanuxem, and from this thought sprang a sudden recollection of the deserted medical career in which he had been regarded as so ignominious a failure. He had never mentioned it since he had cut himself off from the old life, and the women for whose children he had prescribed with some success now and then had considered the ends achieved only the natural results of his multitudinous gifts. But the thought of the desolate young creature lying there alone struck deep. He listened one moment, then made his resolve.

"Go to the stable," he said, "and throw a saddle over the horse you will find there. I know something of such matters myself, and I shall be better than nothing, with a woman's help. I have a woman here who will follow us."

He went into the back room and awakened Aunt Mornin.

"Get up," he said, "and saddle the mule and follow me as soon as you can to the cabin in Blair's Hollow. The wife of a man who lives there needs a woman with her. Come quickly."

When he returned to the door his horse stood there saddled, the stranger sitting on his own and holding the bridle.

Tom mounted in silence, but once finally seated, he turned to his companion.

"Now strike out," he said.

There were four miles of road before them, but they scarcely slackened rein until they were within sight of the Hollow, and the few words they exchanged were the barest questions and answers.

The cabin was built away from the road on the side of the hill, and leaving their horses tethered at the foot of the slope, they climbed it together.

When they reached the door, the stranger stopped and turned to Tom.

"There is no sound inside," he faltered; "I dare not go in."

Tom strode by him and pushed the door open.

In one corner of the room was a roughly made bedstead, and upon it lay a girl, her deathly pale face turned sideways upon the pillow. It was as if she lay prostrated by some wave of agony which had just passed over her; her breath was faint and rapid, and great drops of sweat stood out upon her young drawn face.

Tom drew a chair forward and sat down beside her. He lifted one of her hands, touching it gently, but save for a slight quiver of the eyelids she did not stir. A sense of awe fell upon him.

"It's Death," he said to himself. He had experience enough to teach him that. He turned to the man.

"You had better go out of the room; I will do my best."

* * * * * * * *

In a little over an hour Aunt Mornin dismounted from her mule and tethered it to a sapling at the side of the road below. She looked up at the light gleaming faintly through the pines on the hillside.

"I cum 's fas' 's I could," she said, "but I reckon I'd orter been here afore. De Lord knows dis is a curi's 'casion."

When she crossed the threshold of the cabin, her master pointed to a small faintly moving bundle lying at the foot of the bed over which he was bending.

"Take it into the other room and tell the man to come here," he said. "There's no time to lose."

He still held the weak hand; but the girl's eyes were no longer closed; they were open and fixed on his face. The great fellow was trembling like a leaf. The past hour had been almost more than he could bear. He was entirely unstrung.

"I wasn't cut out for this kind of thing," he had groaned more than once, and for the first time in his life thanked Fate for making him a failure.

As he looked down at his patient, a mist rose before his eyes, blurring his sight, and he hurriedly brushed it away.

She was perhaps nineteen years old, and had the very young look a simple trusting nature and innocent untried life bring. She was small, fragile, and fair, with the pure fairness born of a cold climate. Her large blue-gray eyes had in them the piteous appeal sometimes to be seen in the eyes of a timid child.

Tom had laid his big hand on her forehead and stroked it, scarcely knowing what he did.

"Don't be frightened," he said, with a tremor in his

voice. " Close your eyes and try to be quiet for a few moments, and then——"

He stooped to bend his ear to her lips which were moving faintly.

" He'll come directly," he answered, though he did not hear her; "—directly. It's all right."

And then he stroked her hair again because he knew not what else to do, seeing, as he did, that the end was so very near, and that no earthly power, however far beyond his own poor efforts, could ward it off.

Just at that moment the door opened and the man came in.

That he too read the awful truth at his first glance, Tom saw. All attempts at disguise had dropped away. His thin, scholarly face was as colourless as the fairer one on the pillow, his brows were knit into rigid lines and his lips were working. He approached the bed, and for a few moments stood looking down as if trying to give himself time to gain self-control. Tom saw the girl's soft eyes fixed in anguished entreaty; there was a struggle, and from the slowly moving lips came a few faint and broken words.

" Death!—They—never know."

The man flung himself upon his knees and burst into an agony of such weeping that, seeing it, Tom turned away shuddering.

" No," he said, " they will never know, they who loved you—who loved you—will never know! God forgive me if I have done wrong. I have been false that they might be spared. God forgive me for the sin! "

The poor child shivered; she had become still paler, and the breath came in sharp little puffs through her nostrils.

" God—God!—God! " she panted. But the man did not

seem to hear her. He was praying aloud, a struggling, dis-jointed prayer.

"O God of sinners," he cried, "Thou who forgivest, Thou who hast died, forgive—forgive in this hour of death!"

Tom heard no more. He could only listen to the soft, panting breath sinking lower and lower.

Suddenly the piteous eyes turned towards him—the stranger—as if in great dread: perhaps they saw in the mere human pity of his face what met some sharp last need.

He went to his old place as if in answer to the look, and took the poor little hand once more, closing the warmth of his own over its coldness. He was weeping like a child.

"Don't be afraid," he said; "—not afraid. It's—it's all right."

And almost as he said it, with her eyes still fixed upon his own, and with her hand in his, she gave a low sob—and died.

Tom touched the kneeling man upon the shoulder.

"There's no need of that now," he said; "it's over."

CHAPTER IV

WHEN a few minutes later he went into the back room, he found Aunt Mornin sitting before the big fireplace in which burned a few logs of wood. The light the snapping sticks gave fell full upon her black face, and upon the small bundle upon her spacious knee.

As he entered she turned sharply towards him.

" Don't nobody keer nothin' for this yere? " she said, " ain't nobody comin' nigh? Whar's he? Don't he take no int'rus' in the pore little lonesome child? I 'spect yo'll haf to take it ye'self, Mars' De Willerby, while I goes in dar."

Tom stopped short, stricken with a pang of remorse. He looked down at the small face helplessly.

" Yes," he said, " you'll have to go in there; you're needed."

The woman looked at him in startled questioning.

" Mars De Willerby," she said, " does dat ar mean she's cl'ar gone? "

" Yes," answered Tom. " She's gone, Mornin."

With the emotional readiness of her race, the comfortable creature burst into weeping, clasping the child to her broad bosom.

" Pore chile! " she said, " an' poor chile lef' behin'! De Lord help 'em bofe."

With manifest fear Tom stooped and took the little red flannel bundle from her arms.

40

" Never mind crying," he said. " Go into the room and do what's to be done."

When left alone with his charge, he sat down and held it balanced carefully in his hands, his elbows resting on his knees. He was used to carrying his customers' children, a great part of his popularity being based upon his jovial fondness for them. But he had never held so small a creature as this in his arms before. He regarded it with a respectful timidity.

" It wasn't thought of," he said, reflectively. " Even she—poor thing, poor thing—" he ended, hurriedly, " there was no time."

He was still holding his small burden with awkward kindliness when the door opened and the man he had left in the room beyond came in. He approached the hearth and stood for a few seconds staring at the fire in a stupefied, abstracted way. He did not seem to see the child. At last he spoke.

" Where shall I lay her? " he asked. " Where is the nearest churchyard? "

" Fifteen miles away," Tom answered. " Most of the people like to have their dead near them and lay them on the hillsides."

The man turned to him with a touch of horror in his face.

" In unconsecrated ground? " he said.

" It doesn't trouble them," said Tom. " They sleep well enough."

The man turned to the fire again—he had not looked at the child yet—and made a despairing gesture with his hands.

" That she—" he said, " that she should lie so far from them, and in unconsecrated ground! "

"There is the place I told you of," said Tom.

"I cannot go there," with the gesture again. "There is no time. I must go away."

He made no pretence at concealing that he had a secret to hide. He seemed to have given up the effort.

Tom looked up at him.

"What are you going to do with this?" he asked.

Then for the first time he seemed to become conscious of the child's presence. He turned and gave it a startled sidelong glance, as if he had suddenly been struck with a new fear.

"I—do not know," he stammered. "I—no! I do not know. What have I been doing?"

He sank into a chair and buried his face in his trembling hands.

"God's curse is upon it," he cried. "There is no place for it on earth."

Tom rose with a sudden movement and began to pace the floor with his charge in his arms.

"It's a little chap to lay a curse on," he said. "And helpless enough, by Gad!"

He looked down at the diminutive face, and as he did so, a wild thought flashed through his mind. It had the suddenness and force of a revelation. His big body trembled with some feeling it would have gone hard with him to express, and his heart warmed within him as he felt the light weight lying against it.

"No place for it!" he cried. "By God, there is! There is a place *here*—and a man to stand by and see fairplay!"

"Give her to me," he said, "give her to me, and if there is no place for her, I'll find one."

" What do you mean? " faltered the man.

" I mean what I say," said Tom. " I'll take her and stand by her as long as there is breath in me; and if the day should ever come in spite of me when wrong befalls her, as it befell her mother, some man shall die, so help me God! "

The warm Southern blood which gave to his brothers' love-songs the grace of passion, and which made them renowned for their picturesque eloquence of speech, fired him to greater fluency than was usual with him, when he thought of the helplessness of the tiny being he held.

" I never betrayed a woman yet, or did one a wrong," he went on. " I'm not one of the lucky fellows who win their hearts," with a great gulp in his throat. " Perhaps if there's no one to come between us, she may—may be fond of me."

The man gave him a long look, as if he was asking himself a question.

" Yes," he said at last, " she will be fond of you. You will be worthy of it. There is no one to lay claim to her. Her mother lies dead among strangers, and her father——"

For a few moments he seemed to be falling into a reverie, but suddenly a tremour seized him and he struck one clenched hand against the other.

" If a man vowed to the service of God may make an oath," he said, " I swear that if the day ever dawns when we stand face to face, knowing each other, I will not spare him! "

The child stirred in Tom's arms and uttered its first sharp little cry, and as if in answer to the summons, Aunt Mornin opened the door.

"It's all done," she said. "Gib me de chile, Mars De Willerby, and go in an' look at her."

.　　.　　.　　.　　.　　.　　.

When he entered the little square living room, Tom paused at the foot of the bed. All was straight and neat and cold. Among the few articles in the one small trunk, the woman had found a simple white dress and had put it on the dead girl. It was such a garment as almost every girl counts among her possessions. Tom remembered that his sisters had often worn such things.

"She looks very pretty," he said. "I dare say her mother made it and she wore it at home. O Lord! O Lord!" And with this helpless exclamation, half sigh, half groan, he turned away and walked out of the front door into the open air.

It was early morning by this time, and he passed into the dew and sunlight not knowing where he was going; but once outside, the sight of his horse tethered to a tree at the roadside brought to his mind the necessity of the occasion.

"I'll ride in and see Steven," he said. "It's got to be done, and it's no work for *him!*"

When he reached the Cross-roads there were already two or three early arrivals lounging on the store-porch and wondering why the doors were not opened.

The first man who saw him, opened upon him the usual course of elephantine witticisms.

"Look a' yere, Tom," he drawled, "this ain't a-gwine to do. You a-gittin' up 'fore daybreak like the rest of us folks and ridin' off Goddlemighty knows whar. It ain't a-gwine to do now. Whar air ye from?"

But as he rode up and dismounted at the porch, each

saw that something unusual had happened. He tied his horse and came up the steps in silence.

"Boys," he said, when he stood among them, "I want Steven. I've been out to the Hollow, and there's a job for him there. The—the woman's dead."

"Dead!" they echoed, drawing nearer to him in their excitement. "When, Tom?"

"Last night. Mornin's out there. There's a child."

"Thunder 'n' molasses!" ejaculated the only family man of the group, reflectively. "Thunder 'n' molasses!" And then he began to edge away, still with a reflective air, towards his mule.

"Boys," he explained, "there'd ought to be some women folks around. I'm gwine for Minty, and she'll start the rest on 'em. Women folks is what's needed. They kin kinder organize things whar thar's trouble."

"Well," said Tom, "perhaps you're right; but don't send too many of 'em, and let your wife tell 'em to talk as little as possible and leave the man alone. He's got enough to stand up under."

Before the day was over there were women enough in the hillside cabin. Half a dozen faded black calico riding-skirts hung over the saddles of half a dozen horses tethered in the wood round the house, while inside half a dozen excellent souls disposed themselves in sympathetic couples about the two rooms.

Three sat in the front room, their sunbonnets drawn well down over their faces in the true mourner's spirit, one at the head of the bed slowly moving a fan to and fro over the handkerchief-covered face upon the pillow. A dead silence pervaded the place, except when it was broken by occasional brief remarks made in a whisper.

45

"She was a mighty purty-lookin' young critter," they said. "A sight younger-lookin' than her man."

"What's the child?"

"Gal."

"Gal? That's a pity. Gals ain't much chance of bein' raised right whar they're left."

"Hain't they any folks, neither on 'em?"

"Nobody don't know. Nobody hain't heerd nothin' about 'em. They wus kinder curi's about keepin' to themselves."

"If either on 'em had any folks—even if they wus only sort o' kin—they might take the chile."

"Mebbe they will. Seems to reason they must have some kin—even if they ain't nigh."

Then the silence reigned again and the woman at the bed's head gave her undivided attention to the slow, regular motion of her palm-leaf fan.

In the room beyond a small fire burned in spite of the warmth of the day, and divers small tin cups and pipkins simmered before and upon the cinders of it, Aunt Mornin varying her other duties by moving them a shade nearer to the heat or farther from it, and stirring and tasting at intervals.

Upon a low rocking-chair before the hearth sat the wife of the family man before referred to. She was a tall, angular creature, the mother of fifteen, comprising in their number three sets of twins. She held her snuff-stick between her teeth and the child on her lap, with an easy professional air.

"I hain't never had to raise none o' mine by hand since Martin Luther," she remarked. "I've been mighty glad on it, for he was a sight o' trouble. Kinder colicky and

46

weakly. Never done no good till we got him off the bottle. He'd one cow's milk, too, all the time. I was powerful partickerler 'bout that. I'd never have raised him if I hadn't bin. 'N' to this day Martin Luther hain't what 'Poleon and Orlando is."

" Dis yere chile ain't gwine to be no trouble to nobody," put in Aunt Mornin. " She's a powerful good chile to begin with, 'n' she's a chile that's gwine to thrive. She hain't done no cryin' uv no consequence yit, 'n' whar a chile starts out dat dar way it speaks well for her. If Mornin had de raisin' o' dat chile, dar wouldn't be no trouble 't all. Bile der milk well 'n' d'lute down right, 'n' a chile like dat ain't gwine to have no colick. My young Mistis Mars D'Willerby bought me from, I've raised three o' hern, an' I'm used to bilin' it right and d'lutin' it down right. Dar's a heap in de d'lutin'. Dis yere bottle's ready now, Mis' Doty, ef ye want it."

" It's the very bottle I raised Martin Luther on," said Mrs. Doty. " It brings back ole times to see it. She takes it purty well, don't she? Massy sakes! How f'erce she looks for sich a little thing! "

Later in the day there arose the question of how she should be disposed of for the night, and it was in the midst of this discussion that Tom De Willoughby entered.

" Thar ain't but one room; I s'pose he'll sleep in that," said Mrs. Doty, " 'n' the Lord knows he don't look the kind o' critter to know what to do with a chile. We hain't none o' us seen him since this mornin'. I guess he's kinder wanderin' round. Does any of you know whar he is? We might ax what he 'lows to do."

Tom bent down over the child as it lay in the woman's lap. No one could see his face.

" I know what he's going to do," he said. " He's going away to-morrow after the funeral."

" 'N' take the child? " in a chorus.

" No," said Tom, professing to be deeply interested in the unclosing of the small red fist. " I'm going to take the child."

There were four sharp exclamations, and for a second or so all four women gazed at him with open mouths. It was Mrs. Doty who first recovered herself sufficiently to speak. She gave him a lively dig with her elbow.

" Now, Tom D'Willerby," she said, " none of your foolin'. This yere ain't no time for it."

" Mars D'Willerby," said Aunt Mornin, " dis chile's mother's a-lyin' dead in the nex' room."

Tom stooped a trifle lower. He put out both his hands and took the baby in them.

" I'm not foolin'," he said, rather uncertainly. " I'm in earnest, ladies. The mother is dead and the man's going away. There's nobody else to claim her, he tells me, and so I'll claim her. There's enough of me to take care of her, and I mean to do it."

It was so extraordinary a sensation, that for a few moments there was another silence, broken as before by Mrs. Doty.

" Waal," she remarked, removing her snuff-stick and expectorating into the fire. " Ye've allus been kinder fond o' chillun, Tom, and mebbe she ain't as colicky by natur' as Martin Luther was, but I mus' say it's the curi'sest thing I ever heern—him a-gwine away an' givin' her cl'ar up as ef he hadn't no sort o' nat'ral feelin's—I do say it's curi's."

" He's a queer fellow," said Tom, " a queer fellow! There's no denying that."

That this was true was proven by his conduct during the

48

time in which it was liable to public comment. Until night he was not seen, and then he came in at a late hour and, walking in silence through the roomful of watchers, shut himself up in an inner chamber and remained there alone.

"He's takin' it mighty hard," they said. "Seems like it's kinder onsettled his mind. He hain't never looked at the child once."

He did not appear at all the next day until all was ready and Tom De Willoughby went to him.

He found him lying on the bed, his haggard face turned towards the window. He did not move until Tom touched him on the shoulder.

"If you want to see her——" he said.

He started and shuddered.

"What, so soon?" he said. "So soon?"

"Now," Tom answered. "Get up and come with me."

He obeyed, following him mechanically, but when they reached the door, Tom stopped him.

"I've told them a story that suits well enough," he said. "I've told them that you're poor and have no friends, and can't care for the child, and I've a fancy for keeping it. The mother is to lie out here on the hillside until you can afford to find a better place for her—perhaps at your own home. I've told the tale my own way. I'm not much of a hand at that kind of thing, but it'll do. I've asked you no questions."

"No," said the man, drearily. "You've asked me no questions."

Then they went together into the other room. There were twenty or thirty people in it, or standing about the door. It was like all mountain funerals, but for an air of desolateness even deeper than usual. The slender pine coffin was

49

supported upon two chairs in the middle of the room, and the women stood or sat about, the more easily moved weeping a little under the shadow of their calico sunbonnets. The men leaned against the door-posts, or sat on the wooden steps, bare-headed, silent, and rather restless.

When Tom led his charge into the apartment, there was a slight stir and moving back of chairs to make way for him. He made his way straight to the coffin. When he reached it and looked down, he started. Perhaps the sight of the white dress with its simple girlish frills and homelike prettiness brought back to him some memory of happier days when he had seen it worn before.

The pure, childlike face had settled into utter calm, and across the breast and in the hands were long, slender branches of the thickly flowering wild white clematis. Half an hour before Tom had gone into the woods and returned with these branches, which he gave to one of the younger women.

" Put them on her," he said, awkwardly; " there ought to be some flowers about her."

For a few moments there reigned in the room a dead silence. All eyes were fixed upon the man who stood at the coffin side. He simply looked down at the fair dead face. He bestowed no caresses upon it, and shed no tears, though now and then there was to be seen a muscular contraction of his throat.

At length he turned towards those surrounding him and raised his hand, speaking in a low voice.

" Let us pray."

It was the manner of a man trained to rigid religious observances, and when the words were uttered, something like an electric shock passed through his hearers. The circuit-riders who stopped once or twice a month at the log churches on the roadside were seldom within reach on such an occasion as this, and at such times it was their custom to depend on any good soul who was considered to have the gift of prayer. Perhaps some of them had been wondering who would speak the last words now, as there was no such person on the spot; but the trained manner and gesture, even while it startled them by its unexpectedness, set their minds at rest.

They settled themselves in the conventional posture, the women retiring into their bonnets, the men hanging their heads, and the prayer began.

It was a strange appeal—one which only one man among them could grasp the meaning of, though all regarded its outpouring words with wonder and admiration. It was an outcry full of passion, dread, and anguish which was like despair. It was a prayer for mercy—mercy for those who suffered, for the innocent who might suffer—for loving hearts too tender to bear the bitter blows of life.

" The loving hearts, O God! " he cried, " the loving hearts who wait—who——"

More than one woman looked up from under her bonnet; his body began to tremble—he staggered and fell into a chair, hiding his face, shaking from head to foot in an agony of weeping. Tom made his way to him and bent over him.

" Come with me," he said, his great voice broken. " Come with me into the air, it will quiet you, and we can wait until —until they come."

He put his arm under his and supported him out of the house.

Two or three women began to rock themselves to and fro and weep aloud hysterically. It was only the stronger ones who could control themselves. He was standing at Tom's side then; when they came out a short time afterwards, walking slowly and carrying the light burden, which they lowered into its resting-place beneath the pines.

He was quite calm again, and made no sound or movement until all was over. Then he spoke to Tom.

"Tell them," he said, "that I thank them. I can do no more."

He walked back to the desolate house, and in a little while the people went their ways, each of them looking back a little wistfully at the cabin as he or she rode out of sight.

When the last one was lost to view, Tom, who had loitered about, went into the cabin.

The man was sitting in the empty room, his gaze fixed upon the two chairs left standing in the middle of it a few paces from each other.

Tom moved them away and then approached him.

"The child has been taken to my house," he said. "You don't want to see it?"

"No."

"Is there anything else I can do?"

"No, nothing else," monotonously.

"Are you going away?"

"Yes—to-night."

Tom glanced around him at the desolation of the poor, bare little place, at the empty bed, and the small trunk at the foot of it.

"You are not going to stay here alone, man?" he said.

"Yes," he was answered. "I have something to do; I must be alone."

Tom hesitated a moment.

"Well," he said, at length, "I suppose I've done, then. Good-bye."

"Good-bye," he was answered. "The Lord—the Lord will reward you."

And then Tom crossed the room slowly and reluctantly, passed out, and closed the door after him.

. . . .

When he opened his own door, he struck his foot against something and stumbled over it. It was a primitive wooden cradle—somewhat like a box on rockers—a quilt of patchwork covered it, and upon the small pillow rested the round black head of his new possession. He stopped short to regard it. Aunt Mornin had left it there while she occupied herself with preparing supper in the kitchen. It really looked quite comfortable. Gradually a smile established itself upon Tom's countenance.

"By thunder!" he said, "here you are, youngster, ain't you? You've come to stay—that's what you've come for."

And, being answered by a slight stirring of the patchwork quilt, he put his foot out with much cautiousness, touched the rocker, and, finding to his great astonishment that he had accomplished this much safely, he drew up a chair, and, sitting down, devoted himself with laudable enthusiasm to engineering the small ark with a serious and domestic air.

CHAPTER V

In two days' time the whole country had heard the news. The mystery of Blair's Hollow was revived and became a greater mystery than ever. The woman was dead, the man had disappeared. The cabin stood deserted, save for the few household goods which had been left just as they were on the day of the funeral. Not an article had been moved, though the woman to whom Tom De Willoughby, as the person most concerned, handed over the discarded property, did not find the little trunk, and noticed that articles had been burned in the fireplace in the front room.

" Thar wus a big pile o' ashes on the ha'th," she said to her friends, " sorter like as if he'd been burnin' a heap a little things o' one sort or 'nother. It kinder give me cold chills, it looked so lonesome when I shut the door arter the truck was gone. I left the ashes a-lyin' thar. I kinder had a curi's feelin' about touchin' on 'em. Nothing wouldn't hire me to live thar. D'Willerby said he reckoned I could hev moved right in ef I wanted to, but, Lawsy! I wouldn't have done it fer nothin'."

But that which roused the greatest excitement in the community was Tom De Willoughby's course.

At first Mrs. Doty's story of Big Tom's adoption of the child was scarcely accepted as being a possibility. The first man who heard it received it with a grin of disbelief. This individual was naturally Mr. Doty himself.

"Minty," he said, "don't ye let him fool ye. Don't ye know Tom D'Willerby by this time? Ye'd orter. It's jest some o' his gas. Don't ye s'pose he hain't got no more sense? What'd he do with it?"

"Ye can believe it or not," replied Mrs. Doty, sharply, "but he's gwine to raise that young'n, as shore as your name's Job. Mornin's got her this minute."

Mr. Doty indulged in a subdued chuckle.

"A nice-lookin' feller he is to raise a infant babe!" he remarked. "Lord a massy! if thet thar ain't jest like one o' his doggoned tales! He is the derndest critter," with reflective delight, "the derndest! Thar ain't nothin' in Hamlin to come up to him."

But the next day even Mr. Doty was convinced. After his customary visit to the Cross-roads, he returned to his family wearing a bewildered expression. It became a sheepish expression when his wife confronted him on the doorstep.

"Wal, Job Doty," she remarked, "I guess you've found out by this time whether I was right or wrong."

"Wal," answered Mr. Doty, throwing his saddle down on the porch, "I reckon I hev. She's thar shore enough, 'n' it seems like he's gwine to keep her; but I wouldn't hev believed it ef I hadn't seen it, doggoned ef I would! But, Lord, it's like him, arter all." And he brightened up and chuckled again.

"I reckon he don't scarcely know what he's tuk in hand," said Mrs. Doty.

"Him!" answered Mr. Doty. "Tom! Lord! 'tain't a-gwine to trouble Tom. He'll get along, Tom will. Tom'd jus' as lief as she wus twins as not, mebbe liefer. It'd be a bigger thing for him to engineer 'n' gas about ef she wus. Ef you'd seen him bring her into the store to the boys 'n' brag on her 'n' spread hisself, I reckon ye wouldn't hev minded 'bout Tom. Why, he's set on her, Minty, a'reddy, as set as he kin be."

The Cross-roads post-office had indeed been the scene of a sort of informal *levée* held by the newcomer, who had been thus presented to her fellow-citizens. One man after another had dropped in to hear the truth of the story related, and each one had been dumfounded at the outset by Tom's simple statement of fact.

"Yes, I'm going to keep her, boys," he said. "She's in the back part of the house now. According to my calculations, she's drunk about three quarts of milk since morning, and seems to stand it pretty well, so I suppose she's all right."

There were a great many jokes made at first, and a general spirit of hilariousness reigned, but it was observed by one of the keener witted ones that, despite his jocular tone, there was an underlying seriousness in Tom's air which might argue that he felt the weight of his responsibility. When the women began to come in, as they did later in the day, he received them with much cordiality, rising from his chair to shake hands with each matron as she appeared.

"Come in to see her, have you?" he said. "That's right. She's in the back room. Walk right in. Mis' Simpson and Mis' Lyle, I'd like some of you ladies to have a look at her. I'll go with you myself and hear what you have to say."

He made the journey each time with a slight air of anxiety, leading the way to the wooden cradle, and standing over it like a Herculean guardian angel, listening attentively to all the comments made and all the advice given.

"She seems to be getting on pretty well, doesn't she?" he enquired.

"Lor', yes!" said one matron; "jest keep her kivered up

'n' don't let no air strike her, 'n' ye won't hev no trouble with her, I reckon."

"No air?" enquired Tom, in some trepidation; "none at all?"

"Wal, thet's my way," was the answer. "Some folks does diff'rent, but I didn't never expose 'em none till they was more'n a month old. New-born babies is tender things!"

"Yes," said Tom. "Good Lord, yes!"

His visitor started at him perplexedly for a moment.

"Wal," she said. "My man allus used to say they kinder skeered him 'long at the first—he kinder felt as if they'd mebbe come apart, or sumthin'. They allus sorter 'minded me o' young mice. Wal, you jest tell Mornin to giv' her es much milk as she calls fer, an' don't let it bile too long, 'n' she'll come on fine."

The next visitor that entered uttered an exclamation of dismay.

"Ye're gwine ter kill her!" she said. "Thar ain't a breath o' air in the room, 'n' thar ain't nothin' a new-born baby wants more 'n plenty o' air. They're tender critters, 'n' they cayn't stand to be smothered up. Ye'll hev her in spasms afore the day's over."

Tom flung the doors and windows open in great alarm.

"It is hot," he said. "It's hot enough out of doors, but Mis' Simpson told me to keep her shut up, and I thought she'd had experience enough to know."

"Jane Simpson!" with ill-concealed scorn. "She'd or-ter! She's had six to die in their second summer. I reckon she told ye to give her half-b'iled milk as often as she wanted it?"

Tom reflected in manifest trepidation.

"She did tell me not to boil it too much, and to give it to her when she called for it," he said, slowly.

57

" Wal, if ye don't want ter kill her, take my advice an' bile it a good half hour, 'n' don't give it to her oftener than once in three hours. She'll cry fur it, but ye needn't mind. Ye'll get used ter it. I don't believe in lettin' young uns hev nuthin' out o' their reg'lar time."

The next caller found Tom somewhat discouraged. He preceded her into the reception-chamber with less alacrity than he had shown in his previous visits.

She was a younger woman than the rest, and when she reached the cradle's side, she bent down and rearranged the cover with a soft touch.

" She's gwine to be a purty little thing," she said; " she'll be sorter dark-complected, but she's gwine to hev purty hair 'n' eyes. Ye'll be right proud of her, Tom, when she's grown, 'n' I guess she'll be a heap o' company to you. Lord! " with a motherly sigh, " it seems sorter curi's her bein' left to a man; but you'll do well by her, Tom, you'll do well by her. I hain't no doubt o' that. You was always mighty clever with children."

" I'll do all I can for her," said Tom, " though I suppose that isn't much."

The young woman—she had left her own baby in the store with her husband—patted the little pillow lightly into shape.

" Ye'll larn a heap by watchin' her," she said. " Jest watch her close 'n' she'll teach you herself. What do you do about her milk? " anxiously.

" I've been told to do several things," said Tom. " I've been told to boil it half an hour and not to boil it at all, and to give her all she wanted and not to give her all she wanted. I'm a little mixed about it."

" Wal, I hain't had but five, but I've allus let it come

to a bile an' then kinder used my reason about givin' it. Seems like the mejumer ye air with children, the better. But, Lordy! I guess Mornin knows. She raised her young mistress's."

She kissed the child before she left it, and when she re-entered the store, hurriedly took her own struggling off-spring from its father's arms, settled its pink dress and sunbonnet with a nervous, caressing motion, and, carrying it to the door, stood with it pressed against her breast while she seemed to be looking out at the distant mountains. She did not move until her husband had completed his pur-chases and came to her. And when she followed him out to take her place in the waggon, her eyes were bright and moist.

" Don't ye take the Blair's Holler road, Dave," she said, as he touched up his horses. " Go round by Jones's."

" What's yer notion, Louizy? " he asked.

" 'Tain't nothin' but a notion, I reckon," she answered; " but I don't—I don't want to hev to pass by that thar grave jest to-day. Take the other road."

And being an easy-going, kindly fellow, he humoured her and went the other way.

In the store itself the spirit of hilariousness increased as the day advanced. By mail-time the porch was crowded and Tom had some slight difficulty in maintaining order.

" Say, boys," he said, " there's got to be quiet here. If we can't carry on the establishment without disturbing the head of the household at present asleep in the back room, this post-office has to close and you can get a new postmaster. That'd suit you, I daresay. Some fellow, now, that wouldn't half 'tend to his business, not more than half, and that hadn't legislative ability enough to carry on a precinct, let alone a county. You want a man of that kind, I suppose. That's what you're working for."

" Tom," said one of the younger ones, " bring her out 'n' let's see her. You've been braggin' on her all day, but ye hain't let us see her."

Half a dozen others joined in the cry.

" Yes," they said, " bring her out, Tom."

Tom did not rise from his seat. He tilted his chair back and balanced himself on his heels, his hands thrust into his pockets.

"Boys," he said, " I'll bring her out on one condition, and that is that there shall be no shines. I wouldn't have her scared or upset for a good deal. There's a joke in this sort of thing, I daresay; but it ain't all joke. If I bring her out and show her, there's to be no crowding and no row."

It was agreed that there should be none, and he left his chair and went to the inner room again. When he returned, the men who had been lounging in the porch had come in, though perhaps not one among them understood his own unusual interest in the affair. Babies were not rarities in Hamlin County, every cabin and farmhouse in the region being filled to overflowing with white-headed, sunburnt youngsters. And yet when Tom appeared there was a moment of silence. The child was asleep, its tiny black head resting peacefully against the huge chest of its bearer. There was no trace of confusion or awkwardness in his face, he seemed well content with his burden, and perhaps it was the quiet of his manner as much as anything else which caused the slight hush to fall upon those around him.

At last a middle-aged farmer stepped forward. He gave the child a long and rather curious look.

" Gal, ain't it? " he enquired.

" Yes," Tom answered.

" Wal, 'tain't a bad thing fer her she's got some un to stan' by her; gals needs it."

Tom gave her a long look too. She was sleeping very quietly; it might have been her mother's breast she was lying against.

" Well," he said, " here's a man to stand by her," and then he raised his head and looked at the rest of them.

" Boys," he said, " that's a promise. Remember it."

And he carried her back.

CHAPTER VI

THE rooms at the back had never seemed so quiet before as when, at the close of the day, he went into them. They seemed all the quieter by contrast with the excitement of the past hours. In the kitchen Mornin was giving the final touches to the supper, and in the room which was at once sitting-room and bedroom, the wooden cradle had fitted itself in a corner near the fireplace and wore an air of permanent establishment remarkable to contemplate when one considered how unlooked-for an incident it was.

On the threshold of this apartment Tom paused a moment. Such silence reigned that he could hear the soft, faint breathing of the child as it lay asleep. He stopped a second or so to listen to it. Then he stooped down, and began to loosen his shoes gently. As he was doing it, Mornin caught sight of him in passing the open door.

" Mars Tom," she said, " what's ye a-gwine fer to do? "

" I'm going to take them off," he answered, seriously. " They'll make too much noise."

The good soul in the kitchen chuckled.

" Now," she said, " now, Mars Tom, dar ye go right now a-settin' out to ruinate a good chile, 'stead o' ustin' it ter things—a-settin' out ter ruinate it. Don't never tip aroun' fer no chile. Don't ye never do it, 'n' ye won't never haf ter. Tippin' roun' jest spiles 'em. Tell ye, Mornin never tipped roun' when she had em' ter raise. Mornin started out right from de fust."

Tom looked at the cradle.

" She'll rest easier," he said. " And so shall I. I must get a pair of slippers." And he slipped out of his shoes and stood ready to spend the evening in his stocking-feet. A solitary tallow candle stood upon the table, shedding its yellow light upon all surrounding objects to the best of its ability, and, seeing that its flickering brightness fell upon the small sleeper's face, he placed it at the farther end of the high mantel.

" She'll be more comfortable," he said. And then sat down feeling at ease with his conscience.

Mornin went back to her supper shaking her head.

" By de time she's a year old, dar won't be no managin' her," she said. " Da's allus de way wid de men folks, allus too hard or too soft; better leav' her to Mornin 'n' ust'n her to things right at de start."

There seemed little chance that she would be so " ustened." Having finished his supper, Tom carried his pipe and newspaper into the kitchen.

" I'll sit here awhile," he said. " The smoke might be too much for her, and the paper rustles so. We'd better let her have her sleep out."

But when the pipe was out and the last page of the paper read, he went back to his own room. The small ark stranded in his chimney corner was attractive enough to draw him there. It was a stronger attraction than it would have been to most men. He had always been fond of children and curious concerning them. There was not a child in the surrounding region who had not some remembrance of his rather too lavish good-nature. A visit to the Cross-roads was often held out as a reward for circumspect behaviour, and the being denied the treat was considered punishment heavy enough for most juvenile crimes.

" Ef ye'd had young uns of yer own, Tom, ye'd hev ruined them, shore," the secretly delighted matrons frequently remarked. " You'd let 'em run right over ye. I reckon ye keep that candy thar right a-purpose to feed 'em on now, don't yer? "

His numerous admirers, whose affection for him was founded on their enjoyment of his ponderous witticisms and the humour which was the little leavening of their unexciting lives, had once or twice during the past few days found themselves unprepared for, and so somewhat bewildered by, the new mood which had now and then revealed itself.

" It's kinder outer Tom's way to take things like he takes this; it looks onnat'ral," they said.

If they had seen him as he drew up to the cradle's side, they would have discovered that they were confronting a side of the man of which they knew nothing. It was the man whose youth had been sore-hearted and desolate, while he had been too humble to realise that it was so, and with reason. If he had known lonely hours in the past eight years, only the four walls of the little back room had seen them. He had always enacted his *rôle* well outside; but it was only natural that the three silent rooms must have seemed too empty now and again. As he bent over the cradle, he remembered such times, and somehow felt as if they were altogether things of the past and not to trouble him again.

" She'll be life in the place," he said. " When she sleeps less and is old enough to make more noise, it will be quite cheerful."

He spoke with the self-congratulating innocence of inexperience. A speculative smile settled upon his countenance.

64

"When she begins to crawl around and—and needs looking after, it will be lively enough," he reflected. "She'll keep us busy, I daresay."

It was a circumstance perhaps worthy of mention that he never spoke of the little creature as "it."

"She'll need a good deal of looking after," he went on. "It won't do to let her tumble around and take care of herself, as a boy might. We must be tender of her."

He bent forward and drew the cover cautiously over the red flannel sleeve.

"They think it a good joke, those fellows," he said; "but it isn't a joke with us, is it, young woman? We've a pretty big job to engineer between us, but I daresay we shall come out all right. We shall be good friends in the end, and that's a pretty nice thing for a lonely fellow to look forward to."

Then he arose stealthily and returned to the kitchen.

"I want you to tell me," he said to Mornin, "what she needs. I suppose she needs something or other."

"She needs mos' ev'rything, Mars Tom," was the answer; "seems like she hain't bin pervided fer 't all, no more 'n ef she was a-gwine ter be a youn' tukky dat de Lord hisself hed fitted out at de start."

"Well," said Tom, "I'll go to Barnesville to-morrow and talk to Judge Rutherford's wife about it. She'll know what she ought to have."

And, after a few moments given to apparently agreeable reflection, he went back to the room he had left.

He had barely seated himself, however, when he was disturbed by a low-sounding tap on the side door, which stood so far open as to allow of any stray evening breeze entering without reaching the corner of the chimney.

"Come in!" said Tom, not in a friendly roar, as usual, but in a discreetly guarded voice.

The door was pushed gently open and the visitor stood revealed, blinking with an impartial air at the light within.

"Don't push it wide open," said Tom; "come in if you are going to, and leave it as it was."

Mr. Stamps obeyed without making any noise whatever. It was one of his amiable peculiarities that he never made any noise, but appeared and disappeared without giving any warning, making himself very agreeable thereby at inopportune moments. He slipped in without a sound, deftly left the door in its previous position, and at once slipped into a chair, or rather took possession of one, by balancing himself on the extreme edge of it, arranging his legs on the lower bar with some dexterity.

"Howdy?" he said, meekly, having accomplished this.

Tom's manner was not cordial. He stretched himself, put his hands in his pockets, and made no response to the greeting which was, upon the whole, a rather unnecessary one, as Mr. Stamps had been hanging about the post-office through the whole day, and had only wended his way homeward a few hours before.

"Want anything?" he enquired.

Mr. Stamps turned his hat around in his hands hurriedly.

"No, I don't want nothin', Tom," he said. Then, after a pause, he added, very softly:

"I jest thought I'd step in."

"Where are you going?" asked Tom.

The hat was turned round again.

"Whar wus I a-gwine?" deprecatingly. "Whar? Oh! I—I was a-gwine—I was a-gwine to Marthy's, I guess."

In Connection with
The De Willoughby Claim

" You're pretty late," remarked Tom; " better lose no time; it's a pretty bad road between here and there."

" So 'tis," replied Mr. Stamps, apparently struck with the originality of the suggestion. " So 'tis! " He appeared to reflect deeply for a few seconds, but suddenly his eyes began to wander across the room and rested finally upon the corner in which the cradle stood. He jerked his head towards it.

" It's thar, is it? " he enquired.

" Yes, she's thar," Tom answered, rather crustily. " What of it? "

" Oh! nothin', nothin', Tom, only it's kinder curi's— kinder curi's."

" Well," said Tom, " I've not begun to look at it in that light yet myself."

" Hain't ye, now? " softly. " Hain't ye, Tom? "

Then a faint little chuckle broke from him—not an intrusive chuckle, quite the contrary; a deprecatory and inadvertent sort of chuckle.

" That ain't me," he ventured, inoffensively. " I've been a-thinkin' it was curi's all along."

" That ain't going to hurt anybody," responded Tom.

" Lord, no! " quite in a hurry. " Lord, no! 'tain't likely; but it kinder int'rusted me—int'rusted me, findin' out what I did."

And he ended with a gently suggestive cough.

Tom thrust his hands deeper into his pockets and covered as large an area of floor with his legs as was possible without upsetting Mr. Stamps's chair and at the same time that stealthy little man himself.

" Oh! found out! " he replied, " Found out h——"

He checked himself with much suddenness, glancing at the cradle as he did so.

"What did you find out?" he demanded, unceremoniously, and with manifest contempt. "Let's hear."

Mr. Stamps coughed again.

"'Twan't much, mebbe," he replied, cautiously, "'n' then again, mebbe 'twas. It was kinder int'rusting, though. That —that thar was a good prayer o' his'n, warn't it?"

"Yes," admitted Tom, rather blusteringly. "I daresay it was; I suppose you are a better judge of prayers than I am."

"I'm a purty good judge on 'em," modestly. "I'd orter be, bein' a class-leader 'n' uster kinder critykisin'. I don't never do it much in public myself, but I've allus critikised them as did. Thet sounded more professionaller then they air mostly—unless comin' frum them as has bin raised to it."

"Did it?" said Tom.

"Yes, it was more professionaller."

Then he turned his hat again, setting it more carefully on his knee. He also fixed his eyes on Tom with a harmless smile.

"They wus North'ners."

Tom started, but managed to recover himself.

"You might have mentioned that before," he remarked, with sarcasm.

"I did," said Mr. Stamps, "along at the start, Tom; but ye wouldn't none on ye believe me."

Tom remembered that this was true, it having been Mr. Stamps who suggested the Northern theory which had been so unitedly scouted by his hearers at the time of its propounding.

"I h'ain't stayed as stiddy in North Car'lina as the rest on 'em," repeated Mr. Stamps. "When I was younger, I kinder launched out wunct. I thought I could make money faster ef I wus in a more money-makin'er place, 'n' I launched out. I went North a spell 'n' was thar a right smart while. I sorter stedded the folks' ways 'n' I got to knowin' 'em when I seed 'em 'n' heerd 'em talk. I know'd her for one the minit I set eyes on her 'n' heern her speak. I didn't say nuthin' much to the rest on ye, 'cause I know's ye'd make light on it; but I know'd it wus jest that ar way with the Northerners."

" Well," said Tom, "it's valuable information, I suppose."

Mr. Stamps coughed. He turned his hat over and looked into its greasy and battered crown modestly.

" It mout be," he replied, " 'n' then again it moughtent. It moughtent be if thar' wus nuthin' else to go 'long with it. They wus hidin' sumthin', ye know, 'n' they sot a heap on keepin' it hid. Ef a body know'd the whole thing from the start, thet'd be int'rustin', 'n' it 'ud be vallyable too."

" Valuable be d——" Tom began, but he checked himself once more on glancing at the cradle.

But Mr. Stamps was so far interested that he did not read the warning he might have read in the suddenly repressed outbreak. As he neared his goal he became a little excited and incautious. He leaned forward, blinking rapidly.

" They wasn't no man 'n' wife," he said. " Lord, no! 'N' ef the two as knowed most on 'em 'n' was kinder quickest at readin' signs 'd kinder go partners 'n' heve confidence in one another, 'n' sorter lay to 'n' work it out 'n' foller it up, it ud be vallybler than stores, or post-offices, or farms to both on 'em." And he leaned so far forward and blinked so fast that he lost his balance and almost fell off his chair.

It was Tom who saved him from his fall, but not from

that tender consideration for his physical security which such an act would argue. Tom gathered up his legs and strode across to him almost before he had finished speaking. For the time being he had apparently forgotten the cradle and its occupant. He seized the little man by the back of his collar and lifted him bodily out of his chair and shook him as a huge mastiff might have shaken a rat, agitating the little legs in the large trousers with a force which gave them, for a few seconds, the most active employment.

" You confounded, sneaking, underhanded little thief! " he thundered. " You damned little scoundrel! You—you——"

And he bore him out of doors, set him struggling astride his mule which was cropping the grass, and struck that sagacious animal a blow upon her quarters which sent her galloping along the Barnesville Road at a pace which caused her rider to cling to her neck and body with arms and legs, in which inconvenient posture he remained, unable to recover himself, for a distance of at least half a mile.

Tom returned to the back room in some excitement. As he crossed the threshold, he was greeted by a shrill cry from the cradle. He ruefully regarded the patchwork quilt which seemed to be struggling violently with some unseen agency.

" Doggone him! " he said, innocently, " he's wakened her —wakened her, by thunder! "

And he sat down, breathing heavily from his bodily exertion, and began to rock the cradle with a vigour and gravity which might have been expected to achieve great results, if Mornin had not appeared and taken his charge into her own hands.

CHAPTER VII

THE next day Tom went to Barnesville. He left the Cross-roads on horseback early in the morning, and reached his journey's end at noon. He found on arriving at the town that the story of his undertaking had preceded him.

When he drew rein before Judge Rutherford's house and having dismounted and tied his horse to the fence, entered the gate, the Judge's wife came out upon the porch to meet him with her baby in her arms.

She greeted him with a smile.

"Well," she said, "I must say I am glad to see you. The Judge brought us a nice story from the country yesterday. What have you been doing at the Cross-roads? I told the Judge I didn't believe a word of it. There, sit down in this chair and tell me right away."

"Well," answered Tom in a business-like manner, "it's true or I shouldn't be here to-day. I've come to ask your advice about—well, about things in general."

Mrs. Rutherford uttered a little cry of delighted curiosity and surprise.

"Gracious!" she exclaimed, "I never heard such a thing! Mother!" turning her head to call to someone in the room beyond, "it's all true about the baby. Do come and hear Mr. De Willoughby tell about it."

She sat down on the steps of the porch laughing and yet regarding Tom with a half sympathetic, half curious look. It was not the first time she had found him unexpectedly mysterious.

" Where's the father? " she said. " Didn't he care for the poor little thing at all? The Judge heard that he was so poor that he couldn't take care of it. Hadn't he any friends? It has a kind of heartless sound to me—his going away that way."

" He was poor," said Tom, quietly. " And he had no relatives who could take the child. He didn't know what to do with it. I—I think he had a chance of making a living out West and—the blow seemed to have stunned him."

" And you took the baby? " put in Mrs. Rutherford.

" Yes," Tom answered, " I took the baby."

" Is it a pretty baby? "

" Yes," said Tom, " I think it is."

Just then the Judge's mother came out and he was called upon to tell the story again, when it was received with interest even more excited and wondering than before. The older Mrs. Rutherford exclaimed and looked dubious alternately.

" Are you sure you know what to do with it? " she asked.

" Well, no," said Tom, " I'm not. I suppose I shall have to educate myself up to it gradually. There'll be a good deal to learn, I suppose."

But he did not appear at all discouraged, and presently broached the object of his visit, displaying such modest readiness to accept advice and avail himself of all opportunities for acquiring valuable information, that his young hostess was aroused to the deepest admiration, and when he proceeded to produce quite a large memorandum book with a view to taking an immediate list of all required articles, and established rules, she could scarcely contain her delight.

" I want to do it all up in the proper way," he said.

Thereupon he was borne into the house and a consultation of the most serious practical nature was held. Piles of the last baby's pretty garments being produced to illustrate any obscure point. The sight of those garments with their embroidery and many frills fired Tom with new enthusiasm. He could not resist the temptation to pick up one after another of the prettiest and most elaborate and hold them out at arm's length, his fingers stuck through the sleeves the better to survey and display them to advantage.

" Yes," he kept saying, " that's the kind of thing she wants—pretty and with plenty of frills."

He seemed to set his heart especially upon this abundance of frills and kept it in view throughout the entire arrangements. Little Mrs. Rutherford was to take charge of the matter, purchasing all necessaries and superintending the work of placing it in competent hands.

" Why," she said, laughing at him delightedly, " she'll be the best dressed baby in the county."

" I'd like her to be among the best," said Tom, with a grave face, " among the best."

Whereupon Mrs. Rutherford laughed a little again, and then quite suddenly stopped and regarded him for a moment with some thoughtfulness.

" He has some curious notions about that baby, mother," she said afterwards. " I can see it in all he says. Everyone mightn't understand it. I'm not sure I do myself, but he has a big, kind heart, that Tom de Willoughby, a big, kind heart."

She understood more clearly the workings of the big, kind heart before he left them the next morning.

At night after she had put her child to sleep, she joined him on the front porch, where he sat in the moonlight, and there he spoke more fully to her.

He had seated himself upon the steps of the porch and wore a deeper reflective air, as he played with a spray of honeysuckle he had broken from its vine.

She drew up her rocking-chair and sat down near him.

" I actually believe you are thinking of that baby now," she said, with a laugh. " You really look as if you were."

" Well," he admitted, " the fact is that's just what I was doing—thinking of her."

" Well, and what were you thinking? "

" I was thinking—" holding his spray of honeysuckle between his thumb and forefinger and looking at it in an interested way, " I was thinking about what name I should give her."

" Oh! " she said, " she hasn't any name? "

" No," Tom answered, without removing his eyes from his honeysuckle, " she hasn't any name yet."

" Well," she exclaimed, " they were queer people."

There was a moment's silence which she spent in looking curiously both at him and his honeysuckle.

" What was her mother's name? " she asked at last.

" I don't know."

Mrs. Rutherford sat up in her chair.

" You don't know! "

" She was dying when I saw her first, and I never thought of asking."

" But her father? "

" I didn't think of asking that either, and nobody knew anything of them. I suppose he was not in the frame of mind to think of such things himself. It was all over and done with so soon. He went away as soon as she was buried."

Mrs. Rutherford sank back into her chair.

" It's the strangest story I ever heard of in my life," she commented, with a sigh of amazement. " The man must have been crazed with grief. I suppose he was very fond of his wife? "

" I suppose so," said Tom.

There was another pause of a few moments, and from the thoughts with which they occupied it Mrs. Rutherford roused herself with a visible effort.

" Well," she said, cheerily, " let it be a pretty name."

" Yes," answered Tom, " it must be a pretty one."

He turned the bit of honeysuckle so that the moonlight fell on its faintly tinted flower. It really seemed as if he felt he should get on better for having it to look at and refer to.

" I want it to be a pretty name," he went on, " and I've thought of a good many that sounded well enough, but none of them seemed exactly to hit my fancy in the right way until I thought of one that came into my mind a few moments ago as I sat here. It has a pleasant meaning—I don't know that there's anything in that, of course; but I've got a sort of whim about it. I suppose it's a whim. What do you think—" looking very hard at the honey-suckle, " of Felicia? "

" I think," said his companion, " that it is likely to be the best name you could give her, for if she isn't a happy creature it won't be your fault."

" Well," said Tom, " I've set out to do my best and I'd like to give her a fair start in every way, even in her name, though there mayn't be anything in it, but I'd like to do it.

In Connection with
The De Willoughby Claim

I suppose it's time I should be having some object in life. I've never had one before, and I've been a useless fellow. Well, I've got one now by chance, and I'm bound to hold on to it and do what I can. I want her to have what chances I can give her on her side, and it came into my mind that Felicia——"

He stopped to consult the honeysuckle, as it were, and Jenny Rutherford broke in:

"Yes," she said, "Felicia is the name for her, and it's a beautiful thought——"

"Oh!" interrupted Tom, bestirring himself uneasily, "it's a natural thought. She needs all she can get to balance the trouble she began life with. Most other little chaps begin it in a livelier way—in a way that's more natural, born into a home, and all that. It's a desolate business that she should have no one but a clumsy fellow like me to pick her up, and that there should be a shadow of—of trouble and pain and death over her from the first. Good Lord!" with a sudden movement of his big arm, "let's sweep it away if we can."

The thought so stirred him, that he turned quite around as he sat.

"Look here," he said, "that's what I was aiming at when I set my mind on having her things frilled up and ornamented. I want them to be what they might have been if she had been born of a woman who was happy and well cared for and—and loved—as if she had been thought of and looked forward to and provided for in a—in a tender way—as they say young mothers do such things: you know how that is; I don't, perhaps, I've only thought of it sometimes——" his voice suddenly dropping.

But he had thought of it often, in his lonely back room

one winter a few years ago, when it had drifted to him that his brother De Courcy was the father of a son.

Mrs. Rutherford leaned forward in her seat, tears rose in her eyes, and she put her hand impulsively on his shoulder.

" Oh! " she cried, " you are a good man. You're a good man, and if she lives, she will tell you so and love you with all her heart. I will see to the little clothes just as if they were Nellie's own " (Nellie being the baby, or more properly speaking, the last baby, as there were others in the household). " And if there is anything I can ever do for the little thing, let me do it for her poor young mother's sake."

Tom thanked her gratefully.

" I shall be glad to come to you often enough, I reckon," he said. " I guess she'll have her little sick spells, as they all do, and it'll help wonderfully to have someone to call on. There's her teeth now," anxiously, " they'll be coming through in a few months, and then there'll be the deuce to pay."

He was so overweighted by this reflection, that he was silent for some minutes afterwards and was only roused by a question requiring a reply.

Later the Judge came in and engaged him in political conversation, all the Judge's conversation being of a political nature and generally tending to vigorous denunciations of some candidate for election who belonged to the opposite party. In Barnesville political feeling ran high, never running low, even when there was no one to be elected or defeated, which was very seldom the case, for between such elections and defeat there was always what had been done or what ought to have been done at Washington to discuss, it being strongly felt that without the assistance of Barnesville, Washington would be in a sorry plight indeed.

To-day the Judge had been engaged in a livelier discussion than usual as he rode homeward with a select party of legal brethren from court at Brownsboro, and consequently made his appearance blustering and joyous. He bestowed upon his wife a sounding kiss, and, with one arm around her waist, shook hands with Tom in a gust of hospitality, speaking to both at once.

"Howdy, Jenny? Howdy, Tom? It's a coon's age since we've seen you, Tom. Time you showed yourself. How are the children, Jenny—and what's Tom Scott been doing? What's this we hear about that stray young one? Nice tale that is to tell on a fellow. Fowler heard it at Brownsboro and like to have killed himself. Lord! how hot it's been! I'm ready for supper, Jenny. Sit down, Tom. As soon as I get through supper, we'll have a real old-fashioned talk. I've been suffering for one for three months. Jenny, tell Sophronia to spread herself on her waffles, for I've been getting some mighty poor stuff for the last few days. What do you think of Thatcher running for the Legislature? Lord! Lord! what a fool that fellow is! Most unpopular man in the county, and about the meanest too. Mean? Lord! mean ain't the name for it! He'll be beat so that any other man wouldn't want to show his head, and it won't make a mark on him. Nellie's asleep, ain't she, Jenny? I've got to go and look at her and the rest of them. Don't you want to come along, Tom? You're a family man yourself now, and you ought to take an interest!"

He led the way into the family-room at the back and, taking the candle from the high mantel, moved it triumphantly over the beds in which the children slept.

In Connection with
The De Willoughby Claim

"Here's Tom Scott!" he announced. "Tom Scott's got to have a crib to himself. Look at him now. What do you think of that for a boy? He's five years old next month, and he about runs Barnesville. The boys round here are just ruining him with making much of him and setting him up to tricks. He just lives round at the stores and the post-office. And what Tom Scott don't know ain't worth knowing. Came home with six jack-knives in his pockets the first day Jenny turned him out in pantaloons. The boys tried themselves to see who could do best by him. You could hear them shouting and laughing all over the town at the things they got him to say. I tell you he's a case, Tom is. Last election he was as stirred up as any of us. Hollered ' 'Rah for Collins' until he was hoarse and his mother brought him home and gave him syrup of squills because she thought he had the croup. What do you think he did, now? Went into Barton's store and ordered a bushel of chestnuts to be sent down to my account and brought 'em out and set on the horse-block and gave a treat for Collins. I was coming up home and saw the crowd and heard the hollering and laughing, and there was Tom in the middle baling out his chestnuts and hollering at the top of his voice: 'Come on, boys, all you Collins men, here's a treat for Collins!' I thought Collins would have died when he heard it. He laughed until he choked, and the next day he came to see Tom and gave him a gold eagle and a colt. He says he is going to give him a little nigger to look after it, and he'll do it. Oh, Tom Scott's the boy! He'll be in the White House forty years from now. He's making a bee-line for it right now."

And he bent and kissed the little fellow's sunburnt rosy cheek.

In Connection with
The De Willoughby Claim

" His mother and his grandmother can't do a thing with him," he said, rapturously, " and it's as much as I can do to manage him. Oh, he's a case, is Tom Scott! "

And with this tribute to his character, he left him to his slumbers, with his sturdy little legs occupying an extensive area of crib and his face resting on his small brown arm.

After this, the Judge went to his supper and consumed a large quantity of fried chicken, waffles, and coffee, afterwards joining Tom on the porch, smoking his pipe and stigmatising Thatcher in a loud and jovial voice as the meanest man in Hamlin.

But for this resonant jovialness of voice, his denunciatin of the Democratic Party, which was not his party, might have appeared rather startling.

" There isn't an honest man among them," he announced. " Not a durned one! They're all the same. Cut each other's throats for a dime, the whole caboodle. Oh! damn a Democrat anyhow, Tom, 'tain't in the nature of things that they should be anything but thieves and rascals. Just look at the whole thing. It's founded on lies and corruption and scoundrelism. That's their foundation. They start out on it, and it ain't reasonable to expect anything better of them. Good Lord! If I thought Tom Scott would join the Democrats, I believe I'd blow his brains out in his crib this minute."

Tom's part in this discussion was that of a large-minded and strictly impartial listener. This was the position he invariably assumed when surrounded by political argument. He was not a politician. His comments upon political subjects being usually of a sarcastic nature, and likely to prove embarrassing to both parties.

" Yes," he said in reply to the Judge's outpourings,

"you're right. There ain't a chance for them, not an eternal chance. You can't expect it, and it ain't all their fault either. Where are they to get their decent men from, unless some of you fellows go over? Here you are without a liar or a fool among you—not a durned one—made a clean sweep of all the intellect and honesty and incorruptible worth in the country and hold on to it too, and then let out on these fellows because there isn't any left for 'em. I'm a lazy man myself and not much on argument, but I must say that's a weak place in your logic. You don't give 'em a show at the start—that's their misfortune."

" Oh, go to thunder! " roared the Judge, amiably. " You don't know the first thing about it and never did. That's where you fail—in politics. The country would be in a mighty poor fix if we had many fellows like you—in a mighty poor fix. You're a good citizen, Tom, but you ain't a politician."

" That's so," said Tom. " I ain't good enough for your party or bad enough for the other, when a man's got to be either a seraphim or a Democrat, there isn't much chance for an ordinary fellow to spread himself."

Whereupon the Judge in an altogether friendly manner consigned him to thunder again and, evidently enjoying himself immensely, proceeded to the most frightful denunciations of Thatcher and his party, the mere list of whose crimes and mental incapacities should have condemned them to perdition and the lunatic asylum upon the spot without further delay.

While he was in the midst of this genial loud-voiced harangue, his wife, who had been in the back room with the baby, came out and, on seeing her, he seemed suddenly to forget his animosities and the depraved political condition of the country altogether, becoming a placable, easily pleased, domesticated creature at once.

"Got Nellie to sleep again, have you?" he said, putting his hand on her shoulder. "Well, let's go in and have some music. Come and sing 'The Last Rose of Summer.' That's my favourite; it beats all the new-fangled opera things all to pieces."

He led the way into the parlour, which was a large square room, regarded by Barnesville as the most sumptuous of reception chambers, inasmuch as its floor was covered by a Brussels carpet adorned with exotics of multifarious colours, its walls ornamented with massively framed photographs, and its corners fitted up with whatnots and shining hair-cloth seats known in Hamlin County as "tater-tates," and in that impressive character admired beyond expression. Its crowning glory, however, was the piano, which had belonged to Jenny Rutherford in her boarding-school days, and was the delight of the Judge's heart. It furnished him with his most cherished recreation in his hours of repose from political conflict and argument, inasmuch as he regarded his wife's performance seldom to be equalled and never surpassed, and the soft, pleasant voice with which she sang "The Last Rose of Summer" and other simple and sentimental melodies as that of a cantatrice whose renown might have been world-wide if she had chosen to turn her attention to its development.

"Lord!" he said, throwing himself into one of the shining arm-chairs. "There's nothing like music, nothing under the shining sun. 'Music hath charms to soothe the savage breast.'"

This in his most sonorous quotation tones: "Let a man

get tired or out of sorts, or infernal mad at a pack of cursed fools, and music's the thing that'll set him straight every time, if he's any sort of a fellow. A man that ain't fond of music ain't of any account on God's green earth. I wouldn't trust him beyond a broom-straw. There's a mean streak in a man that don't care for music, sure. Why, the time the Democrats elected Peyton, the only thing that saved me from bursting a blood-vessel was Jenny's playing ' My Lodging's on the Cold Ground ' with variations. I guess she played it for two hours hand-running, because when I found it was sort of soothing me, I didn't want her to break in on the effect by beginning another. Play it for Tom, Jenny, after you've sung awhile. There's one thing I've made up my mind to—if I had fifty girls, I'd have 'em all learn music if they didn't know anything—not the operatic kind, you know, but enough to teach them to sing to a man like Jenny does. Go on, Jenny."

The sustaining and cheering effects of Sophronia's fried chicken and waffles probably added to his comfortable enjoyment, which was without limit. He leaned back in his arm-chair as far as the stiffly ornamented back would admit of his so doing and kept time with his head or his feet, occasionally joining in on a chorus with startling suddenness in an evidently subdued roar, which, though subdued, was still roaring enough, and, despite the excellence of its intention, quite out of tune enough to cause the wax flowers in their wax basket on the table (both done by Jenny at boarding-school) to shake under the glass shade until they tapped against its side with a delicate tinkle.

It was while this was going on that Tom, sitting near a side table, picked up a book and almost unconsciously opened it and read its title. Having read its title, an expression of interest showed itself on his countenance and he turned over a leaf or so, and as he turned them over dipped into them here and there.

He had the book in his hand when Jenny Rutherford ended her last chorus and came towards him.

" Do you go much by this? " he asked.

She took it from him and glanced at it.

" I brought Tom Scott up on it," she said. " Mother wasn't with me then, and I was such a child I did not know what to do with him."

" Seems to be a good sort of book," said Tom, and he turned over the leaves again.

" It is," she answered, smiling at him. " There are lots of things in it every doctor don't know. It was written by a woman."

" That's the reason, I reckon," said Tom.

He laid the book down and seemed to forget it, but about an hour after when his bedroom candle was brought and he was on the point of retiring for the night, he turned upon the threshold of the sitting-room and spoke to his hostess in the tone of one suddenly recollecting himself.

" Where did you say you got that book? " he inquired, snuffing his candle with his thumb and forefinger.

" I didn't say at all," answered Jenny. " I got it from Brough & Bros., Baltimore."

" Oh, there! " he remarked. " Good-night."

When he reached his room and shut himself in, he set his candlestick on a table and proceeded to draw from his pocket the memorandum-book, also producing the stump of a lead pencil.

Then he made as he stood up before the looking-glass and in the flickering light of the candle, an entry which was

as follows: "Advice to Young Mothers, Brough & Bros."
He made it with a grave countenance and a business-like
manner, and somehow, owing it may be to the small size of
the room, its low ceilings and many shadows, or the flickering of the candle, his colossal height and breadth of body
and tremendous look of strength had never seemed so
marked nor appeared so to overpower the objects surrounding him.

Having completed the entry, he shut up the book and returned it to his pocket with a relieved air.

"If a man ain't a young mother," he remarked, "I guess
he can get the good of it, if he gives himself time. And
what she wants"—rather hurriedly—"is to get as good
a start as if she had a young mother."

And he sat down and pulled off his right boot in so absorbed a frame of mind, that he aroused presently with a
start to find that he was holding it as if it had been made
of much less tough material and required handling tenderly.

CHAPTER VIII

HE was on his way homeward early the next morning, and by noon his horse had climbed the rising ground from which he could look down on the Cross-roads and the post-office baking itself brown in the sun. Catching sight of the latter edifice, he smiled a little and shook the bridle against his steed's warm neck.

"Get along, Jake," he said. "I'm in a little more of a hurry to get home than usual—seems that way anyhow."

The eagerness he felt was a new experience with him and stirred his sense of humour even while it warmed his always easily moved heart. It had been his wont during the last eight years to return from any absence readily but never eagerly or with any touch of excited pleasure. Even at their brightest aspect, with the added glow of fire and warmth and good cheer, and contrast to winter's cold and appetite sharpened by it, the back rooms had always suffered from the disadvantage of offering no prospect of companionship or human interest to him. After the supper had been disposed of and the newspapers read and the pipe smoked, there had only been the fire to watch, and it was quite natural to brood as its blaze died down and its logs changed to a bed of glowing cinders. Under such circumstances it was easy to fall into a habit of brooding too much and thinking of things which had better been forgotten. When there was no fire, it had been lonelier still, and he had found the time hang heavily on his hands.

" But now," he said, shaking his bridle again, " there she is, and it's quite queer, by thunder, how much she seems to give a man to think of and what will it be when she begins to talk." And his smile ended in a jovial laugh which rather startled Jake, who was not expecting it, and caused him to shy promptly.

She was not asleep when he entered her presence, which was so unusual a state of affairs that he found it a little alarming.

" Hello! " he exclaimed, " there's nothing wrong, I hope."

" Wid dat chile? " chuckled Mornin, delightedly. " I sh'd think not, Mars' D'Willerby! Dat ar chile's a-thrivin' an' a-comin' 'long jes' like she'd orter. Dar ain't a-gwine to be nothin' wrong wid dat chile."

" That's a good thing," said Tom.

He sat down by the cradle's side and regarded its occupant with an interest as fresh as if she had just appeared for the first time upon his horizon. She had been imbibing a large quantity of milk, and the effect of this nourishment had been to at once compose her spirits and slightly enliven them. So she employed the passing moments by looking at Tom with steadfast and solemn eyes—not, perhaps, very intelligently, but still with a vacant air of interest in him in his character of an object.

" Why," he said, " she's grown; she's grown in thirty-six hours, and she's improved too. Oh, yes! she's coming along nicely."

He touched her very carefully with his large forefinger, a liberty which she did not resent or even notice, unless the fact that she winked both eyes might be regarded as a token of recognition.

" We'll have a box full of things here for her in a couple of weeks," he said. " And then she can start out in life— start out in life."

The last four words seemed to please him; as he repeated them he touched her cheek again, carefully as before.

" And start out fair, too! " he added. " Fair and square —as fair and square as any of them."

He remained a little longer in his seat by the cradle, talking to Mornin, asking her questions and delivering messages laden with advice from little Mrs. Rutherford, which instructions Aunt Mornin plainly regarded as superfluous.

" Now, Mars' D'Willerby," she giggled in amiable scorn, " didn't I raise fo' o' my young Mistes's? Mornin ain't no spring chicken. Dar ain't nuffin 'bout chillun Mornin h'aint heerd. Leeve dis yere chile to Mornin."

" She ain't going to be left to anyone," said Tom, cheerfully, " not to the best woman in Hamlin County. We've got to make up to her for two or three things, and we're going to do it."

Having relieved himself of which sentiment, he went to his place at the table and ate a mighty dinner, during his enjoyment of which meal he did not lose interest in his small silent partner at all, but cast proud glances and jocular sallies at her every few mouthfuls, partaking of her, as it were, with his mountain trout, and finding her add flavour and zest to his hot corn-bread and fried ham.

When he had ended his repast with an astonishing draught of buttermilk, and was ready to go into the store, she had dozed off cosily again and was making the best of her opportunities, so he only paused for a moment to give her a farewell glance.

" Yes," he said, " Felicia—that'll do. When you come

to the meaning of it, I don't know of anything else that'd seem to start her out as fair—Felicia! "

And though he said the word in a whisper it seemed to reach her ear in some mysterious way, for she stirred slightly, though not as through any sense of disturbance, opened her eyes upon his big figure and, closing them the next instant, sank into soft sleep again with the faintest dawn or ghost of a baby smile upon her face.

So, nestling under the patchwork quilt and sleeping the hours away in the small ark stranded in the chimney corner, she began life.

．　　．　　．　　．　　．　　．　　．

Felicia was received by Talbot's Cross-roads with some difference of opinion.

"I'd rather had Mirandy or Lucretia," said Mrs. Doty. "Flishyer ain't nigh as showy as a heap o' other names, 'n' like as not, folks 'll be callin' her F'lish. Now thar's Vangerline 'n' Clementine 'n' Everlyne that'd ha' bin showier then Flishyer."

"Tom," put in Mr. Doty, with his usual enjoyment of his friend's weakness and strength, "Tom he'd a notion 'bout it. He said it meant som'n 'bout her a'bein' happy, 'n' he 'lowed it'd kinder give her a start in the right direction. It's jes' like Tom. He's full o' notions when he gits started. I'll back him agin any man in Hamlin fur notions when he gits started. Lord! it's jes' Tom all over! "

Through a disposition to take even names easily and avoid in all cases any unnecessary exertion, Mrs. Doty's pronunciation was adopted at once, which was perhaps the principal reason for a fanciful change being made not long afterwards.

Against "F'lishyer" Tom rebelled loudly and without ceasing, but without effect.

The fanciful change came about and was adopted in this wise. In the course of a couple of weeks the box of little garments arrived from Barnesville, accompanied by a warm-hearted note from Jenny Rutherford.

The unpacking of the box—which was not a large one, though it seemed to contain an astonishing number of things, most of them of great length and elaborateness— was to Tom a singularly exciting event, so exciting that he found himself wondering and not at all sure that he understood it.

When he opened the box—Mornin standing at his side, her charge in her arms—he did it with tremulous fingers, and when, having laid one article after another in a snowy drift upon the bed, he drew back to look at them, he found it necessary after a few moments' inspection to turn about and pace the floor, not uneasily, but to work off steam as it were, while Mornin uttered her ejaculations of rapture.

" I never seen nuthin' like 'em afore, Mars' D'Willerby," she said with many excitable giggles. " Dis yer chile's a-gwine to take the flo' shore as yo' bawn! Sich a settin' out as dat is! She'll git ter puttin' on airs afore she's a year ole. We'll hev ter give her a settin' down wunce 'n a while to keep her straight. Mis' Rutherford, she wus boun' to do it up in style, she wus ! "

Tom took one hand out of his pocket and ruffled his hair with it, and then put it back again.

" Your young mistresses now," he suggested, " I suppose they are about such things as their mothers made for them."

" Lordy, dey's a heap finer, Mars' D'Willerby—a heap

finer! Dey wus rich folks' chillun, but dey never hed sich a settin' out as dis yere—not one on 'em."

"They didn't?" said Tom, with secretly repressed exultation. "Well, if they didn't, I guess she'll do. They are rather nice, I reckon—and I meant they should be. Say, Mornin, suppose you dress her up and let me show her to the boys."

He himself picked out the sumptuous long-skirted garments she was to wear and watched with the deepest interest the rather slow process of her attiring. He was particularly pleased with a wonderfully embroidered white cloak and lace cap, which latter article he abstractedly tied on his great fist and found much too small for it. His triumph, when she was given to his arms, he did not attempt to conceal, but carried her into the store with the manner of a large victor bearing his spoils.

"Now look here, boys," he announced, being greeted with the usual laughter and jocular remarks. "This ain't the style of thing we want. Hand a man a chair."

His customary support being produced, he seated himself in it, keeping his charge balanced with a dexterity and ease quite wonderful to behold.

"What we want," he proceeded, "is a more respectful tone. Something in the elaborate chivalric style, and we're going to have it. What we want is to come into this establishment feeling that there's no risk of our being scared or upset by any durned fool startling us and setting our delicate machinery wrong. We've come here to stay, and we expect to be more familiar with things as we grow older, and the thing for us is to start out right without any disagreeable impressions. We don't want to say when we're brought in here—' Why, here's the place where that fool gave me such a start last week. I wonder if he's here again?' What we want is to feel that here's a place that's home, and a place that a person's likely to look forward to coming to with the view to ah—I should say to a high old time of an agreeable description."

" She's a-goin' to be a doggoned purty critter," said a lounger who sat on a barrel near by.

" She ain't nuthin' like her mother," said another; " though she wus a purty critter when I seed her."

He had only seen her in her coffin.

" She ain't like her father," put in another.

Tom moved in his chair uneasily.

" She won't be like either of them," he said. " Let that go."

There was a tone in his voice which more than one among them had now and again noticed with some slow bewilderment during the last few weeks—a tone new to them, but which in time they grew used to, though they never understood its meaning.

" Kinder," they used to say, " as ef he wus mad or—ruffed up, though it warn't that exactly, either."

" Black eyes, h'ain't she? " inquired the man on the barrel.

" Yes."

" An har. That's my kind er women, black eyes an' har, and kinder spirity. They've more devil to 'em 'n is better able to take care of 'emselves."

" She's got some one to take care of her," answered Tom. " That's my business."

" You've got her mightily fixed up, Tom," remarked Mr. Doty, who had just entered. " You'll hev all the women in the country flocking up. She sorter makes me think o' the Queen o' Sheby. Sheby, she wus great on fixin'."

In Connection with
The De Willoughby Claim

Every man who entered, seeing her as she lay in state in Tom's lap, was drawn towards her to stand and wonder at her vaguely. There developed a tendency to form small and rather silent groups about her. Infancy was no novelty in this region of numerous progenies, but the fine softness of raiment and delicate sumptuousness of infancy were. More than one man, having looked at her and wandered away, was unable to resist the temptation to wander back again and finally to settle in some seat or box upon a barrel, that he might the better indulge his curiosity and interest.

" Ye must hev spent a heap on her, Tom," was said respectfully again and again.

The fact that " a heap had been spent on her " inspired the audience with a sense of her importance, which amounted to reverence. That she represented an apparently unaccountable expenditure, was considered to reflect credit upon her, however vaguely, and to give her a value not to be lightly regarded. To Mr. Doty the idea of the " Queen of Sheby " appeared to recur persistently, all his imaginings of the poetic, the dramatic, and luxurious being drawn from Scriptural sources.

" I can't think o' nuthin' else but Sheby when I look at her," he remarked several times. " She 'minds me more o' Sheby then anything else 'n Scripter. Minty'll jest hev to come ter see her."

This boldness of imagery struck a chord in the breast of his hearers which responded at once. It was discovered that more than one of them had been reminded in some indefinite manner of the same distinguished personage.

" When she was consider'ble younger then in Solomon's time," said one gentleman with much solemnity.

Tom himself was caught by the fancy and when his

charge was referred to occasionally in a most friendly spirit as "Sheby thar," he made no protest against it.

"It's a thunderation sight better than 'Flishyer,'" he said, "and if it comes easier to you fellows, I've no objection. Sheba ain't bad. There's a kind of swing to it, and you can't get it very far wrong. The other's a good name spoiled, and it's a name I've a fancy for saving for her. I gave it to her—I'll save it for her, and it shall be a thing between us two. Call her Sheba if you like."

So it fell out that Mr. Doty's Oriental imaginings sealed her fate and gradually, by a natural process, Felicia was abandoned for Sheba, even Tom using it upon all ordinary occasions.

Having in this manner begun life, a day rarely passed in which she did not spend an hour or so in the post-office. Each afternoon during the first few months of her existence Tom brought her forth attired in all her broidery, and it was not long before the day came when he began to cherish the fancy that she knew when the time for her visit was near, and enjoyed it when it came.

"She looks as if she did," he said to Mornin. "She wouldn't go to sleep yesterday after I came into the room, and I'll swear I saw her eyes following me as I walked about; and when I carried her in after she was dressed, she turned her head over her shoulder to look round her and smiled when she had done it and found nothing was missing. Oh! she knows well enough when she gets in there."

The fancy was a wonderfully pleasant one to him, and when, as time went on, she developed a bright baby habit of noticing all about her, and expressing her pleasure in divers soft little sounds, he was a happier man than he had ever thought to be. His greatest pleasure was the certain

knowledge that she had first noticed himself—that her first
, greeting had been given to him, that her first conscious
caress had been his. She was a loving little creature, showing her affection earlier than most children do. Before
she could sit upright, she recognised his in-comings and
out-goings, and when he took her in his arms to walk to
and fro with her, as was his habit at night, she dropped
her tiny head upon his shoulders with a soft yielding to
his tenderness which never failed to quicken the beatings
of his heart.

" There's something in her face," he used to say to himself, " something that's not in every child's face. It's a
look about her eyes and mouth that seems to tell a man that
she understands him—whether his spirits are up or down."

But his spirits were not often down in those days. The
rooms at the back no longer wore an air of loneliness, and
the evenings never hung heavily on his hands. In the
course of a few months he sent to Brownsboro for a high
chair and tried the experiment of propping his small companion up in it at his side when he ate his supper. It was
an experiment which succeeded very well and filled him
with triumph. From her place in the kitchen Mornin
could hear during every meal the sound of conversation
of the most animated description. Tom's big, kind voice
rambling cheerily and replied to by the soft and unformed
murmuring of the child. He was never tired of her, never
willing to give her up.

" What I might have given to others if they'd cared for
it," was his thought, " I give to her and she knows it."

It seemed too that she did know it, that from her first
gleaming of consciousness she had turned to him as her
friend, her protector, and her best beloved. When she

heard his footsteps, she turned in Mornin's arms, or in her cradle, to look for him, and when she saw his face her whole little body yearned towards him.

One afternoon when she was about eight months old, he left her at the usual time. Mornin, who was working, had spread a big red shawl upon the floor and seated her upon it, and when Tom went out of the room, she sat still playing in the quiet way peculiar to her, with the gay fringe. She gave him a long earnest look as he crossed the threshold, a look which he remembered afterwards as having been more thoughtful than usual and which must have represented a large amount of serious speculation mingled with desire.

Tom went into the store, and proceeded to the performance of his usual duty of entertaining his customers. He was in a jovial mood, and, having a larger number of visitors than ordinarily, was kept actively employed in settling the political problems of the day and disposing of all public difficulties.

"What's most wanted at the head of things," he proclaimed, "is a man that's capable of exerting himself (Mis' Doty, if you choose that calico, Job can cut it off for you!) a man who ain't afraid of work. (Help yourself, Jim!) Lord! where'd this post-office be if some men had to engineer it—a man who would stand at things and loaf instead of taking right hold. (For Heaven's sake, Bill, don't hurry! Jake'll give you the tea as soon as he's cut off his wife's dress!) That's the kind of men we want in office now—in every kind of office—in every kind of office. If there's one thing I've no use for on God's green earth, it's a man with no energy. (Nicholson, just kick that box over here so I can get my feet on it!)"

He was sitting near the door which connected the back part of the establishment with the front, and it was just at this juncture that there fell upon his ear a familiar sound as of something being dragged over the floor. The next moment he felt his foot touched and then pressed upon by some soft unsteady weight.

He looked down with a start and saw first a small round face upturned, its dark eyes tired but rejoicing and faithful, and then a short white dress much soiled and dusted by being dragged over the bare boards of the two store-rooms.

His heart gave a leap and all the laughter died out of his face.

" My God, boys! " he said, as he bent down, " she's followed me! She's followed me! "

It was quite true. She had never crawled far beyond the limits of the shawl before, but this morning her longing had given her courage and strength, and she had set out upon her journey in search of him.

Those about him burst into loud, admiring laughter, but Tom did not laugh at all. He lifted the child to his knee and held her encircled by one arm. She was weary with her exertion and settled at once into an easy sitting posture, her head resting against him while she gazed quietly from under her upcurled lashes at the faces grouped about her. Their laughter did not disturb her now that she had reached her haven of safety.

" To think of her a-followin' him! " said Mis' Doty, " 'n' her never sot off nowhars afore. The purty little critter! Lord! Tom, she's a-gwine ter be a sight when she's grown —with them eyes and har! An' ter think of her a-slippin' off from Mornin an' makin' up her little mind to follow ye.

I've never had a young 'un to try it that early in all I've
raised."

"Lordy!" said Mr. Doty, "she's as sot on Tom 's he's
on her, 'n' ef ever a man wus a doggoned fool about a young
'un, he is about that'n; 'n' fur bein' a doggoned fool"—
triumphantly—"when he sets out ter be, I'll back Tom
agin any man in Hamlin."

Tom said but little. He made no more jokes. He kept
the child with him through the rest of the day, holding
her upon his knee or carrying her out upon the porch.

When at supper-time he carried her back to the room,
she was asleep and he laid her in her cradle himself. He
moved about very quietly afterwards and ate his supper
alone with frequent glances at the sleeper.

"Don't take her away," he said to Mornin when she
came in; "leave her here."

"'N' hev her a-wakin' 'n' disturbin' uv ye, Mars' Tom!"
she responded.

"Leave her here," he said, laying his hand on the head
of the cradle. "She'll not disturb me. We shall get along
finely together."

She was left, Mornin taking her departure with manifest
disbelief in the practicability of the plan. And then, having drawn the cradle to his bedside, Tom put out the light
and retired himself.

But he did not sleep for some time; having flung his
mighty body upon the couch, he lay with his arms thrown
above his head gazing at the darkness and listening to the
soft breathing at his side. He was thinking over the one
event of the day.

What might have seemed a slight thing to many men
had struck deep into his great heart.

"My God!" he said, a touch of reverential tone in his whisper, " to think of her following me!"

And he stretched out his hand in the darkness and laid it upon the side of the cradle lightly, and afterwards fell asleep.

CHAPTER IX

JUST at this time, which was the year before the Civil War, that fashionable summer resort, the White Briar Springs, was at its gayest. Rarely before had the hotel been filled with so brilliant a company. A few extra cases of yellow fever had been the cause of an unusual exodus from the fever districts, and in consequence the various summer resorts flourished and grew strong. The "White Briar" especially exerted and arrayed itself in its most festive garments. The great dining-room was filled to overflowing, the waiters were driven to desperation by the demands made upon them as they flew from table to table and endeavoured with laudable zeal to commit to memory fifty orders at once and at the same time to answer "Comin', sah" to the same number of snapped fingers. There were belles from Louisiana, beauties from Mississippi, and enslavers from Virginia, accompanied by their mothers, their fathers, their troops of younger brothers and sisters, and their black servants. There were nurses and valets and maids of all shades from ebony to cream-colour, and of all varieties of picturesqueness. All day the immense piazzas were crowded with promenaders, sitters, talkers, fancy-workers, servants attired in rainbow hues and apparently enjoying their idleness or their pretence at work to the utmost. Every morning parties played ten-pins, rode, strolled, gossipped ; every afternoon the daring few who did not doze away the heated hours in the shaded rooms, flirted in couples under trees on the

100

lawn, or in the woods, or by the creek. Every evening there was to be found ardent youth to dance in the ball-room, and twice a week at least did this same youth, arrayed in robes suited to honour the occasion, disport itself joyfully and with transcendent delight in the presence of its elders assembled in rooms around the walls of the same glittering apartment with the intention of bestowing distinction upon what was known as "the hop."

Sometimes, in dull seasons, there was a scarcity of partners upon such occasions; but this year such was not the case. Aside from the brothers of the belles and beauties before referred to, who mustered in full force, there was a reserved corps of cavaliers who, though past the early and crude bloom of their first youth, were still malleable material. Who could desire a more gallant attendant than the agile though elderly Major Beaufort, who, with a large party of nieces, daughters, and granddaughters, made the tour of the watering-places each succeeding year, pervading the atmosphere of each with the subtle essence of his gallantry and hilariousness ?

"I should be a miserable man, sir," proclaimed the Major, chivalrously upon each succeeding Thursday—" I should be a miserable man in seeing before me such grace and youth and beauty, feeling that I am no longer young, if I did not possess a heart which will throb for Woman as long as it beats with life."

Having distinguished himself by which poetic remark, he usually called up a waiter with champagne and glasses, in which beverage he gallantly drank the health of the admiring circle which partook of it with him.

Attached to the Beaufort party were various lesser luminaries, each of whom, it must be confessed, might well, under ordinary circumstances, have formed the centre of a circle himself; legal luminaries, social luminaries, political luminaries, each playing ten-pins and whist, each riding, each showing in all small gallantries, and adding by their presence to the exhilaration of the hour.

There was one gentleman, however, who, though he was not of the Beaufort party, could still not be considered among the lesser luminaries. He was a planet with an orbit of his own. This gentleman had ridden up to the hotel one afternoon on a fine horse, accompanied by a handsome, gloomy boy on another animal as fine, and followed by a well-dressed young negro carrying various necessary trappings, and himself mounted in a manner which did no discredit to his owner. The air of the party was such as to occasion some sensation on the front gallery, where the greater number of the guests were congregated.

"Oh," cried one of the Beauforts, "what a distinguished-looking man. Oh, what a handsome boy! and what splendid horses."

At that moment one of the other ladies—a dark, quiet, clever matron from South Carolina—uttered an exclamation.

"Is it possible," she said. "There is Colonel De Willoughby."

The new arrival recognised her at once and made his way towards her with the most graceful air of ease and pleasure, notwithstanding that it was necessary that he should wind his way dexterously round numerous groups in and out among a dozen chairs.

He was a strikingly handsome man, dark, aquiline, tall and lithe of figure; his clothes fitted him marvellously well at the waist, his slender arched foot was incased in a marvel of a boot, his black hair was rather long, and his superb eyes gained a mysterious depth and mellowness from the length and darkness of their lashes ; altogether, it was quite natural that for the moment the Beauforts and their satellites should pale somewhat by comparison.

When he bowed over Mrs. Marvin's hand, a thrill of pleasure made itself manifest in those surrounding them. He spoke in the most melodious of voices.

"The greatest of pleasures," he was heard to say. "I did not expect this." And then, in response to some question : "My health since—since my loss has been very poor. I hope to recover strength and spirits," with an air of delicate and gentle melancholy. "May I present my boy—Rupert ? "

In response to the summons the boy came forward—not awkwardly, or with any embarrassment, but with a bearing not at all likely to create a pleasant impression. The guests could see that he was even a handsomer boy than he had seemed at a greater distance. He was very like his father in the matter of aquiline features, clear pale-olive skin and superb dark eyes : his face had even a fineness the older man's lacked, but the straight marks of a fixed frown were upon his forehead, and his mouth wore a look which accorded well with the lines.

He approached and bared his head, making his boyish bow in a manner which did credit to his training, but though he blushed slightly on being addressed, his manner was by no means a responsive one, and he moved away as soon as an opportunity presented itself, leaving his father making himself very fascinating in a gently chivalric way, and establishing himself as a planet by the mere manner of his address towards a woman who was neither pretty, young, nor enthusiastic.

In Connection with
The De Willoughby Claim

There was no woman in the hotel so little prone to enthusiasm as this one. She was old enough and clever enough to have few illusions. It was thought singular that though she admitted she had known the Colonel from his youth, she showed very little partiality for his society, and, indeed, treated him with marked reserve. She never joined in the choruses of praise which were chanted daily around her.

"I know the De Willoughbys very well," she said. "Oh, yes, very well indeed—in a way. We hear a good deal of them. De Courcy's wife was a friend of mine. This one is De Courcy, the other is Romaine, and there was one who was considered a sort of black sheep and broke with the family altogether. They don't know where he is and don't care to know, I suppose. They have their own views of the matter. Oh, yes; I know them very well, in a way."

When questioned by enthusiasts, she was obliged to confess that the hero of the hour was bountifully supplied with all outward gifts of nature, was to be envied his charm of manner and the air of romance surrounding him, though, in admitting this, she added a little comment not generally approved of.

"It's a little of the Troubadour order," she said; "but I dare say no woman would deny that it is rather taking. I don't deny it, it is taking—if you don't go below the surface."

Never was a man so popular as the Colonel, and never a man so missed as he on the days of his indisposition. He had such days when he did not leave his room and his negro was kept busy attending to his wants. The nature of his attacks was not definitely understood, but after them he always appeared wearing an interesting air of languor and melancholy, and was more admired than ever.

"The boy seems to feel it very much," the lady remarked. "He always looks so uneasy and anxious, and never goes away from the house at all. I suppose they are very fond of each other."

"I dare say he does feel it very much," said Mrs. Marvin with her reserved little smile. "He is De Willoughby enough for that."

It was not agreed to that he inherited his father's grace of manner however. He was a definitely unamiable boy, if one might judge from appearances. He always wore a dark little scowl, as if he were either on the point of falling into a secret rage or making his way out of one ; instead of allowing himself to be admired and made a pet of, he showed an unnatural preference for prowling around the grounds and galleries alone, sometimes sitting in corners and professing to read, but generally appearing to be meditating resentfully upon his wrongs in a manner which in a less handsome boy would have been decidedly unpleasant. Even Mrs. Marvin's advances did not meet with any show of cordiality, though it was allowed that he appeared less averse to her society than to that of any other woman, including the half dozen belles and beauties who would have enjoyed his boyish admiration greatly.

"I knew your mother," said Mrs. Marvin to him one day as he sat near her upon the gallery.

"Did you ?" he answered, in a rather encouraging way. "When did you know her ?"

"When she was young. We were girls together. She was a beauty and I wasn't, but we were very fond of each other."

He gave his closed book a sullen look.

In Connection with
The De Willoughby Claim

" What makes women break so ? " he asked. " I don't see why they break so. She had pretty eyes when she died, but, —— "

He drew his handsome black brows down and scowled ; and, seeing that he was angry at himself for having spoken, Mrs. Marvin made another remark.

" You miss her very much ? " she said, gravely.

He turned his face away.

" She's better off where she is, I suppose," he said. " That's what they always say of dead people."

And then still frowning he got up and walked away.

The negro servants about the hotel were all fond of him, though his manner towards them was that of a fiery and enthusiastic young potentate, brooking no delay or interference. His beauty and his high-handed way impressed them as being the belongings of one favoured by fortune and worthy of admiration and respect.

" He's a D'Willoughby out and out," said his father's negro, Tip. " Ain't no mistake 'bout dat. He's a young devil when his spirit's up, 'n it's easy raised. But he's a powerful gen'lman sort o' boy — powerful. Throw's you a quarter soon's look at ye, 'n he's got the right kind o' high ways—dough der ain't no sayin' he ain't a young devil ; de Kurnel hisself cayn't outcuss him when his spirit's up."

The Colonel and his son had been at the springs a month, when the fancy-dress ball took place which was the occasion of a very unpleasant episode in the annals of this summer.

For several days before the greatest excitement had prevailed at the hotel. A pleasant air of mystery had prevailed over the preparations that were being made. The rural proprietors of the two stores in which the neighbourhood rejoiced were driven to distraction by constant demands made upon them for articles and materials of which they had never before heard, and which were not procurable within a hundred miles of the place. Bedrooms were overflowing with dresses in process of alteration from ordinary social aspects to marvellous combinations of imagination and ingenuity, while an amiable borrowing and exchanging went on through all the corridors.

On the day before the ball the Colonel's popularity reached its height. As it was the time of a certain local election, there was held upon the grounds a political meeting, giving such individuals as chose to avail themselves of it the opportunity of expressing their opinions to the assembled guests and the thirty or forty mountaineers who had suddenly and without any warning of previous existence appeared upon the scene.

The Colonel had been one of the first called upon, and, to the delight of his admirers, he responded at once with the utmost grace to the call.

When he ascended the little platform with the slow, light step which was numbered among his chief attractions and stood before his audience for a moment looking down at them gently and reflectively from under his beautiful lashes, a throb of expectation was felt in every tender bosom.

His speech fell short of no desire, being decided to be simple perfection. His soft voice, his quiet ease of movement, his eloquence, were all that could be hoped for from mortal man. He mentioned with high-bred depreciation the fact that he could not fairly call himself a politician unless as any son of the fair South must be one at least at heart, however devoid of the gifts which have made her

In Connection with
The De Willoughby Claim

greatest heard from continent to continent. He was only one of the many who had at stake their cherished institutions, the homes they loved, the beloved who brightened those homes, and their own happiness as it was centred in those homes, and irrevocably bound in that of the fairest land upon which the fair sun shone.

The applause at this juncture was so great as to oblige him to pause for a few moments; but it was to be regretted that nine out of ten of the mountaineers remained entirely unresponsive, crossing their jean-covered legs and rubbing their lean and grizzled jaws in a soulless manner. They displayed this apathetic indifference to the most graceful flight of rhetoric, to the most musical appeals to the hearts of all men loving freedom, to the announcement that matters had reached a sad and significant crisis, that the peculiar institutions left as a legacy by their forefathers were threatened by the Northern fanatics, and that in the near future the blood of patriots might be poured forth as a libation upon the soil they loved; to eloquent denunciations of the hirelings and would-be violators of our rights under the constitution. To all these they listened, evidently devoting all their slow energies to the comprehension of it, but they were less moved than might have been expected of men little used to oratory.

But it was the termination of the speech that stirred all hearts. With a dexterity only to be compared to its easy grace, the orator left the sterner side of the question for a tenderer one to which he had already referred in passing, and which was the side of all political questions which presented themselves to such men as he. Every man, it was to be hoped, knew the meaning of home and love and tenderness in some form, however poor and humble and unpatriotic; to every man was given a man's privilege of defending the rights and sacredness of this home, this love, with his strength, with his might, with the blood of his beating heart if need be. To a Southern man, as to all men, his right to be first in his own land in ruling, in choosing rulers, in carrying out the laws, meant his right to defend this home and that which was precious to him within it. There were a few before him upon this summer's day, alas, alas! that Fate should will it so, who had not somewhere a grave whose grass moved in the softness of the wind over dead loves and hopes cherished even in this hour as naught else was cherished. And these graves——"

He faltered and paused, glancing towards the doorway with a singular expression. For a few seconds he could not go on. He was obliged to raise to his lips the glass of water which had been provided for him.

"Oh!" was sighed softly through the room, "his emotion has overpowered him. Poor fellow! how sad he looks."

Mrs. Marvin simply followed the direction his eyes had taken. She was a practical person. The object her eye met was the figure of the boy who had come in a few minutes before. He was leaning against the doorpost, attired in a cool suit of white linen, his hands in his pockets, the expression of his handsome darkling young face a most curious one. He was staring at his father steadily, his fine eyes wide open holding a spark of inward rage, his nostrils dilated and quivering. He seemed bent upon making the orator meet his glance, but the orator showed no desire to do so. He gave his sole attention to his glass of water. To this clever, elderly Southern matron it was an interesting scene.

"If he sprang up in two minutes and threw something deadly and murderous at him," she said to herself, "I should not be in the least surprised ; and I should not be the first to blame him."

But the rest of the audience was intent upon the Colonel, who, recovering himself, finished his harangue with an appeal that the land made sacred by those loves, those homes, those graves, might be left solely in the hands of the men who loved it best, who knew its needs, who yearned for its highest development, and who, when the needful hour arrived, would lay down their lives to save its honour.

When he concluded, and was on the point of seating himself very quietly, without any appearance of being conscious of the great sensation he had created, and still wearing an admirable touch of melancholy upon his fine countenance, Major Beaufort rushed towards him, almost upsetting a chair in his eagerness, and grasped his hand and shook it with a congratulatory ardour so impressive and enthusiastic as to be a sensation in itself.

There were other speeches afterwards. Fired by the example of his friend, Major Beaufort distinguished himself by an harangue overflowing with gallantry and adorned throughout with amiable allusions to the greatest power of all, the power of Youth, Beauty, and Womanhood. The political perspicuity of the address was perhaps somewhat obscured by its being chivalrously pointed towards those fair beings who brighten our existence and lengthen our griefs. Without the Ladies, the speaker found, we may be politicians, but we cannot be gentlemen. He discovered (upon the spot, and with a delicate suggestion of pathos) that by a curious coincidence, the Ladies were the men's mothers, their wives, their sisters, their daughters. This being greatly applauded, he added that over these husbands, these fathers, these brothers—and might be added " these lovers" —the Ladies wielded a mighty influence. The position of

In Connection with
The De Willoughby Claim

Woman, even in the darkest ages, had been the position of one whose delicate hand worked the lever of the world ; but to-day, in these more enlightened times, in the age of advancement and discovery, before what great and sublime power did the nobleman, the inventor, the literary man, the warrior, bow, as he bowed before the shrine of the Ladies ?

But it was the Colonel who bore away the palm and was the hero of the hour. When the audience rose he was surrounded at once by groups of enthusiasts, who shook hands with him, who poured forth libations of praise, who hung upon his every word with rapture.

" How proud of you he must be," said one of the fairest in the group of worshippers ; " boys of his age feel things so strongly. I wonder why he doesn't come forward and say something to you ? He is too shy, I suppose."

" I dare say," said the Colonel with his most fascinating gentle smile. " One must not expect enthusiasm of boys. I have no doubt he thought it a great bore and wondered what I was aiming at."

"Impossible," exclaimed the fair enslaver. " Don't do him an injustice, Colonel de Willoughby."

But as she glanced towards the doorway her voice died down and the expression of her face changed somewhat. The boy—still with his hands in his pockets—was looking on with an air which was as insolent as it was remarkable, an air of youthful scorn and malignant derision which staggered even the enthusiast.

She turned uneasily to the Colonel, who faintly smiled.

" He is a handsome fellow," he said, " and I must own to being a vain parent, but he has a demon of a temper and he has been spoiled. He'll get over it when he is older."

In Connection with
The De Willoughby Claim

It was a great blow to his admirers when it became known the next morning that the Colonel was suffering from one of his attacks, and even a worse one than usual. Nel was shut up in his room with him all day, and it was rumoured that the boy would not come down, but wandered up and down the corridors restlessly, looking miserable enough to have touched the stoniest heart.

During the morning quite a gloom pervaded the atmosphere; only the excitement of preparations for the evening could have proved an antidote to the general depression.

It was to be a brilliant occasion. The county had been scoured for guests, some of whom were to travel in their carriages from other watering-places for twenty or thirty miles. The ball-room had been decorated by a committee of ladies; the costumes, it was anticipated, would be dazzling beyond measure. No disappointment was felt when the festal hour arrived, but the very keen emotion attendant upon the absence of the interesting invalid.

"If he had only been well enough to be here," it was said, "how he would have enjoyed it."

Major Beaufort, attired as a Sultan and appropriately surrounded by his harem in sarsenet trousers and spangled veils, gave universal satisfaction. Minnehaha in feathers and moccasins, and Hiawatha in moccasins and feathers, gave a touch of mild poetry to the evening. Sisters of Charity in white cambric caps told their beads through the mazes of the lancers. Night and Morning, attired respectively in black and white tarletan, and both profusely adorned with silver paper stars, combined their forces to add romance and vividness to the festive scene.

There had been dancing and flirtation, upon which those of the guests who did not join gazed for an hour or so as they sat in the chairs arranged around the walls, doubtless enjoying themselves intensely, and the gaiety was at its height, when some commotion became manifest at one of the doors. Those grouped about it appeared to be startled at finding something or somebody behind them, and almost immediately it was seen that this something or somebody was bent upon crowding past them. A loud, insane-sounding laugh was heard. The dancers stopped and turned towards it with one accord, their alarm and astonishment depicted on their faces. The spectators bent forward in their seats.

"What is it?" was the general exclamation. "Oh! Oh!" This last interjection took the form of a chorus as two of the group at the doorway were pushed headlong into the room, and a tall, unsteady, half-dressed figure made its violent entrance.

At the first glance it was not easy to recognize it; it was simply the figure of a very tall man in an ungirt costume, composed of shirt and pantaloons. He was crushed and dishevelled. His hair hung over his forehead. He strode into the middle of the quadrille, and stood with his hands in his pockets, swaying to and fro, with a stare at once malicious and vacant.

"Oh," he remarked, sardonically, as he took in his surroundings, and then everyone recognized at once that it was Colonel De Willoughby, and that Colonel De Willoughby was mad drunk.

He caught sight of Major Beaufort, and staggered towards him with another frantic laugh.

"Good God, Major," he cried; "how becomin' 'tis, how damned becomin'. Harem an' all. Only trouble is you're too fat—too fat; if you weren't so fat wouldn't look such a damned fool."

It was to be regretted there was no longer an air of refinement about his intoxication, no suggestion of melancholy grace, no ghost of his usual high-bred suavity; with his laugh and stare and unsteady legs he was simply a more drunken lunatic than one generally sees.

There was a rush at him from all sides—Major Beaufort, in his Turkish trousers, being the first to fall upon him and have his turban stamped upon in the encounter. He was borne across the room, shouting and struggling and indulging in profanity of the most frightful kind. Just as they got him to the door his black boy Neb appeared, looking ashen with fright.

"De Lord o' massey," he cried. "I ain't lef' him more'n a minit. He sent me down hisself. One o' his cunnin' ways to get rid o' me when he's at de wust. Opium 'n whiskey, dats what gets him dis way. Bof togedder agwine ter kill him some dese days, 'n de opium am de wustest. For de Lord's sake some o' you gen'men cum 'n hep me till I git him quieted down."

It was all over in a few moments, but the effort made to return to hilariousness was a failure; the shock to the majority of the gay throng had been great. Mrs. Marvin, sitting in her special corner, was besieged with questions, and at length was prevailed upon through the force of circumstances to speak the truth as she knew it.

"Has he ever done it before?" she said. "Yes, he has done it before—he has done it a dozen times since he has been here, only to-night he was madder than usual and got away from his servant. What is it? It is opium when it isn't whiskey, and whiskey when it isn't opium, and oftenest it is both together. He is the worst of a bad lot, and if you haven't understood that miserable angry boy before you may understand him now. His mother died of a broken heart when he was twelve years old, and he watched her die of it and knew what killed her, and is proud enough to feel the shame that rests upon him. That's as much as I care to say, and yet it isn't the half."

When those bearing the Colonel to his room turned into the corridor leading to it they encountered his son, who met them with a white-lipped rage, startling to every man of them in its incongruous contrast to the boyish face and figure.

"What?" he said, panting. "You've got him, have you?"

"Yes," responded the Colonel hilariously; "'ve got me safe 'nuff; pick me up ad' car' me. If man won't go out, tote 'm out."

They carried him into his rooms and laid him down, and more than one among them turned curiously to the boy as he stood near the bed looking down at the dishevelled, incoherent, gibbering object upon it.

"Damn him," he said in a sudden outburst; "damn him."

"Hello, youngster," said one of the party, "that's not the thing exactly."

"Go to the devil," roared the lad, livid with wrath and shame. "Do you think I'll not say what I please? A nice one he is for a fellow to have for a father—to be tied to and dragged about by—drinking himself mad and disgracing himself after his palaver and sentiment and playing the gentleman. He ought to be a gentleman—he's got a gentleman's name, and"— choking a little—" all the rest of it. I hate him! He makes me sick. I wish he was dead. He's a liar and a bully and a fool. I'd kill him if he wasn't my father. I should like to kill him for *being* my father!"

115

Suddenly his voice faltered and his face turned white. He walked to the other side of the room, turning his back to them all, and, flinging himself into a chair, dropped his curly head on his arm on the window-sill and sobbed aloud with a weakness and broken-down fury pitiful to see.

The Colonel burst into a frantic shriek of laughter.

"Queer little devil," he said. "Prou' lit'l devil ! Like's moth'—don' like it. Moth' used er cry. *She* didn't like it."

CHAPTER X

As the Cross-roads had regarded Tom as a piece of personal property to be proud of, so it fell into the habit of regarding his *protégée*. The romance of her history was considered to confer distinction upon the vicinity, and Tom's affection for her was approved of as a sentiment worthy of the largeness of the Cross-roads nature.

"They kinder set one anuther off," it was frequently remarked, "her a-bein' so little and him so big, an' both of 'em stickin' to each other so clost. Lordy! 'tain't no use a-tryin' to part 'em. Sheby, she ain't a-goin' nowhar 'thout Tom, an' Tom, he h'aint a-goin' nowhars 'thout Sheby!"

When the child was five years old the changes which had taken place in the store were followed by still greater changes in the house. Up to her fifth birthday the experiences had balanced themselves between the store and the three back rooms with their bare floors and rough walls. She had had her corner, her small chair behind the counter or near the stove, and there she had amused herself with her playthings through long or short days, and in the evening Tom had taken her upon his shoulder and carried her back to the house, as it was called, leaving his careless, roystering gaiety behind him locked up in the store, ready to be resumed for the edification of his customers the next morning.

"He don't hev no pore folkses ways wid dat chile," said Mornin once to Mrs. Doty; "he don't never speak to her

117

no other then gen'leman way. He's a-raisin' her to be
fitten fur de highes'. He's mighty keerful ob her way ob
speakin' an' settin' to de table. Mornin's got to stand
'hind her cheer an' wait on her hersel'; an' sence she was
big 'nuff to set dar, she's had a silver fork an' spoon
an' napkin-ring same's de President himself. Ah; he's
a-raisin' her keerful, is Mars D'Willerby."

"Waal," said Mrs. Doty, "ef 'twarn't Tom D'Willerby,
I shed say it was a puttin' on airs; but thar ain't no airs
'bout Tom D'Willerby."

From the first Mr. Stamps's interest in Tom's *protégée*
had been unfailing though quiet. When he came into
the store, which he did some three times a week, it was
his habit to fix his small, pale eyes upon her and follow
her movements stealthily but with unflagging watchful-
ness. Occasionally this occupation so absorbed him that
when she moved to her small corner behind the counter,
vaguely oppressed by his surveillance, he sauntered across
the room and took his seat upon the counter itself, per-
sisting in his mild, furtive gaze, until it became too much
for her and she sought refuge at Tom's knee.

"He looks at me," she burst out distressedly on one
such day. "Don't let him look at me."

Tom gave a start and turned round, and Mr. Stamps
gave a start also, at once mildly recovering himself.

"Leave her alone," said Tom, "what are you lookin'
at her for?"

Mr. Stamps smiled.

"Thar's no law agin it, Tom," he replied. "An' she's
wuth a lookin' at. She's that kind, an' it'll grow on her.
Ten year from now thar ain't no law es 'ed keep 'em
from lookin' at her, 'thout it was made an' passed in Con-
grist. She'll hev to git reckonciled to a-bein' looked at."

In Connection with
The De Willoughby Claim

"Leave her alone," repeated Tom, quite fiercely. "I'll not have her troubled."

"I didn't go to trouble her, Tom," said Mr. Stamps, softly; and he slipped down from the counter and sidled out of the store and went home.

With Mr. Stamps Sheba always connected her first knowledge of the fact that her protector's temper could be disturbed. She had never seen him angry until she saw Mr. Stamps rouse him to wrath on the eventful fifth birthday, from which the first exciting events of her life dated themselves. Up to that time she had seen only in his great strength and broad build a power to protect and shield her own fragility and smallness from harm or fear. When he took her in his huge arms and held her at what seemed to be an incredible height from the ordinary platform of existence, she had only felt the cautious tenderness of his touch and recognised her own safety, and it had never occurred to her that his tremendous voice, which was so strong and deep by nature, that it might have been a terrible one if he had chosen to make it so, could express any other feeling than kindliness in its cheery roar.

But on this fifth birthday Tom presented himself to her childish mind in a new light.

She had awakened early to find him standing at her small bedside and a new doll lying in her arms. It was a bigger doll than she had ever owned before, and so gaily dressed, that in her first rapture her breath quite forsook her. When she recovered it, she scrambled up, holding her new possession in one arm and clung with the other around Tom's neck.

"Oh, the lovely, lovely doll!" she cried, and then hid her face on his shoulder.

"Hallo," said Tom, hugging her, "what is she hiding her eyes for?"

She nestled closer to him with a little sob of loving delight.

"Because — because of the doll," she answered, bewildered by her own little demonstration and yet perfect in her confidence that he would understand her.

"Well," said Tom, cheerfully, "that's a queer thing, ain't it? Look here, did you know it was your birthday? Five years old to-day—think of that."

He sat down and settled her in her usual place on his knee, her doll in her arms.

"To think," he said, "of her setting up a birthday on purpose to be five years old and have a doll given her. That's a nice business, ain't it?"

After they had breakfasted together in state, the doll was carried into the store to be played with there. It was a wet day, and, the air being chilled by a heavy mountain rain, a small fire was burning in the stove, and by this fire the two settled themselves to enjoy the morning together, the weather precluding the possibility of their being disturbed by many customers. But in the height of their quiet enjoyment they were broken in upon by the sound of horse's hoofs splashing in the mud outside and Mr. Stamps's hat appeared above the window-sill.

It was Sheba who saw it first, and in the strength of her desire to avoid the wearer, she formed a desperate plan. She rose so quietly that Tom, who was reading a paper, did not hear her, and, having risen, drew her small chair behind the counter in the hope that, finding her place vacant, the visitor would not suspect her presence.

In this she was not disappointed. Having brushed the mud from his feet on the porch, Mr. Stamps appeared at the doorway, and, after his usual precautionary glance about him, made his way to the stove. His manner was at once propitiatory and friendly. He drew up a chair and put his wet feet on the stove, where they kept up a comfortable hissing sound as they dried.

"Howdy, Tom," he said, "howdy?" And from her hiding-place Sheba saw him rubbing his legs from the knee downwards as he said it, with an air of solid enjoyment which suggested that he was congratulating himself upon something he had in his mind.

"Morning" responded Tom.

Mr. Stamps rubbed his legs again quite luxuriously.

"You're a lookin' well, Tom," he remarked. "Lord, yes, ye're a lookin' powerful well."

Tom laid his paper down and folded it on his knee.

"Lookin' well, am I?" he answered. "Well, I'm a delicate weakly sort of fellow in general, I am, and it's encouraging to hear that I'm looking well."

Mr. Stamps laughed rather spasmodically.

"I wouldn't be agin bein' the same kind o' weakly myself," he said, "nor the same kind o' delycate. You're a powerfle hansum man, Tom."

"Yes," replied Tom, drily, "I'm a handsome man. That's what carried me along this far. It's what I've always had to rely on—that and a knock-down intellect."

Mr. Stamps rubbed his legs with his air of luxury again.

"Folks is fond o' sayin' beauty ain't but skin deep," he said; "but I wouldn't hev it no deeper myself—bein' so that it kivers. An', talkin' o' beauty, she's one—Lord, yes. She's one."

"Look here," said Tom, "leave her alone."

"'Tain't a gwine to harm her, Tom," replied Mr. Stamps, "'tain't a gwine to harm her none. What made me think of it was it a bein' jest five years since she was born—a makin' it her birthday an' her jest five years old."

"What," cried Tom, "you've been counting it up, have you?"

"No," replied Mr. Stamps, with true modesty of demeanour, "I ain't ben a countin' of it up, Tom." And he drew a dirty memorandum book softly from his pocket. "I set it down at the time es it happened."

He laid the dirty book on his knee and turned over its pages carefully as if looking for some note.

"I ain't much on readin' an' writin'," he said, "an' 'rithmetick it goes kinder hard with me now an' agin, but a man's got to know suthin' on 'em if he 'lows to keep anyways even. I 'low to keep even, sorter, an' I've give a good deal o' time to steddyin' of 'em. I never went to no school, but I've sot things down es I want to remember, an' I kin count out money. I never was imposed on none I rekin, an' I never lost nothin'. Yere's whar I sot it down about her a-bein' born an' the woman a-dyin' an' him a-gwine away. Ye cayn't read it, mebbe." He bent forward, pointing to the open page and looking up at Tom as if he expected him to be interested. "Thar it is," he added in his thin, piping, little voice, "even to the time o' day. Mornin, she told me that. 'Bout three o'clock in the mornin' in thet thar little front room. Ef anyone shed ever want to know particular, thar it is."

The look in Tom's face was far from being a calm one. He fidgetted in his chair and finally rolled his paper into a hard wad and threw it at the counter as if it had been a missile.

"See here," he exclaimed, "take my advice and let that alone."

Mr. Stamps regarded his dirty book affectionately.

" 'Tain't a-gwine to hurt nothin' to hev it down," he replied, with an air of simplicity.

He shut it up, returned it to his pocket, and clasped his hands about his knees, while he fixed his eyes on the glimmer of red showing itself through a crack in a stove-plate.

"It's kinder curi's I should hev happened along by thar this mornin'," he remarked, reflectively.

"By where?" demanded Tom.

Mr. Stamps hugged his knees as if he enjoyed their companionship.

"By thar," he responded, cheerfully, "the Holler, Tom. An' it 'peared to me it 'ed be kinder int'restin' to take a look through, bein' as this was the day as the thing kinder started. So I hitched my mule an' went in." He paused a moment as if to enjoy his knees again.

"Well," said Tom.

Mr. Stamps looked up at him harmlessly. "Eh?" he enquired.

"I said 'well,'" answered Tom, "that's what I said."

"Oh," replied Mr. Stamps. "Waal, thar wasn't nothin' thar, Tom."

For the moment Tom's expression was one of relief. But he said nothing.

"Thar wasn't nothin' thar," Mr. Stamps continued. Then occurred another pause. "Nothin'," he added after it, "nothin' particular."

The tenderness with which he embraced his knees at this juncture had something like fascination in it.

Tom found himself fixing a serious gaze upon his clasping arms.

"I kinder looked round," he proceeded, "an' if there'd ben anythin' thar I 'low I'd hev seed it. But thar wasn't nothin', nothin' but the empty rooms an' a dead leaf or so es hed blowed in through a broken winder, an' the pile o' ashes in the fireplace beat down with the rain as hed fell down the chimney. Mighty lonesome an' still them ashes looked ; an' thar wasn't nothin' but them an' the leaves,—— an' a bit of a' envelope."

Tom moved his chair back. Sheba thought he was going to get up suddenly. But he remained seated, perhaps because Mr. Stamps began again.

"Thar wasn't nothin' but them an' the bit of a envelope," he remarked. "It was a-sticken in a crack o' the house, low down, like it hed ben swep' or blowed thar an' overlooked. I shouldn't hev seed it"—modestly—"ef I hedn't ben a-goin' round on my hands an' knees."

Then Tom rose very suddenly indeed, so suddenly that he knocked his chair over and amazed Sheba by kicking it violently across the store. For the moment he so far forgot himself as to be possessed with some idea of falling upon Mr. Stamps with the intent to do him bodily injury. He seized him by the shoulders and turned him about so that he had an excellent view of his unprepossessing back. What Mr. Stamps thought it would have been difficult to discover. Sheba fancied that when he opened his mouth he was going to utter a cry of terror. But he did not. He turned his neck about as well as he could under the circumstances, and looking up into Tom's face meekly smiled.

"Tom," he said, "ye ain't a-gwine ter do a thing to me, not a dern thing."

"Yes, I am," cried Tom, furiously, "I'm goin' to kick——"

"Ef ye was jest haaf to let drive at me, ye'd break my neck," said Mr. Stamps, "an ye ain't a-gwine ter do it.

In Connection with
The De Willoughby Claim

Ef ye was, Tom, ye'd be a bigger fool than I took ye fer. Lemme go."

He looked so diminutive and weak-eyed, as he made these remarks, that it was no wonder Tom released him helplessly, though he was obliged to thrust his hands deep into his pockets and keep them under control.

"I thought I'd given you one lesson," he burst forth; "I thought——"

Mr. Stamps interrupted him, continuing to argue his side of the question, evidently feeling it well worth his while to dispose of it on the spot.

"Ye weigh three hundred, Tom," he said, "ef ye weigh a pound, an' I don't weigh but ninety, 'n ye couldn't handle me keerful enuf not to leave me in a fix as wouldn't be no credit to ye when ye was done ; 'n it 'ed look kinder bad for ye to meddle with me, anyhow. An' the madder ye get, the more particular ye'll be not to. Thar's whar ye are, Tom ; an' I ain't sich a fool as not to know it."

His perfect confidence in the strength of his position, and in Tom's helplessness against it, was a thing to be remembered. Tom remembered it long afterwards, though at the moment it only roused him to greater heat.

"Now then," he demanded, "let's hear what you're driving at. What I want to know is what you're driving at. Let's hear."

Mr. Stamps's pale eyes fixed themselves with interest on his angry face. He had seated himself in his chair again, and he watched Tom closely as he rambled on in his simple, uncomplaining way.

"Ye're fond o' laughin' at me round yere at the store, Tom," he remarked, "an' I ain't agin it. A man don't make nothin' much by bein' laughed at, I rekin, but he don't lose nothin' nuther, an' that's what I *am* agin. I

rekin ye laugh 'cos I kinder look like a fool—an' I hain't
nothin' agin thet, nuther, Lord ! not by a heap. A man
ain't a-gwine to lose nothin' by lookin' like a fool. I hain't
never, not a cent, Tom. But I ain't es big a fool es I look,
an' I don't 'low ye air, uther. Thar's whar I argy from.
Ye ain't es big a fool as ye look, an' ye'd be in a bad fix ef
ye was."

"Go on," ordered Tom, "and leave me out."

"I cayn't leave ye out, Tom," said Mr. Stamps, "fer
ye're in. Ye'd be as big a fool as ye look ef ye was doin'
all this yere fer nothin'."

"All what ?" demanded Tom.

"Gals," suggested Mr. Stamps, "is plenty. An' ef
ye take to raisin' 'em as this un's ben raised, ye ain't
makin' much ; an' ef thar ain't nothin' to be made, Tom,
what's yer aim ? "

He put it as if it was a conundrum without an answer.

"What's yer aim, Tom ? " he repeated, pleasantly, "ef
thar ain't nothin' to be made ? "

Tom's honest face flamed into red which was almost
purple, the veins swelled on his forehead, his indignation
almost deprived him of his breath. He fell into a chair
with a concussion which shook the building.

"Good—good Lord ! " he exclaimed ; "how I wish you
weighed five hundred pounds."

It is quite certain that if Stamps had, he would have de-
molished him utterly upon the spot, leaving him in such a
condition that his remains would hardly have been a source
of consolation to his friends. He pointed to the door.

"If you want to get out," he said, "start. This is getting the better of me—and if it does——"

Mr. Stamps rose.

"Ye wouldn't do a dern thing, Tom," he said, peaceably, "not a dern thing."

He sidled towards the door, and reaching it, paused to reflect, shaking his head.

"Ef thar ain't nothin' to be made," he said, "ye'v got ter hev a aim, an' what is it?"

Observing that Tom made a move in his chair, he slipped through the doorway rather hurriedly. Sheba thought he was gone, but a moment later the door re-opened and he thrust his head in and spoke, not intrusively—simply as if offering a suggestion which might prove of interest.

"It begun with a 'L,'" he said; "thar was a name on it, and it begun with a 'L'."

CHAPTER XI

It was upon the evening after this interview with Mr. Stamps that Tom broached to his young companion a plan which had lain half developed in his mind for some time.

They had gone into the back room and eaten together the supper Mornin had prepared with some extra elaboration to do honour to the day, and then Sheba had played with her doll Lucinda while Tom looked on, somewhat neglecting his newspaper and pipe in his interest in her small pretence of maternity.

At last, when she had put Lucinda to sleep in the wooden cradle which had been her own, he called her to him.

"Come here," he said, "I want to ask you a question."

She came readily and stood at his knee, laying her hands upon it and looking up at him, as she had had a habit of doing ever since she first stood alone.

"How would you like some new rooms?" he said, suggestively.

"Like these?" she answered, a pretty wonder in her eyes.

"No," said Tom, "not like these—bigger and brighter and prettier. With flowers on the walls and flowers on the carpets, and all the rest to match."

He had mentioned this bold idea to Molly Hollister the day before, and she had shown such pleasure in it, that he had been quite elated.

In Connection with
The De Willoughby Claim

"It's not that I need anything different," he had said, "but the roughness and bareness don't seem to suit her. I've thought it often when I've seen her running about."

"Seems like thar ain't nothin' you don't think of, Tom," said Molly, admiringly.

"Well," he admitted, "I think about her a good deal, that's a fact. She seems to have given me a kind of imagination. I used to think I hadn't any."

He had imagination enough to recognise at the present moment in the child's uplifted face some wistful thought she did not know how to express, and he responded to it by speaking again.

"They'll be prettier rooms than these," he said. "What do you say?"

Her glance wandered across the hearth to where the cradle stood in the corner with Lucinda in it. Then she looked up at him again.

"Prettier than this," she repeated, "with flowers. But don't take this away." The feeling which stirred her flushed her childish cheek and made her breath come and go faster. She drew still nearer to him.

"Don't take this away," she repeated, and laid her hand on his.

"Why?" asked Tom, giving her a curious look.

She met the look helplessly. She could not have put her vague thought into words.

"Don't—don't take it away," she said again, and suddenly laid her face upon his great open palm.

For a minute or two there was silence. Tom sat very still and looked at the fire.

"No," he said at length, "we won't take it away."

In a few days, however, it was well known for at least fifteen miles around the Cross-roads that Tom D'Willerby was going to build a new house, and that it was going to be fitted up with great splendour with furniture purchased at Brownsboro.

"Store carpetin' on every floor an' paper on every wall," said Dave Hollister to Molly when he went home after hearing the news. "An' Sheby's a-goin' with him to choose 'em. He says he'll bet fifty dollars she has her notions about things, an' he's a-goin to hev 'em carried out, fer it's all fer her, an' she's the one to be pleased."

It was not many weeks before the rooms were so near completion that the journey to Brownsboro was made, and it was upon this day of her first journeying out into the world that Sheba met with her first adventure. She remembered long afterwards the fresh brightness of the early morning when she was lifted into the buggy which stood before the door, while Mornin ran to and fro in the agreeable bustle attendant upon forgetting important articles and being reminded of them by shocks. When Tom climbed into his seat and they drove away, the store-porch seemed quite crowded with those who watched their triumphant departure. Sheba looked back and saw Mornin showing her teeth and panting for breath, while Molly Hollister waved the last baby's sun-bonnet, holding its denuded owner in her arms. The drive was a long one, but the travellers enjoyed it from first to last. Tom found his companion's conversation quite sufficient entertainment to while away the time, and when at intervals she refreshed herself from Mornin's basket and fell asleep, he enjoyed driving along quietly while he held her small, peacefully relaxed body on his knee, quite as much as another man might have enjoyed a much more exciting occupation.

"There's an amount of comfort in it," he said, reflectively, as the horse plodded along on the shady side of the road, "an amount of comfort that's astonishing. I don't know, but I'd like to have her come to a standstill just about now and never grow any older or bigger. But I thought the same thing three years ago, that's a fact. And when she gets to blooming out and enjoying her bits of girl finery there'll be pleasure in that too, plenty of it."

She awakened from one of these light sleeps just as they were entering Brownsboro, and her delight and awe at the dimensions and business aspect of the place pleased Tom greatly, and was the cause of his appearing a perfect mine of reliable information on the subject of large towns and the habits of persons residing in them.

Brownsboro contained at least six or seven hundred inhabitants, and, as Court was being held, there were a good many horses to be seen tied to the hitching-posts; groups of men were sitting before the stores and on the sidewalks, while something which might almost have been called a crowd was gathered before the Court-house itself.

Sheba turned her attention to the tavern they were approaching with a view to spending the night, and her first glance alighted upon an object of interest.

"There's a big boy," she said. "He looks tired."

He was not such a very big boy, though he was perhaps fourteen years old and tall of his age. He stood upon the plank-walk which ran at the front of the house, and leaned against the porch with his hands in his pockets. He was a slender, lithe boy, well dressed in a suit of fine white linen. He had a dark, spirited face, and long-lashed dark eyes, but, notwithstanding these advantages, he looked far from amiable as he stood lounging discontentedly and knitting his brows in the sun.

But Sheba admired him greatly and bent forward that she might see him better, regarding him with deep interest.

"He's a pretty boy," she said, softly, "I—I like him."

Tom scarcely heard her. He was looking at the boy himself, and his face wore a troubled and bewildered expression. His gaze was so steady that at length the object of it felt its magnetic influence and lifted his eyes. That his general air of discontent did not belie him, and that he was by no means an amiable boy, was at once proved. He did not bear the scrutiny patiently, his face darkened still more, and he scowled without any pretence of concealing the fact.

Tom turned away uneasily.

"He'd be a handsome fellow if he hadn't such an evil look," he said. "I must have seen him before; I wonder who he is?"

There were many strangers in the house, principally attenders upon the Court being held. Court week was a busy time for Brownsboro, which upon such occasions assumed a bustling and festive air, securing its friends from less important quarters, engaging in animated discussions of the cases in hand, and exhibiting an astonishing amount of legal knowledge, using the most mystical terms in ordinary conversation, and secretly feeling its importance a good deal.

"Sparkses" was the name of the establishment at which the travellers put up, and, being the better of the two taverns in which the town rejoiced, Sparkses presented indeed an enlivening spectacle. It was a large frame house with the usual long verandah at the front, upon which verandah there were always to be seen customers in rocking-chairs, their boots upon the balustrade, their hands clasped easily on the tops of their heads. During

Court week these customers with their rocking-chairs and boots seemed to multiply themselves indefinitely, and, becoming exhilarated by the legal business transacted around them, bestirred themselves to jocularity and argument, thus adding to the liveliness of the occasion.

At such periods Mr. Sparkes was a prominent feature. Attired in an easy costume seemingly composed principally of suspenders, and bearing a pipe in his hand, he permeated the atmosphere with a business-like air which had long stamped him in the minds of his rural guests as a person of administrative abilities rarely equalled and not at all to be surpassed.

"He's everywhar on the place, is Sparkes," had been said of him. "He's at dinner, 'n supper, 'n breakfast, 'n out on the porch, 'n in the bar, an' kinder sashiatin' through the whole thing. Thet thar tavern wouldn't be nothin' ef he wasn't thar."

It was not to be disputed that he appeared at dinner and breakfast and supper, and that on each appearance he disposed of a meal of such proportions as caused his countenance to deepen in colour and assume a swelled aspect, which was, no doubt, extremely desirable under the circumstances, and very good for the business, though it could scarcely be said to lighten the labour of Mrs. Sparkes and her daughters, who apparently existed without any more substantial sustenance than the pleasure of pouring out cups of coffee and tea and glasses of milk, and cutting slices of pie, of which they possibly partook through some process of absorption.

To the care of Mrs. Sparkes Tom confided his charge when, a short time after their arrival, he made his first pilgrimage for business purposes.

"She's been on the road all day," he said, "and I won't

take her out till to-morrow ; so if you don't mind, I'll leave her with you until I come back. She'll be all right and happy, won't you, Sheba ? "

Secretly Sheba felt some slight doubt of this ; but in her desire to do him credit, she summed up all her courage and heroically answered that she would, and so was borne off to the dining-room, where two girls were cutting bread and slicing ham for supper. They were Mrs. Sparkes's daughters, and when they saw the child, dropped their knives and made a good-natured rush at her, for which she was not at all prepared.

" Now, mother," they cried, " whar's she from, 'n who does she b'long to ? "

Mrs. Sparkes cast a glance at her charge, which Sheba caught and was puzzled by. It was a mysterious glance, with something of cautious pity in it.

" Set her up in a cheer, Luce," she said, " 'n give her a piece of cake. Don't ye want some, honey ? "

Sheba regarded her with uplifted eyes as she replied. The glance had suggested to her mind that Mrs. Sparkes was sorry for her, and she was anxious to know why.

" No," she answered, " no, thank you, I don't want any."

She sat quite still when they put her into a chair, but she did not remove her eyes from Mrs. Sparkes.

" Who does she b'long to, anyhow ? " asked Luce.

Mrs. Sparkes lowered her voice as she answered :

" She don't b'long to nobody, gals," she said. " It's thet little critter big Tom D'Willerby from Talbot's Cross-roads took to raise."

" Ye don't say. Pore little thing," exclaimed the girls. And while one of them stooped to kiss her cheek, the other hurriedly produced a large red apple, which she laid on the long table before her.

But Sheba did not touch it. To hear that she belonged to nobody was a mysterious shock to her. There had never seemed any doubt before that she belonged to her Uncle Tom, but Mrs. Sparkes had quite separated her from him in her statement. Suddenly she began to feel a little tired, and not quite so happy as she had been. But she sat still and listened, rendered rather tremulous by the fact that the speakers seemed so sure they had reason to pity her.

" Ef ever thar was a mystery," Mrs. Sparkes proceeded, " thet thar was one ; though Molly Hollister says D'Willerby don't like it talked over. Nobody knowed 'em, not even their names, an' nobody knowed whar they come from. She died, 'n he went away—nobody knowed whar ; 'n the child wasn't two days old when he done it. Ye cayn't tell me thar ain't a heap at the back o' that. They say D'Willerby's jest give himself up to her ever since, an' 'tain't no wonder, nuther, for she's a' out 'n out beauty, ain't she, now ? Just look at her eyes. Why don't ye eat yer apple, honey ?"

Sheba turned towards the window and looked out on the porch. A bewildering sense of desolation had fallen upon her.

"I don't want it," she said ; and her small voice had a strange sound even in her own ears. " I want Uncle Tom. Let me go out on the porch and see if he's coming."

She saw them exchange rapid glances and was troubled afresh by it.

" D'ye reckin she understands ?" the younger daughter said, cautiously.

"Lordy, no !" answered the mother ; "we ain't said nothin'. Ye kin go ef ye want to, Sheba," she added, cheerfully. " Thar's a little rocking-cheer that ye kin set in. Help her down, Luce."

But she had already slipped down and found her way to the door opening out on to the street. The porch was deserted for a wonder, the reason being that an unusually interesting case was being argued in the Court-house across the street, where groups of men were hanging about the doors. The rocking-chair stood in a corner, but Sheba did not sit down in it. She went to the steps and stood there, looking out with a sense of pain and loneliness still hanging over her; and at last, without knowing why, only feeling that they had a dreary sound and contained a mystery which somehow troubled her, she began to say over softly the words the woman had used.

"She died and he went away, nobody knows where. She died and he went away, nobody knows where."

Why those words should have clung to her and made her feel for the moment desolate and helpless, it would be difficult to say, but as she repeated them half unconsciously, the figures of the woman who had died and the man who had wandered so far away alone, that he seemed to have wandered out of life itself, cast heavy shadows on her childish heart.

"I am glad," she whispered, "that it was not Uncle Tom that went away." And she looked up the street with an anxious sigh.

Just at this moment she became conscious that she was not alone. In bending forward that she might see the better, she caught sight of someone leaning against the balustrades which had before concealed him—the boy, in short, who was standing just as he had stood when they drove up, and who looked as handsome in a darkling way as human boy could look.

For a few seconds the child regarded him with bated breath. The boys she had been accustomed to seeing were

136

not of this type, and were more remarkable for gifts less ornamental than beauty. This boy, with his graceful limbs and haughtily carried head, filled her with awe and admiration. She admired him so much, that, though her first impulse was to run away, she did not obey it, and almost immediately he glanced up and saw her. When this occurred, she was greatly relieved to find that his gloom did not lead him to treat her unkindly, indeed, he was amiable enough to address her with an air of one relenting and condescending somewhat to her youth.

" Didn't you know I was here ? " he asked.

" No," Sheba answered, timidly.

" Whom are you looking for ? "

" For my Uncle Tom."

He glanced across the street, still keeping his hands in his pockets and preserving his easy attitude.

" Perhaps he is over there," he suggested.

" Perhaps he is," she replied, and added, shyly, " Are you waiting for anyone ?"

He frowned so darkly at first, that she was quite alarmed and wished that she had run away as she had at first intended ; but he answered, after a pause :

" No—yes ; " he said, " yes—I'm waiting for my father."

He did not even speak as the boys at the Cross-roads spoke. His voice had a clear, soft ring, and his mode of pronunciation was one Tom had spent much time in endeavouring to impress upon herself as being more desirable than that she had heard most commonly used around her. Up to this time she had frequently wondered why she must speak differently from Mornin and Molly Hollister, but now she suddenly began to appreciate the wisdom of his course. It was very much nicer to speak as the boy spoke.

"I haven't any father," she ventured, "or any mother. That's queer, isn't it?" And as she said it, Mrs. Sparkes's words rushed into her mind again, and she looked up the street towards the sunset and fell into a momentary reverie, whispering them to herself.

"What's that you are saying?" asked the boy.

She looked at him with a rather uncertain and troubled expression.

"It was only what they said in there," she replied, pointing towards the dining-room.

"What did they say?"

She repeated the words slowly, regarding him fixedly, because she wondered if they would have any effect upon him.

"She died and he went away, nobody knows where. What does it mean?"

"I don't know," he admitted, staring at her with his handsome, long-lashed eyes. "Lots of people die and go away." Then, after a pause, in which he dropped his eyes, he added:

"My mother died two years ago."

"Did she?" answered Sheba, wondering why he looked so gloomy again all at once. "I don't think I ever had any mother, but I have Uncle Tom."

He stared at her again, and there was silence for a few minutes. This he broke by asking a question.

"What is your name?" he demanded.

"De Willoughby," she replied, "but I'm called Sheba."

"Why, that's my name," he said, surprisedly. "My name is De Willoughby. I— Hallo, Neb——"

This last in a tone of proprietorship to a negro servant, who was advancing towards them from a side-door and who hurried up with rather a frightened manner.

"Ye'd best get ready ter start right away, Mars Ralph,"
he said. "He's wake at las', an' der's de debbil to pay,
a-cussin' an' roarin' an' wantin' opium ; an' he wants to
know whar ye bin an' what ye mean, an' ses de hosses mus'
be at de do' in ten minits. Oh, de cunnel he's in de
wustest kin' o' humour, dar's no doin' nuffin right fer
him."

"Tell him to go to h——" burst forth the lad, flying
into a rage and looking so wickedly passionate in a boyish
way that Sheba was frightened again. "Tell him I won't
go until I'm ready ; I've been dragged round till I'm sick
of it, and——"

In the midst of his tempest he checked himself, turned
about and walked suddenly into the house, the negro following him in evident trepidation.

His departure was so sudden that Sheba fancied he
would return and say something more to her. Angry as
he looked, she wished very much that he would, and so
stood waiting wistfully.

But she was doomed to disappointment. In a few
minutes the negro brought to the front three horses, and
almost immediately there appeared at the door a tall,
handsome man, who made his way to the finest horse and
mounted it with a dashing vault into the saddle.

He had a dark aquiline face like the boy's, and wore a
great sweeping mustache which hid his mouth. The boy
followed, looking wonderfully like him, as he sprang into
his own saddle with the same dare-devil vault.

No one spoke a word, and he did not even look at Sheba,
though she watched him with admiring and longing eyes.
As soon as they were fairly in their seats the horses, which
were fine creatures, needing neither whip nor spur, sprang
forward with a light, easy movement, and so cantered down

the street towards the high road which stretched itself over a low hill about a quarter of a mile away.

Sheba laid her cheek against the wooden pillar and looked after them with a return of the sense of loneliness she had felt before.

"He went away," she whispered, "nobody knows where—nobody knows where."

She felt Tom's hand laid on her shoulder as she said the words, and turned her face upward with a consciousness of relief, knowing she would not be lonely any longer.

"Have I been gone long?" he asked. "Where's Mrs. Sparkes?"

"She's in there," Sheba answered, eagerly, "and I've been talking to the boy."

"To the boy?" he repeated. "What boy?"

"To the one we saw," she replied, holding his hand and feeling her cheeks flush with the excitement of relating her adventure. "The nice boy. His name is like mine—and his mother died. He said it was De Willoughby, and it is like mine. He has gone away with his father. See them riding."

He dropped her hand and, taking a step forward, stood watching the receding travellers. He watched them until they reached the rising ground. The boy had fallen a few yards behind. Presently the others passed the top of the hill, and, as they did so, he turned in his saddle as if he had suddenly remembered something, and glanced back at the tavern porch.

"He is looking for me," cried Sheba, and ran out into the brightness of the setting sun, happy because he had not quite forgotten her.

He saw her, waved his hand with a careless, boyish gesture and disappeared over the brow of the hill.

In Connection with
The De Willoughby Claim

Tom sat down suddenly on the porch - step. When Sheba turned to him he was pale and his forehead was damp with sweat. He spoke aloud, but to himself, not to her.

"Good Lord," he said, "it's De Courcy and—and the boy. That was why I knew his face."

.   .   .   .

When they went in to supper later on, there was a great deal of laughing and talking going on down the long table. Mr. Sparkes was finishing a story as they entered, and he was finishing it in a loud voice.

"They're pretty well known," he said ; "an' the Colonel's the worst o' the lot. The nigger told me thar'd been a reg'lar flare-up at the Springs. Thar was a ball an' he got on a tear an' got away from 'em an' bust right into the ball-room an' played Hail Columby. He's a pop'lar man among the ladies, is the Colonel, but a mixtry of whiskey an' opium is apt to spile his manners. Nigger says he's the drunkest man when he is drunk that the Lord ever let live. Ye cayn't do nothin' with him. The boy was thar, an' they say 'twas a sight ter see him. He's his daddy's son, an' a bigger young devil never lived, they tell me. He's not got to the whiskey an' opium yet, an' he jes' takes his'n out in pride an' temper. Nigger said he jest raved an' tore that night—went into the Colonel's room an' cussed an' dashed round like he was gone mad. Kinder shamed, I reckin. But Lord, he'll be at it himself in ten years from now. It's in the blood."

"Who's that you're talking of ?" asked Tom from his end of the table. He had not recovered his colour yet and looked pale as he put the question.

"Colonel De Willoughby of Delisleville," answered Mr. Sparkes. "Any kin o' your'n ? Name's sorter like. He

141

jest left here this evenin' with his boy an' nigger. They've ben to Whitebriar, an' they're on their way home."

"I saw them ride over the hill," said Tom. "I thought I wasn't mistaken in the man. I've seen him before."

But he made a very poor supper, and a shadow seemed to have fallen upon his cheery mood of the morning. Sheba recognised this and knew, too, that her new friend and his father were in some vague way responsible for it, and the knowledge oppressed her so that when they sat out upon the porch together after the meal was over, she in her accustomed place on his knee, she grew sad under it herself and, instead of talking as usual, leaned her small head against his coat and watched the few stars whose brightness the moon had not shut out.

She went to bed early, but did not sleep well, dreaming dreary dreams of watching the travellers riding away towards the sunset, and of hearing the woman talk again. One of the talkers seemed at last to waken her with her voice, and she sat up in bed suddenly and found that it was Tom, who had roused her by speaking to himself in a low tone as he stood in a flood of moonlight before the window.

"She died," he was saying; "she died."

Sheba burst into a little sob, stretching out her hands to him without comprehending her own emotion.

"And he went away," she cried, "nobody knows where—nobody knows where—" And even when he came to her hurriedly and sat down on the bedside, soothing her and taking her in his arms to sink back into slumber, she sobbed drearily two or three times, though, once in his clasp, she felt, as she had always done, the full sense of comfort, safety, and rest.

CHAPTER XII

THE New England town of Willowfield was a place of great importance. Its importance—religious, intellectual, and social—was its strong point. It took the liberty of asserting this with unflinching dignity. Other towns might endeavour to struggle to the front, and, indeed, did so endeavour, but Willowfield calmly held its place and remained unmoved. Its place always had been at the front from the first, and there it took its stand. It had, perhaps, been hinted that its sole title to this position lay in its own stately assumption; but this, it may be argued, was sheer envy and entirely unworthy of notice.

" Willowfield is not very large or very rich," its leading old lady said, " but it is important and has always been considered so."

There was society in Willowfield, society which had taken up its abiding-place in three or four streets and confined itself to developing its importance in half a dozen families—old families. They were always spoken of as the " old families," and, to be a member of one of them, even a second or third cousin of weak mind and feeble understanding, was to be enclosed within the magic circle outside of which was darkness, wailing, and gnashing of teeth. There were the Stornaways, who had owned the button factory for nearly a generation and a half—which was a long time; the Downings, who had kept the feed-store for quite thirty years; and the Burtons, who had been doctors for almost as long,

143

not to mention the Larkins, who had actually founded the Willowfield *Times*, and kept it going, which had scarcely been expected of them at the outset.

Their moral, mental, and social gifts notwithstanding, there was nothing connected with the Stornaways, the Downings, the Burtons, and the Larkins of such importance as their antiquity. The uninformed outsider, on hearing it descanted upon, might naturally have been betrayed into the momentary weakness of expecting to see Mr. Downing moulder away, and little old Doctor Burton crumble into dust.

"They belong," it was said, with the temperateness of true dignity, "to our old families, and that is something, you know, even in America."

"It has struck me," an observing male visitor once remarked, "that there are a good many women in Willowfield, and that altogether it has a feminine tone."

It was certainly true that among the Stornaways, the Downings, the Burtons, and the Larkins, the prevailing tone was feminine; and as the Stornaways, the Downings, the Burtons, and the Larkins comprised Willowfield society, and without its society Willowfield lost its significance, the observing male visitor may not have been far wrong. If mistakes were made in Willowfield society, they were always made by the masculine members of it. It was Mr. Stornaway who had at one time been betrayed into the blunder of inviting to a dinner-party at his house a rather clever young book-keeper in his employ, and it was Doctor Burton who had wandered still more glaringly from the path of rectitude by taking a weak, if amiable, interest in a little music teacher with a sweet, tender voice, even going so far as to request his family to call upon her and ask her to take tea with them. It was Mr. Downing, who, when this last incident occurred and created some sensation, had had the temerity to intimate that he thought the Doctor was entirely in the right; though, to be sure, he had afterwards been led to falter in this opinion and subside into craven silence, being a little gentleman of timorous and yielding nature, and rather overborne by a large and powerful feminine majority in his own household. Mr. Larkin was, it is to be regretted, the worst of the recreant party, being younger and more unmanageable, having not only introduced to public notice certain insignificant though somewhat talented persons in the shape of young men and women who talked well, or sang well, or wielded lively pens, but had gone to the length of standing by them unflinchingly, demanding civility for them at the hands of his own family of women in such a manner as struck a deadly blow at the very foundations of the social structure. But Mr. Larkin—he was known as Jack Larkin to an astonishing number of people—was a bold man by nature and given to deeds of daring, from the fatal consequences of which nothing but the fact that he was a member of one of the " old families " could have saved him. As he was a part—and quite a large part—of one of these venerable households, and, moreover, knew not the fear of man—or woman—his failings could be referred to as " eccentricities."

" Mr. Larkin," Mrs. Stornaway frequently observed, with long-suffering patience, " is talented but eccentric. You are never quite sure what he will do next."

Mrs. Stornaway was the head and front of all Willowfield's social efforts, and represented the button factory with a lofty grace and unbending dignity of demeanour which were the admiration and envy of all aspirants to social fame. It was said that Mrs. Stornaway had been a beauty in her youth, and there were those who placed confidence in the rumour. Mrs. Stornaway did so herself, and it had been intimated that it was this excellent lady who had vouched for the truth of the statement in the first instance; but this report having been traced to a pert young relative who detested and derided her, might have had its origin in youthful disrespect and malice.

At present Mrs. Stornaway was a large blonde woman whose blondness was not fairness, and whose size was not roundness. She was the leader of all religious and charitable movements, presiding with great vigour over church matters, fairs, concerts, and sewing societies. The minister of her church submitted himself to her advice and guidance. All the modest members of the choir quailed and quavered before her, while even the bold ones, meeting her eye when engaged in worldly conversation between their musical efforts, momentarily lost their interest and involuntarily straightened themselves.

Towards her family Mrs. Stornaway performed her duty with unflinching virtue. She had married her six daughters in a manner at once creditable to herself, themselves, and Willowfield. Five of them had been rather ordinary, depressed-looking girls, who, perhaps, were not sorry to obtain their freedom. The sixth had narrowly escaped being dowered with all the charms said to have adorned Mrs. Stornaway's own youth.

"Agnes is very like what I was at her age," said her mother, with dignity; and perhaps she was, though no one had been able to trace any resemblance which had defied the ravages of time.

Agnes had made a marriage which in some points was better than those of her sisters. She had married a brilliant man, while the other five had been obliged to make the best of things as far as brilliancy was concerned. People always said of John Baird that he was a brilliant man and that a great career lay before him. He was rather remarkable for a curious subtle distinction of physical good looks. He was not of the common, straight-featured, personable type. It had been said by the artistic analyst of form and line that his aspect did not belong to his period, that indeed his emotional, spirited face, with its look of sensitiveness and race, was of the type once connected with fine old steel engravings of young poets not quite beyond the days of powdered hair and frilled shirt-bosoms.

"It is absurd that he should have been born in America and in these days," a brilliant person had declared. "He always brings to my mind the portraits in delightful old annuals, ' So-and-so—at twenty-five.' "

His supple ease of movement and graceful length of limb gave him an air of youth. He was one of the creatures to whom the passage of years would mean but little, but added charm and adaptability. His eyes were singularly living things—the eyes that almost unconsciously entreat and whose entreaty touches one; the fine, irregular outline of his profile was the absolute expression of the emotional at war with itself, the passionate, the tender, the sensitive, and complex. The effect of these things was almost the effect of peculiar physical beauty, and with this he combined the allurements of a compelling voice and an enviable sense of the fitness of things. He never lost a thought through the inability to utter it. When he had left college, he had left burdened with honours and had borne with him the enthusiastic admiration of his fellow-students. He had earned and worn his laurels with an ease and grace which would be remembered through years to come.

In Connection with
The De Willoughby Claim

"It's something," it was once said, "to have known a fellow to whom things came so easily."

When he had entered the ministry, there had been some wonder expressed among the men who had known him best, but when he preached his first sermon at Willowfield, where there was a very desirable church indeed, with whose minister Mrs. Stornaway had become dissatisfied, and who in consequence was to be civilly removed, the golden apple fell at once into his hand.

Before he had arrived he had been spoken of rather slightingly as "the young man," but when he rose in the pulpit on the eventful Sunday morning, such a thrill ran through the congregation as had not stirred it at its devotions for many a summer day. Mrs. Stornaway mentally decided for him upon the spot.

"He is of one of our oldest families," she said. "This is what Willowfield wants."

He dined with the Stornaways that day, and when he entered the parlour the first figure his eyes fell upon was that of Agnes Stornaway, dressed in white muslin, with white roses in her belt. She was a tall girl, with a willowy figure and a colourless fairness of skin, but when her mother called her to her side and Baird touched her hand, she blushed in such a manner that Mrs. Stornaway was a little astonished. Scarcely a year afterward she became Mrs. Baird, and people said she was a very fortunate girl, which was possibly true.

Her husband did not share the fate of most ministers who had presided over Mrs. Stornaway's church. His power over his congregation increased every year. His name began to be known in the world of literature; he was called upon to deliver in important places the lectures he had delivered to his Willowfield audiences, and the result was one startling triumph after another. There was every indication of the fact that a career was already marked out for him.

Willowfield looked forward with trepidation to the time when the great world which stood ready to give him fame would absorb him altogether, but in the meantime it exerted all its power of fascination, and was so far successful that the Reverend John Baird felt that his lines had indeed fallen in pleasant places.

But after the birth of her little daughter his wife was not strong, and was so long in regaining vitality that in the child's second year she was ordered abroad by the physician. At this time Baird's engagements were such that he could not accompany her, and accordingly he remained in America. The career was just opening up its charmed vistas to him; his literary efforts were winning laurels; he was called upon to lecture in Boston and New York, and he never rose before an audience without at once awakening an enthusiasm.

Mrs. Baird went to the south of France with her child and nurse and a party of friends, and remained there for a year. At the termination of that time, just as she thought of returning home, she was taken seriously ill. Her husband was sent for and went at once to join her. In a few months she had died of rapid decline. She had been a delicate girl, and a far-off taint of consumption in her family blood had reasserted itself. But though Mrs. Stornaway bewailed her with diffuse and loud pathos and for a year swathed her opulence of form in deepest folds and draperies of crape, the quiet fairness and slightness which for some five and twenty years had been known as Agnes Stornaway, had been a personality not likely to be a marked and long-lingering memory.

The child was placed with a motherly friend in Paris.

For a month after his wife's death Baird had been feverishly, miserably eager to return to America. Those about him felt that the blow which had fallen upon him might affect his health seriously. He seemed possessed by a desperate, morbid desire to leave the scene of the calamity behind him. He was restless and feverish in his anxiety, and scarcely able to endure the delay which the arrangement of his affairs made necessary. He had not been well when he had left Willowfield, and during his watching by his wife's bedside he had grown thin and restless-eyed.

" I want to get home. I must get home," he would exclaim, as if involuntarily. His entire physical and mental condition were strained and unnatural. His wife's doctor, who had become his own doctor as his health deteriorated, was not surprised, on arriving one day, to find him prostrated with nervous fever. He was ill for months, and he rose from his sick-bed a depressed shadow of his former self and quite unable to think of returning to his charge, even if his old desire had not utterly left him with his fever. He was absent from Willowfield for two years, and when at length he turned his face homeward, it was with no eagerness. He had passed through one of those phases which change a man's life and being. If he had been a rich man he would have remained away and would have lived in London, seeing much of the chief continental cities. As it was, he must at least temporarily return to Willowfield and take with him his little girl.

On the day distinguished by his return to his people, much subdued excitement prevailed in Willowfield. During the whole of the previous week Mrs. Stornaway's carriage had paid daily visits to the down-town stores. There was a flourishing New England thrift among the Stornaways, the Lar-

kins, the Downings, and the Burtons, which did not allow
of their delegating the ordering of their households to assistants. Most of them were rigorous housewives, keen
at a bargain and sharp of tongue when need be, and there
was rarely any danger of their getting less than their money's
worth.

To celebrate his arrival, Mrs. Stornaway was to give an
evening party which was to combine congratulatory welcome
with a touch of condolence for the past and assurance for
the future.

" We must let him see," said Mrs. Stornaway, " that Willowfield has its attractions."

Its attractions did not present themselves as vividly to
John Baird as might have been hoped, when he descended
from the train at the depot. He had spent two or three
days in Boston with a view to taking his change gradually,
but he found himself not as fully prepared for Willowfield
as he could have wished. He was not entirely prepared for
Mrs. Stornaway, who hurried towards them with exultation
on her large, stupid face, and, after effusive embraces, bus-
iled with them towards an elderly woman who had evidently accompanied her.

" See, here's Miss Amory Starkweather! " she exclaimed.
" She came with me to meet you. Just see how Annie's
grown, Miss Amory."

Miss Amory was a thin woman with a strong-featured
countenance and deep-set, observing eyes. They were eyes
whose expression suggested that they had made many painful discoveries in the course of their owner's life.

John Baird rather lighted up for a moment when he
caught sight of her.

" I am glad to see you, Miss Amory," he said.

"Thank you," she answered. "I hope you are as well as you look."

"We're so delighted," Mrs. Stornaway announced, as if to the bystanders. "Everybody in Willowfield is so delighted to have you back again. The church has not seemed the same place. The man who took your place—Mr. Jeramy, you know—you haven't any idea how unpopular——"

"Excuse me," said Baird, "I must speak to Latimer. Where is Latimer, Annie?"

"Who is Latimer?" asked Mrs. Stornaway.

"Excuse me," said Baird again, and turning back towards the platform, he disappeared among the crowd with Annie, who had clung to his hand.

"Why, he's gone!" proclaimed Mrs. Stornaway. "But where's he gone? Why didn't he stay? Who's Latimer?"

"Latimer!" Miss Amory echoed, "you ought to know him. His family lives in Willowfield. He is the man who was coming home to take charge of the little church at Janway's Mills. He has evidently crossed the Atlantic with them."

"Well, now, I declare," proclaimed Mrs. Stornaway. "It must be the man who took his sister to Europe. It was a kind of absurd thing. She died away—the girl did, and people wondered why he did not come back and how he lived. Why, yes, that must be the man." And she turned to look about for him.

Miss Amory Starkweather made a slight movement.

"Don't look," she said. "He might not like to be stared at."

"They're quite common people," commented Mrs. Stornaway, still staring. "They live in a little house in a side street. They had very silly ideas about the girl. They thought she was a genius and sent her to the School of Art

152

in Boston, but it wasn't long before her health failed her. Ah! I guess that must be the man talking to Mr. Baird and Annie. He looks as if he would go off in a consumption."

He was a tall, hollow-chested man, with a dark, sallow face and an ungainly figure. There were suggestions of both ill-health and wretchedness in his appearance, and his manner was awkward and embarrassed. Two human beings more utterly unlike each other than himself and the man who held his hand could not possibly have been found. It was Baird who held his hand, not he Baird's, and it was Baird who seemed to speak while he listened, while with his free hand he touched the hair of the child Annie.

" Well," remarked Mrs. Stornaway, " Mr. Baird seems to have taken a fancy to him. I don't think he's attractive myself. Are they going to talk to him all day?"

" No," said Miss Amory, " he is going now."

He was going. Baird had released his hand and he was looking in a gloomy, awkward way at Annie, as if he did not know how to make his adieux. But Annie, who was a simple child creature, solved the difficulty for him with happy readiness. She flung both her small arms about his ungainly body and held up her face.

" Kiss me three times," she said; " three times."

Latimer started and flushed. He looked down at her and then glanced rather timidly at Baird.

" Kiss her," said Baird, " it will please her—and it will please me."

Latimer bent himself to the child's height and kissed her. The act was without grace, and when he stood upright he was more awkward and embarrassed than ever. But the caress was not a cold or rough one, and when he turned and strode away the flush was still on his sallow cheek.

CHAPTER XIII

THE Stornaway parlours were very brilliant that evening in a Willowfield sense. Not a Burton, a Larkin, or a Downing was missing, even Miss Amory Starkweather being present. Miss Amory Starkweather was greatly respected by the Stornaways, the Downings, the Larkins, and the Burtons, the Starkweathers having landed upon Plymouth Rock so early and with such a distinguished sense of their own importance as to lead to the impression in weak minds that they had not only founded that monumental corner-stone of ancestry, but were personally responsible for the Mayflower. This gentlewoman represented to the humorous something more of the element of comedy than she represented to herself. She had been born into a world too narrow and provincial for the development of the powers born with her. She had been an ugly girl and an ugly woman, marked by the hopeless ugliness of a long, ill-proportioned face, small eyes, and a nose too large and high—that ugliness which even love's eyes can scarcely ameliorate into good drawing.

The temperament attached to these painful disabilities had been warm and strongly womanly. Born a century or so earlier, in a French Court, or any great world vivid with picturesque living, she would in all probability have been a remarkable personage, her ugliness a sort of distinction; but she had been born in Willowfield, and had lived its life and been bound by its limits. She had been com-

fortably well off—she had a large square house with a garden, an income sufficient to provide for extremely respectable existence in Willowfield, but not large enough to allow
of experiments with the outside world. She had never met
a man whom she could have loved, who would have loved
her, and she was essentially—though Willowfield would
never have dreamed it—a woman who should have loved
and mated. A lifetime of narrow, unstimulating years and
thwarted instincts had made age treat her ill. She was a
thin woman with burning eyes, and a personality people
were afraid of.

She had always found an interest in John Baird. When
he had come to Willowfield she had seen in him that element
which her whole long life had lacked. His emotional poten-
tialities had wakened her imagination. If she had been a
young woman she knew that she might have fallen tragi-
cally and hopelessly in love with him; as an old woman
she found it well worth her while to watch him and specu-
late upon him. When he had become engaged to Agnes
Stornaway, she had watched him and secretly wondered how
the engagement would end; when it had ended in marriage
she had not wondered, but she had seen many things other
people did not see. " He is not in love with her," had been
her mental decision, " but he is emotional, and he is in love
with her being in love with him. There is no foretelling
what will come of it."

Baird had found himself attracted by Miss Amory. He
did not know that if she had been young she would, despite
her ugliness, have had a powerful feminine effect on him.
He used to go and talk to her, and he was not conscious that
he went when he was made restless by a lack of something
in the mental atmosphere about him. He could talk to her

155

as he could not talk to the rest of Willowfield. She read and thought and argued with herself, and as a product of a provincial dogmatic New England town was a curious development.

"Were you once a brilliant, wicked, feminine mover of things in some old French court?" he said to her once.

They had been plunging deep into the solving of unsolvable problems, and she turned her burning old eyes on him as she answered.

"God knows what I was," she said, "but it was nothing like this—nothing like this—and I was not wicked."

"No," Baird replied, "you were not wicked; but you broke laws."

"Yes, I broke laws," she agreed; "but they were hideous laws—better broken than kept."

She had been puzzled by the fact that after his wife left him he had had a restless period and had seemed to pass through a miserable phase, such as a man suffering from love and longing might endure.

"Has he fallen in love with her because she has gone away?" she wondered; "men are capable of it at times."

But later she decided mentally that this was not his special case. She saw, however, that he was passing through some mental crisis which was a dangerous struggle. He was restless and often away from Willowfield for two or three days at a time.

"To provide the place with orthodox doctrine once a week is more than he can bear, and to be bored to extinction into the bargain makes him feel morbid," she said to herself. "I hope he won't begin to be lured by things which might produce catastrophe."

Once he came and spent a long, hot summer evening with

her, and when he went away she had arrived at another decision, and it made her wretched.

"He is lured," she thought. "I cannot help him, and God knows Willowfield could not. After this—perhaps the Deluge."

She saw but little of him for two months, and then he was called across the Atlantic by his wife's illness and left the place.

"Write to me now and then," he said, when he came to bid her good-bye.

"What can I write about from Willowfield to a man in Paris?" she asked.

"About Willowfield," he answered, holding her hand and laughing a little gruesomely. "There will be a thrill in it when one is three thousand miles away. Tell me about the church—about the people—who comes, who goes—your own points of view will make it all worth while. Will you?" almost as if a shade anxiously.

She felt the implied flattery just enough to be vaguely pleased by it.

"Yes, I will," she answered.

She kept her word, and the letters were worth reading. It was, as he had said, her points of view which gave interest to the facts that unexciting people had died, married, or been born. Her sketch of the trying position of the unpopular man who filled his pulpit and was unfavourably compared with him every Sunday morning was full of astute analysis and wit; her little picture of the gloomy young theological student, Latimer, his efforts for his sister, and her innocent, pathetic death in a foreign land had a wonderful realism of touch. She had by pure accident made the child's acquaintance and had been strongly touched and moved. She did not write often, but he read her letters many times over.

Upon this evening of his home-coming she thought he had sometimes the look of a man who felt that he walked in a dream. More than once she saw him involuntarily pass his hand with a swift movement over his eyes as if his own touch might waken him. It was true he did not greatly enjoy the festivities. His occasional views of Mrs. Stornaway as she rambled among her guests, talking to them about him in audible tones, were trying. She dispensed him with her hospitalities, as it were, and was diffuse upon the extent of his travels and the attention paid him, to each member of the company in turn. He knew when she was speaking of himself and when of her daughter, and the alternate decorous sentiment and triumphant pleasure marked on her broad face rasped him to the extent of making him fear lest he might lose his temper.

"She is a stupid woman," he found himself saying half aloud once; "the most stupid woman I think I ever met."

Towards the end of the evening, as he entered the room, he found himself obliged to pass her. She stood near the door, engaged in animated conversation with Mrs. Downing. She had hit upon a new and absorbing topic, which had the additional charge of savouring of local gossip.

"Why," he heard her say, "I mean to ask him. He can tell us, I guess. I haven't a doubt but he heard the whole story. You know he has a way of drawing people out. He's so much tact and sympathy. I used to tell Agnes he was all tact and sympathy."

Feeling quite sure that it was himself who was "all tact and sympathy," Baird endeavoured to move by unobserved, but she caught sight of him and checked his progress.

"Mr. Baird," she said, "we're just talking about you."

"Don't talk about me," he said, lightly; "I am not half so culpable as I look."

He often found small change of this order could be made useful with Mrs. Stornaway, and he bestowed this upon her with an easy air which she felt to be very delightful.

"He's so ready," she observed, enraptured; "I often used to say to Agnes——"

But Mrs. Downing was not to be defrauded.

"We were talking about those people on Bank Street," she said, "the Latimers. Mrs. Stornaway says you crossed the Atlantic with the son, who has just come back. Do tell us something about him."

"I am afraid I cannot make him as interesting to you as he was to me," answered Baird, with his light air again.

"He does not look very interesting," said Mrs. Stornaway. "I never saw anyone so sallow; I can't understand Annie liking him."

"He is interesting," responded Baird. "Annie took one of her fancies to him, and I took something more than a fancy. We shall be good friends, I think."

"Well, I'm sure it's very kind of you to take such an interest," proclaimed Mrs. Stornaway. "You are always finding something good in people."

"I wish people were always finding something good in me," said John Baird. "It was not difficult to find good in this man. He is of the stuff they made saints and martyrs of in the olden times."

"What did the girl die of?" asked Mrs. Downing.

"What?" repeated Baird. "The girl? I don't know."

"And where did she die?" added Mrs. Downing.

"I was just saying," put in Mrs. Stornaway, "that you

had such a sympathetic way of drawing people out that I
was sure he had told you the whole story."

"There was not much story," Baird answered, "and it
was too sad to talk over. The poor child went abroad
and died in some little place in Italy—of consumption,
I think."

"I suppose she was sick when they went," commented
Mrs. Downing. "I heard so. It was a queer thing for
them to go to Europe, as inexperienced as they were and
everything. But the father and mother were more inexperienced still, I guess. They were perfectly foolish about
the girl—and so was the brother. She went to some studio
in Boston to study art, and they had an idea her bits of
pictures were wonderful."

"I never saw her myself," said Mrs. Stornaway. "No
one seems to have seen anything of her but Miss Amory
Starkweather."

"Miss Starkweather!" exclaimed Baird. "Oh, yes—in
her letters she mentioned having met her."

"Well, it was a queer thing," said Mrs. Downing, "but
it was like Miss Amory. They say the girl fainted in the
street as Miss Amory was driving by, and she stopped her
carriage and took her in and carried her home. She took
quite a fancy to her and saw her every day or so until she
went away."

It was not unnatural that at this juncture John Baird's
eyes should wander across the room to where Miss Amory
Starkweather sat, but it was a coincidence that as his eye
fell upon her she should meet it with a gesture which called
him to her side.

"It seems that Miss Amory wishes to speak to me," he
said to his companions.

" He'll make himself just as interesting to her as he has made himself to us," said Mrs. Stornaway, with heavy sprightliness, as he left them. " He never spares himself trouble."

He went across the room to Miss Amory.

" Can you sit down by me? " she said. " I want to talk to you about Lucien Latimer."

" What is there in the atmosphere which suggests Latimer? " he inquired. " We have been talking about him at the other side of the room. Do you know him? "

" I never saw him," she replied, " but I knew her."

" Her! " he repeated.

" The little sister." She leaned forward a little. " What were the details of her death? " she asked. " I want to know—I want to know."

Somehow the words sounded nervously eager.

" I did not ask him," he answered; " I thought he preferred to be silent. He is a silent man."

She sat upright again, and for a moment seemed to forget herself. She said something two or three times softly to herself. Baird thought it was " Poor child! Poor child! "

" She was young to die," he said, in a low voice. " Poor child, indeed."

Miss Amory came back to him, as it were.

" The younger, the better," she said. " Look at me! " Her burning eyes were troubling and suggestive. Baird found himself trying to gather himself together. He assumed the natural air of kindly remonstrance.

" Oh, come," he said. " Don't take that tone. It is unfair to all of us."

Her reply was certainly rather a startling one.

"Very well then," she responded. "Look at yourself. If you had died as young as she did——"

He looked at her, conscious of a little coldness creeping over his body. She was usually lighter when they were not entirely alone. Just now, in the midst of this commonplace, exceedingly middle-class evening party, with the Larkins, the Downings, and the Burtons chattering, warm, diffuse, and elate, about him, she stirred him with a little horror—not horror of herself, but of something in her mood.

"Do you think I am such a bad fellow?" he said.

"No," she answered. "Worse, poor thing. It is not the bad fellows who produce the crudest results. But I did not call you here to tell you that you were bad or good. I called you to speak about Lucien Latimer. When you go to him—you are going to him?"

"To-morrow."

"Then tell him to come and see me."

"I will tell him anything you wish," said Baird. "Is there anything else?"

"Tell him I knew her," she answered, "Margery—Margery!"

"Margery," Baird said slowly, as if the sound touched him. "What a pretty, simple name!"

"She was a pretty, simple creature," said Miss Amory.

"Tell me——" he said, "tell me something more about her."

"There is nothing more to tell," she replied. "She was dying when I met her. I saw it—in her eyes. She could not have lived. She went away and died. She—I——"

John Baird heard a slight sharp choking sound in her throat.

In Connection with
The De Willoughby Claim

" There! " she said presently, " I don't like to talk about it. I am too emotional for my years. Go to Mrs. Stornaway. She is looking for you."

He got up and turned and left her without speaking, and a few minutes later, when Mrs. Stornaway wanted him to give an account of his interview with the Pope, she was surprised to see him approaching her from the door as if he had been out of the room.

His story of the interview with the Pope was very interesting, and he was more " brilliant " than ever during the remainder of the evening, but when the last guest had departed, followed by Mrs. Stornaway to the threshold, that lady, on her return to the parlour, found him standing by the mantel looking at the fire with so profoundly wearied an air, that she uttered an exclamation.

" Why," she said, " you look tired, I must say. But everything went off splendidly and I never saw you so brilliant."

" Thank you," he answered.

" I've just been saying," with renewed spirit of admiration, " that your crossing with that Latimer has quite brought him into notice. It will be a good thing for him. I heard several people speak of him to-night and say how kind it was of you to take him up."

Baird stirred uneasily.

" I should not like to have that tone taken," he said. " Why should I patronise him? We shall be friends—if he will allow it." He spoke with so much heat and impatience that Mrs. Stornaway listened with a discomfited stare.

" But nobody knows anything about them," she said. " They're quite ordinary people. They live in Bank Street."

In Connection with
The De Willoughby Claim

"That may settle the matter for Willowfield," said Baird, "but it does not settle it for me. We are to be friends, and Willowfield must understand that."

And such was the decision of his tone that Mrs. Stornaway did not recover herself and was still staring after him in a bewildered fashion when he went upstairs.

"But it's just like him," she remarked, rather weakly to the room's emptiness. "That's always the way with people of genius and—and—*mind*. They're always humble."

CHAPTER XIV

She had renewed opportunity for remarking upon the generous humility the next morning when he left the house with the intention of paying his visit to Bank Street.

"He's actually going," she said. "Well, I must say again it's just like him. There are very few men in his position who would think it worth while, but he treats everybody with just as much consideration as if—as if he was nobody."

The house on Bank Street was just what he had expected to find it—small, unornamental, painted white, and modestly putting forth a few vines as if with a desire to clothe itself, which had not been encouraged by Nature. The vines had not flourished and they, as well as the few flowers in the yard, were dropping their scant foliage, which turned brown and rustled in the autumn wind.

Before ringing the bell, Baird stood for a few moments upon the threshold. As he looked up and down the street, he was pale and felt chilly, so chilly that he buttoned his light overcoat over his breast and his hands even shook slightly as he did it. Then he turned and rang the bell.

It was answered by a little woman with a girlish figure and gray hair. For a moment John Baird paused before speaking to her, as he had paused before ringing the bell, and in the pause, during which he found himself looking into her soft, childishly blue eyes, he felt even chillier than at first.

"Mrs. Latimer. I think," he said, baring his head.

"Yes," she answered, "and you are Mr. Baird and have come to see Lucien, I'm sure."

She gave him her small hand with a smile.

"I am very glad to see you," she said, "and Lucien will be glad, too. Come in, please."

She led the way into the little parlour, talking in a voice as soft and kindly as her eyes. Lucien had been out, but had just come in, she fancied, and was probably upstairs. She would go and tell him.

So, having taken him into the room, she went, leaving him alone. When she was gone, Baird stood for a moment listening to her footsteps upon the stairs. Then he crossed the room and stood before the hearth looking up at a picture which hung over the mantel.

．　　．　　．　　．　　．　　．　　．

He was still standing before it when she returned with her son. He turned slowly to confront them, holding out his hand to Latimer with something less of alert and sympathetic readiness than was usual with him. There was in his manner an element which corresponded with the lack of colour and warmth in his face.

"I've been looking at this portrait of your—of——" he began.

"Of Margery," put in the little mother. "Everyone looks at Margery when they come in. It seems as if the child somehow filled the room." And though her soft voice had a sigh in it, she did not speak in entire sadness.

John Baird looked at the picture again. It was the portrait of a slight small girl with wistful eyes and an innocent face.

"I felt sure that it was she," he said in a lowered voice, "and you are quite right in saying that she seems to fill the room."

The mother put her hand upon her son's arm. He had turned his face towards the window. It seemed to Baird that her light touch was at once an appeal and a consolation.

"She filled the whole house when she was here," she said; "and yet she was only a quiet little thing. She had a bright way with her quietness and was so happy and busy. It is my comfort now to remember that she was always happy—happy to the last, Lucien tells me."

She looked up at her son's averted face as if expecting him to speak, and he responded at once, though in his usual mechanical way.

"To the last," he said; "she had no fear and suffered no pain."

The little woman watched him with tender, wistful eyes; two large tears welled up and slipped down her cheeks, but she smiled softly as they fell.

"She had so wanted to go to Italy," she said; "and was so happy to be there. And at the last it was such a lovely day, and she enjoyed it so and was propped up on a sofa near the window, and looked out at the blue sky and the mountains, and made a little sketch. Tell him, Lucien," and she touched his arm again.

"I shall be glad to hear," said Baird, "but you must not tire yourself by standing," and he took her hand gently and led her to a chair and sat down beside her, still holding her hand.

But Latimer remained standing, resting his elbow upon the mantel and looking down at the floor as he spoke.

"She was not well in England," the little mother put

in, "but in Italy he thought she was better even to the very last."

"She was weak," Latimer went on, without raising his eyes, "but she was always bright and—and happy. She used to lie on the sofa by the window and look out and try to make sketches. She could see the Apennines, and it was the chestnut harvest and the peasants used to pass along the road on their way to the forests, and she liked to watch them. She used to try to sketch them too, but she was too weak; and when I wrote home for her, she made me describe them——"

"In her bright way!" said his mother. "I read the letters over and over again and they seemed like pictures—like her little pictures. It scarcely seems as if Lucien could have written them at all."

"The last day," said Latimer, "I had written home to say that she was better. She was so well in the morning that she talked of trying to take a drive, but in the afternoon she was a little tired——"

"But only a little," interrupted the mother eagerly, "and quite happy."

"Only a little—and quite happy," said Latimer. "There was a beautiful sunset and I drew her sofa to the windows and she lay and looked at it—and talked; and just as the sun went down——"

"All in a lovely golden glory, as if the gates of heaven were open," the gentle voice added.

Latimer paused for an instant. His sallow face had become paler. He drew out his handkerchief and touched his forehead with it and his lips.

"All in a glow of gold," he went on a little more hoarsely, "just as it went down, she turned on her pillow and began to speak to me. She said ' How beautiful it all is, and how glad—, And her voice died away. I thought she was looking at the sky again. She had lifted her eyes to it and was smiling: the smile was on her face when I—bent over her—a few moments after—and found that all was over."

"It was not like death at all," said his mother with a soft breathlessness. "She never even knew." And though tears streamed down her cheeks, she smiled.

Baird rose suddenly and went to Latimer's side. He wore the pale and bewildered face of a man walking in a dream. He laid his hand on his shoulder.

"No, it was not like death," he said; "try and remember that."

"I do remember it," was the answer.

"She escaped both death and life," said John Baird, "both death and life."

The little mother sat wiping her eyes gently.

"It was all so bright to her," she said. "I can scarcely think of it as a grief that we have lost her—for a little while. Her little room upstairs never seems empty. I could fancy that she might come in at any moment smiling as she used to. If she had ever suffered or been sad in it, I might feel as if the pain and sadness were left there; but when I open the door it seems as if her pretty smile met me, or the sound of her voice singing as she used to when she painted."

She rose and went to her son's side again, laying her hand on his arm with a world of tenderness in her touch.

"Try to think of that, Lucien, dear," she said; "try to think that her face was never any sadder or older than we see it in her pretty picture there. She might have lived to be tired of living, and she was saved from it."

" Try to help him," she said, turning to Baird, " perhaps you can. He has not learned to bear it yet. They were very near to each other, and perhaps he is too young to think of it as we do. Grief is always heavier to young people, I think. Try to help him."

She went out of the room quietly, leaving them together.

When she was gone, John Baird found himself trying, with a helpless feeling of desperation, to spur himself up to saying something; but neither words nor thoughts would come. For the moment his mind seemed a perfect blank, and the silence of the room was terrible.

It was Latimer who spoke first, stiffly, and as if with difficulty.

"I should be more resigned," he said, "I should be resigned. But it has been a heavy blow."

Baird moistened his dry lips but found no words.

" She had a bright nature," the lagging voice went on, " a bright nature—and gifts—which I had not. God gave me no gifts, and it is natural to me to see that life is dark and that I can only do poorly the work which falls to me. I was a gloomy, unhappy boy when she was born. I had learned to know the lack in myself early, and I saw in her what I longed for. I know the feeling is a sin against God and that His judgment will fall upon me—but I have no power against it."

" It is a very natural feeling," said Baird, hoarsely. " We cannot resign ourselves at once under a great sorrow."

" A just God who punishes rebellion demands it of His servants."

" Don't say that! " Baird interrupted, with a shudder; " we need a God of Mercy, not a God who condemns."

" Need! " the dark face almost livid in its pallor, " *We*

need! It is not He who was made for our needs, but we for His. For His servants there is only submission to the anguish chosen for us."

"That is a harsh creed," said Baird, "and a dark one. Try a brighter one, man!"

"There is no brighter one for me," was the answer. "She had a brighter one, poor child—and mine was a heavy trouble to her. Why should we deceive ourselves? What are we in His sight—in the sight of Immutable, Eternal God? We can only do His will and await the end. We have reason which we may not use; we can only believe and suffer. There is agony on every side of us which, if it were His will, He might relieve, but does not. It is His will, and what is the impotent rebellion of Nature against that? What help have we against Him?"

His harsh voice had risen until it was almost a cry, the lank locks which fell over his sallow forehead were damp with sweat. He put them back with a desperate gesture.

"Such words of themselves are sin," he said, "and it is my curse and punishment that I should bear in my breast every hour the crime of such rebellion. What is there left for me? Is there any labour or any pang borne for others that will wipe out the stain from my soul?"

John Baird looked at him as he had looked before. His usual ready flow of speech, his rapidity of thought, his knowledge of men and their necessities seemed all to have deserted him.

"I—" he stammered, "I am not—fit—not fit——"

He had not known what he was going to say when he began, and he did not know how he intended to end. He heard with a passionate sense of relief that the door behind

171

them opened, and turned to find that Mrs. Latimer stood upon the threshold as if in hesitancy.

"Lucien," she said, "it is that poor girl from Janway's Mills. The one Margery was so sorry for—Susan Chapman. She wants to see you. I think the poor child wants to ask about Margery."

Latimer made a movement forward, but checked himself.

"Tell her to come in," he said.

Mrs. Latimer went to the front door, and in a few seconds returned. The girl was with her and entered the room slowly. She was very pale and her eyes were dilated and she breathed fast as if frightened. She glanced at John Baird and stopped.

"I didn't know anyone else was here," she said.

"I will go away, if you wish it," said Baird, the sympathetic tone returning to his voice.

"No," said Latimer, "you can do her more good than I can. This gentleman," he added to the girl, "is my friend, and a Minister of God as well as myself. He is the Rev. John Baird."

There was in his eyes, as he addressed her, a look which was like an expression of dread—as if he saw in her young yet faded face and figure something which repelled him almost beyond self-control.

Perhaps the girl saw, while she did not comprehend it. She regarded him helplessly.

"I—I don't know—hardly—why I came," she faltered, twisting the corner of her shawl.

She had been rather pretty, but the colour and freshness were gone from her face and there were premature lines of pain and misery marking it here and there.

Baird moved a chair near her.

"Sit down," he said. "Have you walked all the way from Janway's Mills?"

She started a little and gave him a look, half wonder, half relief, and then fell to twisting the fringe of her poor shawl again.

"Yes, I walked," she answered; "but I can't set down. I h'ain't but a minute to stay."

Her clothes, which had been shabby at their best, were at their worst now, and, altogether, she was a figure neither attractive nor picturesque.

But Baird saw pathos in her. It was said that one of his most charming qualities was his readiness to discover the pathetic under any guise.

"You came to ask Mr. Latimer some questions, perhaps?" he said.

She suddenly burst into tears.

"Yes," she answered, "I—I couldn't help it."

She checked herself and wiped her tears away with the shawl corner almost immediately.

"I wanted to know something about *her*," she said. "Nobody seemed to know nothin', only that she was dead. When they said you'd come home, it seemed like I couldn't rest until I'd heard something."

"What do you want to hear?" said Latimer.

It struck Baird that the girl's manner was a curious one. It was a manner which seemed to conceal beneath its shame-faced awkwardness some secret fear or anxiety. She gave Latimer a hurried, stealthy look, and then her eyes fell. It was as if she would have read in his gloomy face what she did not dare to ask.

"I'd be afraid to die myself," she stammered. "I can't bear to think of it. I'm afraid. Was she?"

" No," Latimer answered.

The girl gave him another dull, stealthy look.

" I'm glad of that," she said; " she can't have minded so much if she wasn't afraid. I'd like to think she didn't mind it so much—or suffer."

" She did not suffer," said Latimer.

" I never saw nothin' of her after the last day she came to Janway's Mills," the girl began.

Latimer lifted his eyes suddenly.

" She went to the Mills? " he exclaimed.

" Yes," she answered, her voice shaking. " I guess she never told. After that first night she stood by me. No one else did. Seemed like other folks thought I'd poison 'em. She'd come an' see me an'—help me. She was sick the last day she came, and when she was going home she fainted in the street, I heard folks say, I never saw her after that."

She brushed a tear from her face with the shawl again.

" So as she didn't mind much, or suffer," she said, " t'ain't so bad to think of. She wasn't one to be able to stand up against things. She'd have died if she'd been me. I'd be glad enough to die myself, if I wasn't afraid. She'd cry over me when I wasn't crying over myself. I've been beat about till I don't mind, like I used. They're a hard lot down at the Mills."

" And you," said Latimer, " what sort of a life have you been leading? "

His voice was harsh and his manner repellant only because Nature had served him the cruel turn of making them so. He was bitterly conscious as he spoke of having chosen the wrong words and uttered them with an appearance of relentless rigour which he would have made any effort to soften.

Baird made a quick movement towards the girl.

"Have you any work?" he asked. "Do you need help? Don't mind telling us. My friend is to take charge of your church at the Mills."

The girl interrupted him. She had turned miserably pale under Latimer's question.

"'Tain't no church of mine!" she said, passionately; "I h'ain't nothin' to do with it. I never belonged to no church anyhow, an' I'm leadin' the kind o' life any girl'd lead that hadn't nothin' nor nobody. I don't mean," with a strangled sob, "to even myself with *her;* but what'ud she ha' done if she'd ha' slipped like I did—an' then had nothin' nor—nor nobody?"

"Don't speak of her!" cried Latimer, almost fiercely.

"'Twon't hurt her," said the girl, struggling with a sob again; "she's past bein' hurt even by such as me—an' I'm glad of it. She's well out of it all!"

She turned as if she would have gone away, but Baird checked her.

"Wait a moment," he said; "perhaps I can be of some service to you."

"You can't do nothin'," she interrupted. "Nobody can't!"

"Let me try," he said; "take a note to Miss Starkweather from me and wait at the house for a few minutes. Come, that isn't much, is it? You'll do that much, I'm sure."

She looked down at the floor a few seconds and then up at him. It had always been considered one of his recommendations that he was so unprofessional in his appearance.

"Yes," she said, slowly, "I can do that, I suppose."

He drew a note-book from his breast-pocket and, having written a few words on a leaf of it, tore it out and handed it to her.

"Take that to Miss Starkweather's house and say I sent you with it."

When she was gone, he turned to Latimer again.

"Before I go," he said, "I want to say a few words to you—to ask you to make me a promise."

"What is the promise?" said Latimer.

"It is that we shall be friends—friends."

Baird laid his hand on the man's gaunt shoulder with a nervous grasp as he spoke, and his voice was unsteady.

"I have never had a friend," answered Latimer, monotonously; "I should scarcely know what to do with one."

"Then it is time you had one," Baird replied. "And I may have something to offer you. There may be something in—in my feeling which may be worth your having."

He held out his hand.

Latimer looked at it for a second, then at him, his sallow face flushing darkly.

"You are offering me a good deal," he said, "I scarcely know why—myself."

"But you don't take my hand, Latimer," Baird said; and the words were spoken with a faint loss of colour.

Latimer took it, flushing more darkly still.

"What have I to offer in return?" he said. "I have nothing. You had better think again. I should only be a kind of shadow on your life."

"I want nothing in return—nothing," Baird said. "I don't even ask feeling from you. Be a shadow on my life, if you will. Why should I have no shadows? Why should all go smoothly with me, while others——" He paused, checking his vehemence as if he had suddenly recognised it. "Let us be friends," he said.

CHAPTER XV

THE respectable portion of the population of Janway's Mills believed in church-going and on Sunday-school attendance—in fact, the most entirely respectable believed that such persons as neglected these duties were preparing themselves for damnation. They were a quiet, simple, and unintellectual people. Such of them as occasionally read books knew nothing of any literature which was not religious. The stories they had followed through certain inexpensive periodicals were of the order which describes the gradual elevation of the worldly-minded or depraved to the plane of church-going and Sunday-school. Their few novels made it their *motif* to prove that it is easier for a camel to pass through the eye of a needle than for a rich man to enter into the Kingdom of Heaven. Any hero or heroine of wealth who found peace of mind and married happily, only attained these objects through the assistance of some noble though humble unsecular person whose example and instruction led them to adopt unsecular views. The point of view of Janway's Mills was narrow and far from charitable when it was respectable; its point of view, when it was not respectable, was desperate. Even sinners, at Janway's Mills, were primitive and limited in outlook. They did not excuse themselves with specious argument for their crimes of neglecting church-going, using bad language, hanging about bar-rooms, and loose living. They were not brilliant wrongdoers and made no attempt at defending themselves or pretending that they did not know they were going to perdition. The New England mind is not broad or versatile, and, having begun life in a Puritan atmosphere, it is not quick to escape its influence. Society at the Mills recognised no social distinction which was not founded upon the respectability of church-going and the observance of social laws made by church-goers; it recognised none because it absolutely *knew* of none. The great world was not far from Janway's Mills, but they did not touch each other. Willowfield was near, Boston and New York themselves were not far distant, but the curious fact being that millions of human minds may work and grow and struggle as if they were the minds of dwellers upon another planet, though less than a hundred miles may separate them, the actual lives, principles, and significances of the larger places did not seem to touch the smaller one. The smaller one was a village of a few streets of small houses which had grown up about the Mills themselves. The Mills gave employment to a village full of hands, so the village gradually evolved itself. It was populated by the uneducated labouring class; some were respectable, some were dissolute and lived low and gross lives, but all were uneducated in any sense which implies more than the power to read, write, and make a few necessary calculations. Most of them took some newspaper. They read of the multi-millionaires who lived in New York and Chicago and California, they read of the politicians in Washington, they found described to them the great entertainments given by millionaires' wives and daughters, the marvellous dresses they wore, the multifarious ways in which they amused themselves, but what they read seemed so totally unlike anything they had ever seen, so far apart from their own lives, that though they were not aware of the fact, the truth was that they believed in them with about the same degree of realisation with which they believed in what they heard in the pulpit of the glories of the New Jerusalem. No human being exists without an ambition, and the ambition of Janway's Millers of the high-class was to possess a neat frame-house with clean Nottingham lace curtains at the windows, fresh oilcloth on the floor of the front hall, furniture covered with green or red reps in the parlour, a tapestry Brussels carpet, and a few lithographs upon the walls. It was also the desire of the owners of such possessions that everyone should know that they attended one of the churches, that their house-cleaning was done regularly, that no member of the family frequented bar-rooms, and that they were respectable people. It was an ambition which was according to their lights, and could be despised by no honest human being, however dull it might appear to him. It resulted oftener than not in the making of excellent narrow lives which brought harm to no one. The lives which went wrong on the street-corners and in the bar-rooms often did harm. They produced discomfort, unhappiness, and disorder; but as it is also quite certain that no human being produces these things without working out his own punishment for himself while he lives on earth, the ends of justice were doubtless attained.

If a female creature at the Mills broke the great social law, there was no leaning towards the weakness of pity for her, Janway's was not sufficiently developed, mentally, to deal with gradations or analysis of causes and impelling powers. The girl who brought forth a child without the pale of orthodox marriage was an outcast and a disgraced creature, and nobody flinched from pronouncing her both.

"It's disgustin', that's what I call it," it was the custom for respectable wives and mothers to say. "It's disgustin'! A nice thing she's done for herself. I h'ain't no patience with girls like her, with no fear o' God or religion in them an' no modesty and decency. She deserves whatever comes to her!"

Usually every tragedy befell her which could befall a woman. If her child lived, it lived the life of wretchedness and was an outcast also. The outcome of its existence was determined by the order of woman its mother chanced to be. If the maternal instinct was warm and strong within her and she loved it, there were a few chances that it might fight through its early years of struggle and expand into a human being who counted as *one* at least among the world's millions. Usually the mother died in the gutter or the hospital, but there had been women who survived, and when they did so it was often because they made a battle for their children. Sometimes it was because they were made of the material which is not easily beaten, and then they learned as the years went by that the human soul and will may be even stronger than that which may seem at the outset overwhelming fate.

When the girl Susan Chapman fell into misfortune and disgrace, her path was not made easy for her. There were a few months when the young mill hand who brought disaster upon her, made love to her, and hung about her small home, sometimes leaning upon the rickety gate to talk and laugh with her, sometimes loitering with her in the streets or taking her to cheap picnics or on rather rowdy excursions. She wore the excited and highly pleased air seen in young women of her class when the masculine creature is paying court. She spent her wages in personal decoration, she bought cheap feathers and artificial flowers and remnants on " bargain days," and decked herself with them. Her cheap, good looks reached their highest point because she felt the glow of a promotive triumph and her spirits were exhilarated. She was nearer happiness than she had ever been before. The other girls, who were mill hands like herself, were full of the usual rather envious jokes about her possible marriage. To be married was to achieve a desirable distinction and to work at home instead of at the Mills. The young man was not an absolute villain, he was merely an ignorant, foolish young animal. At first he had had inchoate beliefs in a domestic future with the girl. But the time came when equally inchoate ideas of his own manhood led him to grow cool. The New England atmosphere which had not influenced him in all points, influenced him in the matter of feeling that the woman a man married must have kept herself respectable. The fact that he himself had caused her fall from the plane of decency was of comparatively small moment.

A man who married a woman who had not managed to keep straight, put himself into a sort of ridiculous position. He lost masculine distinction. This one ceased to lean on the gate and talk at night, and went to fewer picnics. He was in less high spirits, and so was the girl. She often looked pale and as if she had been crying. Then Jack Williams gave up his place at the Mill and left the village. He did not tell his sweetheart. The morning after he left, Susan came to her work and found the girls about her wearing a mysterious and interested air.

" What are you whispering about? " she asked. " What's the secret? "

" 'Tain't no secret," was the answer. " Most everybody's heard it, and I guess it ain't no secret to you. I guess he told you when he made up his mind to go."

" Who? " she asked.

" Jack Williams. He's gone out to Chicago to work somewhere there. He kept it pretty dark from us, but when he went off on the late train last night, Joe Evans saw him, and he said he'd had the offer of a first-rate job and was going to it. How you stare, Sue! Your eyes look as if they'd pop out o' yer head."

She was staring and her skin had turned blue-white. She broke into a short hysteric laugh and fell down. Then she was very sick and fainted and had to be taken home trembling so that she could scarcely crawl as she walked, with great tears dropping down her cold face. Janway's Mills knew well enough after this that Jack Williams had deserted her, and had no hesitation in suggesting a reason for his defection.

The months which followed were filled with the torments of a squalid Inferno. Girls who had regarded her with envy, began to refuse to speak to her or to be seen in her company. Jack Williams's companions were either impudent or disdainful, the married women stared at her and commented on her as she passed; there were no more picnics or excursions for her; her feathers became draggled and hung broken in her hat. She had no relatives in the village, having come from a country place. She was thankful that she had not a family of aunts on the spot, because she knew they would have despised her and talked her over more than the rest. She lived in a bare little room which she rented from a poor couple, and she used to sit alone in it, huddled up in a heap by the window, crying for hours in the evening as she watched the other girls go by laughing and joking with their sweethearts.

One night when there was a sociable in the little frame Methodist church opposite, and she saw it lighted up and the people going in dressed in their best clothes and excited at meeting each other, the girls giggling at the sight of their favourite young men—just as she had giggled six months before—her slow tears began to drip faster and the sobs came one upon another until she was choked by them and she began to make a noise. She sobbed and cried more convulsively, until she began to scream and went into something like hysterics. She dropped down on her face and rolled over and over, clutching at her breast and her sides and throwing out her arms. The people of the house had gone to the sociable and she was alone, so no one heard or came near her. She shrieked and sobbed and rolled over and over, clutching at her flesh, trying to gasp out words that choked her.

" O, Lord! " she gasped, wild with the insensate agony of a poor, hysteria torn, untaught, uncontrolled thing, " I don't know what I've done! I don't! 'Tain't fair! I didn't go to! I can't bear it! He h'ain't got nothin' to bear, he ain't! O, Lord God, look down on me! "

She was the poor, helpless outcome of the commonest phase of life, but her garret saw a ghastly tragedy as she choked through her hysterics. Who is to blame for and who to prevent such tragedies, let deep thinkers strive to tell.

The day after this was the one on which little Margery Latimer came into her life. It was in the early spring, just before the child had gone to Boston to begin her art lessons. She had come to Janway's Mills to see a poor woman who had worked for her mother. The woman lived in the house in which Susan had her bare room. She began to talk about the girl half fretfully, half contemptuously.

"She's the one Jack Williams got into trouble and then left to get out of it by herself as well as she could," she said. "She might ha' known it. Gals is fools. She can't work at the Mills any more, an' last night when we was all at the Sosherble, she seems to've had a spasm o' some kind; she can't get out o' bed this mornin' and lies there lookin' like death an' moanin'. I can't 'tend to her, I've got work o' my own to do. Lansy! how she was moanin' when I passed her door! Seemed like she'd kill herself!"

"Oh, poor thing!" cried Margery; "let me go up to her."

She was a sensitive creature, and the colour had ebbed out of her pretty face.

"Lor, no!" the woman cried; "she ain't the kind o' gal you'd oughter be doing things for, she was allus right down common, an' she's sunk down 'bout as low as a gal can."

But Margery went up to the room where the moaning was going on. She stood outside the door on the landing for a few moments, her heart trembling in her side before she went in. Her life had been a simple, happy, bright one up to this time. She had not seen the monster life close at hand. She had large, childish eyes which were the colour of harebells and exquisitely sympathetic and sweet. There were tears in them when she gently opened the door and stood timidly on the threshold.

"Let me, please let me come in," she said. "Don't say I mayn't."

The moaning and low choking sobs went on, and in a very few moments they so wrought upon her, that she pushed the door farther open and entered the room. What she saw was a barren, common little place, and on the bed a girl lying utterly prostrated by an hysteric tempest which had lasted hours. Her face was white and swollen and covered with red marks, as if she had clutched and torn it with her fingers, her dress was torn open at the bosom, and her hair tumbled, torn, and loose about the pillow; there was a discoloured place upon her forehead which was settling into a bruise. Her eyes were puffed with crying until they were almost closed. Her breast rose with short, exhausted, but still convulsive sobs. Margery felt as if she was drawn into a vortex of agony. She could not resist it. She went to the bed, stood still a second, trembling, and then sank upon her knees and put her face down upon the wretched hand nearest and kissed it with piteous impulsive sympathy.

" Oh! don't cry like that," she said, crying herself. " Oh, don't! Oh, don't! I'm so sorry for you—I'm *so* sorry for you."

She did not know the girl at all, she had never even heard of her before, but she kissed her hand and cried over it and fondled it against her breast. She was one of those human things created by Nature to suffer with others, and for them, and through them.

She did not know how long it was before the girl became sufficiently articulate to speak to her. She herself was scarcely articulate for some time. She could only try to find words to meet a need so far beyond her ken. She had never come in contact with a woman in this strait before.

But at last Susan was lying in the bed instead of on its

tossed and tumbled outside. Margery had done the nearest, simple things for her. She had helped her to bathe her face with cold water, to undress and put on her nightgown; she had prepared her narrow bed for her decently, and smoothed and wound up her hair. Then she had gone downstairs, got her a cup of tea, and sat by her and made her drink it. Then she set the room in order and opened the window to air it.

"There is a bruise on your forehead," she had said, as she was arranging the torn hair. "You must have struck it against something when you were ill last night."

"I struck it against the wall," Susan answered, in a monotonous voice. "I did it on purpose. I banged my head against the wall until I fell down and was sick."

Margery's face quivered again.

"Don't think about it," she said. "You ought not to have been alone. Some—some friend ought to have been with you."

"I haven't got any friends," Susan answered. "I don't know why you came up to me. I don't guess you know what's the matter with me."

"Yes, I do," said Margery. "You are in great trouble."

"It's the worst kind o' trouble a woman can get into," said Susan, the muscles of her face beginning to be drawn again. "I don't see why—why Jack Williams can skip off to Chicago to a new, big job that's a stroke o' luck—an' me left lie here to bear everything—an' be picked at, an' made fun of, an' druv mad with the way I'm kicked in the gutter. I don't see no *right* in it. There *ain't* no right in it; I don't believe there's no God anyhow; I won't never believe it again. No one can't make me. If I've done what gives folks a right to cast me off, so's Jack Williams."

In Connection with
The De Willoughby Claim

" You haven't pretended to love a person and then run away and left them to—to suffer," said little Margery, on the verge of sobs again.

" No, I haven't! " said the girl, her tears beginning to stream anew. " I'm not your kind. I'm not educated. I'm only a common mill hand, but I did love Jack Williams all I knew how. He had such a nice way with him—kind of affectionate, an'—an' he was real good-lookin' too when he was fixed up. If I'd been married to him, no one would have said nothin', an'—an' 'tain't nothin' but a minister readin' somethin' anyhow—marryin' ain't."

CHAPTER XVI

This was before Margery went to Boston to try to develop her gift for making pretty sketches. Her father and mother and her brother strained every nerve to earn and save the money to cover her expenses. She went away full of innocent, joyous hope in the month of May. She boarded in a plain, quiet house, and had two rooms. One was her workroom and studio. She worked under a good-natured artist, who thought her a rather gifted little creature and used to take her to look at any pictures that were on exhibition. Taking into consideration her youth and limited advantages, she made such progress as led him to say that she had a future before her.

She had never deserted Sue Chapman after that first morning in which she had gone to her rescue. Janway's Mills was bewildered when it found that the Reverend Lucien Latimer's sister went to see Jack Williams' deserted sweetheart, and did not disdain to befriend her in her disgrace. The church-going element, with the Nottingham lace curtains in its parlour windows, would have been shocked, but that it was admitted that " the Latimers has always been a well-thought-of family, an' all of 'em is members in good standin'. They're greatly respected in Willowfield; even the old fam'lies speak to 'em when they meet 'em in the street or at Church.

" Not that I'd be willin' for my Elma Ann to 'sociate with a girl that's gone wrong. Maybe it's sorter different with a minister's sister. Ministers' families has to 'sociate out o' charity an' religion; go to pray with 'em, an' that, an' read the Scripture to make 'em sense their sinfulness an' the danger they're in."

But Margery did not pray with Susan Chapman, or read the Bible to her. The girl held obstinately to her statement of unbelief in a God, and Margery did not feel that her mood was one to which reading the Gospel would appeal. If she could have explained to her the justice of the difference between Jack Williams' lot and her own, she felt they might have advanced perhaps, but she could not. She used to go to see her and try to alleviate her physical discomfort and miserable poverty. She saved her from hunger and cold when she could no longer work at all, and she taught her to feel that she was not utterly without a friend.

"What I'd have done without you, God knows—or what ought to be God," Sue said. "He didn't care, but you did. If there *is* one, He's got a lot to learn from some of the people He's made Himself. 'After His own image created He them '—that's what the Bible says; but I don't believe it. If He was as good and kind-hearted as the best of us, He wouldn't sit upon His throne with angels singing round an' playin' on harps, an' Him too much interested to see how everythin's sufferin' down below. What did He make us for, if He couldn't look after us? I wouldn't make a thing I wouldn't do my best by—an' I ain't nothin' but a factory girl. This—this poor thing that's goin' to be born an' hain't no right to, I'll do my level best by it—I will. It sha'n't suffer, if I can help it "—her lips jerking.

Sometimes Margery would talk to her a little about Jack Williams—or, rather, she would listen while Susan talked. Then Susan would cry, large, slow-rolling tears slipping down her cheeks.

"I don't know how—how it happened like this," she
would say. "It seems like a kind o' awful dream. I don't
know nothin'. He was common—just like I am—an' he
didn't know much; but it didn't seem like he was a bad
feller—an' I do b'lieve he liked me. *Seemed* like he did,
anyways. They say he's got a splendid job in Chicago. He
won't never know nothin' about what happens."

Margery did not leave her unprovided for when she went
to Boston. It cost very little to keep her for a few months
in her small room. The people of the house promised to be
decently kind to her. Margery had only been away from
home two weeks when the child was born. The hysterical
paroxysms and violent outbreaks of grief its mother had
passed through, her convulsive writhings and clutchings and
beating of her head against the walls had distorted and exhausted the little creature. The women who were with her
said its body looked as if it were bruised in spots all over,
and there was a purple mark on its temple. It breathed
a few times and died.

"Good thing, too!" said the women. "There's too many
in the world that's got a right here. It'd hev' had to go
to ruin."

"Good thing for *it*," said Susan, weakly but sullenly,
from her bed; "but if it's God as makes 'em, how did He
come to go to the trouble of making this one an' sendin'
it out, if it hadn't no right to come? He *does* make 'em
all, doesn't he? You wouldn't darst to say He didn't—you,
Mrs. Hopp, that's a church member!" And her white face
actually drew itself into a ghastly, dreary grin. "Lawsy!
He's kept pretty busy!"

When she was able to stand on her feet she went back to
the mill. She was a good worker, and hands were needed.

In Connection with
The De Willoughby Claim

The girls and women fought shy of her, and she had no chance of enjoying any young pleasures or comforts, even if she had not been too much broken on the rack of the misery of the last year to have energy to desire them. No young man wanted to be seen talking to her, no young woman cared to walk with her in the streets. She always went home to her room alone, and sat alone, and thought of what had happened to her, trying to explain to herself how it had happened and why it had turned out that she was worse than any other girl. She had never felt like a bad girl. No one had ever called her one before this last year.

Three months after the child was born and died, Margery came back to Willowfield to spend a week at home. She came to see Susan, and they sat together in the tragic little bare room and talked. Though the girl had been so delicately pretty before she left home, Susan saw that she had become much prettier. She was dressed in light, softly tinted summer stuffs, and there was something about her which was curiously flower-like. Her long-lashed, harebell blue eyes seemed to have widened and grown lovelier in their innocent look. A more subtle mind than Susan Chapman's might have said that she seemed to be looking farther into Life's spaces, and that she was trembling upon the verge of something unknown and beautiful.

She talked about Boston and the happiness of her life there, and of her work and her guileless girlish hopes and ambitions.

"I am doing my very best," she said, a spot of pink flickering on her cheek; "I work as hard as I can, but you see I am so ignorant. I could not have learned anything about art in Willowfield. But people are so good to me—people who know a great deal. There is one gentleman who comes sometimes to see Mr. Barnard at the studio. He is so wonderful, it seems to me. He has travelled, and knows all about the great galleries and the pictures in them. He talks so beautifully that everyone listens when he comes in. Nobody can bear to go on with work for fear of missing something. You would think he would not notice a plain little Willowfield girl, but he has been *lovely* to me, Susan. He has even looked at my work and criticised it for me, and talked to me. He nearly always talks to me a little when he comes in, and once I met him in the Gardens, and he stopped and talked there, and walked about looking at the flowers with me. They had been planting out the spring things, and it was like being in fairyland to walk about among them and hear the things he said about pictures. It taught me so much."

She referred to this friend two or three times, and once mentioned his name, but Susan forgot it. She was such a beautiful, happy little thing, and seemed so exquisite an expression of spring-like, radiant youth and its innocent joy in living that the desolate and stranded creature she had befriended could think of nothing but her own awkward worship and the fascination of the flower-like charm. She used to sit and stare at her.

"Seems so queer to see anyone as happy an' pretty as you," she broke out once. "Oh, Lawsy, I hope nothing won't ever come to spoil it. It hadn't ought to be spoiled."

A month or so later Margery paid a visit to her home again. She stayed a longer time, but Susan only saw her once. She had come home from Boston with a cold and had been put to bed for a day or two.

One morning Susan was in Willowfield and met her walking in a quiet street. She was walking slowly and looking down as she went, as if some thought was abstracting her. When Susan stopped before her, she looked up with a start. It was a start which revealed that she had been brought back suddenly from a distance, as it were a great distance.

" Oh, Susan! " she said. " Oh, Susan! "

She held out her hand in her pretty, affectionate way, but she was actually a little out of breath.

" I'm sorry I came on you so sudden," Susan said, " I startled you."

" Yes," she answered, " I was—I was thinking of things that seem so far off. When I'm in Willowfield it seems as if—as if they can't be true. Does anything ever seem like that to you, Susan? "

" Yes," said Susan. One of her hopeless looks leaped into her eyes. She did not say what the things were, but she stared at Margery in a helpless, vacant way for a moment.

" Are you well, Susan, and have you got work? " asked Margery. " I am coming to see you to-morrow."

They spoke of common things for a few minutes, and then went their separate ways.

Why it was that when she paid the promised visit the next day and they sat together in their old way and talked, Susan felt a kind of misery creeping slowly upon her, she could not in the least have explained. She was not sufficiently developed mentally to have been capable of saying to herself that there was a difference between this visit and the last, between this Margery and the one who had sat with her before. Her dull thoughts were too slow to travel to a point so definite in so short a length of time as one afternoon afforded.

"Your cold was a pretty bad one, wasn't it?" she asked, vaguely, once.

"Yes," was the answer. "It made me feel weak. But it has gone now. I am quite well again."

After that Susan saw her but once again. As time went on she heard a vague rumour that the Latimers were anxious about Margery's health. Just at that time the mill hands gossiped a good deal about Willowfield, because the Reverend John Baird was said to be going to Europe. That led to talk on the subject of other Willowfield people, and the Latimers among them. In the rare, brief letters Margery wrote to her *protégée*, she did not say she was ill. Once she said her brother Lucien had quite suddenly come to Boston to see how she was, because her mother imagined she must have taken cold.

She had been in Boston about a year then. One afternoon Susan was in her room, standing by her bed forlornly, and, in a vacant, reasonless mood, turning over the few coarse little garments she had been able to prepare for her child—a few common little shirts and nightgowns and gray flannels—no more. She heard someone at the door. The handle turned and the door opened as if the person who came in had forgotten the ceremony of knocking. Susan laid down on the bed the ugly little night-dress she had been looking at; it lay there stiff with its coarseness, its short arms stretched out. She turned about and faced Margery Latimer, who had crossed the threshold and stood before her.

Susan uttered a low, frightened cry before she could speak a word.

The girl looked like a ghost. It was a ghost Susan thought of this time, and not a flower. The pure little face was white and drawn, the features were sharpened, the harebell-coloured eyes had almost a look of wildness; it was as if they had been looking at something frightening for a long time, until they could not lose the habit of expressing fear.

"Susan," she said, in a strange, uncertain voice, "you didn't expect to see me."

Susan ran to her.

"No, no," she said, "I didn't know you was here. I thought you was in Boston. What's the matter? Oh, Lawsy, Margery, what's happened to make you look like this?"

"Nobody knows," answered Margery. "They say it's the cold. They are frightened about me. I'm come to say good-bye to you, Susan."

She sank into a chair and sat there, panting a little.

"Lucien's going to take me to Europe," she said, her voice all at once seeming to sound monotonous, as if she was reciting a lesson mechanically. "I always wanted to go there —to visit the picture galleries and study. They think the climate will be good for me. I've been coughing in the mornings—and I can't eat."

"Do they think you might be going into—a consumption?" Susan faltered.

"Mother's frightened," said Margery. "She and the doctor don't know what to think. Lucien's going to take me to Europe. It's expensive, but—but he has managed to get the money. He sold a little farm he owned."

"He's a good brother," said Susan.

Suddenly Margery began to cry as if she could not help it.

"Oh," she exclaimed. "No one knows what a good brother he is—nobody but myself. He is willing to give up everything to—to save me—and to save poor mother from awful trouble. Sometimes I think he is something like Christ—even like Christ! He is willing to suffer for other people—for their pain—and weakness—and sin."

It was so evident that the change which had taken place in her was a woeful one. Her bright loveliness was gone—her simple, lovable happiness. Her nerves seemed all unstrung. But it was the piteous, strained look in her childlike eyes which stirred poor Susan's breast to tumult.

"Margery," she said, almost trembling, "if—if—if you was to go in a consumption and die—you're not like me—you needn't be afraid."

The next moment she was sorry she had said the crude thing. Margery burst into a passion of weeping. Susan flew to her and caught her in her arms, kneeling down by her.

"I oughtn't to have said it," she cried. "You're too ill to be made to think of such things. I was a fool not to see—Margery, Margery, don't!"

But Margery was too weak to be able to control her sobbing.

"They say that—that God forgives people," she wept. "I've prayed and prayed to be forgiven for—for my sins. I've never meant to be wicked. I don't know—I don't know how——"

"Hush!" said Susan, soothing and patting her trembling shoulder. "Hush, hush! If there *is* a God, Margery, He's a heap sight better than we give Him credit for. He don't make people a' purpose, so they can't help things somehow —an' don't know—an' then send 'em to burning hell for *bein'* the way He made 'em. *We* wouldn't do it, an' He won't. You hain't no reason to be afraid of dyin'."

Margery stayed with her about half an hour. There was a curious element in their conversation. They spoke as if their interview was a final one. Neither of them actually expressed the thought in words, but a listener would have felt vaguely that they never expected to meet each other again on earth. They made no references to the future; it was as if no future could be counted upon. Afterwards, when she was alone, Susan realised that she had never once said " when you come back from Europe."

As she was leaving the room, Margery passed the bed on which the small, coarse garments lay. The little nightgown, with its short sleeves stiffly outstretched, seemed to arrest her attention specially. She caught at Susan's dress as if she was unaware that she made the movement or of the sharp shudder which followed it.

" Those—are its things, aren't they, Susan? " she said.

" Yes," Susan answered, her sullen look of pain coming back to her face.

" I—don't know—how people *bear* it! " exclaimed Margery. It was an exclamation, and her hand went quickly up to her mouth almost as if to press it back.

" They don't *bear* it," said Susan, stonily. " They have to go through it—that's all. If you was standin' on the gallows with the rope round your neck and the trap-door under your feet, you wouldn't be bearin' it, but the trap-door would drop all the same, an' down you'd plunge—into the blackness."

It was on this morning, on her way through the streets, that Margery dropped in a dead faint upon the pavement, and Miss Amory Starkweather, passing in her carriage, picked her up and carried her home.

Susan Chapman never saw her again. Some months afterwards came the rumour that she had died of consumption in Italy.

CHAPTER XVII

WHEN, in accordance with Baird's instructions, Susan Chapman took the note to Miss Starkweather, she walked through the tree-shaded streets, feeling as if she had suddenly found herself in a foreign country. To the inhabitants of Janway's Mills, certain parts of Willowfield stood for wealth, luxury, and decorous splendour. The Mills, which lived within itself, was easily impressed. Its—occasionally resentful—respect for Willowfield was enormous. It did not behold it as a simple provincial town, whose business establishments were primitive, and whose frame houses, even when surrounded by square gardens with flower-beds adorning them, were merely comfortable middle-class abodes of domesticity. It was awed by the Willowfield *Times*, it revered the button factory, and bitterly envied the carriages driven and the occasional festivities held by the families of the representatives of these monopolies. The carriages were sober and middle-aged, and so were the parties, but to Janway's Mills they illustrated wealth and gaiety. People drove about in the vehicles and wore fine clothes and ate cakes and ice-cream at the parties—neither of which things had ever been possible or ever would become possible to Janway's.

And Susan, who had been a Pariah and an outcast at the Mills, was walking through the best streets, carrying a note from the popular minister to the rich Miss Starkweather, who had an entire square white frame house and garden, which were her own property.

The girl felt a little sullen and a little frightened. She

did not know what would happen to her; she did not know how she would be expected to carry herself in a house so representative of wealth and accustomedness to the good things of life. Perhaps if she had not been desperate, and also, if she had not known that Miss Starkweather had been fond of Margery, she would have evaded going to her.

"I wonder what she'll say to me," she thought. "They say she's queer."

She still felt uncertain and resentful when she stood upon the threshold and rang the bell. She presented a stolid countenance to the maid servant who opened the door and received her message. When she was at last taken to Miss Amory, she went with an unresponding bearing, and, being led into a cheerful room where the old woman sat, stood before her waiting, as if she had really nothing to do with the situation.

Miss Amory looked rather like some alert old hawk, less predatory by instinct than those of his species usually are.

"You are Susan Chapman, and come from Mr. Baird," she said.

Susan nodded.

"He says he met you at Mr. Latimer's."

"Yes. I went there to ask something. I couldn't bear not to know—no more than I did."

"About——?" asked Miss Amory.

"About Margery," her voice lowering unconsciously.

"How much did you know?" Miss Amory asked again.

"Nothin'," rather sullenly, "but that she was ill—an' went away an' died."

"In Italy, they say," put in Miss Amory—"lying on a sofa before an open window—on a lovely day, when the sun was setting."

In Connection with
The De Willoughby Claim

Susan Chapman started a little, and her face changed. The unresponsiveness melted away. There was something like a glow of relief in her look. She became human and lost sight of Miss Amory's supposed grandeur.

" Was it like that? " she exclaimed. " Was it? I'm thankful to you for telling me. Somehow I couldn't ask properly when I was face to face with her brother. You can't talk to him. I never knew where—or how—it was. I wanted to find out if—if it was all right with her. I wanted to know she hadn't suffered."

" So did I," Miss Amory answered. " And that was what they told me."

She passed her withered hand across her face.

" I was fond of her," she said.

" I'd *reason* to be," returned Susan. " She was only a delicate little young thing—but she came an' stayed by me when I was in hell an' no one else would give me a drop of water to cool my tongue."

" I know something about that," said Miss Amory; " I have heard it talked of. Where's your child? "

Susan did not redden, but the hard look came back to her face for a moment.

" It didn't live but a few minutes," she answered.

" What are you doing for your living? "

A faint red showed itself on the girl's haggard cheeks, and she stared at her with indifferent blankness.

" I worked in the mill till my health broke down for a spell, an' I had to give up. I'm better now, but I've not got a cent to live on, an' my place was filled up right away."

" Where's the man? " Miss Amory demanded.

" I don't know. I've never heard a word of him since he slid off to Chicago."

In Connection with
The De Willoughby Claim

"Humph!" said Miss Amory.

For a moment or so she sat silent, thinking. She held her chin in her hand and pinched it. Presently she looked up.

"Could you come and live with me for a month?" she enquired. "I believe we might try the experiment. I daresay you would rub me when I want rubbing, and go errands and help me up and down stairs and carry things for me. It just happens that my old Jane has been obliged to leave me because she's beginning to be as rheumatic as I am myself, and her daughter offers her a good home. Would you like to try? I don't promise to do more than make the experiment."

The girl flushed hot this time, as she looked down on the floor.

"You may guess whether I'm likely to say 'yes' or not," she said. "I ain't had a crust to-day. I believe I could *learn* to suit you. But I never expected anything as good as this to happen to me. Thank you, ma'am. May I— when must I come?"

"Take off your bonnet and go and have your dinner, and stay now," answered Miss Amory.

When John Baird called later in the day, Miss Amory was walking in the sun in her garden and Susan was with her, supporting her stiff steps. She had been fed, her dress had been changed for a neat print, and the dragged lines of her face seemed already to have relaxed. She no longer wore the look of a creature who is hungry and does not know how long her hunger may last and how much worse it may become.

"I am much obliged to you, Miss Amory," Baird said when he joined her, and he said it almost impetuously. To-day he was in the state of mind when even vicarious good deeds are a support and a consolation. To have been a means of doing a good turn even to this stray creature was a comfort.

Miss Amory removed her hand from Susan's arm and allowed Baird to place it on his own. The girl went away in obedience to a gesture.

" She will do," said Miss Amory, " and it is a home for her. She's not stupid. If she fulfils the promise of her first day I may end by interesting myself in developing her brains. She has brains. The gray matter is there, but it has never moved much so far. It will be interesting to set it astir. But it was not that I thought of when I took her."

" You took her out of the kindness of your heart," said Baird.

" I took her for that poor, dead child's sake," returned Miss Amory.

" For——" Baird began.

" For Margery's sake," put in Miss Amory. " Margery Latimer. When Susan was in trouble the child was a tender little angel to her. Lord! what a pure little heart it was! "

" As pure as young Eve's in the Garden of Eden—as pure as young Eve's," murmured Baird.

" Just that! " said Miss Amory, rather sharply. " How do you know it? " And she turned and looked at him. " You have heard her brother say a good deal of her."

" Yes, yes," Baird answered. " She seems to have been the life of him."

" Well, well! " with emotional abruptness. " I took this girl for her sake. Her short life was not wasted if another's is built upon it. That's one of my fantastic fancies, I suppose. Stop a minute."

The old woman paused a few moments on the garden

walk and turned her face upward to look at the blue height and expanse of sky. There was a shade of desperate appeal or question on her uplifted, rugged countenance.

" When the world gets too much for me," she said, " and I lose my patience with the senselessness of the tragedy of it, I get a sort of courage from looking up like this—into the height and the still, clear blueness. It sends no answer back to me—that my human brain can understand—but it makes me feel that perhaps there is no earth at all. I get out of it and away."

" I know—I know—though I am not like you," Baird said, slowly.

Miss Amory came back to earth with a curious look in her eyes.

" Yes," she answered, " I should think that perhaps you are one of those who know. But one has to have been desperate before one turns to it as a resource. It's a last one —and the unmerciful powers only know why we should feel it a resource at all. As I said, it does not answer back. And we want answers—answers."

Then they went on walking.

" That poor thing has been a woman at least," said Miss Amory. " I have been a sort of feminine automaton. I have been respectable and she has not. All good women are not respectable and all respectable women are not good. That's a truism so absolute that it is a platitude, and yet there still exist people to whom it would appear a novel statement. That poor creature has loved and had her heart broken. She has suffered the whole gamut of things. She has been a wife without a name, a mother without a child. She is full of crude tragedy. And I have found out already that she is good—good."

" What is goodness? " asked Baird.

Miss Amory gave him another of her sharp looks.

" You are drawing me out," she said. " I'm not really worth it. Goodness is quite different from respectability. Respectability is a strict keeping of the laws men have made to oblige other men to do or not to do the things they want done or left undone. The large meaning of the law is punishment. No law, no punishment; no punishment, no law. And man made both for man. If you keep man's law you will be respectable, but you may not be good. Jesus Christ was not respectable—no one will deny that. Goodness, after all, means doing all kindness to all creatures, and, above all, doing no wrong to any. That's all. Are you good? "

" No," he answered, " I am not."

" You would probably find it more difficult to be so than I should," she responded. " And I find it hard enough—without being handicapped by beauty and the pleasure-loving temperament. You were started well on the road to the devil when you were born. Your very charms and virtues were ready to turn out vices in disguise. But when such things happen——" and she shrugged her lean shoulders. " As we have no one else to dare to blame, we can only blame ourselves. In a scheme so vague every man must be his own brake."

Baird drew a sharp breath. " If one only knew that early enough," he exclaimed.

Miss Amory laughed harshly.

" Yes," she said, " part of the vagueness of the scheme— if it *is* a scheme—is that it takes half a lifetime to find it out. Before that, we are always either telling ourselves that we are not going to do any harm, or that we are under the guidance of a merciful Providence."

In Connection with
The De Willoughby Claim

" That we are not going to do any harm," Baird repeated,
" that we are not going to do any harm. And suddenly it's
done."

" And can't be undone," Miss Amory added. " That's it."

The girl, Susan Chapman, was watching them from a window as they walked and talked. She bit her lips anxiously
as she stood behind the curtain. She was trying to imagine
what they might be saying to each other. Suppose it was
something which told against her. And why should it not
be so? What good could be said? Janway's Mills had borne
in upon her the complete sense of her outcast state. While
professing a republican independence of New England spirit,
the place figuratively touched its forehead to the earth before Miss Starkweather. She lived on an income inherited
from people who had owned mills instead of working them;
who employed—and discharged—hands. She would have
been regarded as an authority on any subject, social or moral.
And yet it was she who had spoken the first lenient word
to a transgressor of the unpardonable type. Susan had been
dumfounded at first, and then she had begun to be afraid
that the leniency arose from some mistake Miss Amory
would presently discover.

" Perhaps he's heard and he's telling her now," she said,
breathlessly, as she looked into the garden. " Maybe she'll
come in and order me out." She looked down at her clean
dress, and a sob rose in her throat at the realisation of the
mere physical comfort she had felt during the last hour or
two—the comfort of being fed and clothed and enclosed
within four walls. If she was to be cast back into outer
darkness again it would be better to know at once.

When Baird had gone away and Miss Amory was sitting
by her window, Susan appeared before her again with an

ashen complexion and a set look. She stood a moment, hesitating, her hands clasping her elbows behind her back.

" You want to say something to me? " said Miss Amory.

" Yes," the girl answered. " Yes, I do—an' I don't know how. Are you sure, ma'am, are you sure you know quite how bad I have been? "

" No," said Miss Amory; " sit down and tell me, Susan."

She said it with an impartiality so serenely free from condemnation that Susan's obedient sitting down was almost entirely the result of not being able to stand up. She, so to speak, fell into a chair and leaned forward, covering her face with her hands.

" I don't believe you know," she whispered.

" By experience I know next to nothing," Miss Amory answered, " but my imagination and my reason tell me a great deal. You were not married and you had a child. You lost your health and your work——"

" I would have worked," said the girl from behind her hands, sobbingly, but without tears. " Oh, I would have worked till I dropped—I did work till I dropped. I kept fainting—Oh! I would have been glad and thankful and grateful——"

" Yes," said Miss Amory, " life got worse and worse—they all treated you as if you were a dog. Those common virtuous people are like the torturers of the Inquisition. You were hungry and cold—cold and hungry——"

" You don't know what it's like," Susan moaned. " You don't know. When you get sick and hollow and cramped, and stagger about in your bare room—and call out to yourself to ask what made you and where is it. And the wind's like ice—and you huddle in a heap——"

" And there are lights in the streets," said Miss Amory,

" and it seems as if there must be something there to be given to you by somebody—somebody. And you go out."

Susan got up, panting, and stared at her.

" You do know," she cried, almost with passion. " Somehow you've found out what it's like. I wanted you to know. I don't want you—not to understand and then of a sudden to send me away. I'm so *afraid* of you sending me away."

" I shall not send you away for anything you have done in the past," said Miss Amory.

" I don't know what I should have done in the future, if you hadn't taken me in," Susan said. " Perhaps I should have thrown myself under a train. But, oh! " with starting dampness in her skin, which she wiped off with a sick gesture, " I did *hate* to let myself think of it. It wasn't the being killed—that's nothing—but feeling yourself crushed and torn and twisted—I used to stand and shake all over thinking of it. And I couldn't have gone on. I hated myself—I hated everything—most of all I hated the Thing that made me. What right had it? I hadn't done nothing to it before I was born. Seemed like it had made me just for the fun of pushing me under them wheels and seeing them tear and grind me. Oh! how I hated it! "

" So have I," said Miss Amory, her steady eyes looking more like a hawk's than ever.

Susan stared more than before. " I suppose I ought to have hated Jack Williams," she went on, her throat evidently filling, " but I never did. I loved him. Seemed like I was just his wife, that it did. I believe it always will. That's the way girls get into trouble. Some man that's got an affectionate way makes 'em believe they're as good as married. An' then they find out it's all a lie."

In Connection with
The De Willoughby Claim

"Perhaps some day you may see Jack Williams again," said Miss Amory.

"He wouldn't look at me," answered Susan.

"Perhaps you wouldn't look at him," Miss Amory remarked, with speculative slowness.

"Yes, I would," said Susan, "yes I would. I couldn't trust him same as I did before—'cause he's proved he ain't to be trusted. But if he wanted me to marry him I couldn't hold out, Miss Starkweather."

"Couldn't you?" Miss Amory said, still speculative. "No —perhaps you couldn't."

The girl wiped her eyes and added, slowly, almost as if she was thinking aloud:

"I'm not one of the strong ones—I'm not one of the strong ones—no more than little Margery was."

She said the last words with a kind of unconscious consciousness. While she uttered them her mind had evidently turned back to other times—not her own, but little Margery's.

Miss Amory drew a deep breath. She took up her knitting. She asked a question.

"You knew her very well—Margery?"

Susan drew her chair closer and looked in the old face with uncertain eyes.

"Miss Starkweather," she said, "do you think that a girl's being—like me—would make her evil-minded? Would it make her suspicion things, and be afraid of them —when there wasn't nothin'? I should think that it would," quite wistfully.

"It might," answered Miss Amory, her knitting-needles flying; "but for God's sake don't call yourself evil-minded. You'd be evil-minded if you were *glad* to suspect—not if you were sorry and afraid."

"Glad!" with a groan. "Oh, Lord, I guess not. But I might be all wrong all the same, mightn't I?"

"Yes, you might."

"I loved her—oh, Lord, I did love her! I'd reason to," the girl went on, and her manner had the effect of frightened haste. "I've suffered awful sometimes—thinkin' in the night and prayin' there wasn't nothin'. She was such a delicate, innocent little thing. It would have killed her."

"What were you afraid of?"

"Oh, I don't know," Susan answered, hysterically. "I don't. I only knew she couldn't bear nothin' like—like lyin' awake nights gaspin' an' fightin' with awful fear. She couldn't—she couldn't."

"But there are girls—women, who have to bear it," said Miss Amory. "Good God, who *have* to!"

"Yes—yes—yes," cried Susan. She drew her hand across her brow as if suddenly it felt damp, and for a moment her eyes looked wild with a memory of some awful thing. "I told her so," she said.

Miss Amory Starkweather turned in her chair with something like a start.

"You told her so," she exclaimed.

Susan stared out of the window and her voice fell.

"I didn't go to," she answered. "It was like this. That last time she came to see me—to tell me how ill she was and how Lucien was going to take her away—I'd been lookin' at the little clothes I'd got ready for—it." The tears began to roll fast down her cheeks. "Oh, Miss Starkweather! they was lyin' on the bed—an' she saw 'em an' turned as white as a sheet."

"Ugh!" the sound broke from Miss Amory like a short, involuntary groan.

In Connection with
The De Willoughby Claim

" She said she didn't know how people could *bear* it,"
Susan hurried on, " an' I said—just like you did—that they
had to bear it."

She suddenly hid her face in her arms.

" You were thinking of yourself," said Miss Amory. She
felt and looked a little sick.

" Yes," said Susan, " I was thinkin' of how it is when
•a girl's goin' to have a child an' can't get away from it—
can't—can't. She's got to go through with it—an' no one
can't save her. But I suppose it made her think of her death
that was comin'—her death that I b'lieve she knowed she
was struck for. When I'd said it she looked like some little
hunted animal dogs was after—that had run till its breath
was gone an' its eyes was startin' from its head. Her little
chest went up an' down with pantin'. I didn't wonder when
I heard after that she'd dropped in the street in a dead faint."

" Was that the day I picked her up as she lay on the
pavement? " Miss Amory asked.

Susan nodded, her face still hidden.

Old Miss Starkweather put out her hand and laid it on
the girl's shoulder.

" She has had time to forget," she said, rather as if she
was out of breath—" forget and grow quiet. She is dust
by now—peaceful dust. Let us—my good girl—let us remember that happy story of how she died."

" Yes," answered Susan, " in Italy—lying before the open
window—with the sunset all rosy in the sky."

But her head rested on her folded arms upon her knee,
and she sobbed a low, deep sob.

CHAPTER XVIII

Just before the breaking out of the Civil War, Delisle-ville had been provided with a sensation in a piece of singularly unexpected good fortune which befell one of its most prominent citizens. It was indeed good fortune, wearing somewhat the proportions of a fairy tale, and that such things could happen in Delisleville and to a citizen who possessed its entire approval was considered vaguely to the credit of the town.

One of the facts which had always been counted as an added dignity to the De Willoughbys had been their well-known possession of property in land. "Land" was always felt to be dignified, and somehow it seemed additionally so when it gained a luxuriously superfluous character by merely lying in huge, uncultivated tracts, and representing nothing but wide areas and taxes.

"Them big D'Willerbys of D'lisleville owns thousands of acres as never brings 'em a cent," Mr. Stamps had said to his friends at the Cross-roads at the time Big Tom had first appeared among them. It was Mr. Stamps who had astutely suggested that the stranger was possibly "kin" to the De-lisleville family, and in his discreet pursuit of knowledge he had made divers discoveries.

"'Twarn't Jedge D'Willerby bought the land," he went on to explain, "'n' it seems like he would hev bin a fool to hev done it, bein' as 'tain't worked an' brings in nothin'. But ye never know how things may turn out. 'Twas the

Jedge's gran'father, old Isham D'Willerby bought it fer a kinder joke. Some said he was blind drunk when he done it, but he warn't so drunk but what he got a cl'ar title, an' he got it mighty cheap too. Folks ses as he use ter laugh an' say he war goin' to find gold on it, but he never dug fer none—nor fer crops nuther, an' thar it lies to-day in the mountains, an' no one goin' nigh it."

In truth, Judge De Willoughby merely paid his taxes upon it from a sense of patriarchal pride.

" My ancestor bought it," he would say. " I will hand it to my sons. In England it would be an estate for an earldom, here it means merely tax-paying.` Still, I shall not sell it."

Nobody, in fact, would have been inclined to buy it in those days. But there came a time when its value increased hour by hour in the public mind, until it was almost beyond computation.

A chance visitor from the outside world made an interesting discovery. On this wild tract of hill and forest was a vein of coal so valuable that, to the practical mind of the discoverer, the Judge's unconsciousness of its existence was amazing. He himself was a practical, driving, business schemer from New York. He knew the value of what he saw, and the availability of the material in consequence of a certain position in which the mines lay. Before he left Delisleville he had explained this with such a presenting of facts that the Judge had awakened to an enthusiasm as Southern as his previous indifference had been. He had no knowledge of business methods; he had practised his profession in a magnificent *dilettante* sort of way which had worn an imposing air and impressed his clients, and, as he was by inheritance a comparatively rich man, he had not been driven by necessity to alter his methods. The sudden prospect of becoming a multimillionaire excited him. He made Napoleonic plans, and was dignified and eloquent.

"Why should I form a company?" he said. "If I am willing to make the first ventures myself, the inevitable returns of profit will do the rest, and there will be no complications. The De Willoughby Mine will be the De Willoughby Mine alone. I prefer that it should be so."

The idea of being sole ruler in the scheme made him feel rather like a king, and he privately enjoyed the sensation. He turned into money all the property he could avail himself of; his library table was loaded with books on mining; he invested in tons of machinery, which were continually arriving from the North, or stopping on the way when it should have been arriving. He sent for engineers from various parts of the country and amazed them with the unprofessional boldness of his methods. He really indulged in a few months of dignified riot, of what he imagined to be a splendidly executive nature. The plans were completed, the machinery placed, the engineers and cohorts of workmen engaged in tremendous efforts, the Judge was beginning to reflect on the management of his future millions, when—the first gun was fired on Fort Sumter.

That was the beginning, and apparently the end. Suddenly the storm of war broke forth, and its tempest, surging through the land, swept all before it. The country was inundated with catastrophes, capitalists foundered, schemes were swamped, the armies surged to and fro. The De Willoughby land was marched and fought over; scores of hasty, shallow graves were dug in it and filled; buildings and machinery were destroyed as if a tornado had passed by. The Judge was a ruined man; his realisable property he had allowed to pass from his hands, his coal remained in the bowels of the earth, the huge income he was to have drawn from it had melted into nothingness.

Nothing could have altered the aspect of this tragedy; but there was a singular fact which added to its intensity and bitterness. In such a hot-bed of secession as was De-lisleville, the fact in question was indeed not easily explainable, except upon the grounds either of a Quixotic patriotism or upon those of a general disposition to contradictoriness. A Southern man, the head of a Southern family, the Judge opposed the rebellion and openly sided with the Government. That he had been a man given to argument and contradiction, and always priding himself upon refusing to be led by the majority was not to be denied.

" He is fancying himself a Spartan hero, and looking forward to laurels and history," one of his neighbours remarked. " It is like De Willoughby after all. He would have been a Secessionist if he had lived in Boston."

" The Union General George Washington fought for and handed down to us *I* will protect," the Judge said loftily himself.

But there was no modifying the outburst of wonder and condemnation which overwhelmed him. To side with the Union—in an aristocratic Southern town—was to lose social caste and friends, to be held a renegade and an open, degraded traitor to home and country. At that period, to the Southerner the only country was the South—in the North reigned outer darkness. Had the Judge been a poor white, there would have been talk of tar and feathers. As a man who had been a leader among the aristocratic classes, he was ostracized. In the midst of his financial disasters he was treated as an outlaw. He had been left a widower a few years before, during the war his son De Courcy died of fever, Romaine fell in battle, and his sole surviving daughter lost her life through diphtheria contracted in a soldiers' hospital. The family had sunk into actual poverty; the shock of sorrows and disappointment broke the old man's spirit. On the day that peace was finally declared he died in his room in the old house which had once been so full of young life and laughter and spirit.

The only creature with him at the time was his grandson, young Rupert De Willoughby, who was De Courcy's son. The sun was rising, and its first beams shone in at the open window rosily. The old Judge lay rubbing his hands slowly together, perhaps because they were cold.

"Only you left, Rupert," he said, "and there were so many of us. If Tom—if Tom had not been such a failure—don't know whether he's alive—or dead. If Tom——"

His hands slowly ceased moving and his voice trailed off into silence. Ten minutes later all was over, and Rupert stood in the world entirely alone.

.   .   .   .

For the next two years the life the last De Willoughby lived in the old house, though distinctly unique, was not favourable to the development of youth. Having been prepared for the practice of the law, after the time-honoured De Willoughby custom, and having also for some months occupied a corner in the small, unbusiness-like, tree-shaded, brick building known as the Judge's "office," Rupert sat now at his grandfather's desk and earned a scant living by endeavouring to hold together the old man's long-diminished practice. The profession at the time offered nothing in such places as Delisleville, even to older and more experienced men. No one had any money to go to law with, few had any property worth going to law about.

Both armies having swept through it, Delisleville wore in those days an aspect differing greatly from its old air of hospitable well-being and inconsequent good spirits and good cheer. Its broad verandahed houses had seen hard usage, its pavements were worn and broken, and in many streets tufted with weeds; its fences were dilapidated, its rich families had lost their possessions, and those who had not been driven away by their necessities were gazing aghast at a future to which it seemed impossible to adjust their ease-loving, slave-attended, luxurious habits of the past. Houses built of wood, after the Southern fashion, do not well withstand neglect and ill-fortune. Porticos and pillars and trellis-work which had been picturesque and imposing when they had been well cared for, and gleamed white among creepers and trees, lost their charm drearily when paint peeled off, trees were cut down, and vines were dragged away and died. Over the whole of the once gay little place there had fallen an air of discouragement, desolation, and decay. Financial disaster had crippled the boldest even in centres much more energetic than small, unbusiness-like Southern towns; the country lay, as it were, prostrate to recover strength, and all was at a standstill.

Finding himself penniless, Rupert De Willoughby lived in a corner of the house he had been brought up in. Such furniture as had survived the havoc of war and the entire dilapidation of old age, he had gathered together in three or four rooms, which he occupied with the one servant good fortune brought to his door at a time when the forlornness of his changed position was continually accentuated by the untidy irregularity of his life and surroundings. He was only able to afford to engage the shiftless services of a slatternly negro girl, rendered insubordinate by her newly acquired freedom, and he had begun to feel that he should never again find himself encompassed by the decorous system of a well-managed household.

It was at this juncture that Uncle Matthew arrived and presented his curious petition, which was that he should be accepted as general servant, with wages or without them.

He had not belonged to Judge De Willoughby, but to a distant relative, and, as he was an obstinate and conservative old person, he actually felt that to be " a free nigger " was rather to drop in the social scale.

" Whar's a man stand, sah, if he ain't got no fambly? " he said to Rupert when he came to offer his services to him. " He stan' nowhar, that's war he stan'; I've got to own up to it, Marse Rupert, I'se a 'ristycrat bawn an' bred, an' I 'low to stay one, long's my head's hot. Ef my old mars's fambly hadn't er gone fo'th en' bin scattered to de fo' win's of de university, I'd a helt on, but when de las' of 'um went to dat Europe, dey couldn't 'ford to take me, an' I had ter stay. An' when I heerd as all yo' kin was gone an' you was gwine to live erlone like dis yere, I come to ax yer to take me to wait on yer—as a favier, Marse Rupert—as a *favier*. 'Tain't pay I wants, sah; it's a fambly name an' a fambly circle."

" It's not much of a circle, Uncle Matt," said Rupert, looking round at the bareness of the big room he sat in.

" 'Tain't much fer you, suh," answered Uncle Matthew, " but it's a pow'fle deal fer me in dese yere days. Ef yer don't take me, fust thing I knows I'll be drivin' or waitin' on some Mr. Nobody from New York or Boston, an' seems like I shouldn't know how to stand it. 'Scuse me a-recom-

mendin' myself, sah—I *look* ole, but I ain't as ole as I look;
I'se l'arnt to cook, sah, from three womens what I was
married to, an' I knows my place an' how to keep house
like it orter be kep'. Will you try me a mont', Marse De
Willoughby—will you try me a week? "

Rupert tried him and never regretted the venture. In
fact, Uncle Matt's accomplishments were varied for practical
reasons. He had been in his time first house servant, then
coachman; he had married at twenty a woman of forty,
who had been a sort of female mulatto Vatel. When she
had died, having overheated herself and caught cold on the
occasion of a series of great dinners given at a triumphant
political crisis, he had taken for his second wife the woman
whose ambition it had been to rival her in her culinary arts.
His third marriage had been even more distinguished. His
wife had been owned by some extravagantly rich Creoles in
New Orleans, and had even lived with them during a year
spent in France, thereby gaining unheard-of culinary accomplishments. Matthew had always declared that he loved her
the best of the three. Those matrimonial ventures had been
a liberal education to him. He had learned to cook almost
as well as his first, and from his second and third he had
inherited methods and recipes which were invaluable. He
seemed to have learned to do everything. He dismissed the
slatternly negro girl and took upon himself the duties of
both man and woman servant. The house gradually wore
a new aspect—dust disappeared, windows were bright, the
scant furniture was arranged to the best possible advantage,
the scant meals were marvels of perfect cookery and neat
serving. Having prepared a repast, Uncle Matt donned an
ancient but respectable coat and stood behind his young
master's chair with dignity. The dramatic nature of his

race was strongly appealed to by the situation in which he found himself. A negro of his kind is perfectly capable of building a romance out of much smaller materials. The amiable vanity which gave such exalted value to all the belongings of their masters in their days of slavery, and which so delighted in all picturesqueness of surrounding, is the best of foundations for romances. From generation to generation certain circumstances and qualities had conferred a sort of distinction upon their humbleness; to be owned by an aristocrat, to live in a great house, to wait upon young masters who were handsome and accomplished and young mistresses who were beautiful and surrounded by worshippers, to be indispensable to " de Jedge " or " de Cun'l," or to travel as attendant because some brilliant young son or lovely young daughter could find no one who would wait on them as " Uncle Matt " or " Aunt Prissy " could—these things made life to be desired and filled it with excitement and importance.

To the halcyon days in which such delights were possible Uncle Matt belonged. He was too old to look forward; he wanted his past again; and to find himself the sole faithful retainer in a once brilliant household, with the chance of making himself indispensable to the one remaining scion of an old name, assisted him to feel that he was a relic of departed grandeur.

His contrivances were numberless. In a corner of what he called the " back gyarden " he constructed an enclosure for chickens. He bought two or three young fowls, and by marvels of management founded a family with them. The family once founded, he made exchanges with friendly coloured matrons of the vicinity, with such results in breeding that " Uncle Matt's " chickens became celebrated fowls. He

219

displayed the same gifts in the management of the garden. In a few months after his arrival, Rupert began to find himself sitting down before the kind of meal he had not expected to contemplate again.

" Uncle Matt," he said, " where do I get fried chicken and vegetables like these—and honey and fresh butter and cream? I don't pay for them."

" Yes, you do, sah. Yo' property pays for 'em. Dat 'ar gyarden, sah, is black with richness—jest black. It's a forchen for a pusson what kin contrive an' make fren's, an' trade, an' kin flourish a spade. Dar's fruit-trees an' grape-vines dar—an' room enuf to plant anything—an' richness enuf to make peas an' taters an' beets an' cabbages jest jump out o' de yarth. I've took de liberty of makin' a truck patch, an' I've got me a chicken coop, an' I've had mighty good luck with my aigs an' my truck—an' I've got things to trade with the women folks for what I *ain't* got. De ladies likes tradin', an' dey's mighty neighbourly about yeah, 'memberin' yo' fambly, sah."

Rupert leaned back in his chair and broke into a hearty, boyish laugh, which it was very good both to see and hear. He very seldom laughed.

" I wish I was a genius like you, Matt," he said. " What luck I'm in to have you. Raising chickens and vegetables, and negotiating with your lady friends for me! I feel like a caliph with a grand vizier. I never tasted such chicken or such waffles in my life! "

" I'm settin' some tukkey-eggs now—under de yaller hen," said Matt, with a slyly exultant grin. " She's a good mother, the yaller hen; an' de way dem fruit-trees is gwine ter be loaded is a sight. Aunt Mary Field, she's tradin' with me a'ready agin fruit puttin'-up time."

Rupert got up from his chair. He caught old Matt's dusky, yellow-palmed paw in his hand and shook it hard. His gloomy young face had changed its aspect, his eyes suddenly looked like his mother's—and Delia Vanuxem had been said to have the loveliest soft eyes in all the South.

"Matt," he said, "I couldn't do without you. It isn't only *that*," with a gesture towards the table, "you—it's almost as if you had come to save me."

"Ole nigger man like me, Marse Rupert," said Uncle Matt, "savin' of a fine young gentleman like what you is! How's I gwine ter do it?" But his wrinkled face looked tremulous with emotion. "Times is gwine ter change for you, they is, an' Matt's gwine ter stay by yer till dat come to pass. Marse Rupert," looking at him curiously, "I 'clar to Gawd you look like yo' young mammy did. Yo' ain't always, but jes' dish yer minnit yo' does—an' yer did jes' now when yer laf'."

"Do I look like her?" said Rupert. "I'm glad of it. I want to be like her. Say, Uncle Matt, whenever I look or speak or act like her, you tell me."

When in the course of neighbourly conversation Matt mentioned this to his friend Aunt Mary Fields, she put a new colour upon it.

"He worshipped his maw, an' she jest 'dored down on him," she said; "but 'tain't only he want look like her, he *doan'* want look like his paw. Ev'one know what Cun'l de Courcy was—an' dat chile jest 'spise him. He was allus a mons'ous proud chile, and when de Cun'l broke loose an' went on one o' his t'ars, it mos' 'stroyed dat boy wid de disgracefulness. Dar's chil'en as doan' keer or notice— but dat boy, it 'most 'stroyed him."

The big, empty-sounding house was kept orderly and

spotless, the back garden exhibited such vegetables as no one else owned, the fruit-trees and grape-vines throve, in time the flower-beds began to bloom brilliantly, the rose-bushes and shrubs were trimmed, the paths swept, and people began to apply to Uncle Matt for slips and seeds. He himself became quite young again, so inspired was he by his importance and popularity. When he went into the town upon errands, people stopped to talk to him; the young business or professional men called him into their offices to have a chat with him. He was such a respectable relic of the times which had been " better days " to all of them, that there were those who were almost confidential with him. Uncle Matt would always understand their sentiments and doctrines, and he was always to be relied on for any small service. Such a cocktail or julep no one else could prepare, and there were numerous subtle accomplishments in the matter of mixing liquid refreshments which would have earned a reputation for any man.

There was no more familiar figure than his in the market or business streets of the hot, sunshine-flooded little town, which the passing armies had left so battered and deserted.

Uncle Matt knew all the stories in Delisleville. He knew how one house was falling to pieces for lack of repairs; he heard of the horses that had been sold or had died of old age and left their owners without a beast to draw their rickety buggies or carriages; he was deeply interested in the failing fortunes of what had once been the most important " store " in the town, and whose owner had been an aristocratic magnate, having no more undignified connection with the place than that of provider of capital.

As he walked up Main Street on his way to market, with his basket on his arm, he saw who had been able to " lay in new stock" and who had not. He saw the new sign-boards hung outside small houses which had been turned into offices. He knew what young scion of a respectable family had begun "doctoring" or "set up as a lawyer." Sometimes he even dropped in and made brief visits of respectful congratulation.

"But," he said privately to his young master, "de air ob de atmosphere, it's jest full of dem young lawyers an' doctors. Dar don't seem to be nothin' else for a gen'leman's sons to do but to kyore people or go to law for 'em. Of cose dey oughtn't ter hab ter work, gen'lemen oughtn't ter. Dey didn't usen to heb ter, but now dey *is* gotter. Lawdy, Marse Rupert, you'll hatter 'scuse me, but de young lawyers, an' de young doctors, dey is scattered about dish yer D'lisleville!"

There were certain new sign-boards which excited him to great interest. There was one he never passed without pausing to examine and reflect upon it.

When he came within range of it on his way up the street, his pace would slacken, and when he reached it he would stop at the edge of the pavement and stand with his basket on his arm, gazing at the lettering with an absorbed air of interest and curiosity. It read, "Milton January, Claim Agent." He could not read, but he had heard comments made upon the profession of the owner of this sign-board which had filled him with speculative thought. He shared the jealousy of strangers who came from "the North" to Delisleville and set up offices, which much more intelligent persons than himself burned with. He resented them as intruders, and felt that their well-dressed air and alert, business-like manner was an insult to departed fortunes.

"What they come fer?" he used to grumble. "Takin'

away trade an' business when they ain't none left for de proper people nohow. How's we gwine ter live if all New York City an' Bos'n an' Philadelphy pours in?"

"They are not pouring in very fast, Uncle Matt," Rupert answered him once. "Perhaps it would be better for us if they did. They bring *some* money, at any rate. There are only one or two of them, and one is a claim agent."

"Dat's jest what I wants ter know," said Matt. "What's dey layin' claim to? What right dey got ter claim anythin'? Gawd knows dar ain't much ter claim."

Rupert laughed and gave him a friendly, boyish slap on the back.

"They are not claiming things *from* people, but *for* them. They look up claims against the Government and try to get indemnity for them. They prove claims to back pay, and for damages and losses, and try to make the Government refund."

Uncle Matt rubbed his head a minute, then he looked up eagerly.

"Cun'l De Willoughby, now," he said; "doan' you s'pose dar's some back pay owin' to him for de damage dat yaller fever done him wot he done cotch from de army?"

Rupert laughed a little bitterly.

"No," he said, "I'm afraid not."

"What dey gwine to refun', den?" said Matt. "Dat's what I'd like ter fin' out. Dis hyer idee of refun'in' please me mightily. I'd be pow'fle glad to come bang up agin' some refun'in' myself."

From that time his interest in Milton January, Claim Agent, increased week by week. He used to loiter about talking groups if he caught the sound of his name, in the hope of gathering information. He was quite shrewd enough to realise his own entire ignorance of many subjects, and he had the pride which prevented his being willing to commit himself.

"I ain't nothin' but a ole nigger," he used to say. "I ain't had no eddication like some er dese yere smarties what kin read an' cipher an' do de double shuffle in de copy-book. Matt ain't never rub his back 'gin no college wall. Bes' thing he knows is dat he doan' know nothin'. Dat's a pow'fle useful piece o' l'arnin' to help a man, black or white, from makin' a fool er hesself bigger dan what de good Lawd 'tended him fer ter be. Matt he gradyuated in dat 'ar knowledge an' got he stiffikit. When de good Lawd turn a man out a fool, he got ter *be* a fool, but he needn' ter be a bigger fool den what he *gotter*."

So he listened in the market, where he went every morning to bargain for his bit of beefsteak, or fish, or butter, and where the men and women who kept the stalls knew him as well as they knew each other. They all liked him and welcomed him as he approached in his clean old clothes, his market basket on his arm, his hat set rather knowingly upon his grizzled wool. He was, in fact, rather a flirtatious old party, and was counted a great wit, and was full of a shrewd humour as well as of grandiloquent compliment.

"I has a jocalder way er talkin', I ain't gwine ter deny," he would say when complimented upon his popularity with the fair sex, "an' dey ain't nothin' de ladies likes mo' dan a man what's jocalder. Dey loves jokin' an' dey loves to laff. It's de way er de sect. A man what cayn't be jocalder with 'em, he hain't no show."

"What dis hyer claim agentin' I's hearin' so much talk about?" he enquired of a group one morning. "What *I* wants is ter get inter de innards of de t'ing, an' den I'se gwine to claim sump'n fer myse'f. If dar's claimin' gwine on, I'se a gen'leman what's gwine to be on de camp-meetin' groun', an' fo'most 'mong de shouters."

"What did ye lose by the war, Uncle Matt?" said a countryman, who was leaning against his market waggon of "produce" and chewing tobacco. "If ye kin hunt up suthin' ye lost, ye kin put in a claim fer the vally of it, an' mebbe get Government to give ye indemnity. Mebbe ye kin an' mebbe ye cayn't. They ain't keen to do it, but mebbe ye could work it through a smart agent like January. They say he's as smart as they make 'em."

It was a broiling July morning; only the people who were obliged to leave their houses for some special reason were to be seen in the streets; the market waggons which had come in from the country laden with vegetables and chickens and butter were drawn up under the shadow of the market house, that their forlorn horses or mules might escape the glaring hot sun. The liveliest business hour had passed, and about the waggons a group of market men and women and two or three loiterers were idling in the shade, waiting for chance-belated customers. There was a general drawing near when Uncle Matt began his conversation. They always wanted to hear what he had to say, and always responded with loud, sympathetic guffaws to his "jocalder" remarks.

"He's sech a case, Uncle Matt is," the women would say; "I never seen sich a case."

When the countryman spoke, Uncle Matt put on an expression of dignified thoughtfulness. It was an expression his audience were entirely familiar with and invariably greeted with delight.

"Endurin' of de war," he said, "I los' severial things. Fust thing I memberize of losin' was a pa'r of boots. Dar was a riggiment passin' at de time, an' de membiers of dat riggiment had been footin' it long enough to have wo' out a good deal er shoe-leather. They was thusty an' hungry, an' come to de halt near my cabin to require if dar warn't no vittles lyin' roun' loose for de good er de country. When dey was gone, my new boots was gone, what I'd jest brung home from de cobbler."

His audience broke into a shout of enjoyment.

" Dat 'ar incerdent stirred up my paketriotit feelin's con-sider'ble at de moment. I couldn't seem to see it in de light what p'raps I oughter seen it in. I rared roun' a good deal, an' fer a moment er two, I didn't seem tar mind which side beat de oder. Jest dat 'casion. I doan' say de sentiment continnered on, but jest dat 'casion seemed ter me like dar was a Yank somewhars es I wouldn't hev ben agin seein' takin' a whuppin' from some'un, Secesh or no Secesh."

" What else did ye lose, Unc' Matt? " someone said when the laugh died down.

" Well, I lose a wife—kinder cook dat dar ain't no 'dem-nity kin make up fer when de Lawd's removed 'em. An' 'pears to me right dar, dat if I wusn't a chu'ch member, I shed be led on ter say dat, considerin' what a skaseness er good cooks dar is, seems like de good Lawd's almost wasteful an' stravagant, de way he lets 'em die off. Three uv 'em he 'moved from me to a better worl'. Not as I'm a man what'd wanter be sackerligious; but 'pears to me dar was mo' wuk fur 'em to do in dis hyer dark worl' er sin dan in de realms er glory. I may be wrong, but dat's how it seem to a pore nigger like me."

" The Government won't pay for yer wife, Matt," said the owner of the market waggon.

" Dat dey won't, en dat dey cayn't," said Matt. " Dat

las' woman's gumbo soup warn't a thing to be 'demnified fer, dat it warn't. But what I'm a aimin' at is to fin' out what dey *will* pay fer, en how much. Dar was one mawnin' I sot at my do' reflectin' on de Gawsp'l, an' de Yanks come jest a tarin' down de road, licketty switch, licketty switch, yellin' like de debil let loose, en firin' of dere pistols, an' I gotter 'fess I los' a heap a courage dat time—an' I los' a heap o' breath runnin' 'way from 'em en outer sight. Now I know de Gov'ment not gwine ter pay me fer losin' dem things, but what *is* dey gwine pay for losin'? "

" Property, they say—crops 'n' houses, 'n' barns, 'n' truck wuth money."

Uncle Matt removed his hat, and looked into the crown of it as if for instruction before he wiped his forehead and put it on again.

" Aye-yi! Dey is, is dey? " he said. " Property—en houses, en barns, en truck wuth money? Dey'll hev a plenty to pay, ef dey begins dat game, won't dey? Dey'll hev ter dig down inter de Gov'ment breeches pocket pretty deep, dat dey will. Doan' see how de Pres'dent gwine ter do it out'n what dey 'lows him, less'n dey 'lows him mighty big pocket money."

" 'Tain't the President, Matt," said one of the crowd. " It's the Nation."

" Oh, it's de Nation! " said Matt. " De Nation. Well, Mr. Nation gwine fin' he got plenty ter do—early *en* late."

This was not the last time he led the talk in the direction of Government claims, and in the course of his marketings and droppings into various stores and young lawyers' offices, he gathered a good deal of information. Claims upon the Government had not been so far exploited in those days as they were a little later, and knowledge of such business and

its processes was not as easily obtainable by unbusinesslike
persons.

One morning, as he stood at the street corner nearest the
Claim Agent's office, a little man came out of the place, and
by chance stopped to cool himself for a few moments under
the shade of the very maple tree Uncle Matt had chosen.

He was a very small man, wearing very large pantaloons, and he had a little countenance whose expression
was a curious combination of rustic vacancy and incongruous slyness. He was evidently from the country, and
Uncle Matt's respectable, in fact, rather aristocratic air, apparently attracted his attention.

" 'Scuse me, sah," said Matt, " 'scuse me addressin' of you,
but dem ar Claim Agents——? "

" Hev ye got a claim? " said the little man in words that
were slow, but with an air that was sharp. " I mean, has
anyone ye work fur got one? "

" Well, sah," answered Matt, " I ain't sartain, but——"

" Ye'd better make sartain," said the little man. " Bein'
es the thing's started the way it hes, anyone es might hev a
claim an' lets it lie, is a derned fool. I come from over the
mountain. My name's Stamps, and *I've* got one."

Uncle Matt regarded him with interest—not exactly with
respect, but with interest.

Stamps took off his battered broad-brimmed hat, wiped
his moist forehead and expectorated, leaning against the
tree.

" Thar's people in this town as is derned fools," he remarked, sententiously. " Thar's people in most every town
in the Union as is derned fools. Most everybody's got a
claim to suthin', if they'd only got the common horse sense
ter look it up. Why, look at that yoke o' oxen o' mine—the

finest yoke o' steers in Hamlin County. Would hev took fust ticket at any Agricultural Fair in the United States. I ain't goin' to sacceryfist them steers to no Stars an' Stripes as ever floated. The Guv'ment's *got* to pay me the wuth of 'em down to the last cent."

He gave Matt a sharp look with a hint of inquiry in it, as if he was asking either his hearer or himself a question, and was not entirely certain of the answer.

"Now thar's D'Willerby," he went on. "Big Tom— Tom D'Willerby lost enough, the Lord knows. Fust one army, 'n' then another layin' holt on his stock as it come over the road from one place an' another, a-eatin' of it up 'n' a-wearin' his goods made up into shirts 'n' the like— 'n' him left a'most cleaned out o' everythin'. Why, Tom D'Willerby——"

"'Scuse me, sah," interrupted Matt, "but did you say De Willoughby?"

"I said D'Willerby," answered Mr. Stamps. "That's what he's called at the Cross-roads."

There he stopped and stared at Matt a moment.

"My young master's name's De Willoughby, sah," Matt said; "'n' de names soun's mighty simulious when dey's spoke quick. My young Marse, Rupert De Willoughby, he de gran'son er Jedge De Willoughby, an' de son an' heir er Cun'l De Courcy De Willoughby what died er yaller fever at Nashville."

"Well, I'm doggoned," the little man remarked, "I'd orter thought er thet. This yere's Delisleville, 'n' I recker- lect hearin' when fust he come to Hamlin thet he was some kin to some big bugs down ter D'lisleville, 'n' his father was a Jedge—doggoned ef I didn't!"

CHAPTER XIX

RUPERT DE WILLOUGHBY was lying upon the grass in the garden under the shade of a tree. The "office" had been stifling hot, and there had been even less to suggest any hope of possible professional business than the blankness of most days held. There never was any business, but at rare intervals someone dropped in and asked him a question or so, his answers to which, by the exercise of imagination, might be regarded as coming under the head of "advice." His clients had no money, however—nobody had any money; and his affairs were assuming a rather desperate aspect.

He had come home through the hot streets with his straw hat pushed back, the moist rings of his black hair lying on a forehead lined with a rather dark frown. He went into the garden and threw himself on the grass in the shade. He could be physically at ease there, at least. The old garden had always been a pleasure to him, and on a hot summer day it was full of sweet scents and sounds he was fond of. At this time there were tangles of honeysuckle and bushes heavy with mock-orange; an arbour near him was covered by a multiflora rose, weighted with masses of its small, delicate blossoms; within a few feet of it a bed of mignonette grew, and the sun-warmed breathing of all these fragrant things was a luxurious accompaniment to the booming of the bees, blundering and buzzing in and out of their flowers, and the summer languid notes of the stray birds which lit on the branches and called to each other among the thick leaves.

In Connection with
The De Willoughby Claim

At twenty-three a man may be very young. Rupert was both young and old. His silent resentment of the shadow which he felt had always rested upon him, had become a morbid thing. It had led him to seclude himself from the gay little Delisleville world and cut himself off from young friendships. After his mother—who had understood his temperament and his resentment—had died, nobody cared very much for him. The youth of Delisleville was picturesque, pleasure-loving, and inconsequent. It had little parties at which it danced; it had little clubs which were vaguely musical or literary; and it had an ingenuous belief in the talents and graces displayed at these gatherings. The feminine members of these societies were sometimes wonderfully lovely. They were very young, and had soft eyes and soft Southern voices, and were the owners of the tiniest arched feet and the slenderest little, supple waists in the world. Until they were married—which usually happened very early—they were always being made love to and knew that this was what God had made them for—that they should dance a great deal, that they should have many flowers and bonbons laid at their small feet, that beautiful youths with sentimental tenor voices should serenade them with guitars on moonlight nights, which last charming thing led them to congratulate themselves on having been born in the South, as such romantic incidents were not a feature of life in New York and Boston. The masculine members were usually lithe and slim, and often of graceful height; they frequently possessed their share of good looks, danced and rode well, and could sing love songs. As it was the portion of their fair companions to be made love to, it was theirs to make love. They often wrote verses, and they also were given to arched insteps and eyes with very perceptible fringes.

In Connection with
The De Willoughby Claim

For some singular reason, it seems that Southern blood tends to express itself in fine eyes and lashes.

But with this simply emotional and happy youth young De Willoughby had not amalgamated. Once he had gone to a dance, and his father the Colonel had appeared upon the scene as a spectator in a state of exaggeratedly graceful intoxication. He was in the condition when he was extremely gallant and paid flowery compliments to each pair of bright eyes he chanced to find himself near.

When he first caught sight of him, Rupert was waltzing with a lovely little creature who was a Vanuxem and was not unlike the Delia Tom De Willoughby had fallen hopelessly in love with. When he saw his father a flash of scarlet shot over the boy's face, and, passing, left him looking very black and white. His brow drew down into its frown, and he began to dance with less spirit. When the waltz was at an end, he led his partner to her seat and stood a moment silently before her, glancing under his black lashes at the Colonel, who had begun to quote Thomas Moore and was declaiming "The Young May Moon" to a pretty creature with a rather alarmed look in her uplifted eyes. It was the first dance at which she had appeared since she had left school.

Suddenly Rupert turned to his partner. He made her a bow; he was a graceful young fellow.

"Thank you, Miss Vanuxem. Thank you for the dance. Good-night. I am going home."

"Are you?" exclaimed little Miss Vanuxem. "But it is so early, Mr. De Willoughby."

"I have stayed just ten minutes too long now," said Rupert. "Thank you again, Miss Vanuxem. Good-night."

He walked across the room to Colonel De Willoughby.

" I am going home," he said, in a low, fierce voice; " you had better come with me."

" No sush thing," answered the Colonel, gaily. " On'y just come. Don't go to roosh with shickens. Just quoting Tom Moore to Miss Baxter.

> " Bes' of all ways to lengthen our days
> Is to steal a few hours from the night, my dear."

The little beauty, who had turned with relieved delight to take the arm of a new partner, looked at her poetic admirer apologetically.

" Mr. Gaines has come for me, Colonel De Willoughby," she said; " I am engaged to him for this dance." And she slipped away clinging almost tenderly to the arm of her enraptured escort, who felt himself suddenly transformed into something like a hero.

" Colonel De Willoughby is so flattering," she said; " and he has such a queer way of paying compliments. I'm almost frightened of him."

" I will see that he does not speak to you again," said her partner, with an air of magnificent courage. " He should not have been allowed to come in. You, of course, could not understand, but—the men who are here will protect the ladies who are their guests."

Rupert gave his father a long look and turned on his heel. He went home, and the next time the Terpsichorean Society invited him to a dance he declined to go.

" Nice fellow I am to go to such places," he said to himself. " Liable to bring a drunken lunatic down upon them at any minute. No, the devil take it all, I'm going to stay at home! "

He stayed at home, and gradually dropped out of the young, glowing, innocently frivolous and happy world altogether, and it carried on its festivities perfectly well without him. The selfishness of lovely youth is a guileless, joyous thing, and pathetic inasmuch as maturity realises the undue retribution which befalls it as it learns of life.

When poverty and loneliness fell upon him, the boy had no youthful ameliorations, even though he was so touchingly young. Occasionally some old friend of his grandfather's encountered him somewhere and gave him rather florid good advice; some kindly matron, perhaps, asked him to come and see her; but there was no one in the place who could do anything practical. Delisleville had never been a practical place, and now its day seemed utterly over. Its gentlemanly pretence at business had received blows too heavy to recover from until times had lapsed; in some of the streets tiny tufts of grass began to show themselves between the stones.

As he had walked back in the heat, Rupert had observed these tiny tufts of green with a new sense of their meaning. He was thinking of them as he lay upon the grass, the warm scent of the mock-orange blossoms and roses, mingled with honeysuckle in the air, the booming of the bees among the multiflora blooms was in his ears.

"What can I do?" he said to himself. "There is nothing to be done here. There never was much, and now there is nothing. I can't loaf about and starve. I won't beg from people, and if I would, I haven't a relation left who isn't a beggar himself—and there are few enough of them left."

He put his hand in his pocket and pulled out a well-worn greenback. He straightened out its creases cautiously and looked at it.

" I've got two dollars," he said, " and no prospect of getting any more. Even Matt can't make two dollars last long."

The latch of the side gate clicked and the gate opened. Presently Uncle Matt appeared round the rose-bushes. He had his market basket on his arm and wore a thoughtful countenance.

" Uncle Matt! " Rupert called out to him. " I wish you would come here."

Notwithstanding his darkling moods, he was in a subtle way singularly like Delia Vanuxem. He needed love and tenderness, and he was boy enough yet to be unhappy and desolate through lack of them, though without quite knowing why. He knew Uncle Matt loved him, and the affectionate care the old man surrounded him with was like a warm robe wrapped about a creature suffering from chill. He had not analyzed his feeling himself; he only knew that he liked to hear his footsteps as he pottered about the house, and when he was at his dreariest, he was glad to see him come in, and to talk a little to him.

Uncle Matt came towards him briskly. He set his basket down and took off his hat.

" Marse Rupert," he said, " dis hyer's a pow'fle scorcher of a mawnin'. Dem young lawyers as shets up dey office an' comes home to lie in de grass in de shade, dey is follerin' up dey perfession in de profitablest way—what'll be likely to bring 'em de mos' clients, 'cause, sho's yo' bawn, dere's sunstroke an' 'cussion or de brain just lopin' roun' dis town—en a little hot brick office ain't no place for a young man what got any dispect fur his next birfday. Dat's so."

" I haven't much respect for mine," said Rupert; " I've had twenty-two too many—just twenty-two."

In Connection with
The De Willoughby Claim

" 'Scusin' me sayin' it, sah, but dat ain't no way ter talk. A man boun' to have some dispect for his birfday—he *boun'* to! Birfdays gotter be took keer on. Whar's a man when he runs out of 'em? "

" He'd better run out of them before he runs out of everything else," said Rupert. " Matt, I've just made two dollars this month."

He looked at the old man with a restless appeal in his big, deer-like eyes.

" I'm very sorry, Matt," he said, " I'm terribly sorry, but you know—we can't go on."

Uncle Matthew looked down at the grass with a reflective air.

" Marse Rupert, did you never heah nothin' 'bout your Uncle Marse Thomas De Willoughby? "

Rupert was silent a moment before he answered, but it was not because he required time to search his memory.

" Yes," he said, and then was silent again. He had heard of poor Tom of the big heart from his mother, and there had been that in her soft speech of him which had made the great, tender creature very real. Even in his childhood his mother had been his passion, as he had been hers. Neither of them had had others to share their affection, and they were by nature creatures born to love. His first memory had been of looking up into the soft darkness of the tender eyes which were always brooding over him. He had been little more than a baby when he had somehow known that they were very sorrowful, and had realised that he loved them more because of their sorrow. He had been little older when he found out the reason of their sadness, and from that time he had fallen into the habit of watching them and knowing their every look. He always remembered the

look they wore when she spoke of Tom De Willoughby,
and it had been a very touching one.

"Yes," he said to Uncle Matt, "I have heard of him."

"Dar was a time, a long way back, Marse Rupert—'fore
you was borned—when I seemed to year a good deal 'bout
Marse Thomas. Dat was when he went away in dat curi's
fashion. Nobody knowed *whar* he went, an' nobody knowed
quite *why*. It wus jes' afore ye' maw an' paw wus married.
Some said him an' de Jedge qua'lled 'cause Marse Thomas
he said he warn't gwine ter be no medical student, an'
some said he was in love with some young lady dat wouldn't
'cept of him."

"Did they?" said Rupert.

"Dat dey did," Matt said; "an' a lot moah. But ev'ry-
body think it mighty strange him a-gwine, an' no one never
huntin' him up afterwards. Seemed most like dey didn't
keer nothin' 'bout him."

"They didn't, damn them!" said Rupert, with sudden
passion. "And he was worth the whole lot."

"Dat what make I say what I gwine ter," said Matt, with
some eagerness. "What I heerd about Marse Thomas make
me think he must be er mighty fine gen'leman, an' one
what'd be a good fren' to anyone. An' dishyer ve'y mawnin'
I heerd sump'n mo' about him."

Rupert raised himself upon his elbow.

"About Uncle Tom!" he exclaimed. "You have heard
something about Uncle Tom to-day?"

"I foun' out whar he went, Marse Rupert," said Matt,
much roused. "I foun' out whar he *is* dishyer ve'y instep.
He's in Hamlin County, keepin' sto' an' post-office at Talbot's Cross-roads; an', frum what I heah, Marse Tom De
Willoughby de mos' pop'larist gen'leman an' mos' looked
up ter in de county."

In Connection with
The De Willoughby Claim

" Who—who did you hear it from? " demanded Rupert.

Uncle Matt put his foot upon a rustic seat near and leaned forward, resting his elbow on his knee and making impressive gestures with his yellow-palmed old hand.

" It was dishyer claimin' dat brung it about," he said; " dishyer claimin' an' 'demnification what's been a-settin' pow'fle heavy on my min' fur long 'nuff. Soon's I yeerd tell on it, Marse Rupert, it set me ter steddyin'. I been a-watchin' out an' axin' questions fur weeks, an' when I fin' out——"

" But what has that to do with Uncle Tom? " cried Rupert.

" A heap, Marse Rupert. Him an' you de onliest heirs to de De Willoughby estate; an' ef a little hoosier what's los' a yoke er oxen kin come down on de Guv'ment for 'demnification, why can't de heirs of a gen'leman dat los' what wus gwine ter be de biggest fortune in de South'n States. What's come er dem gold mines, Marse Rupert, dat wus gwine ter make yo' grandpa a millionaire—whar is dey? What de Yankees done with dem gol' mines? "

" They weren't gold mines, Uncle Matt," said Rupert; " they were coal mines; and the Yankees didn't carry them away. They only smashed up the machinery and ruined things generally."

But he laid back upon the grass again with his hands clasped behind his head and his brow drawn down thoughtfully.

" Coal mines er gol' mines," said Uncle Matt. " Guv'ment gotter 'demnify ef things er managed right; en dat what make me think er Marse Thomas De Willoughby when dat little Stamps feller said somep'n dat soun' like his name. ' Now dar's D'Willerby,' he ses, ' big Tom D'Willerby,' en

I jest jumped on him. ' Did you say De Willoughby, sah?' I ses, an' from dat I foun' out de rest."

" I should like to see him," said Rupert; " I always thought I should like to know where he was—if he was alive."

" Why doan' you go an' see him, den? " said Matt. " Jest take yo' foot in yo' han' an' start out. Hamlin County ain't fur, Marse Rupert, an' de Cross-roads Pos'-office mighty easy to fin'; and when you fin' it an' yo' uncle settin' in de do', you jest talk ter him 'bout dem gol' mines an' dat claimin' business an' ax his devise 'bout 'em. An' ef yer doan' fin' yo'se'f marchin' on ter Wash'n'ton city an' a-talkin' to de Pres'dent an' de Senators, de whole kit an' bilin' of 'em, Marse Thomas ain't de buz'ness gen'l'man what I believe he is."

Rupert lay still and looked straight before him, apparently at a bluebird balanced on a twig, but it was not the bird he was thinking of.

" You'se young, Marse Rupert, an' it 'ud be purty dan-g'rous for a onexperienced young gen'l'man ter lan' down in de midst er all dem onprinciple' Yankees with a claim to hundreds of thousan's of dollars. Marse Thomas, he's a settled, stiddy gen'l'man, en, frum what I hears, I guess he's got a mighty 'stablished-lookin' 'pearance."

" I should like to see him," Rupert reflected aloud. " I should like to see him."

CHAPTER XX

THE years had passed for the child Sheba so sweetly, and had been so full of simple joys and pleasures, that they seemed a panorama of lovely changing seasons, each a thing of delight. There was the spring, when she trotted by Tom's side into the garden and he showed her the little, pale-green points of the crocuses, hyacinths, and tulips pushing their way up through the moist brown earth, and when he carried her in his big arms into the woods on the hillsides, and they saw the dogwood covered with big white flowers and the wild plum-trees snowed over with delicate blooms, and found the blue violets thick among the wet grass and leaves, and the frail white wind-flowers quivering on their stems. As they went about in this new fairyland, which came every year, and which still seemed always a surprise, it was their habit to talk to each other a great deal. The confidences they had exchanged when the child had not been able to speak, and which Tom had nevertheless understood, were enchanting things when she became older and they strayed about together or sat by the fire. Her child thoughts and fancies might have been those of some little faun or dryad. She grew up among green things, with leaves waving above and around her, the sun shining upon her, and the mountains seeming to stand on guard, looking down at her from day to day, from year to year. From behind one mountain the sun rose every morning, and she always saw it; and behind another it sank at night. After the spring came the summer, when the days were golden and drowsy and

241

hot, and there were roses and other flowers everywhere; wild roses in the woods and by the waysides, heavy-headed beauties in their own garden, and all the beds and vines a fine riot of colour. After these there were blackberries thick on their long brambles, and wild grapes in the woods, and presently a delicious snap of cold in the clear air night and morning, and the trees were dropping golden, amber, and scarlet leaves, while under the pale yellow ones which rustled beneath the chestnut-trees, there were brown, glossy nuts, which fell one by one with a delightful suddenness of sound at irregular intervals. There were big chestnut-trees in the woods near their house, and Tom and Sheba used to go before breakfast to look for the nuts which had fallen in the night. Hamlin County always rose at sunrise, or before it, and to go out in the heavenly fresh morning air and walk through the rustling, thickly fallen yellow leaves under the trees, making little darts of joy at the brown, glossy things bursting through their big burrs, was a delicious, exciting thing. Mornin's hot breakfast held keen delights when they returned to it.

When the big wood-fires were lighted and there was snow and rain outside, and yams and chestnuts to roast in the ashes, and stories to be told and talked over in the glow of the red birch-log and snapping, flaming hickory sticks, the child used to feel as if she and Uncle Tom were even nearer together and more comfortable than at any other time.

"Uncle Tom," she said to him, as she was standing in the circle of his arm on one such night, when she was about ten years old. "Uncle Tom, we do love each other in the winter, don't we?"

"Yes, we do, Sheba," answered Tom. "And we're pretty partial to each other even in the summer."

In Connection with
The De Willoughby Claim

"We love each other at all the times," she said. "And every morning that I get up I love you more than I did when I went to bed—*every* morning, Uncle Tom."

Tom kissed her. He remembered what he had said one morning in the cabin in Blair's Hollow ten years before.

"Perhaps, if there's no one to come between us, she may be fond of me."

She was fond of him. He was her very little life itself. No one had ever come between—nothing ever could.

She had by that time shot up into a tall, slender slip of a girl-child. She was passing, even with a kind of distinction, through the stage of being all long, slim legs and big eyes. The slim legs were delicately modelled and the big eyes were like pools of gold-brown water, fringed with rushes.

"I never seen a young 'un at thet thar young colty age es was es han'some es thet child o' Big Tom's," Mis' Doty often remarked.

By the frequenters of the Cross-roads Post-office she was considered, as was her protector, a county institution. When she had reached three years old, she had been measured against the wall, and each year her increase of inches was recorded amid lively demonstrations of interest. The smallness of her feet had also been registered, and the thickness and growth of her curling hair ranked as a subject of discussion only second in interest to the development of crops.

But this affection notwithstanding, a curious respect for her existed. She had played among them in the store in her little dusty pinafore; one and all of them had given her rustic offerings, bringing her special gifts of yellow popcorn ears, or abnormal yams unexpectedly developed in their own gardens, or bags of hickory nuts; but somehow they did not think or speak of her as they did of each other's children.

Tom had built a comfortable white house, over whose verandah honeysuckles and roses soon clambered and hung. In time the ground enclosed about it had a curious likeness to the bowery unrestraint of the garden he had played in during his childhood. It was a pleasure to him to lay it out on the old plan and to plant japonicas, flowering almonds, and syringa bushes, as they had grown in the days when he had played under them as a child, or lounged on the grass near them as a boy. He and Sheba planted everything themselves—or, rather, Sheba walked about with him or stood by his side and talked while he worked. In time she knew almost as well as he did the far-away garden he took as his model. She learned to know the place by heart.

" Were you a little boy then, Uncle Tom? " she would say, " when there was a mock-orange and a crape myrtle next to the big yellow rose-bush? "

There were even times when he found her memory was better than his own, and she could correct him.

" Ah! no, Uncle Tom," she would say; " the pansies were not in the little heart-shaped bed; they were all round the one with the pink harp-flower in the middle."

When she was six years old he sent for some books and began seriously to work with a view to refreshing his memory on subjects almost forgotten.

" I'm preparing myself for a nursery governess, Sheba," he said. " What we want is a nursery governess, and I don't know where to find one. I shouldn't know how to manage her if I did find her, so I've got to post up for the position myself."

The child was so happy with him in all circumstances,

that it was easy to teach her anything. She had learned to read and write before she discovered that the process she went through to acquire these accomplishments was not an agreeable pastime specially invented by Tom for her amusement. At eleven years old she had become so interested in her work that she was quite an excited little student. By the time she was twelve Tom began to shake his head at her.

" If you go on like this," he said, " I sha'n't be able to keep up with you, and what I've got to do is to keep ahead. If I can't, I shall have to send you to the Academy at Ralston; and how should we stand that? "

She came and sat upon his big knee—a slim little thing, as light as a bird.

" We couldn't stand it, Uncle Tom," she said. " We *have* to be together. We always have been, haven't we? " And she rubbed her ruffled head against his huge breast.

" Yes, we always have been," answered Tom; " and it would go pretty hard with us to make a change, Sheba."

She was not sent to Ralston. The war broke out and altered the aspect of things even at the Cross-roads. The bank in which Tom's modest savings were deposited was swept away by misfortune; the primitive resources of Hamlin County were depleted, as the resources of all the land were. But for the existence of the white, vine-embowered house and the garden full of scents and bloom, Tom's position at the close of the rebellion was far less fortunate than it had been at the time the mystery of Blair's Hollow had occurred. In those old, happy-go-lucky days the three rooms behind the store and the three meals Mornin cooked for him had been quite sufficient for free and easy peace. He had been able to ensure himself these primitive comforts with so little expenditure that money had scarcely seemed an object. He had taken eggs in exchange for sugar, bacon in exchange for tea, and butter in exchange for everything. Now he had no means of resource but the store, and the people were poorer than they had been. Farms had gone to temporary ruin through unavoidable neglect during the absence of their masters. More than one honest fellow had marched away and never returned, and their widows were left to struggle with the land and their children. The Cross-roads store, which had thriven so wonderfully for a year or two before the breaking out of the war, began to wear a less cheerful aspect. As far as he himself was concerned, Tom knew that life was a simple enough thing, but by his side there was growing up a young goddess. She was not aware that she was a young goddess. There was no one in the vicinity of the Cross-roads who could have informed her that she presented somewhat of that aspect, and that she was youth and happiness and Nature's self at once.

Tom continually indulged in deep reflection on his charge after she was twelve years old. She shot up into the tall suppleness of a lovely young birch, and she was a sweetly glowing thing. A baby had been a different matter; the baby had not been so difficult to manage; but when he found himself day by day confronting the sweetness of child-womanhood in the eyes that were gold-brown pools, and the softening grace of the fair young body, he began to be conscious of something like alarm. He was not at all sure what he ought to do at this crisis, and whether life confining its experiences entirely to Talbot's Cross-roads was all that was required.

"I don't know whether it's right, by thunder," he said. "I don't know whether it's right; and that's what a man who's taken the place of a young mother ought to know."

In Connection with
The De Willoughby Claim

There came a Sunday when one of the occasional "preach-ings" was to be held at the log-cabin church a few miles distant, and they were going together, as they always did.

It was a heavenly, warm spring morning, and Sheba, hav-ing made herself ready, wandered into the garden to wait among the flowers. The rapturous first scents of the year were there, drawn by the sun and blown by vagrant puffs of wind from hyacinths and jonquils, white narcissus and blue violets. Sheba walked among the beds, every few min-utes kneeling down upon the grass to bury her face in pink and yellow and white clusters, inhaling the breath of flowers and the pungent freshness of the sweet brown earth at the same time. She had lived among leaves and growing things until she felt herself in some unexplainable way a part of the world they belonged to. The world beyond the moun-tains she knew nothing of; but this world, which was the brown earth springing forth into green blades and leaves and little streaked buds, warming into bloom and sun-drenched fragrance, setting the birds singing and nest-building, giv-ing fruits and grain, and yellow and scarlet leaves, and folding itself later in snow and winter sleep—this world she knew as well as she knew herself. The birds were sing-ing and nest-building this morning, and, as she hung over a bed of purple and white hyacinths, kneeling on the grass and getting as close to them as she could, their perfume mounted to her brain and she began to kiss them.

"I love you," she said, dwelling on their sweet coolness with her lips; "I love and love you!" And suddenly she made a little swoop and kissed the brown earth itself. "And, oh! I love you, too!" she said. "I love you, too!"

She looked like young spring's self when she stood up as Tom came towards her. Her smile was so radiant a thing that he felt his heart quake with no other reason than this sight of her happy youth.

" What are you thinking of, Sheba? " he asked.

" I am thinking," she said, as she glanced all about her, the smile growing more entrancing, " I am thinking how happy I am, and how happy the world is, and how I love you, and," with a pretty laugh, " the flowers, and the sun, and the earth—and everything in the world! "

" Yes," said Tom, looking at her tenderly. " It's the spring, Sheba."

She caught his arm and clung to it, laughing again.

" Yes," she answered; " and when it isn't the spring, it is the summer; and when it isn't the summer, it is the autumn; and when it isn't the autumn, it is the winter; and we sit by the fire and know the spring is making its way back every day. Everything is beautiful—everything is happy, Uncle Tom."

" Good Lord! " exclaimed Tom.

" Why do you say that? " Sheba asked. " Why do you look so—so puzzled, Uncle Tom? "

" Well," said Tom, holding her out at arm's length before him, " the truth is, I've suddenly realised something. I'd like to know what I'm to do with *this!* "

" This? " laughed Sheba. " Am I ' this '? You look at me as if I was ' this '."

" You are," Tom answered, ruefully. " Here you suddenly change to a young woman on a man's hands. Now, what am I to do with a grown-up young woman? I'm used to babies, and teething, and swallowing kangaroos out of Noah's arks—and I know something of measles and letting tucks out of frocks; but when it comes to a beautiful young woman, there you have me! "

In Connection with
The De Willoughby Claim

He shook his head as he ended, and, though his face wore the affectionate, humorous smile which had never failed her, there was a new element in its kindness which, it must be confessed, bordered on bewilderment.

" A beautiful, grown-up young woman," he said, glancing reflectively over her soft, swaying slimness, her white frock with its purple ribbon and golden jonquils, and up to her tender cheek.

Sheba blushed with sweet delight.

" Am I beautiful, Uncle Tom? " she inquired, with a lovely anxiousness in her eyes.

" Yes, you are," admitted Tom; " and it isn't a drawback to you, Sheba, but it's likely to make trouble for me."

" But why? " she said.

" In novels, and poetry, and sometimes in real life, beautiful young women are fallen in love with, and then trouble is liable to begin," explained Tom with amiable gravity.

" There is no one to fall in love with me at the Cross-roads," said Sheba, sweetly. " I wish there was."

" Good Lord," exclaimed Tom, devoutly. " Come along to church, Sheba, and let's go in for fasting and prayer."

He took her to the " preaching " in the log cabin and noticed the effect of her entry on the congregation as they went in. There were a number of more or less awkward and raw-boned young male creatures whose lives were spent chiefly in cornfields and potato patches. They were uncomely hewers of wood and drawers of water, but they turned their heads to look at her, and their eyes followed her as she went to her seat. When she had sat down, those who could catch glimpses of her involuntarily craned their necks and sat in discomfort until the sermon was over. Tom recognised this fact, and in secret reflected upon it in all its bearings.

"Yes," he found himself saying, mentally; "I'd like to know how I'm going to do my duty by *this*. I don't believe there's a derned thing about it in 'Advice to Young Mothers.'"

The day wore on to its lovely end, and lost itself in one of the sunsets which seem to flood the sky with a tide of ripples of melted gold, here and there tipped with flame. When this was over, a clear, fair moon hung lighted in the heavens, and, flooding with silver what had been flooded with gold, changed the flame-tips to pearl.

Sheba strayed in the garden among the flowers. Tom, sitting under the vines of the porch, watched her white figure straying in and out among the shrubbery. At last he saw her standing on the grass in the full radiance of the moonlight, her hands hanging clasped behind her and her face turned upward to the sky. As she had wandered about, she had done a fanciful thing. She had made a wreath of white narcissus and laid it on her hair, and she had twisted together a sort of long garland of the same blossoms and cast it loosely round her waist.

"She never did that before," Tom said, as he watched her. "Good Lord! what a picture she is, standing there with her face lifted. I wonder what she's thinking of."

"Uncle Tom," she said, when she sauntered back to him, "does the moonlight make you feel sad without being unhappy at all? That is what it does to me."

"It's the spring, Sheba," he said, as he had said it in the morning; "it's the spring."

She saw that he was looking at her flower garlands, and she broke into a shy little laugh.

In Connection with
The De Willoughby Claim

"You see what you have done to me, Uncle Tom," she said; "now you have told me I am a beautiful young woman, I shall always be doing things to—to make myself look prettier."

She came on to the verandah to him, and he held out his hand to her.

"That's the spring, too, Sheba," he said.

She yielded as happily and naturally to the enfolding of his big arm in these days as she had done when she was a baby. No one but themselves knew what they were to each other. They had always talked things over together—their affection, their pleasures, their simple anxieties and responsibilities. They had discussed her playthings in the first years of their friendship and her lessons when she had been a little girl. To-night the subject which began to occupy them had some seriousness of aspect. The changes time and the tide of war had made were bringing Tom face to face with a difficulty his hopeful, easy-going nature had never contemplated with any realising sense—the want of money, even the moderate amount the requirements of their simple lives made necessary.

"It's the taxes that a man can't stand up against," Tom said. "You may cut off all you like, and wear your old clothes, but there's a liveliness about taxes that takes the sand out of you. Talk about the green bay-tree flourishing and increasing, all a tax wants is to be let alone a few years. It'll come to its full growth without any sunning or watering. Mine have had to be left alone for a while, and—well, here we are—another year, and——"

"Will the house be taken?" Sheba asked.

"If I can't pay up, it'll all go—house and store and all," Tom answered. "Then *we* shall have to go too."

In Connection with
The De Willoughby Claim

He turned and looked ruefully at the face beneath the wreath of white narcissus.

" I wish it hadn't come on us just now," he said. " There's no particular season that trouble adds a charm to; but it seems to me that it's not entitled to the spring."

When she went upstairs she did not go to bed. The moonlight lured her out into the night again. Outside her window there was a little balcony. It was only of painted wood, as the rest of the house was, but a multiflora rose had climbed over it and hung it with a wonderful drapery, and, as she stood upon it, she unconsciously made herself part of a picture almost strange in its dramatic quality.

She looked out over the sleeping land to the mountains standing guard.

" Where should we go? " she said. " The world is on the other side."

She was not in the mood to observe sound, or she would have heard the clear stroke of a horse's hoofs on the road. She did not even hear the opening of the garden gate. She was lost in the silver beauty of the night, and a vague dreaming which had fallen upon her. On the other side of the purple of the mountains was the world. It had always been there and she had always been here. Presently she found herself sighing aloud, though she could not have told why.

" Ah! " she said as softly as young Juliet. " Ah, me! "

As she could not have told why she sighed, so there was no explanation of the fact that, having done so, she looked downward to the garden path, as if something had drawn her eyes there. It is possible that some attraction had so drawn them, for she found herself looking into a young, upturned face—the dark, rather beautiful face of a youth who stood and looked upward as if he had stopped involuntarily at sight of her.

She drew back with a little start and then bent her Narcissus-crowned head forward.

" Who—who is it? " she exclaimed.

He started himself at the sound of her voice. She had indeed looked scarcely a real creature a few moments ago. He took off his hat and answered:

" I am Rupert De Willoughby," he said. " I beg pardon for disturbing you. It startled me to see you standing there. I came to see Mr. Thomas De Willoughby."

It was a singular situation. Perhaps the moonlight had something to do with it; perhaps the spring. They stood and looked at each other quite simply, as if they did not know that they were strangers. A young dryad and faun meeting on a hilltop or in a forest's depths by moonlight might have looked at each other with just such clear, unstartled eyes, and with just such pleasure in each other's beauty. For, of a truth, each one was thinking the same thing, innocently and with a sudden gladness.

As he had come up the garden-path, Robert had seen a vision and had stopped unconsciously that instant. And Sheba, looking down, had seen a vision too—a beautiful face as young as her own, and with eyes that glowed.

" You don't know what you looked like standing there," said Rupert, as simply as the young faun might have spoken. " It was as if you were a spirit. The flowers in your hair looked like great white stars."

" Did they? " she said, and stood and softly gazed at him.

How the boy looked up at her young loveliness! He had never so looked at any woman before. And then a thought

253

detached itself from the mists of memory and he seemed
to remember.

"Are you Sheba?" he asked.

"Yes, I am Sheba," she answered, rather slowly. "And
I remember you, too. You are the boy."

He drew nearer to the balcony, laying his hand upon the
multiflora rose creeper.

"Yes, yes," he said, almost tremulous with eagerness.
"You bring it all back. You were a little child, and I——"

"You rode away," she said, "over the hill."

"Will you come down to me?" he said.

"Yes," she answered, and that moment disappeared.

He stood in the moonlight, his head bared, his straw hat
in his hand. He felt as if he was in a dream. His face had
lost its gloom and yearning, and his eyes looked like his
mother's.

When he heard a light foot nearing him, he went forward,
and they met with strange young smiles and took each other's
hands. Nearer than the balcony, she was even a sweeter
thing, and the scent of her white flowers floated about her.

As they stood so, smiling, Tom came and joined them.
Sheba had called him as she passed his door.

Rupert turned round and spoke, vaguely conscious, as
he did so, that his words sounded somewhat like words uttered in a dream and were not such as he had planned.

"Uncle Tom," he said, "I—Delia Vanuxem was my
mother."

CHAPTER XXI

THE moment ceased to be so fanciful and curiously exalted when his hand was grasped and a big, kind palm laid on his shoulder, though Tom's face was full of emotion.

"I think I should have known it," he said. "Welcome to you. Yes," looking at him with an affection touched with something like reverence. "Yes, indeed—Delia Vanuxem!"

"I've come to you," the young fellow said, with fine simplicity, "because I am the only De Willoughby left except yourself. I am young and I'm lonely—and my mother always said you had the kindest heart she ever knew. I want you to advise me."

"Come in to the porch," said Tom, "and let us sit down and talk it over."

He put his arm about Sheba and kept his hand on Rupert's shoulder, and walked so, with one on either side, to the house. Between their youthful slimness he moved like a protecting giant.

"Where did you come from?" he asked when they sat down.

"From Delisleville," Rupert answered. "I did not think of coming here so late to-night, but it seems I must have missed my road. I was going to ask for lodgings at a place called Willet's Farm. I suppose I took the wrong turning; and when I saw this house before me, I knew it must be yours from what I had heard of it. It seemed as if Fate had brought me here. And when I came up the path I saw Sheba. She was standing on the little verandah in the moonlight with the roses all around her; and she looked so white that I stopped to look up at her."

" Uncle Tom," said Sheba, " we—we knew each other."

" Did you? " said Tom. " That's right."

His middle-aged heart surprised him by giving one quick, soft beat. He smiled to himself after he had felt it.

" The first moment or so I only stood and looked," Rupert said; " I was startled."

" And so was I," said Sheba.

" But when she leaned forward and looked down on me," he went on, " I remembered something——"

" So did I," said Sheba. " I leaned forward like that and looked down at you from the porch at the tavern—all those years ago, when I was a little child."

" And I looked up at you—and afterwards I asked about you," said Rupert. " It all came back when you spoke to-night, and I knew you must be Sheba."

" You knew my name, but I did not know yours," said Sheba. " But, after all," rather as if consoling herself, " Sheba is not my real name. I have another one."

" What is it? " asked the young fellow, quite eagerly. His eyes had scarcely left her face an instant. She was standing by Tom's chair and her hands were on his shoulders.

" It is Felicia," she said. " Uncle Tom gave it to me— because he wanted me to be happy." And she curved a slim arm round Tom's neck and kissed him.

It was the simplest, prettiest thing a man could have seen. Her life had left her nature as pure and translucent as the clearest brook. She had had no one to compare herself with or to be made ashamed or timid by. She knew only her own heart and Tom's love, and she smiled as radiantly into the lighting face before her as she would have smiled at a rose, or at a young deer she had met in the woods. No one had ever looked at her in this way before, but being herself a thing which had grown like a flower, she felt no shyness, and was only glad. Eve might have smiled at Adam so in their first hours.

Big Tom, sitting between them, saw it all. A man cannot live a score of years and more, utterly cut off from the life of the world, without having many a long hour for thought in which he will inevitably find himself turning over the problems which fill the life he has missed. Tom De Willoughby had had many of them. He had had no one to talk to whose mind could have worked with his own. On winter nights, when Sheba had been asleep, he had found himself gazing into the red embers of his wood fire and pondering on the existence he might have led if fate had been good to him.

"There must be happiness on the earth somewhere," he would say. " Somewhere there ought to have been a woman I belonged to, and who belonged to me. It ought all to have been as much nature as the rain falling and the corn ripening in the sun. If we had met when we were young things—on the very brink of it all—and smiled into each other's eyes and taken each other's hands, and kissed each other's lips, we might have ripened together like the corn. What is it that's gone wrong?" All the warm normal affections of manhood, which might have remained undeveloped and been cast away, had been lavished on the child Sheba. She had represented his domestic circle.

"You mayn't know it, Sheba," he had said once to her, "but you're a pretty numerous young person. You're a man's wife and family, and mother and sisters, and at least half a dozen boys and girls."

All his thoughts had concentrated themselves upon her—all his psychological problems had held her as their centre, all his ethical reasonings had applied themselves to her.

" She's got to be happy," he said to himself, " and she's got to be strong enough to stand up under unhappiness, if —if I should be taken away from her. When the great thing that's—that's the meaning of it all—and the reason of it—comes into her life, it ought to come as naturally as summer does. If her poor child of a mother—Good Lord! Good Lord! "

And here he sat in the moonlight, and Delia Vanuxem's son was looking at her with ardent, awakened young eyes.

How she listened as Rupert told his story, and how sweetly she was moved by the pathos of it. Once or twice she made an involuntary movement forward, as if she was drawn towards him, and uttered a lovely low exclamation which was a little like the broken coo of a dove. Rupert did not know that there was pathos in his relation. He made only a simple picture of things, but as he went on Tom saw all the effect of the hot little town left ruined and apathetic after the struggle of war, the desolateness of the big house empty but for its three rooms, its bare floors echoing to the sound of the lonely pair of feet, the garden grown into a neglected jungle, the slatternly negro girl in the kitchen singing wild camp-meeting hymns as she went about her careless work.

" It sounds so lonely," Sheba said, with tender mournfulness.

" That was what it was—lonely," Rupert answered. " It's been a different place since Matt came, but it has always been lonely. Uncle Tom," putting his hand on the big knee

near him, as impulsively as a child, " I love that old Matt—
I love him! "

" Ah, so do I! " burst forth Sheba. " Don't you, Uncle
Tom? " And she put her hand on the other knee.

Rupert looked down at the hand. It was so fair and soft
and full of the expression of sympathy—such an adorably
womanly little hand, that one's first impulse was to lay
one's own upon it. He made a movement and then remembered, and looked up, and their eyes met and rested on
each other gently.

When the subject of the claim was broached, Sheba
thought it like a fairy tale. She listened almost with bated
breath. As Rupert had not realised that he was pathetic
in the relation of the first part of his story, so he did not
know that he was picturesque in this. But his material had
strong colour. The old man on the brink of splendid fortune, the strange, unforeseen national disaster sweeping all
before it and leaving only poverty and ruin, the untouched
wealth of the mines lying beneath the earth on which battles
had been fought—all the possibilities the future might hold
for one penniless boy—these things were full of suggestion
and excitement.

" You would be rich," said Sheba.

" So would Uncle Tom," Rupert answered, smiling; " and
you, too."

Tom had been listening with a reflective look on his face.
He tilted his chair back and ran his hand through his hair.

" At all events, we couldn't *lose* money if we didn't gain
any," he said. " That's where we're safe. When a man's
got to the place where he hasn't anything to lose, he can
afford to take chances. Perhaps it's worth thinking over.
Let's go to bed, children. It's midnight."

In Connection with
The De Willoughby Claim

When they said good-night to each other, the two young hands clung together kindly and Sheba looked up with sympathetic eyes.

"Would you like to be very rich?" she asked.

"To-night I am rich," he answered. "That is because you and Uncle Tom have made me feel as if I belonged to someone. It is so long since I have seemed to belong to anyone."

"But now you belong to us," said Sheba.

He stood silently looking down at her a moment.

"Your eyes look just as they did when you were a little child," he said. He lifted her hand and pressed his warm young lips to it.

CHAPTER XXII

HE awoke the next morning with a glow in his heart which should not be new to youth, but was new to him. He remembered feeling something rather like it years before when he had been a little boy and had wakened on the morning of his birthday and found his mother kissing him and his bed strewn with gifts.

He went downstairs and, strolling on to the porch, saw Sheba in the garden. As he went to join her, he found himself in the midst of familiar paths and growths.

"Why," he exclaimed, stopping before her, "it is the old garden!"

"Yes," Sheba answered; "Uncle Tom made it like this because he loved the other one. You and I have played in the same garden. Good-morning," laughing.

"Good-morning," he said. "It is a good-morning. I —somehow I have been thinking that when I woke I felt as I used to do when I was a child and woke on my birthday."

That morning she showed him her domain. To the imaginative boy she led with her, she seemed like a strange young princess, to whom all the land belonged. She loved it so and knew so well all it yielded. She showed him the cool woods where she always found the first spring flowers, the chestnut and walnut trees where she and Tom gathered their winter supply of nuts, the places where the wild grapes grew thickest, and those where the ground was purple-carpeted with violets.

They wandered on together until they reached a hollow

in the road, on one side of which a pine wood sloped up a hillside, looking dark and cool.

"I come here very often," she said, quite simply. "My mother is here."

Then he saw that a little distance above the road a deserted log cabin stood, and not far from it two or three pine trees had been cut down so that the sun could shine on a mound over and about which flowers grew. It was like a little garden in the midst of the silent wildness.

He followed her to the pretty spot, and she knelt down by it and removed a leaf or a dead flower here and there. The little mound was a snowy mass of white blossoms standing thick together, and for a yard or so about the earth was starred with the same flowers.

"You see," she said, "Uncle Tom and I plant new flowers for every month. Everything is always white. Sometimes it is all lilies of the valley or white hyacinths, and then it is white roses, and in the autumn white chrysanthemums. Uncle Tom thought of it when I was a little child, and we have done it together ever since. We think she knows."

She stopped, and, still kneeling, looked at him as if suddenly remembering something.

"You have not heard," she said; "she died when I was born, and we do not even know her name."

"Not her name!" Rupert said; but the truth was that he had heard more of the story than she had.

"My father was so stunned with grief, that Uncle Tom said he seemed to think of nothing but that he could not bear to stay. He went away the very night they laid her here. I suppose," she said slowly, and looking at the mass of white narcissus instead of at him, "I suppose when people love each other, and one dies, the other cannot—cannot——"

Rupert saw that she was unconsciously trying to explain something to herself, and he interposed between her and her thoughts with a hurried effort.

" Yes, yes," he said; " it must be so. When they love each other and one is taken, how *can* the other bear it? "

Then she lifted her eyes from the flowers to his again, and they looked very large and bright.

" You see," she said, in an unsteady little voice, " I had only been alive a few hours when he went away."

Suddenly the brightness in her eyes welled up and fell in two large crystal drops, though a smile quivered on her lips.

" Don't tell Uncle Tom," she said; " I never let him know that it—it hurts my feelings when I think I had only been alive such a few hours—and there was nobody to care. I must have been so little. If—if there had been no Uncle Tom——"

He knelt down by her side and took her hand in his.

" But there was," he said; " there was! "

" Yes," she answered, her sweet face trembling with emotion; " and, oh! I love him so! I love him so! "

She put her free hand on the earth among the white flowers on the mound.

" And I love her, too," she said; " somehow I know *she* would not have forgotten me."

" No, no, she would not! " Rupert cried; and they knelt together, hand in hand, looking into each other's eyes as tenderly as children.

" I have been lonelier than you," he said; " I have had nobody."

" Your mother died, too, when you were very young? "

" Yes, Sheba," hesitating a moment. " I will tell you something."

"Yes?"

"Uncle Tom loved her. He left his home partly because he could not stay and see her marry a man who—did not deserve her."

"Did she marry someone like that?" she asked.

His forehead flushed.

"She married my father," he said, "and he was a drunken maniac and broke her heart. I saw it break. When I first remember her, she was a lovely young girl with eyes like a gazelle's—and she cried all their beauty away, and grew tired and old and haggard before I was twelve. He is dead, but I hate him!"

"Oh!" she said; "you have been lonely!"

"I have been something worse than that!" he answered, and the gloom came back to his face. "I have been afraid."

"Afraid!" said Sheba. "Of what?"

"That I might end like him. How do I know? It is in my blood."

"Oh, no!" she cried.

"We have nearly all been like that," he said. "He was the maddest of them all, but he was only like many of the others. We grow tall, we De Willoughbys, we have black eyes, we drink and we make ourselves insane with morphine. It's a ghastly thing to think of," he shuddered. "When I am lonely, I think of it night and day."

"You must not," she said. "I—I will help you to forget it."

"I have often wondered if there was anyone who could," he answered. "I think perhaps you might."

When they returned to the Cross-roads there were several customers loitering on the post-office porch, awaiting their arrival, and endeavouring to wear an air of concealing no object whatever. The uneventful lives they led year after year made men and women alike avid for anything of the nature of news or incident. In some mysterious way the air itself seemed to communicate to them anything of interest which might be impending. Big Tom had not felt inclined to be diffuse on the subject of the arrival of his nephew, but each customer who brought in a pail of butter or eggs, a roll of jeans or a pair of chickens, seemed to become enlightened at once as to the position of affairs.

" Ye see," Tom heard Doty confiding to a friend as they sat together outside a window of the store; " ye see, it's this way—the D'Willerbys was born 'ristycrats. I dunno as ye'd think it to look at Tom. Thar's a heap *to* Tom, but he ain't *my* idee of a 'ristycrat. My idee is thet mebbe he let out from D'lisleville kase he warn't 'ristycratic enough fur 'em. Thar wus a heap of property in the family, 'pears like. An' now the hull lot of 'em's dead 'cept this yere boy that come last night. Stamps hes seen him in D'lisleville, an' he says he's a-stavin' lookin' young feller, an' thet thar's somethin' about a claim on the Guv'ment thet ef Tom an' him don't foller up, they're blamed fools. Now Tom, he ain't no blamed fool. Fur *not* bein' a blamed fool, I'll back Tom agin any man in Hamlin."

So, when the two young figures were seen sauntering along the road towards the store, there were lookers-on enough to regard them with interest.

" Now *he's* my idee of a 'ristycrat," remarked Mr. Doty, with the manner of a connoisseur. " Kinder tall an' slim, an' high-sperrity lookin'; Sheby's a gal, but she's got it too —thet thar sorter racehorse look. Now, hain't she?"

" I want you to see the store and the people in it," Sheba was saying. " It's my home, you know. Uncle Tom took me there the day after I was born. I used to play on the floor behind the counter and near the stove, and all those men are my friends."

Rupert had never before liked anything so much as he liked the simple lovingness of this life of hers. As she knew the mountains, the flowers, and the trees, she knew and seemed known by the very cows and horses and people she saw.

"That's John Hutton's old gray horse," she had said as she caught sight of one rider in the distance. "That is Billy Neil's yoke of oxen," at another time. "Good-morning, Mrs. Stebbins," she called out, with the prettiest possible cheer, to a woman in an orange cotton skirt as she passed on the road. "It seems to me sometimes," she said to Rupert, "as if I belonged to a family that was scattered over miles and lived in scores of houses. They all used to tell Uncle Tom what would disagree with me when I was cutting my teeth."

They mounted the steps of the porch, laughing the light, easy laugh of youth, and the loiterers regarded them with undisguised interest and admiration. In her pink cotton frock, and blooming like a rose in the shade of her frilled pink sunbonnet, Sheba was fair to see. Rupert presented an aspect which was admirably contrasting. His cool pallor and dense darkness of eyes and hair seemed a delightful background to her young tints of bloom.

"Thet thar white linen suit o' his'n," Mr. Doty said, "might hev been put on a-purpose to kinder set off her looks as well as his'n."

It was to Mr. Doty Sheba went first.

"Jake," she said, "this is my cousin Mr. Rupert De Willoughby from Delisleville."

"Mighty glad to be made 'quainted, sir," said Jake. "Tom's mightily sot up at yer comin'."

They all crowded about him and went through the same ceremony. It could scarcely be called a ceremony, it was such a simple and actually affectionate performance. It was so plain that his young good looks and friendly grace of manner reached their hearts at once, and that they were glad that he had come.

"They *are* glad you have come," Sheba said afterwards. "You are from the world over there, you know," waving her hand towards the blue of the mountains. "We are all glad when we see anything from the outside."

"Would you like to go there?" Rupert asked.

"Yes," she answered, with a little nod of her head. "If Uncle Tom will go—and you."

They spent almost an hour in the store holding a sort of *levée*. Every new-comer bade the young fellow welcome and seemed to accept him as a sort of boon.

"He's a mighty good-lookin' young feller," they all said, and the women added: "Them black eyes o' his'n an' the way his hair kinks is mighty purty."

"Their feelings will be hurt if you don't stay a little," said Sheba. "They want to look at you. You don't mind it, do you?"

"No," he answered, laughing; "it delights me. No one ever wanted to look at me before. But I should hardly think they would want to look at me when they might look at you instead."

"They have looked at me for eighteen years," she answered. "They looked at me when I had the measles, and saw me turn purple when I had the whooping-cough."

As they were going away, they passed a little man who

had just arrived and was hitching to the horse-rail a raw-boned "clay-bank" mare. He looked up as they neared him and smiled peacefully.

"Howdy?" he said to Rupert. "Ye hain't seen me afore, but I seen you when I was to Delisleville. It wuz me as told yer nigger ye'd be a fool if ye didn't get Tom ter help yer to look up thet thar claim. Ye showed horse sense by comin'. Wish ye luck."

"Uncle Tom," said Sheba, as they sat at their dinner and Mornin walked backwards and forwards from the kitchen stove to the dining-room with chicken fried in cream, hot biscuits, and baked yams, "we saw Mr. Stamps and he wished us luck."

"He has a claim himself, hasn't he?" said Rupert. "He told Matt it was for a yoke of oxen."

Tom broke into a melodious roar of laughter.

"Well," he said, "if we can do as well by ours as Stamps will do by his, we shall be in luck. That yoke of oxen has grown from a small beginning. If it thrives as it goes on, the Government's in for a big thing."

"It has grown from a calf," said Sheba, "and it wasn't six weeks old."

"A Government mule kicked it and broke its leg," said Tom. "Stamps made veal of it, and in two months it was 'Thet heifer o' mine'—in six months it was a young steer——"

"Now it's a yoke of oxen," said Rupert; "and they were the pride of the county."

"Lord! Lord!" said Tom, "the United States has got something to engineer."

CHAPTER XXIII

It was doubtless Stamps who explained the value of the De Willoughby claim to the Cross-roads. Excited interest in it mounted to fever heat in a few days. The hitching rail was put to such active use that the horses shouldered each other and occasionally bit and kicked and enlivened the air with squeals. No one who had an opportunity neglected to appear at the post-office, that he or she might hear the news. Judge De Willoughby's wealth and possessions increased each time they were mentioned. The old De Willoughby place became a sort of princely domain, the good looks of the Judge's sons and daughters and the splendour of their gifts were spoken of almost with bated breath. The coal mines became gold mines, the money invested in them something scarcely to be calculated. The Government at Washington, it was even inferred, had not money enough in its treasury to refund what had been lost and indemnify for the injury done.

"And to think o' Tom settin' gassin' yere with us fellers," they said, admiringly, " jest same es if he warn't nothin'. A-settin' in his shirt sleeves an' tradin' fer eggs an' butter. Why, ef he puts thet thar claim through, he kin buy up Hamlin."

"I'd like ter see the way he'd fix up Sheby," said Mis' Doty. " He'd hev her dressed in silks an' satins—an' diamond earrings soon as look."

" Ye'll hev to go ter Washin'ton City sure enough, Tom," was the remark made oftenest. " When do ye 'low to start? "

In Connection with
The De Willoughby Claim

But Tom was not as intoxicated by the prospect as the rest of them. His demeanour was thoughtful and unexhilarated.

" Whar do ye 'low to build yer house when ye come into yer money, Tom? " he was asked, gravely. " Shall ye hev a cupoly? Whar'll ye buy yer land? "

The instinct of Hamlin County tended towards expressing any sense of opulence by increasing the size of the house it lived in, or by building a new one, and invariably by purchasing land. Nobody had ever become rich in the neighbourhood, but no imagination would have found it possible to extend its efforts beyond a certain distance from the Crossroads. The point of view was wholly primitive and patriarchal.

Big Tom was conscious that he had become primitive and patriarchal also, though the truth was that he had always been primitive.

As he sat on the embowered porch of his house in the evening and thought things over, while the two young voices murmured near him, his reflections were not greatly joyful. The years he had spent closed in by the mountains and surrounded by his simple neighbours had been full of peace. Since Sheba had belonged to him they had even held more than peace. The end had been that the lonely unhappiness of his youth had seemed a thing so far away that it was rather like a dream. Only Delia Vanuxem was not quite like a dream. Her pitying girlish face and the liquid darkness of her uplifted eyes always came back to him clearly when he called them up in thought. He called them up often during these days in which he was pondering as to what it was best to decide to do.

" It's the boy who brings her back so," he told himself.

In Connection with
The De Willoughby Claim

"Good Lord, how near she seems! The grass has been growing over her for many a year, and I'm an old fellow, but she looks just as she did then."

The world beyond the mountains did not allure him. It was easier to sit and see the sun rise and set within the purple boundary than to face life where it was less simple, and perhaps less kindly. It was from a much less advanced and concentrated civilisation he had fled in his youth, and the years which had passed had not made him more fitted to combat with what was more complex.

"Trading for butter and eggs over the counter of a country store, and discussing Doty's corn crop and Hayworth's pigs hasn't done anything particular towards fitting me to shine in society," he said. "It suits *me* well enough, but it's not what's wanted at a ball or a cabinet minister's reception." And he shook his head. "I'd rather stay where I am—a darned sight."

But the murmuring voices went on near him, and little bursts of laughter rang out, or two figures wandered about the garden, and his thoughts always came back to one point —a point where the sun seemed to shine on things and surround them with a dazzling radiance.

"Yes, it's all very well for *me*," he concluded more than once. "It's well enough for *me* to sit down and spend the rest of my life looking at the mountains and watching summer change into winter; but they are only beginning it all —just beginning."

So one night he left his chair and went out and walked between them in the moonlight, a hand resting on a shoulder of each.

"See," he said, "I want you two to help me to make up my mind."

"About going away?" asked Rupert, looking round at him quickly.

"Yes. Do you know we may have a pretty hard time? We've no money. We should have to live scant enough, and, unless we had luck, we might come back here worse off than we left."

"But we should have tried, and we should have been on the other side of the mountains," said Sheba.

"So we should," said Tom, reflectively. "And there's a good deal in seeing the other side of the mountains when people are young."

Sheba put her hand on his and looked at him with a glowing face.

"Uncle Tom," she said, "oh, let us go!"

"Uncle Tom," said Rupert, "I *must* go!"

The line showed itself between his black brows again, though it was not a frown. He put his hand in his pocket and held it out, open, with a solitary twenty-dollar bill lying in it.

"That's all I've got," he said, "and that's borrowed. If the claim is worth nothing, I must earn enough to pay it back. All right. We'll all three go," said Tom.

The next day he began to develop the plans he had been allowing to form vaguely as a background to his thoughts. They were not easy to carry out in the existing condition of general poverty. But at Lucasville, some forty miles distant, he was able to raise a mortgage on his land.

"If the worst comes to the worst," he said to Sheba, "after we have seen the other side of the mountains, do you think you could stand it to come back and live with me in the rooms behind the store?"

Sheba sat down upon his knee and put her arms round his neck, as she had done when she was ten years old.

In Connection with
The De Willoughby Claim

"I could live with you anywhere," she said. "The only thing I couldn't stand would be to have to live away from you."

Tom laughed and kissed her. He laughed that he might smother a sigh. Rupert was standing near and looking at her with the eyes that were so like Delia Vanuxem's.

CHAPTER XXIV

FOR an imaginative or an untravelled person to approach the city of Washington at sunrise on a radiant morning, is a thing far from unlikely to be remembered, since a white and majestic dome, rising about a white structure set high and supported by stately colonnades, the whole gleaming fair against a background of blue sky, forms a picture which does not easily melt away.

Those who reared this great temple of white stone and set it on a hilltop to rule and watch over the land, builded better than they knew. To the simple and ardent idealist its white stateliness must always suggest something symbolic, and, after all, it is the ardent and simple idealist whose dreams and symbols paint to prosaic human minds the beautiful impossibilities whose unattainable loveliness so allures as to force even the unexalted world into the endeavour to create such reproductions of their forms as crude living will allow.

Tom leaned against the side of the car window and watched the great dome with an air of curious reflection. Sheba and Rupert leaned forward and gazed at it with dreaming eyes.

" It looks as the capitol of a great republic ought to look," Rupert said. " Spotless and majestic, and as if it dominated all it looks down upon with pure laws and dignity and justice."

" Just so," said Tom.

In the various crises of political excitement in Hamlin

274

In Connection with
The De Willoughby Claim

County he had taken the part of an unbiassed but humorous observer, and in that character had gained much experience of a primitive kind. What he had been led chiefly to remark in connection with the " great republic " was that the majesty and spotlessness of its intentions were not invariably realised by mere human units.

" Well," he said, as he took down his valise from the rack, " we're coming in here pretty well fixed for leaving the place millionaires. If we had only fifteen cents in our pockets, it would be a dead sure thing, according to all the biographers *I* ever read. The only thing against us is that we have a little more—but it's not enough to spoil our luck, that I'll swear."

He was not without reason in the statement. Few voyagers on the ocean of chance could have dared the journey with less than they had in their possession.

" What we've got to do," he had said to Rupert, " is to take care of Sheba. We two can rough it."

They walked through the awakening city, finding it strange and bare with its broad avenues and streets ill-paved, bearing traces everywhere of the tragedy of war through which it had passed. The public buildings alone had dignity; for the rest, it wore a singularly provincial and uncompleted aspect; its plan was simple and splendid in its vistas and noble spaces, but the houses were irregular and without beauty of form; negro shanties huddled against some of the most respectable, and there were few whose windows or doors did not announce that board and lodging might be obtained within. There was no look of well-being or wealth anywhere; the few equipages in the streets had seen hard service; the people who walked were either plainly dressed or shabby genteel; about the doors of the principal hotels there were groups of men who wore, most of them, dispirited or anxious faces. Ten years later the whole aspect of the place was changing, but at this time it was passing through a period of natural fatigue and poverty, and was not an inspiring spectacle to penniless new-comers.

"It reminds me a little of Delisleville, after all," said Rupert.

Beyond the more frequented quarters of the town, they found broad, unkempt, and as yet unlevelled avenues and streets, where modest houses straggled, perched on high banks with an air of having found themselves there quite by accident. The banks were usually grass-covered, and the white picket fences enclosed bits of ground where scant fruit-trees and disorderly bushes grew; almost every house possessed a porch, and almost every porch was scrambled over by an untidy honeysuckle or climbing rose which did its best to clothe with some grace the dilapidated woodwork and the peeled and blistered paint.

Before one of these houses Tom stopped to look at a lop-sided sign in the little garden, which announced that rooms were to be rented within.

"Perhaps we can find something here," he said, "that may suit the first ventures of millionaires. It's the sort of thing that will appeal to the newspaper man who writes the thing up; 'First home of the De Willoughbys when they arrived in Washington to look up their claim.' It'll make a good woodcut to contrast with 'The great De Willoughby mansion in Fifth Avenue. Cost five hundred thousand!'"

They mounted the wooden steps built into the bank and knocked at the door. Rupert and Sheba exchanged glances with a little thrill. They were young enough to feel a sort of excitement even in taking this first modest step.

A lady with a gentle, sallow face and a faded black cotton gown, opened the door. Her hair hung in depressed but genteel ringlets on each side of her countenance; at the back it formed a scant coil upheld by a comb. Tom thought he observed a gleam of hope in her eye when she saw them. She spoke with the accent of Virginia.

" Yes, suh, we have rooms disengaged. Won't you come in? " she said.

She led them into a neat but rather painful little parlour. The walls were decorated with photographs of deceased relatives in oval frames, and encased in glass there was a floral wreath made of hair of different shades and one of white, waxen-looking flowers, with a vaguely mortuary suggestion in their arrangement. There was a basket of wax fruit under a shade on the centre table, a silver ice-water pitcher on a salver, and two photograph albums whose binding had become loosened by much handling. There was also a book with a red and gold cover, bearing in ornate letters the title " Life of General Robert Lee."

" The rooms are not lawge," the lady said, " but they are furnished with the things I brought from my fawther's house in Virginia. My fawther was Judge Burford, of the Burford family of England. There's a Lord Burford in England, we always heard. It is a very old family."

She looked as if she found a vague comfort in the statement, and Tom did not begrudge it to her. She looked very worn and anxious, and he felt it almost possible that during the last few months she might not always have had quite enough to eat.

" I never thawt in the days when I was Judge Burford's

dawtah of Burfordsville," she explained, "that I should come to Washington to take boarders. There was a time when it was thawt in Virginia that Judge Burford might reach the White House if he would allow himself to be nominated. It's a great change of circumstances. Did you want board with the rooms?"

"Well——" began Tom.

She interrupted him in some little hurry.

"I'm afraid it wouldn't be convenient for me to board anyone," she said; "I've not been accustomed to providing for boarders, and I'm not conveniently situated. If—if you preferred to economize——"

"We do," said Tom. "We have come to look up a claim, and people on that business are pretty safe to have to economize, I've been told!"

"Ah, a claim!" she ejaculated, with combined interest and reverence. "Indeed, you are quite right about its being necessary to economize. Might I enqu'ah if it is a large one?"

"I believe it is," Tom answered; "and it's not likely to be put through in a month, and we have not money enough to keep us in luxury for much more. Probably we shall be able to make it last longer if we take rooms and buy our own food."

"I'm sure you would, suh," she answered, with a little eager flush on her cheek. "When people provide for themselves, they can sometimes do without—things." She added the last word hurriedly and gave a little cough which sounded nervous.

It was finally agreed that they should take three little rooms she showed them, in one of which there was a tiny stove, upon which they could prepare such simple food as they could provide themselves with. The arrangement was not a luxurious one, but it proved to be peculiarly suitable to the owners of the great De Willoughby claim.

As they had not broken fast, Tom went out to explore the neighbourhood in search of food. He thought he remembered having seen in a side street a little store. When he returned, after some wanderings, a wood fire was crackling in the stove and Sheba had taken off her hat and put on a white apron.

"Hello!" exclaimed Tom.

"I borrowed it from Miss Burford," she said. "I went down to see her. She let us have the wood, too. Rupert made the fire."

She took the paper bags from Tom's hands and stood on tiptoe to kiss him, smiling sweetly at his rather troubled face.

"All my life you have been doing things for me. Now it is my turn," she said. "I have watched Mornin ever since I was born. I am going to be your servant."

In an hour from the time they had taken possession of their quarters, they were sitting at a little table before an open window, making a breakfast of coffee and eggs. Sheba was presiding, and both men were looking at her flushed cheeks adoringly.

"Is the coffee good, Uncle Tom?" she said. "Just tell me it is good."

"Well," said Tom, "for the first effort of a millionairess, I should say it was."

CHAPTER XXV

THE year before this Judge Rutherford had been sent to Congress by the Republican Party of Hamlin County. His election had been a wildly exciting and triumphant one. Such fiery eloquence as his supporters displayed had rarely, if ever, been poured forth before. It was proved by each orator that the return of the Democratic candidate would plunge the whole country into the renewal of bloodshed and war. This catastrophe having been avoided by the Judge's election, the nation—as represented by Hamlin County— had settled down with prospects of peace, prosperity, and the righting of all old grievances. The Judge bought a new and shining valise, a new and shining suit of broadcloth, and a silk hat equally shining and new, and went triumph- antly to Washington, the sole drawback to his exultation being that he was obliged to leave Jenny behind him with the piano, the parlour furniture, and the children.

"But he'll hev ye thar in the White House, ef ye give him time," said an ardent constituent who called to con- gratulate.

There seemed no end to a political career begun under such auspices but the executive mansion itself. The confi- dence of the rural communities in their representatives was great and respectful. It was believed that upon their arrival at the capital, business in both Houses was temporarily post- poned until it had been supported by their expression of opinion and approval. It was believed also that the luxury and splendour of a Congressman's life was such as ancient Rome itself might have paled before and envied.

" A man in Washin'ton city with a Congristman's wages has got to be a purty level-headed feller not to get into high-falutin' ways of livin' an' throwin' money about. He's got to keep in his mind that this yere's a republic an' not a 'ristycratic, despotic monarchy."

This was a sentiment often expressed, and Tom De Willoughby himself had had vaguely respectful views of the circumstances and possible surroundings of a representative of his country.

But when he made his first visit to Judge Rutherford, he did not find him installed in a palatial hotel and surrounded by pampered menials. He was sitting in a back room in a boarding-house—a room which contained a folding bedstead and a stove. He sat in a chair which was tilted on its hind legs, and his feet rested on the stove's ornamental iron top. He had just finished reading a newspaper which lay on the floor beside him, and his hands were thrust into his pockets. He looked somewhat depressed in spirits.

When Tom was ushered into the room, the Judge looked round at him, uttered a shout of joy, and sprang to his feet.

" Tom," he cried out, falling upon him and shaking his hand rather as if he would not object to shaking it off and retaining it as an agreeable object forever. " Tom! Old Tom! Jupiter, Tom! I don't know how you got here or where you came from, but—Jupiter! I'm glad to see you."

He went on shaking his hand as he dragged him across the room and pushed him into a dingy armchair by the window; and when he had got him there, he stood over him grasping his shoulder, shaking his hand still. Tom saw that his chin was actually twitching in a curious way which made his goatee move unsteadily.

"The legislation of your country hasn't made you forget home folks, has it?" said Tom.

"Forget 'em!" exclaimed the Judge, throwing himself into a seat opposite and leaning forward excitedly with his hands on his knees. "I never remembered anything in my life as I remember them. They're never out of my mind, night or day. I've got into a way of dreaming I'm back to Barnesville, talking to the boys at the post-office, or listening to Jenny playing 'Home, Sweet Home' or 'The Maiden's Prayer.' I was a bit down yesterday and couldn't eat, and in the night there I was in the little dining-room, putting away fried chicken and hot biscuits as fast as the nigger girl could bring the dishes on the table. Good Lord! how good they were! There's nothing like them in Washington city," he added, and he heaved a big sigh.

"Why, man," said Tom, "you're home-sick!"

The Judge heaved another sigh, thrusting his hands deeper into his pockets and looking out of the window.

"Yes, by Jingo!" he said; "that's what I am."

He withdrew his gaze from the world outside the window and returned to Tom.

"You see," he said, "I've lived different. When a man has been born and brought up among the mountains and lived a country life among folks that are all neighbours and have neighbourly ways, city life strikes him hard. Politics look different here; they *are* different. They're not of the neighbourly kind. Politicians ain't joking each other and having a good time. They don't know anything about the other man, and they don't care a damn. What's Hamlin County to them? Why, they don't know anything *about*

In Connection with
The De Willoughby Claim

Hamlin County, and, as far as I've got, they don't want to. They've got their own precincts to attend to, and they're going to do it. When a new man comes in, if he ain't a pretty big fellow that knows how to engineer things and say things to make them listen to him, he's only another greenhorn. Now, I'm not a big fellow, Tom; I've found that out! and the first two months after I came, blamed if I wasn't so home-sick and discouraged that if it hadn't been for seeming to go back on the boys, durned if I don't believe I should have gone home."

Big Tom sat and regarded his honest face thoughtfully.

"Perhaps you're a bigger man than you know," he said. "Perhaps you'll find that out in time, and perhaps other people will."

The Judge shook his head.

"I've not got education enough," he said. "And I'm not an orator. All there is to *me* is that I'm not going back on the boys and Hamlin. I came here to do the square thing by them and the United States, and blamed if I ain't going to do it as well as I know how."

"Now, look here," said Big Tom, "that's pretty good politics to start with. If every man that came here came to stand by his party—*and* the United States—and do the square thing by them, the republic would be pretty safe, if they couldn't do another durned thing."

The Judge rubbed his already rather rough head and seemed to cheer up a little.

"Do you think so?" he said.

Big Tom stood up and gave him a slap on his shoulder.

"Think so?" he exclaimed, in his great, cheerful voice. I'm a greenhorn myself, but, good Lord! I *know* it. Making laws for a few million people is a pretty big scheme, and it's the fellows who intend to do the square thing who are going to put it through. This isn't ancient Greece, or Sparta, but it's my impression that the men who planned and wrote the Constitution, and did the thinking and orating in those days, had a sort of idea of building up a thing just as ornamental and good to write history about as either one; and, what's more, they counted on just such fellows as you to go on carrying the stones and laying them plumb, long after they were gone."

"Jupiter, Tom!" the Judge said, with something actually like elation in his voice, "it's good to hear you. It brings old Hamlin back and gaves a man sand. You're an orator, yourself."

"Am I?" said Tom. "No one ever called my attention to it before. If it's true, perhaps it'll come in useful."

"Now, just think of me sitting here gassing," exclaimed the Judge, "and never asking what you are here for. What's your errand, Tom?"

"Perhaps I'm here to defraud the Government," Tom answered, sitting down again; "or perhaps I've got a fair claim against it. That's what I've come to Washington to find out—with the other claimant."

"A claim!" cried the Judge. "And you've left the Cross-roads—and Sheba?"

"Sheba and the other claimant are in some little rooms we've taken out near Dupont Circle. The other claimant is the only De Willoughby left beside myself, and he is a youngster of twenty-three. He's my brother De Courcy's son."

The Judge glowed with interest. He heard the whole story, and his excitement grew as he listened. The elements of the picturesque in the situation appealed to him greatly.

In Connection with
The De Willoughby Claim

The curiously composite mind of the American contains a strong element of the romantic. In its most mercantile forms it is attracted by the dramatic; when it hails from the wilds, it is drawn by it as a child is drawn by colour and light.

"It's a big thing," the Judge ejaculated at intervals. "When I see you sitting there, Tom, just as you used to sit in your chair on the store-porch, it seems as if it could hardly be you that's talking. Why, man, it'll mean a million!"

"If I get money enough to set the mines at work," said Tom, "it may mean more millions than one."

The dingy square room, with its worn carpet, its turned-up bedstead, shabby chairs, and iron stove, temporarily assumed a new aspect. That its walls should contain this fairy tale of possible wealth and power and magnificence made it seem quite soberly respectable, and that Big Tom, sitting in the second-hand looking armchair, which creaked beneath his weight, should, in matter-of-fact tones, be relating such a story, made Judge Rutherford regard him with a kind of reverent trouble.

"Sheba, now," he said, "Sheba may be one of the biggest heiresses in the States. Lord! what luck it was for her that fellow left her behind!"

"It was luck for me," said Tom. And a faint, contemplative grin showed itself on his countenance. He was thinking, as he often did, of the afternoon when he returned from Blair's Hollow and opened the door of the room behind the store to find the wooden cradle stranded like a small ark in the corner.

CHAPTER XXVI

NATURALLY Judge Rutherford gravitated towards the little house near Dupont Circle. The first night he mounted the stairs and found himself in the small room confronting the primitive supper he had been invited to share with big Tom and his family, his honest countenance assumed a cheerfulness long a stranger to it.

The room looked such a simple, homely place, with its Virginia made carpet, its neat, scant furnishing, and its table set with the plain little meal. The Judge's homesick heart expanded within him.

He shook hands with Tom with fervour. Rupert he greeted with friendly affection. Sheba—on her entering the room with a plate of hot biscuits which she had been baking in Miss Burford's stove—he almost kissed.

"Now this is something like," he said. "I didn't know there was anything so like Barnesville in all Washington city. And there wasn't till you people brought it. I don't know what it is, but, by thunder, it does a man's heart good."

He sat down with the unconventional air of ease he wore in Barnesville when he established himself in one of Jenny's parlour chairs for the evening.

"Lord, Lord!" he said; "you're home folks, and you've got home ways, that's what it is. A month in one of these fashionable hotels would just about kill me. Having to order things written out on a card and eat 'em with a hundred folks looking on—there's no comfort in it. Give me

In Connection with
The De Willoughby Claim

a place where you can all sit up together round the table and smell the good hot coffee and biscuit cooking and the ham and chicken being fried in the kitchen."

Sheba had cooked the supper in Miss Burford's kitchen. Her hot biscuits and coffee were made after Mornin's most respected recipes, and her housewifely air was tenderly anxious.

"If it is not very good, Judge Rutherford," she said, standing shyly at the head of the table before she took her place, "it is because I am only learning."

"You have learned, Sheba," said the Judge, looking at the plate of light golden brown and cream white biscuit with the sensitive eye of a connoisseur. "That plate of biscuit is Barnesville and Sophrony all over."

Sheba blushed with joy.

"Oh, Uncle Tom," she said; "do you think it is? I should so like to remind him of Barnesville."

"Good Lord!" said the Judge. "Fact is, you've made me feel already as if Tom Scott might break out yelling in the back yard any minute."

After the supper was over and the table clear the party of four sat down to talk business and make plans. The entire inexperience of the claimants was an obstacle in their path, but Judge Rutherford, though not greatly wiser than themselves, had means of gaining information which would be of value. As he looked over the papers and learned the details of the story, the good fellow's interest mounted to excitement. He rubbed his head and grew flushed and bright of eye.

"By Jupiter, Tom!" he exclaimed, "I believe I can be of some use to you—I swear I believe I can. I haven't had much experience, but I've seen something of this claim business, and if I set my wits to work I can find out from other fellows who know more. I'll—" After a moment's reflection. "I'll have a talk with Farquhar to-morrow. That's what I'll do. Great Scott!" in a beaming outburst, "if I could push it through for you, how pleased Jenny would be."

When he went away Tom accompanied him downstairs. Sheba and Rupert followed them, and all three found themselves lured out into the moonlit night to saunter with him a few yards down the light avenue, talking still about their fairy story. The Judge himself was as fascinated by it as if he had been a child.

"Why, it's such a good story to tell," he expatiated; "and there must be a great deal in that. I never heard a better story for gaining sympathy—that fine old Southern aristocrat standing by the Union in a red-hot secessionist town—actually persecuted on account of it. He *was* persecuted, wasn't he?" he enquired of Rupert.

"Well," Rupert answered, "everybody was furious at him, of course—all his friends. People who had known him all his life passed him in the street without speaking. He'd been very popular, and he felt it terribly. He never was the same man after it began. He was old, and his spirit gave way."

"Just so!" exclaimed the Judge, stopping upon the pavement, elated even to oratory by the picture presented. "Fine old Southern aristocrat—on the brink of magnificent fortune—property turned into money that he may realise it —war breaks out, ruins him—Spartan patriotism—one patriot in a town of rebels hated and condemned by everybody—but faithful to his country. Friends—*old* friends—refuse to recognise him. Fortune gone—friends lost—heart

broken." He snatched Tom's big hand and shook it enthusi-
astically. "Tom!" he said; "I'd like to make a speech to
the House about it myself. I believe they would listen to
me. How set up Jenny would be—how set up she'd be."

He left them all in a glow of enthusiasm; they could see
him gesticulating a little to himself as he walked down the
avenue in the moonlight.

"That's just like him," said Tom; "he'd rather please
Jenny than set the House of Representatives on fire. And
he'd undertake the whole thing—work to give a man a
fortune for mere neighbourliness. We were a neighbourly
lot in Hamlin, after all."

The Judge went home to his boarding-house and sat late
in his shabby armchair, his legs stretched out, his hands
clasped on the top of his rough head. He was thinking the
thing out, and as he thought it out his excitement grew.
Sometimes he unclasped his hands and rubbed his hair with
restless sigh; more than once he unconsciously sprang to
his feet, walked across the floor two or three times, and
then sat down again. He was not a sharp schemer, he had
not even reached the stage of sophistication which would
have suggested to him that sharp scheming might be a
necessary adjunct in the engineering of such matters as
Government claims. From any power or tendency to diplo-
matise he was as free as the illustrative bull in a china shop.
His bucolic trust in the simple justice and honest disinter-
estedness of the political representatives of his native land
(it being granted they were of the Republican party) might
have appeared a touching thing to a more astute and experienced person who had realised it to its limits. When
he rubbed his hair excitedly or sprang up to walk about,
these manifestations were indications, not of doubt or dis-

trust, but of elated motion. It was the emotional aspect
of the situation which delighted and disturbed him, the dramatic picturesqueness of it. Here was Tom—good old Tom
—all Hamlin knew Tom and his virtues and witticisms—
Lord! there wasn't a man in the county who didn't love
him—yes, *love* him. And here was Sheba that Tom had
been a father to. And what a handsome little creature
she'd grown into—and, but for Tom, the Lord knew what
would have become of her. And there was that story of
the De Willoughbys of Delisleville—handsome, aristocratic
lot, among the biggest bugs in the State—the fine old
Judge with his thousands of acres lying uncultivated, and
he paying his taxes on them through sheer patriarchal
pleasure in being a big landowner. For years the Government had benefited by his taxpaying, while he had
gained nothing. And then there was the accidental discovery of the splendid wealth hidden in the bowels of the earth
—and the old aristocrat's energy and enterprise. Why, if
the war had not brought ruin to him and he had carried
out his plans, the whole State would have been the richer
for his mines. Capital would have been drawn in, labour
would have been in demand—things would have developed
—outsiders would have bought land—new discoveries would
have been made—the wealth of the country's resources
would have opened up—the Government itself would have
benefited by the thing. And then the war had ruined all.
And yet the old Judge, overwhelmed with disaster as he
was, had stood by the Government and had been scorned
and deserted, and had died broken-hearted at the end,
and here were his sole descendants—good old Tom and his
little beauty of a protégée—(no, Sheba wasn't a descend-
ant, but somehow she counted), and this fine young De Wil-

loughby—all of them penniless. Why, the justice of the thing stared a man in the face; a claim like that *must* go through.

At this juncture of his thought Judge Rutherford was standing upright in the middle of his room. His hair was in high disorder and his countenance flushed. He struck his right fist hard against the palm of his left hand.

"Why, the whole thing's as straight as a string," he said. "It's got to go through. I'll go and see Farquhar to-morrow."

.   .   .   .

Farquhar was a cleverer man than the representative from Hamlin County. He had been returned several times by his constituents, and his life had been spent in localities more allied to effete civilization than was Barnesville. He knew his Washington and had an astute interest in the methods and characteristics of new members of Congress, particularly perhaps such as the rural districts loomed up behind as a background. Judge Rutherford he had observed at the outset of his brief career, in the days when he had first appeared in the House of Representatives in his new broadcloth with its new creases, and with the uneasy but conscientious expression in his eye.

"There's a good fellow, I should say," he had remarked to the member at the desk next to him. "Doesn't know what to do, exactly—isn't quite sure what he has come for—but means to accomplish it, whatsoever it may turn out to be, to the best of his ability. He'd be glad to make friends. He's used to neighbours and unceremonious intimacies."

He made friends with him himself and found the acquaintance of interest at times. The faithfully reproduced atmosphere of Barnesville had almost a literary colour. Occasionally, though not frequently, he encouraged delineation of Jenny and Tom Scott and Thacker and "the boys." He had even inhaled at a distance vague whiffs of Sophronia's waffles.

On the morning after the evening spent at Dupont Circle Judge Rutherford frankly buttonholed him in the lobby.

"Farquhar," he said, "I'm chock full of a story. It kept me awake half the night. I want to ask your advice about it. It's about a claim."

"You shouldn't have let it keep you awake," replied Farquhar. "Claims are not novel enough. It's my opinion that Washington is more than half populated just now with people who have come to present claims."

Judge Rutherford's countenance fell a little as the countenance of an enthusiast readily falls beneath the breath of non-enthusiasm.

"Well," he said, "I guess there are plenty of them—but there are not many like this. You never heard such a story. It would be worth listening to, even if you were in the humour to walk ten miles to kick a claim."

Farquhar laughed.

"I have been in them, Guv'nor," he said. "The atmosphere is heavy with carpet-baggers who all have a reason for being paid for something by the Government. There's one of them now—that little Hoosier hanging about the doorway. He's from North Carolina, and wants pay for a herd of cattle."

In the hall outside the lobby a little man stood gazing with pale small eyes intent upon the enchanted space within. He wore a suit of blue jeans evidently made in the domestic circle. He scanned each member of Congress who went in or out, and his expression was a combination of furtive eagerness and tentative appeal.

"I believe I've seen him before," remarked Judge Rutherford, "but I don't know him."

"He's been hanging about the place for weeks," said Farquhar. "He's always in the strangers' gallery when claims come up for discussion. He looks as if he'd be likely to get what he has come for, Hoosier as he is."

"I want to talk to you about the De Willoughbys," said Rutherford. "I can't rest until I've told someone about it. I want you to advise me what to do."

Farquhar allowed himself to be led away into a more secluded spot. He was not, it must be confessed, greatly interested, but he was well disposed towards the member from Hamlin and would listen. They sat down together in one of the rooms where such talk might be carried on, and the Judge forthwith plunged into his story.

It was, as his own instincts had told him, a good story. He was at once simple and ornate in the telling—simple in his broad directness, and ornate in his dramatic and emotional touches. He began with the picture of the De Willoughbys of Delisleville—the autocratic and aristocratic Judge, the two picturesque sons, and the big, unpicturesque one who disappeared from his native town to reappear in the mountains of North Carolina and live his primitive life there as the object of general adulation. He unconsciously made Big Tom the most picturesque figure of the lot. Long before he had finished sketching him, Farquhar—who had been looking out of the window—turned his face towards him. He began to feel himself repaid for his amiable if somewhat casual attention. He did not look out of the window again. The history of big Tom De Willoughby alone was worth hearing. Farquhar did not find it necessary to call Judge Rutherford's attention to the fact that Sheba and the mystery of Blair's Hollow were not to be regarded as evidence. He realised that they adorned the situation and seemed to prove things whether it was strictly true that they did so or not. The discovery of the coal, the fortunes and disasters of Judge de Willoughby, the obstinate loyalty abhorred and condemned of his neighbours, his loneliness and poverty and death—his wasted estates, the big, bare, empty house in which his sole known heir lived alone, were material to hold any man's attention, and, enlarged upon by the member from Hamlin, were effective indeed.

"Now," said the Judge, wiping his forehead when he had finished, " what do you think of that? Don't you think these people have a pretty strong claim?"

"That story sounds as if they had," answered Farquhar; "but the Government isn't eager to settle claims—and you never know what will be unearthed. If Judge De Willoughby had not been such a blatantly open old opposer of his neighbour's political opinions these people wouldn't have a shadow of a chance."

"By Jupiter!" exclaimed Rutherford, delightedly; "he was persecuted—persecuted."

"It was a good thing for his relatives," said Farquhar. "Did you say the people had come to Washington?"

"All three of them," answered the Judge, and this time his tone was exultant; "Tom, and Sheba, and Rupert. They've rented some little rooms out near Dupont Circle."

"I should like to be taken to see them," said Farquhar, reflectively. "I should like to have a look at Big Tom De Willoughby."

"Would you?" cried the Judge. "Why, nothing would

suit me better—or them either, for that matter. I'll take you any day you say—any day."

"It ain't the easiest thing in the world to put a claim through," said Farquhar. "It means plenty of hard knocks and hard work and anxiety. Do you know that?"

"I don't know anything about it," answered the Judge. "But I'm going to get this one through if there's a way of doing it."

"You'll be misunderstood and called names and slandered," said Farquhar, regarding his rugged, ingenuous face with some curiosity. "There may be people—even in Hamlin County—who won't believe you are not up to some big deal. What are you doing it for?"

"Why, for Tom and Sheba and Rupert," said the Judge, in an outburst of neighbourliness. "That's folks enough to do it for, ain't it? There's three of 'em—and I'd do it for ary one—as we say in Barnesville," in discreet correction of the colloquialism.

Farquhar laughed a little, and put a hand on his shoulder as they moved away together. "I believe you would," he said; "perhaps that sort of thing is commoner in Barnesville than in Washington. I believe you would. Take me to see the claimants to-morrow."

CHAPTER XXVII

WHEN Judge Rutherford piloted him up the broad, unpaved avenue towards the small house near Dupont Circle, the first objects which caught Farquhar's gaze were two young people standing among the unkempt rose and syringa bushes in the little front garden. The slim grace and bloom of their youth would have caught any eye. They were laughing happily, and the girl held a branch of rosy blossoms in her hand.

"Are they the claimants?" Farquhar enquired.

"One of them is," answered Rutherford. "But Sheba— Sheba counts somehow."

Sheba looked at the stranger with the soft gaze of deer-like eyes when he was presented to her. There was no shyness in her woodland smile.

"Judge Rutherford," she said, "Uncle Matt has come— Rupert's Matt, you know. We can't help laughing about it, but we can't help being happy."

The boyish Southern face at her side laughed and glowed. Matt represented to Rupert the Lares and Penates his emotional nature required and had been denied.

"If he were not such a practical creature," he said, "I might not know what to do with him. But he worked his way here by engaging himself for the journey as a sort of nurse to an invalid young man who wanted to join his family in Washington and was too weak to travel alone."

The further from romance the world drifts, the fairer

it becomes in its fagged eyes. So few stories unfold themselves sweetly from beginning to end that a first chapter is always more or less alluring, and as he marked the youth and beauty of those two and saw how their young eyes and smiles met in question and response at every thought, to Farquhar, who still retained the fragments of an imagination not wholly blighted by the House of Representatives, it seemed rather as if he had wandered into a world where young Cupid and Psyche still moved and breathed in human guise. As central figures of a government claim, the pair were exquisitely incongruous. Their youth was so radiant and untried, their bright good looks so bloomed, that the man looking at them felt—with a realising sense of humour as well as fanciful sentiment—as if a spring wind wafted through a wood close grown with wild daffodils had swept into a heated manufactory where machinery whirred and ill-clad workers bent over their toil.

"Uncle Tom will be very glad to see you," said Sheba, as they went into the house. "Judge Rutherford says you will tell us what to do."

An interesting feature of the situation to Farquhar was the entire frankness and simplicity of those concerned in it. It was so clear that they knew nothing of the complications they might be called upon to face, that their ignorance was of the order of charm. If he had been some sharper claimant come to fleece them, their visitor knew this young dryad's eyes would have smiled at him just as gratefully.

As they mounted the stairs, a huge laugh broke forth above, and when they entered the small sitting-room Uncle Matt stood before Big Tom, holding forth gravely, his gray wool bared, his decently shabby hat in his hand.

"I'd er come as lady's maid, Marse Thomas De Wil-

loughby," he was saying, " ef I couldn't er got here no other
way. Seemed like I jest got to honin' atter Marse Rupert,
an' I couldn't er stayed nohow. I gotter be whar dat boy
is—I jest *gotter*."

Big Tom, rising to his full height to shake hands with
his visitor, appeared physically to cast such disparagement
on the size of the room as was almost embarrassing. Farquhar saw all his values as he met his honest, humourous eye.

" I've been talking to my nephew's body-guard," he said.
" All right, Uncle Matt. You just go to Miss Burford and
ask her to find you a shake-down. There's always a place
to be found for a fellow like you."

" Marse Thomas De Willoughby," said Matt, " dish yer
niggah man's not gwine to be in no one's way. I come yere
to work—dat's what I come yere for. An' work's a thing
dat kin be hunted down—en a man ain't needin' no gun
to hunt it neder—an' he needn't be no mighty Nimrod."
And he made his best bow to both men and shuffled out of
the room.

To Farquhar his visit was an interesting experience and
a novel one. For months he had been feeling that he lived
in the whirl of a maelstrom of schemes and jobberies, the
inevitable result of the policy of a Government which had
promised to recoup those it had involuntarily wronged during a national convulsion. Upon every side there had sprung
up claimants—many an honest one, and hordes of those not
honest. There were obvious thieves and specious ones, brilliant tricksters and dull ones. Newspaper literature had been
incited by the number and variety of claims, and claims—
to a jocularity which spread over all the land. Farquhar
had seen most of the types—the greenhorn, the astute plan-
ner, the man who had a wrong burning in his breast, the

man who knew how to approach his subject and the man who did not, the man who buttonholed everybody and was diffuse and hopeful, and the man who was helpless before the task he had undertaken. He had never, however, seen anything like the De Willoughby claimants—big Tom telling his straightforward story with his unsanguine air, the attractive youngster adding detail with simple directness, and the girl, Sheba, her roe's eyes dilated with eager interest hanging upon their every word.

" It is one of the best stories I've heard," he said to Rutherford, on their way back. " But it's a big claim—it's a huge claim, and the Government is beginning to get restive."

" But don't you think they'll get it through?" exclaimed Judge Rutherford. " Ain't they *bound* to get it? It's the Lord's truth—every word they speak—the Lord's truth! "

" Yes," answered Farquhar, " that's how it struck me; but, as a rule, it isn't the Lord's truth that carries a big claim through."

He broke into a short laugh, as if at an inward realisation of the aspect of the situation.

" They are as straightforward as a lot of children," he said. " They have nothing to hide, and they wouldn't know how to hide it if they had. It would be rather a joke if——"
And he laughed again.

" If what? " asked Rutherford.

" Ah, well! if that very fact was the thing which carried them through," his laugh ending in a shrewd smile.

This carried the ingenuous mind of his companion beyond its depth.

" I don't see where the joke would come in," he said, rather ruefully. " I should have thought nothing else would do it for them."

Farquhar slapped him on the shoulder.

"So you would," he said. "That's why you are the best advocate they could have. You are all woven out of the same cloth. You stand by them—and so will I."

Judge Rutherford seized his hand and shook it with affectionately ardent pumpings.

"That's what I wanted to make sure of," he said. "I'm going to work at this thing, and I want a man to help me who knows the ropes. Lord, how I should like to go back to Hamlin and tell Jenny and the boys that I'd put Tom through."

And as they walked up the enclosed road to the Capitol he devoted himself to describing anew Big Tom's virtue, popularity, and witticisms.

. . . .

For weeks Talbot's Cross-roads found itself provided with a conversational topic of absorbing interest. Ethan Cronan, who had temporarily "taken on" the post-office and store, had no cause to fear that the old headquarters was in danger of losing popularity. The truth was that big Tom had so long presided over the daily gatherings that the new occupant of the premises was regarded merely as a sort of friendly representative. Being an amiable and unambitious soul, Ethan in fact regarded himself in the same light, and felt supported and indeed elevated by the fact that he stood in the shoes of a public character so universally popular and admired.

"I ain't Tom, an' I cayn't never come a-nigh him," he said; "but I kin do my best not to cast no disgrace on his place, an' allus tradin' as fair as I know how. It's a kinder honor to set in his chairs an' weigh sugar out in the scales he used—an' it drors trade too."

In Connection with
The De Willoughby Claim

During the passage of the first few weeks, horses, wag-gons, and ox-teams crowded about the hitching-posts, while excitement ran high at mail-time. The general opinion was that any post might bring the news that Congress was "sit-ting on" the great De Willoughby claim, and that Wash-ington waited breathless for its decision. That all other national business should be suspended seemed inevitable. That any mail should come and go without bringing some news was not contemplated. The riders of the horses and owners of the waggons sat upon the stone porch and dis-cussed probabilities. They told each other stories they had gathered of the bygone glories of the De Willoughbys, of the obstinate loyalty of the old Judge and the bitter indig-nation of his neighbours, and enlarged upon the strength of the claim this gave him to the consideration of the Government.

"Tom won't have no trouble with his claim," was the general opinion. "He'll just waltz it through. Thar won't be a hitch."

But after the first letter in which he announced his safe arrival in the Capital City, Tom wrote no more for a week or so, which caused a disappointment only ameliorated by the belief that he was engaged in "waltzing" the claim through. Each man felt it necessary to visit the Cross-roads every day to talk over the possible methods employed, and to make valuable suggestions. Interest never flagged, but it was greatly added to when it was known that Judge Ruth-erford had ranged himself on Tom's side.

"He's the pop-larest man in Hamlin County," it was said, "an' he's bound to be a pop'lar man in Congress, an' have a pull."

But when the summer had passed, and a touch of frost in

the night air loosened the chestnuts in their burrs, and a stray morning breeze shook them in showers down upon the carpet of rustling yellowed leaves, Tom's letters had become few and far between, and none of them had contained any account of the intentions of the legislative body with regard to the claim.

"There's nothing to tell, boys," he wrote. "As far as I've gone, it seems a man gets a claim through Congress by waiting about Washington and telling his story to different people until he wears them out—or they wear him out."

For some time after this they did not hear from him at all. The winter set in, and the habitués of the Cross-roads Post-office gathered about the glowing stove. Under the influence of cold gray skies, biting air, leafless trees, and bare land, the claim seemed somehow to have receded into the distance. The sanguine confidence of the community had not subsided into doubt so much as into helpless mystification. Months had passed and nothing whatsoever had happened.

"Seems somehow," said Jabe Doty one night, as he tilted his chair forward and stared at the fire in the stove, "seems somehow as if Tom was a right smart ways off—es ef he got furder as the winter closed in—a'most like Washin'ton city hed moved a thousand miles or so out West somewhars, an' took him with it."

CHAPTER XXVIII

To Tom himself it seemed that it was the old, easy-going mountain life which had receded. The days when he had sat upon the stone porch and watched the sun rise from behind one mountain and set behind another seemed to belong to a life lived centuries ago. But that he knew little of occult beliefs and mysteries, he would have said to himself that all these things must have happened in a long past incarnation.

The matter of the De Willoughby claim was brought before the House. Judge Rutherford opened the subject one day with a good deal of nervous excitement. He had supplied himself with many notes, and found some little difficulty in managing them, being new to the work, and he grew hot and uncertain because he could not secure an audience. Claims had already become old and tiresome stories, and members who were unoccupied pursued their conversation unmovedly, giving the speaker only an occasional detached glance. The two representatives of their country sitting nearest to him were, not at all furtively, eating apples and casting their cores and parings into their particular waste-paper baskets. This was discouraging and baffling. To quote the Judge himself, no one knew anything about Hamlin County, and certainly no one was disturbed by any desire to be told about it.

That night Rutherford went to the house near Dupont Circle. Big Tom was sitting in the porch with Rupert and Sheba. Uncle Matt was digging about the roots of a

303

rose-bush, and the Judge caught a glimpse of Miss Burford looking out from behind the parlour curtains.

The Judge wore a wearied and vaguely bewildered look as he sat down and wiped his forehead with a large, clean white handkerchief.

" It's all different from what I thought—it's all different," he said.

" Things often are," remarked Tom, " oftener than not."

Rupert and Sheba glanced at each other questioningly and listened with anxious eyes.

" And it's different in a different way from what I expected," the Judge went on. " They might have said and done a dozen things I should have been sort of ready for, but they didn't. Somehow it seemed as if—as if the whole thing didn't matter."

Tom got up and began to walk about.

" That's not the way things begin that are going to rush through," he said.

Sheba followed him and slipped her hand through his arm.

" Do you think," she faltered, " that perhaps we shall not get the money at all, Uncle Tom? "

Tom folded her hand in his—which was easily done.

" I'm afraid that if we do get it," he answered, " it will not come to us before we want it pretty badly—the Lord knows how badly."

For every day counts in the expenditure of a limited sum, and on days of discouragement Tom's calculation of their resources left him a troubled man.

When Judge Rutherford had gone Rupert sat with Sheba in the scented summer darkness. He drew his chair opposite to hers and took one of her hands in both of his own.

In Connection with
The De Willoughby Claim

"Suppose I have done a wrong thing," he said. "Suppose I have dragged you and Uncle Tom into trouble?"

"I am glad you came," in a quick, soft voice. "I am glad you came." And the slight, warm fingers closed round his.

He lifted them to his lips and kissed them over and over again. "Are you glad I came?" he murmured. "Oh, Sheba! Sheba!"

"Why do you say 'Oh, Sheba'?" she asked.

"Because I love you so—and I am so young—and I don't know what to do. You know I love you, don't you?"

She leaned forward so that he saw her lovely gazelle eyes lifted and most innocently tender. "I want you to love me," she said; "I could not bear you not to love me."

He hesitated a second, and then suddenly pressed his glowing face upon her palm.

"But I don't love you as Uncle Tom loves you, Sheba," he said. "I love you—young as I am—I love you—differently."

Her swaying nearer to him was a sweetly unconscious and involuntary thing. Their young eyes drowned themselves in each other.

"I want you," she said, the note of a young ring-dove answering her mate murmuring in her voice, "I want you to love me—as you love me. I love your way of loving me."

"Darling!" broke from him, his boy's heart beating fast and high. And their soft young lips were, through some mystery of power, drawn so near to each other that they met like flowers moved to touching by the summer wind.

Later Rupert went to Tom, who sat by an open window in his room and looked out on the moonlit stretch of avenue.

In Connection with
The De Willoughby Claim

The boy's heart was still beating fast, and, as the white light struck his face, it showed his eyes more like Delia Vanuxem's than they had ever been. Their darkness held just the look Tom remembered, but could never have described or explained to himself.

"Uncle Tom," he began, in an unsteady voice, "I couldn't go to bed without telling you."

Tom glanced up at him and learned a great deal. He put a big hand on his shoulder.

"Sit down, boy," he said, his kind eyes warming. Rupert sat down.

"Perhaps I ought not to have done it," he broke forth. "I did not know I was going to do it. I suppose I am too young. I did not mean to—but I could not help it."

"Sheba?" Tom inquired, simply.

"Her eyes were so lovely," poured forth the boy. "She looked at me so like an angel. Whenever she is near me, it seems as if something were drawing us together."

"Yes," was Tom's quiet answer.

"I want to tell you all about it," impetuously. "I have been so lonely, Uncle Tom, since my mother died. You don't know how I loved her—how close we were to each other. She was so sweet and wonderful—and I had nothing else."

Tom nodded gently.

"I remember," he said. "I never forgot."

He put the big hand on the boy's knee this time. "I loved her too," he said, "and *I* had nothing else."

"Then you know—you know!" cried Rupert. "You remember what it was to sit quite near her and see her look at you in that innocent way—how you longed to cry out and take her in your arms."

In Connection with
The De Willoughby Claim

Tom stirred in his seat. Time rolled back twenty-five years.

"Oh, my God, yes—I remember!" he answered.

"It was like that to-night," the young lover went on. "And I could not stop myself. I told her I loved her—and she said she wanted me to love her—and we kissed each other."

Big Tom got up and stood before the open window. His hands were thrust deep into his pockets and he stared out at the beauty of the night.

"Good Lord!" he said. "That's what *ought* to come to every man that lives—but it doesn't."

Rupert poured forth his confession, restrained no more.

"From that first night when I rode through the mountains over the white road and stopped at your gate—since I looked up and saw her standing on the balcony with the narcissus in her hair it has always been the same thing. It began that very moment—it was there when she leaned forward and spoke to me. I had never thought of a woman before—I was too poor and sad and lonely and young. And there she was—all white—and it seemed as if she was *mine*."

Tom nodded his head as if to a white rose-bush in the small garden.

"I am as poor as ever I was," said Rupert. "I am a beggar if we lose our claim; but I am not sad, and I am not lonely—I can't be—I can't be! I am happy—everything's happy—because she knows—and I have kissed her."

"What did you think I would say when you told me?" Tom asked.

"I don't know," impetuously; "but I knew I must come to you. It seems a million years ago since that hot morning

307

in the old garden at Delisleville—when I had never seen her."

" One of the things I have thought about a good deal," said Tom, with quite a practical manner, " has been love. I had lots of time to think over things at the Cross-roads, and I used to work them out as far as my mind would carry me. Love's as much an element as the rest of them. There's earth, air, fire, water—and love. It has to be calculated for. What I've reasoned out is that it has not been calculated for enough. It's going to *come* to all of us—and it will either come and stay, and make the old earth bloom with flowers—or it will come and go, and leave it like a plain swept by fire. It's not a trivial thing that only boys and girls play with; it's better—and worse. It ought to be prepared for and treated well. It's not often treated well. People have got into the way of expecting trouble and tragedy to come out of it. We are always hearing of its unhappiness in books. Poets write about it that way."

" I suppose it is often unhappy," said Rupert; " but just now it seems as if it *could* not be."

" What *I've* been wanting to see," said Tom, " is young love come up like a flower and be given its dew and sun and rain—and bloom and bloom its best."

He drew a big sigh.

" That poor child who lies on the hillside under the pines," he went on, " Sheba's mother—hers was young love—and it brought tragedy and death. Delia," his voice was unsteady, " your mother's was young love, and her heart was broken. No, it's not often well treated. And when you and Sheba came to me that night with your boy and girl eyes shining with gladness just because you had met each other, I said to myself, ' By the Lord, here is what it springs from. Perhaps it may come to them; I wonder if it will?'"

"You thought it might, even then," Rupert cried.

"Yes, I did," was Tom's answer. "You were young— you were drawn together—it seemed natural. I used to watch you, and think it over, making a kind of picture to myself of how it would be if two young things could meet each other and join hands and wander on among roses until they reached the gate of life—and it swung open for them and they passed through and found another paradise."

He stopped a second and turned to look at Rupert's dreamy face with a smile not all humorous. "I'm a sentimental chap for my size," he added. "That's what I wanted for Sheba and you—that's what I want. That sort of thing was left out of my life; but I should like to see it before I'm done with. Good God! why can't people be *happy?* I want people to be *happy.*"

The boy was trembling.

"Uncle Tom," he said, "Sheba and I are happy to-night."

"Then God have mercy on the soul of the man who would spoil it for you," said Big Tom, with actual solemnity. "I'm not that man. You two just go on being happy; try and make up for what your two mothers had to bear."

Rupert got up from his chair and caught the big hand in his. It was a boy's action, and he looked particularly like a boy as he did it. "It is just like you," he broke forth. "I did not know what you would say when I told you—but I ought to have known you would say something like this. It's—it's as big as you are, Uncle Tom," ingenuously.

That was his good-night. When he went away Big Tom

settled into his chair again and looked out for some time longer at the bright night. He was going back to two other nights which lay in the years behind. One was the night he turned his back on Delisleville and rode towards the mountain with a weight on his kindly heart which he had grimly told himself seemed to weigh a ton; the other was the night he had been wakened from his sleep by the knock on the door of the bedroom behind the Cross-roads Post-office and had ridden out under the whiteness of the moon to find in the bare cabin at Blair's Hollow the little fair girl who had sobbed and died as she clung to his warm hand.

CHAPTER XXIX

THE world had heard and talked much of the Reverend John Baird in the years which followed his return to Willow-field. During the first few months after his reappearance among them, his flock had passed through a phase of rest-less uncertainty with regard to him. Certain elder members of his congregation had privately discussed questions of doctrine with anxiousness. Had not Nature already arraigned herself upon the man's side by bestowing upon him a powerful individuality, heads might have been shaken, and the matter discussed openly instead of in considerately confidential conclave. It was, however, less easy to enter into argument with such a man than with one slow and uncertain of tongue, and one whose fortunes rested in the hands of the questioners. Besides, it was not to be denied that even the elderly and argumentative found themselves listening to his discourses. The young and emotional often thrilled and quaked before them. In his hour he was the pioneer of what to-day we call the modern, and seemed to speak his message not to a heterogeneous mental mass, but to each individual man and woman who sat before him with upturned face. He was daringly human for the time in which he lived, it being the hour when humanity was over-powered by deity, and to be human was to be iconoclastic. His was not the doctrine of the future—of future repentance for the wrongs done to-day, of future reward for the good to-day achieves, all deeds being balanced on a mercantile account of profit and loss. His was a cry almost fierce, demanding, in the name of human woe, that to-day shall hold no cruelty, no evil done, even to the smallest and most unregarded thing.

By some chance—though he alone realised the truth of the fact—the subjects of his most realistic and intense appeals to his hearers had the habit of developing themselves in his close talks with Latimer. Among the friends of the man on whom all things seemed to smile, the man on whom the sun had never shone, and who faithfully worshipped him, was known as his Shadow. It was not an unfitting figure of speech. Dark, gloomy, and inarticulate, he was a strange contrast to the man he loved; but, from the hour he had stood by Latimer's side, leaning against the rail of the returning steamer, listening to the monotonously related story of the man's bereavement, John Baird had felt that Fate herself had knit their lives together. He had walked the deck alone long hours that night, and when the light of the moon had broken fitfully through the stormily drifting clouds, it had struck upon a pallid face.

"Poor fellow!" he had said between his teeth; "poor darkling, tragic fellow! I must try—try—oh, my God! I must try——"

Then their lives had joined currents at Willowfield, and the friendship Baird had asked for had built itself on a foundation of stone.

There was nothing requiring explanation in the fact that to the less fortunate man Baird's every gift of wit and ease was a pleasure and comfort. His mere physical attractions were a sort of joy. When Latimer caught sight of his own lank, ill-carried figure and his harshly rugged sallow face, he never failed to shrink from them and avert his eyes.

In Connection with
The De Willoughby Claim

To be the companion of a man whose every movement suggested strength and grace, whose skin was clear and healthful, his features well balanced and admirable in line—to be the friend of a human being built by nature as all human beings should be built if justice were done to them, was nourishment to his own starved needs.

When he assumed his charge at the squalid little town of Janway's Mills, his flock looked askance at him. He was not harsh of soul, but he was gloomy and had not the power to convey encouragement or comfort, though he laboured with strenuous conscientiousness. Among the sordid commonness of the every-day life of the mill hands and their families he lived and moved as Savonarola had moved and lived in the midst of the picturesque wickedness and splendidly coloured fanaticism of Italy in dim, rich centuries past; but his was the asceticism and stern self-denial of Savonarola without the uplifting power of passionate eloquence and fire which, through their tempest, awakened and shook human souls. He had no gifts of compelling fervor; he could not arouse or warm his hearers; he never touched them. He preached to them, he visited them at their homes, he prayed beside their dying and their dead, he gave such aid in their necessities as the narrowness of his means would allow, but none of them loved him or did more than stoically accept him and his services.

"Look at us as we stand together," he said to Baird on an evening when they stood side by side within range of an old-fashioned mirror. "Those things your reflection represents show me the things I was born without. I might make my life a daily crucifixion of self-denial and duty done at all costs, but I could not wear your smile or speak with your voice. I am a man, too," with smothered passion; "I am a man, too! And yet—what woman looks smilingly at *me*—what child draws near unafraid?"

"You are of the severe monastic temperament," answered Baird. "It is all a matter of temperament. Mine is facile and a slave to its emotions. Saints and martyrs are made of men like you—never of men such as I am."

"Are you sure of the value to the world of saints and martyrs?" said Latimer. "I am not. That is the worst of it."

"Ah! the world," Baird reflected. "If we dare to come back to the world—to count it as a factor——"

"It is only the world we know," Latimer said, his harsh voice unsteady; "the world's sorrow—the world's pain—the world's power to hurt and degrade itself. That is what seems to concern us—if we dare to say so—we, who were thrust into it against our wills, and forced to suffer and see others suffer. The man who was burned at the stake, or torn in the arena by wild beasts, believed he won a crown for himself—but it was for *himself*."

"What doth it profit a man," quoted Baird, vaguely, but as if following a thought of his own, "if he gain the whole world and lose his own soul?"

Latimer flung back his shock of uneven black locks. His hollow eyes flashed daringly.

"What doth it profit a man," he cried, "if he save his own soul and lose the whole world, caring nothing for its agony, making no struggle to help it in its woe and grieving? A Man once gave His life for the world. Has any man ever given his soul?"

"You go far—you go far!" exclaimed Baird, drawing a short, sharp breath.

Latimer's deep eyes dwelt upon him woefully. "Have

you known what it was to bear a heavy sin on your soul?" he asked.

"My dear fellow," said John Baird, a little bitterly, "it is such men as I, whose temperaments—the combination of forces you say you lack—lead them to the deeds the world calls 'heavy sins'—and into the torment of regret which follows. You can bear no such burden—you have no such regret."

Latimer, whose elbow rested on the mantel, leaned a haggard forehead on his hand.

"I have sinned," he said. "It was that others might be spared; but I have put my soul in peril. Perhaps it is lost—lost!"

Baird laid a hand on his shoulder and shook him. It was a singular movement with passion in it.

"No! No!" he cried. "Rouse, man, and let your reason speak. In peril? Lost—for some poor rigid law broken to spare others? Great God! No!"

"Reason!" said Latimer. "What you and I must preach each week of our lives is that it is not reason a man must be ruled by, but blind, wilful faith."

"I do not preach it," Baird interposed. "There are things I dare to leave unsaid."

"I have spoken falsely," Latimer went on, heavily. "I have lived a lie—a lie—but it was to save pure hearts from breaking. They would have broken beneath the weight of what I have borne for them. If I must bear punishment for that, I—Let me bear it."

The rigid submission of generations of the Calvinistic conscience which presumed to ask no justice from its God and gave praise as for mercy shown for all things which were not damnation, and which against damnation's self dared not lift its voice in rebellion, had so far influenced the very building of his being that the revolt of reason in his brain filled him with gloomy terror. There was the appeal of despair on his face as he looked at Baird.

"Your life, your temperament have given you a wider horizon than mine," he said. "I have never been in touch with human beings. I have only read religious books—stern, pitiless things. Since my boyhood I have lived in terror of the just God—the just God—who visits the sins of the fathers upon the children even to the third and fourth generation. I—Baird—" his voice dropping, his face pallid, "I have *hated* Him. I keep His laws, it is my fate to preach His word—and I cower before Him as a slave before a tyrant, with hatred in my heart."

"Good God!" Baird broke forth, involuntarily. The force of the man's desperate feeling, his horror of himself, his tragic truthfulness, were strange things to stand face to face with. He had never confronted such a thing before, and it shook him.

Latimer's face relaxed into a singular, rather pathetic smile.

"Good God!" he repeated; "we all say that—I say it myself. It seems the natural human cry. I wonder what it means? It surely means something—something."

John Baird looked at him desperately.

"You are a more exalted creature than I could ever be," he said. "I am a poor thing by comparison; but life struck the wrong note for you. It was too harsh. You have lived among the hideous cruelties of old doctrines until they have wrought evil in your brain."

He stood up and threw out his arms with an involuntary gesture, as if he were flinging off chains.

In Connection with
The De Willoughby Claim

"Ah, they are not true! They are not true!" he exclaimed. "They belong to the dark ages. They are relics of the days when the upholders of one religion believed that they saved souls by the stake and the rack and thumbscrew. There were men and women who did believe it with rigid honesty. There were men and women who, believing in other forms, died in torture for their belief. There *is* no God Who would ask such demoniac sacrifice. We have come to clearer days. Somewhere—somewhere there is light."

"You were born with the temperament to see its far-off glimmer even in your darkest hour," Latimer said. "It is for such as you to point it out to such as I am. Show it to me—show it to me every moment if you can!"

Baird put his hand on the man's shoulder again.

"The world is surging away from it—the chained mind, the cruelty, the groping in the dark," he said, "as it surged away from the revengeful Israelitish creed of 'eye for eye and tooth for tooth' when Christ came. It has taken centuries to reach, even thus far; but, as each century passed, each human creature who yearned over and suffered with his fellow has been creeping on dragging, bleeding knees towards the light. But the century will never come which will surge away from the Man who died in man's agony for men. In thought of Him one may use reason and needs no faith."

The germ of one of the most moving and frequently quoted of Baird's much-discussed discourses sprang—he told his friends afterwards—from one such conversation, and was the outcome of speech of the dead girl Margery. On a black and wet December day he came into his study, on his return from some parish visits, to find Latimer sitting before the fire, staring miserably at something he held in his hand. It was a little daguerrotype of Margery at fifteen.

"I found it in an old desk of mine," he said, holding it out to Baird, who took it and slightly turned away to lean against the mantel, as he examined it.

The child's large eyes seemed to light up the ugly shadows of the old-fashioned mushroom hat she wore, the soft bow of her mouth was like a little Love's, she bloomed with an angelic innocence, and in her straight sweet look was the unconscious question of a child-woman creature at the dawn of life.

John Baird stood looking down at the heavenly, tender little face.

There was a rather long silence. During its passing he was far away. He was still far away when at length an exclamation left his lips. He did not hear his words himself—he did not remember Latimer, or notice his quick movement of surprise.

"How sweet she was!" he broke forth. "How sweet she was! How sweet!"

He put his hand up and touched his forehead with the action of a man in a dream.

"Sometimes," he said, low and passionately, "sometimes I am sick with longing for her—*sick!*"

"You!" Latimer exclaimed. "*You* are heart-sick for her!"

Baird came back. The startled sound in the voice awoke him. He felt himself, as it were, dragged back from another world, breathless, as by a giant's hand. He looked up, dazed, the hand holding the daguerrotype dropping helplessly by his side.

"It is not so strange that it should come to that," he said.

"I seem to know her so well. I think," there was a look of sharp pain on his face—"I think I know the pitiful child-like suffering her dying eyes held." And the man actually shuddered a little.

"I know it—I know it!" Latimer cried, and he let his forehead drop upon his hands and sat staring at the carpet.

"I have heard and thought of her until she has become a living creature," John Baird said. "I hear of her from others than yourself. Miss Starkweather—that poor girl from the mills, Susan Chapman—you yourself—keep her before me, alive. I seem to know the very deeps of her lovingness—and understand her. Oh, that she should have *died!*" He turned his face away and spoke his next words slowly and in a lowered voice. "If I had found her when I came back free—if I had found her here, living—we two might have been brothers."

"No, no!" Latimer cried, rising. "You—it could not——"

He drew his hand across his forehead and eyes.

"What are we saying?" he exclaimed, stammeringly. "What are we thinking of? For a moment it seemed as if she were alive again. Poor little Margery, with her eyes like blue flowers, she has been dead years and years and years."

. . . .

It was not long after this that the Reverend John Baird startled a Boston audience one night by his lecture, "Repentance." In it he unfolded a new passionate creed which produced the effect of an electric shock. Newspapers reported it, editorials discussed it, articles were written upon it in monthly magazines. "Repentance is too late," was the note his deepest fervour struck with virile, almost terrible, intensity. "Repent before your wrong is done."

"Repentance comes too late," he cried. "We say a man saves his soul by it—*his* soul! We are a base, cowardly lot. Our own souls are saved—yes! And we hug ourselves and are comforted. But what of the thing we have hurt—for no man ever lost his soul unless he lost it by the wound he gave another—by inflicting in some other an agony? What of the one who has suffered—who has wept blood? I repent and save *myself;* but repentance cannot undo. The torture has been endured—the tears of blood shed. It is not to God I must kneel and pray for pardon, but to that one whose helplessness I slew, and, though he grant it me, he still has been slain."

The people who sat before him stirred in their seats; some leaned forward, breathing quickly. There were those who turned pale; here and there a man bent his head and a woman choked back a sob, or sat motionless with streaming eyes. "Repentance is too late—except for him who buys hope and peace with it. A lifetime of it cannot *undo.*" The old comfortable convention seemed to cease to be supporting. It seemed to cease to be true that one may wound and crush and kill, and then be admirable in escaping by smug repentance. It seemed to cease to be true that humanity need count only with an abstract, far-off Deity Who can easily afford to pardon—that one of his poor myriads has been done to death. It was all new—strange—direct—and each word fell like a blow from a hammer, because a strong, dramatic, reasoning creature spoke from the depths of his own life and soul. In him Humanity rose up an awful reality, which must itself be counted with—not because it could punish and revenge, but because the laws of nature cried aloud as a murdered man's blood cries from the ground.

As Baird crossed the pavement to reach his cab, the first night he delivered this lecture, a man he knew but slightly stepped to his side and spoke to him.

" Mr. Baird," he said, " will you drive me to the station? "

Baird turned and looked at him in some surprise. There were cabs enough within hailing distance. The man was well known as a journalist, rather celebrated for his good looks and masculine charm. He was of the square-shoul-dered, easy-moving, rich-coloured type; just now his hand-some eye looked perturbed.

" I am going away suddenly," he said, in answer to Baird's questioning expression. " I want to catch the next train. I want you to see me off—*you*."

" Let us get in," was Baird's brief reply. He had an instant revelation that the circumstance was not trivial or accidental.

As the door closed and the cab rolled away his companion leaned back, folding his arms.

" I had an hour to pass before keeping an appointment," he said. " And I dropped in to hear you. You put things before a man in a new way. You are appallingly vivid. I am not going to keep my appointment. It is not easy *not* to keep it! I shall take the train to New York and catch to-morrow's steamer to Liverpool. Don't leave me until you have seen me off. I want to put the Atlantic Ocean and a year of time between myself and——"

" Temptation," said Baird, though he scarcely realised that he spoke.

" Oh, the devil! " exclaimed the other man savagely. " Call her that if you like—call me that—call the whole

321

thing that! She does not realise where we are drifting. She's a lovely dreamer and has not realised that we are human. I did not allow myself to realise it until the passion of your words brought me face to face with myself. I am repenting in time. Don't leave me! I can't carry it through to-night alone."

John Baird leaned back in the corner of the carriage and folded his arms also. His heart was leaping beneath them.

" Great God! " he said, out of the darkness. " I wish someone had said such words to me—years ago—and not left me afterwards! Years ago! "

" I thought so," his companion answered, briefly. " You could not have painted it with such flaming power—otherwise."

They did not speak again during the drive. They scarcely exchanged a dozen words before they parted. The train was in the station when they entered it.

Five minutes later John Baird stood upon the platform, looking after the carriages as they rolled out noisily behind trailing puffs of smoke and steam.

He had asked no questions, and, so far as his own knowledge was concerned, this was the beginning, the middle, and the end of the story. But he knew that there had been a story, and there might have been a tragedy. It seemed that the intensity of his own cry for justice and mercy had arrested at least one of the actors in it before the curtain fell.

A few nights later, as they sat together, Baird and Latimer spoke of this incident and of the lecture it had followed upon.

" Repentance! Repentance! " Latimer said. " What led *you* to dwell upon repentance? "

"Thirty years of life," was Baird's answer. "Forty of them." He was leaning forward gazing into the red-hot coals. "And after our talk," he added, deliberately. "Margery."

Latimer turned and gazed at him.

Baird nodded.

"Yes," he said. "Her picture. Her innocent face and the soft, helpless youth of it. Such young ignorance is helpless—helpless! If in any hour of ruthlessness—or madness—a man had done such tenderness a wrong, what repentance—*what* repentance could undo?"

"None," said Latimer, and the words were a groan. "None—through all eternity."

It was not a long silence which followed, but it seemed long to both of them. A dead stillness fell upon the room. Baird felt as if he were waiting for something. He knew he was waiting for something, though he could not have explained to himself the sensation. Latimer seemed waiting too—awaiting the power and steadiness to reach some resolve. But at length he reached it. He sat upright and clutched the arms of his chair. It was for support.

"Why not now?" he cried; "why not now? I trust you! I trust you! Let me unburden my soul. I will try."

It was Baird's involuntary habit to sink into easy attitudes; the long, supple form of his limbs and body lent themselves to grace and ease. But he sat upright also, his hands unconsciously taking hold upon the arms of his chair as his companion did.

For a moment the two gazed into each other's eyes, and the contrast between their types was a strange one—the one man's face dark, sallow, harsh, the other fine, sensitive, and suddenly awake with emotion.

"I trust you," said Latimer again. "I would not have confessed the truth to any other living creature—upon the rack."

His forehead looked damp under his black locks.

"You would not have confessed the *truth,*" Baird asked, in a hushed voice, "about what?"

"Margery," answered Latimer. "Margery."

He saw Baird make a slight forward movement, and he went on monotonously.

"She did not die in Italy," he said. "She did not die lying smiling in the evening sun."

"She—did not?" Baird's low cry was a thing of horror.

"She died," Latimer continued, in dull confession, "in a log cabin in the mountains of North Carolina. She died in anguish—the mother of an hour-old child."

"My God! My God! My God!"

Three times the cry broke from Baird.

He got up and walked across the room and back.

"Wait—wait a moment!" he exclaimed. "For a moment don't go on."

As the years had passed, more than once he had been haunted by a dread that some day he might come upon some tragic truth long hidden. Here he was face to face with it. But what imagination could have painted it like this?

"You think my lie—a damnable thing," said Latimer.

"No, no!" answered the other man, harshly. "No, no!"

He moved to and fro, and Latimer went on.

"I never understood," he said. "She was a pure creature, and a loving, innocent one."

"Yes," Baird groaned; "loving and innocent. Go on— go on! It breaks my heart—it breaks my heart!"

Remembering that he had said "You might have been

my brother," Latimer caught his breath in a groan too. He understood. He had forgotten—forgotten. But now he must go on.

"At home she had been always a bright, happy, tender thing. She loved us and we loved her. She was full of delicate gifts. We are poor people; we denied ourselves that we might send her to Boston to develop her talent. She went away, radiant and full of innocent gratitude. For some time she was very happy. I was making every effort to save money to take her abroad that she might work in the studios there. She had always been a delicate little creature—and when it seemed that her health began to fail, we feared the old terrible New England scourge of consumption. It always took such bright things as she was. When she came home for a visit her brightness seemed gone. She drooped and could not eat or sleep. We could not bear to realise it. I thought that if I could take her to France or Italy she might be saved. I thought of her day and night —day and night."

He paused, and the great knot in his throat worked convulsively in the bondage of his shabby collar. He began again when he recovered his voice.

"I thought too much," he said. "I don't know how it was. But just at that time there was a miserable story going on at the mills—I used to see the poor girl day by day—and hear the women talk. You know how that class of woman talks and gives you details and enlarges on them? The girl was about Margery's age. I don't know how it was; but one day, as I was standing listening to a gossipping married woman in one of their squalid, respectable parlours, and she was declaiming and denouncing and pouring forth anecdotes, suddenly—quite suddenly—I felt as if something had struck me. I turned sick and white and had to sit down. Oh, God! what an afternoon that was! and how long it seemed before I got back home."

He stopped again. This time he wiped sweat from his forehead before he continued, hoarsely:

"I cannot go over it—I cannot describe the steps by which I was led to—horrid fear. For two weeks I did not sleep a single night. I thought I was going mad. I laid awake making desperate plans—to resort to in case—in case——!"

His forehead was wet again, and he stopped to touch it with his handkerchief.

"One day I told my mother I was going to Boston to see Margery—to talk over the possibility of our going abroad together with the money I had worked for and saved. I had done newspaper work—I had written religious essays—I had taught. I went to her."

It was Baird who broke the thread of his speech now. He had been standing before a window, his back to the room. He turned about.

"You found?" he exclaimed, low and unsteady. "You found——?"

"It was true," answered Latimer. "The worst."

Baird stood stock still; if Latimer had been awake to externals he would have seen that it was because he could not move—or speak. He was like a man stunned.

Latimer continued:

"She was sitting in her little room alone when I entered it. She looked as if she had been passing through hours of convulsive sobbing. She sat with her poor little hands clutching each other on her knees. Hysteric shudders were shaking her every few seconds, and her eyes were blinded with weeping. A child who had been beaten brutally might

326

have sat so. She was too simple and weak to bear the awful terror and woe. She was not strong enough to conceal what there was to hide. She did not even get up to greet me, but sat trembling like an aspen leaf."

"What did you say to her?" Baird cried out.

"I only remember as one remembers a nightmare," the other man answered, passing his hand over his brow. "It was a black nightmare. I saw before I spoke, and I began to shake as she was shaking. I sat down before her and took both her hands. I seemed to hear myself saying, ' Margery—Margery, don't be frightened—don't be afraid of Lucian. I will help you, Margery; I have come to talk to you —just to talk to you.' That was all. And she fell upon the floor and lay with her face on my feet, her hands clutching them."

For almost five minutes there was no other word spoken, but the breathing of each man could be heard.

Then Latimer's voice broke the stillness, lower and more monotonous.

"I had but one resolve. It was to save her and to save my mother. All the soul of our home and love was bound up in the child. Among the desperate plans I had made in the long nights of lying awake there had been one stranger than the rest. I had heard constantly of Americans encountering each other by chance when they went abroad. When one has a secret to keep one is afraid of every chance, however remote. Perhaps my plan was mad, but it accomplished what I wanted. Years before I had travelled through the mountain districts of North Carolina. One day, in riding through the country roads, I had realised their strange remoteness from the world, and the fancy had crossed my mind that a criminal who dressed and lived as the rudely scattered population did, and who chose a lonely spot in the woods, might be safer there than with the ocean rolling between him and his secret. I spent hours in telling her the part she was to play. It was to be supposed that we had gone upon the journey originally planned. We were to be hidden—apparently man and wife—in some log cabin off the road until all was over. I studied the details as a detective studies his case. I am not a brilliant man, and it was intricate work; but I was desperate. I read guide-books and wrote letters from different points, and arranged that they should be sent to our mother at certain dates for the next few months.

" My stronghold was that she was quite ignorant of travel and would think of nothing but that the letters came from me and were about Margery. I made Margery write two or three. Then I knew I could explain that she was not strong enough to write herself. I was afraid she might break down before we could leave home; but she did not. I got her away. By roundabout ways we travelled to the North Carolina mountains. We found a deserted cabin in the woods, some distance from the road. We dressed ourselves in the rough homespun of the country. She went barefooted, as most of the women did. We so secluded ourselves that it was some time before it was known that our cabin was inhabited. The women have a habit of wearing deep sunbonnets when about their work. Margery always wore one and kept within doors. We were thought to be only an unsociable married pair. Only once she found herself facing curious eyes. A sharp-faced little hoosier stopped one day to ask for a drink of water when I was away. He stared at her so intently that she was frightened; but he never came again. The child was born. She died."

"When it was born," Baird asked, "who cared for her?"

"We were alone," answered Latimer. "I did not know whom to call. I read medical books—for hours each day I read them. I thought that perhaps I might be able to do— what was necessary. But on the night she was taken ill— I was stricken with terror. She was so young and childlike —she had lived through months of torture—the agony seemed so unnatural to me, that I knew I must go for help —that I was not mentally calm enough to go through the ordeal. A strange chance took me to a man who had years before studied medicine as a profession. He was a singular being, totally unlike his fellows. He came to her. She died with her hand in his."

"Did the child die too?" Baird asked, after a pause.

"No; it lived. After she was laid in the earth on the hillside, I came away. It was the next day, and I was not sane. I had forgotten the child existed, and had made no plans for it. The man I spoke of—he was unmarried and lonely, and a strange, huge creature of a splendid humaneness—he had stood by me through all—a mountain of strength—the man came to my rescue there and took the child. It would be safe with him. I know nothing more."

"Do you not know his name?" Baird asked.

"Yes; he was called Dwillerby by the country people. I think he had been born a gentleman, though he lived as the mountaineers did."

"Afterwards," said Baird, "you went abroad as you had planned?"

"Yes. I invented the story of her death. I wrote the details carefully. I learned them as a lesson. It has been my mother's comfort—that story of the last day—the open window—the passing peasants—the setting sun—I can see it all myself. That is my lie. Did you suspect it when I told it?"

"No, God knows!" Baird answered. "I did not."

"Never?" inquired Latimer.

"What I have thought was that you had suffered much more than you wished your mother to know; that—perhaps —your sister had suffered more than you would reveal; and that you dreaded with all your being the telling of the story. But never such tragedy as this—never—never!"

"The man—the man who wrought that tragedy," began Latimer, staring darkly before him, "somewhere he stands to-night—unless his day is done. Somewhere he stands—as real a man as *you*."

"With all his load upon him," said Baird; "and he may have loved her passionately."

"It should be a heavy load," said Latimer, with bitter gloom; "heavy—heavy."

"You have not once uttered his name," said Baird, the thought coming to him suddenly.

"No," said Latimer; "I never knew it. She prayed so piteously that I would let her hide it. She knelt and sobbed upon my knee, praying that I would spare her that one woe. I could spare her no other, so I gave way. She thanked me, clinging to me and kissing my hand. Ah, her young, young heart wrung with sobs and tears!"

He flung himself forward against the table, hiding his face upon his arms, and wept aloud. Baird went and stood by him. He did not speak a word or lay his hand upon the shaking shoulders. He stood and gazed, his own chest heaving and awful tears in his eyes.

CHAPTER XXX

In later years, one at least of the two men never glanced back upon the months which followed without a shudder. And yet outwardly no change took place in their relations, unless they seemed drawn closer. Such a secret being shared between two people must either separate or bind them together. In this case it became a bond. They spoke of it but little, yet each was well aware that the other remembered often. Sometimes, when they sat together, Latimer recognised in Baird's eyes a look of brooding and felt that he knew what his thought was; sometimes Baird, glancing at his friend, found his face darkened by reverie, and understood. Once, when this was the case, he said, suddenly:

"What is your feeling about—the man? Do you wish to kill him?"

"It is too late," Latimer answered. "It would undo nothing. If by doing it I could bring her back as she was before she had seen his face—if I could see her again, the pretty, happy child, with eyes like blue convolvulus, and laughing lips—I would kill him and gladly hang for it."

"So would I," said Baird, grimly.

"To crucify him would not *undo* it," said Latimer, looking sickly pale. She was crucified—she lived through terror and shame; she died—afraid that God would not forgive her."

"That God would not——!" Baird gasped.

Latimer's bony hands were twisted together.

"We were brought up to believe things like that," he said.

331

"I was afraid, too. That was the damnable part of it. I could not help her. I have changed since then—I have changed through knowing you. As children we had always been threatened with the just God! The most successful preachers gained their power by painting pictures of the torments of hell. That was the fashion then," smiling horribly.

"It is a wonderful thing that even the fashion in Gods changes. When we were shut up together in the cabin on the hillside, she used to be overwhelmed by paroxysms of fear. She read the Bible a great deal—because sinners who wanted to repent always read it—and sometimes she would come upon threats and curses, and cry out and turn white and begin to shiver. Then she would beg me to pray and pray with her. And we would kneel down on the bare floor and pray together. My prayers were worse than useless. What could I say? I was a black sinner, too—a man who was perjuring his soul with lies—and they were told and acted for her sake, and she knew it. She used to cling about my neck and beg me to betray her—to whiten my soul by confession—not to allow her wickedness to destroy me—because she loved me—loved me. ' Go back to them and tell them, Lucien,' she would cry, ' I will go with you if I ought—I have been wicked—not you—I have been shameful; I must bear it—I must bear it.' But she could not bear it. She died."

"Were you never able to give her any comfort?" said Baird. His eyes were wet, and he spoke as in bitter appeal. "This had been a child in her teens entrapped into bearing the curse of the world with all its results of mental horror and physical agony."

"What comfort could I give?" was the answer. "My

religion and my social creed had taught me that she was a vile sinner—the worst and most shameful of sinners—and that I was a criminal for striving to save her from the consequences of her sin. I was defying the law of the just God, who would have punished her with heart-break and open shame. He would not have spared her, and He would not spare me since I so strove against Him. The night she died—through the long hours of horrible, unnatural convulsions of pain—when cold sweat stood in drops on her deathly childish face, she would clutch my hands and cry out: 'Eternal torments! For ever and ever and ever—could it be like this, Lucien—for ever and ever and ever?' Then she would sob out, 'God! God! God!' in terrible, helpless prayer. She had not strength for other words."

Baird sprang to his feet and thrust out his hand, averting his pallid face.

"Don't tell me any more," he said. "I cannot—I cannot bear it."

"*She* bore it," said Latimer, "until death ended it."

"Was there no one—to save her?" Baird cried. "Was she terrified like that when she died?"

"The man who afterwards took her child—the man D'Willerby," Latimer answered, "was a kindly soul. At the last moment he took her poor little hand and patted it, and told her not to be frightened. She turned to him as if for refuge. He had a big, mellow voice, and a tender, protecting way. He said: 'Don't be frightened. It's all right,' and his were the last words she heard."

"God bless the fellow, wheresoever he is!" Baird exclaimed. "I should like to grasp his hand."

. . . .

The Reverend John Baird delivered his lectures in many

cities that year. The discussion they gave rise to had the natural result of awakening a keen interest in them. There were excellent souls who misinterpreted and deplored them, there were excellent souls who condemned; there were even ministers of the gospel who preached against the man as an iconoclast and a pagan, and forbade their congregations to join his audiences. But his lecture-halls were always crowded, and the hundreds of faces upturned to him when he arose upon his platform were the faces of eager, breathless, yearning creatures. He was a man speaking to men, not an echo of old creeds. He uttered no threats, he painted no hells, he called aloud to that God in man which is his soul.

"That God which is in you—in me," he proclaimed, "has lain dormant because undeveloped man, having made for himself in the dark ages gods of wood and stone, demanding awful sacrifice, called forth for himself later a deity as material, though embodied in no physical form—a God of vengeance and everlasting punishments. This is the man-created deity, and in his name man has so clamoured that the God which is man's soul has been silenced. Let this God rise, and He will so demand justice and noble mercy from all creatures to their fellows that temptation and suffering will cease. What! can we do no good deed without the promise of paradise as reward? Can we refrain from no evil unless we are driven to it by the threat of hell? Are we such base traffickers that we make merchandise of our souls and bargain for them across a counter? Let us awake! I say to you from the deepest depths of my aching soul—if there were no God to bargain with, then all the more awful need that each man constitute himself a god—of justice, pity, and mercy—until the world's wounds are healed and each human thing can stand erect and claim the joy of life which is his own."

On the morning of the day he said these words to the crowd which had flocked to hear him, he had talked long with Latimer. For some weeks he had not been strong. The passion of intensity which ruled him when he spoke to his audiences was too strong an emotion to leave no physical trace. After a lecture or sermon he was often pallid and shaken.

"I have things to say," he exclaimed feverishly to Latimer. "There are things which must be said. The spoken word lives—for good or evil. It is a sound sent echoing through all the ages to come. Some men have awakened echoes which have thrilled throughout the world. To speak one's thought—to use mere words—it seems such a small thing—and yet it is my conviction that nothing which is said is really ever forgotten."

And his face was white, his eyes burning, when at night he leaned forward to fling forth to his hearers his final arraignment.

"I say to you, were there no God to bargain with, then all the more awful need that each man constitute *himself* a god of justice, pity, and mercy—until the world's wounds are healed and each human thing can stand erect and claim the joy of life which is his own."

The people went away after the lecture, murmuring among themselves. Some of them carried away awakening in their eyes. They all spoke of the man himself; of his compelling power, the fire of meaning in his face, and the musical, far-reaching voice, which carried to the remotest corner of the most crowded buildings.

"It is not only his words one is reached by," it was said.

"It is the man's self. Truly, he cries out from the depths of his soul."

This was true. It was the man himself. Nature had armed him well—with strength, with magnetic force, with a tragic sense of the anguish of things, and with that brain which labours far in advance of the thought of the hour. Men with such brains—brains which work fiercely and unceasingly even in their own despite—reach conclusions not yet arrived at by their world, and are called iconoclasts. Some are madly overpraised, some have been made martyrs, but their spoken word passes onward, and if not in their own day, in that to-morrow which is the to-day of other men, the truth of their harvest is garnered and bound into sheaves.

At the closing of his lectures, men and women crowded about him to speak to him, to grasp his hand. When they were hysterical in their laudations, his grace and readiness controlled them; when they were direct and earnest, he found words to say which they could draw aid from later.

"Am I developing—or degenerating—into a popular preacher?" he said once, with a half restless laugh, to his shadow.

"You are not popular," was Latimer's answer. "Popular is not the word. You are proclaiming too new and bold a creed."

"That is true," said Baird. "The pioneer is not popular. When he forces his way into new countries he encounters the natives. Sometimes they eat him—sometimes they drive him back with poisoned arrows. The country is their own; they have their own gods, their own language. Why should a stranger enter in?"

"But there is no record yet of a pioneer who lived—

or died—in vain," said Latimer. "Some day—some day——"

He stopped and gazed at his friend, brooding. His love for him was a strong and deep thing. It grew with each hour they spent together, with each word he heard him speak. Baird was his mental nourishment and solace. When they were apart he found his mind dwelling on him as a sort of habit. But for this one man he would have lived a squalid life among his people at Janney's Mills—squalid because he had not the elasticity to rise above its narrow, uneducated dulness. The squalor so far as he himself was concerned was not physical. His own small, plain home was as neat as it was simple, but he had not the temperament which makes a man friends. Baird possessed this temperament, and his home was a centre of all that was most living. It was not the ordinary Willowfield household. The larger outer world came and went. When Latimer went to it he was swept on by new currents and felt himself warmed and fed.

There had been scarcely any day during years in which the two men had not met. They had made journeys together; they had read the same books and encountered the same minds. Each man clung to the intimacy.

"I want this thing," Baird had said more than once; "if you want it, I want it more. Nothing must rob us of it."

"The time has come—it came long ago—" his Shadow said, "when I could not live without it. My life has grown to yours."

It was Latimer's pleasure that he found he could be an aid to the man who counted for so much to him. Affairs which pressed upon Baird he would take in hand; he was able to transact business for him, to help him in the development of his plans, save him frequently both time and fatigue. It fell about that when the lectures were delivered at distant points the two men journeyed together.

Latimer entered Baird's library on one occasion just as a sharp-faced, rather theatrical-looking man left it.

" You'll let me know your decision, sir, as soon as possible," the stranger departed, saying. " These things ought always to be developed just at the right moment. This is your right moment. Everybody is talking you over, one way or another." When the stranger was gone, Baird explained his presence.

" That is an agent," he said; " he proposes that I shall lecture through the States. I—don't know," as if pondering the thing.

" The things you say should be said to many," remarked Latimer.

" The more the better," said Baird, reflectively; " I know that—the more the better."

They sat and talked the matter over at length. The objections to it were neither numerous nor serious.

" And I want to say these things," said Baird, a little feverishly. " I want to say them again and again."

Before they parted for the night it was decided that he should accede to the proposal, and that Latimer should arrange to be his companion.

" It is the lecture ' Repentance,' he tells me, is most in demand," Baird said, as he walked to the door, with a hand in Latimer's.

CHAPTER XXXI

FREQUENTERS of the Capitol—whether loungers or politicians—had soon become familiar with the figure of one of the De Willoughby claimants. It was too large a figure not to be quickly marked and unavoidably remembered. Big Tom slowly mounting the marble steps or standing on the corridors was an object to attract attention, and inquiries being answered by the information that he was a party to one of the largest claims yet made, he not unnaturally was discussed with interest.

" He's from the depths of the mountains of North Carolina," it was explained; " he keeps a cross-roads store and post-office, but he has some of the best blood of the South in his veins, and his claim is enormous."

" Will he gain it? "

" Who knows? He has mortgaged all he owns to make the effort. The claim is inherited from his father, Judge De Willoughby, who died at the close of the war. As he lived and died within the Confederacy, the Government holds that he was disloyal and means to make the most of it. The claimants hold that they can prove him loyal. They'll have to prove it thoroughly. The Government is growing restive over the claims of Southerners, and there is bitter opposition to be overcome."

" Yes. Lyman nearly lost his last election because he had favoured a Southern claim in his previous term. His constituents are country patriots, and they said they weren't sending a man to Congress to vote for Rebs."

" That's the trouble. When men's votes are endangered

by a course of action they grow ultra-conservative. A vote's
a vote."

That was the difficulty, as Tom found. A vote was a
vote. The bitterness of war had not yet receded far enough
into the past to allow of unprejudiced judgment. Members
of political parties were still enemies, wrongs still rankled,
graves were yet new, wounds still ached and burned. Men
who had found it to their interest to keep at fever heat
the fierce spirit of the past four years of struggle and bloodshed, were not willing to relinquish the tactics which had
brought fortunes to them. The higher-minded were determined that where justice was done it should be done where
it was justice alone, clearly proved to be so. There had been
too many false and idle claims brought forward to admit
of the true ones being accepted without investigation and
delay. In the days when old Judge De Willoughby had
walked through the streets of Delisleville, ostracized and
almost hooted as he passed among those who had once been
his friends, it would not have been difficult to prove that
he was loyal to the detested Government, but in these later
times, when the old man lay quiet in what his few remaining
contemporaries still chose to consider a dishonoured grave,
undeniable proof of a loyalty which now would tend to the
honour and advantage of those who were of his blood was
not easy to produce.

"The man lived and died in the Confederacy," was said
by those who were in power in Washington.

"He was constructively a rebel. We want proof—proof."

Most of those who might have furnished it if they would,
were either scattered as to the four winds of the earth, or
were determined to give no aid in the matter.

"A Southerner who deserted the South in its desperate

struggle for life need not come to Southern gentlemen to ask them to help him to claim the price of his infamy." That was the Delisleville point of view, and it was difficult to cope with. If Tom had been a rich man and could have journeyed between Delisleville and the Capital, or wheresoever the demands of his case called him, to see and argue with this man or that, the situation would have simplified itself somewhat, though there would still have remained obstacles to be overcome.

"But a man who has hard work to look his room rent in the face, and knows he can't do that for more than a few months, is in a tight place," said Tom. " Evidence that will satisfy the Government isn't easily collected in Dupont Circle. These fellows have heard men talk before. They've heard too many men talk. There's Stamps, now—they've heard Stamps talk. Stamps is way ahead of me where lobbying is concerned. He knows the law, and he doesn't mind having doors shut in his face or being kicked into the street, so long as he sees a chance of getting indemnified for his 'herds of cattle.' I'm not a business man, and I mind a lot of things that don't trouble him. I'm not a good hand at asking favours and sitting down to talk steadily for a solid hour to a man who doesn't want to hear me and hasn't five minutes to spare." But for Rupert and Sheba he would have given up the claim in a week and gone back to Talbot's Cross-roads content to end his days as he began them when he opened the store—living in the little back rooms on beans and bacon and friend chicken and hominy.

" That suited me well enough," he used to say to himself, when he thought the thing over. " There were times when I found it a bit lonely—but, good Lord! loneliness is a small thing for a man to complain of in a world like this.

It isn't fits or starvation. When a man's outlived the habit of expecting happiness, it doesn't take much to keep him going."

But at his side was eager youth which had outlived nothing, which believed in a future full of satisfied yearnings and radiant joys.

" I am not alone now," said Rupert; " I must make a place and a home for Sheba. I must not be only a boy in love with her; I must be a man who can protect her from everything—from everything. She is so sweet—she is so sweet. She makes me feel that I am a man."

She was sweet. To big Tom they were both sweet in their youth and radiant faith and capabilities for happiness. They seemed like children, and the tender bud of their lovely young passion was a thing to be cherished. He had seen such buds before, but he had never seen the flower.

" I'd like to see the flower," he used to say to himself. " To see it would pay a man for a good deal he'd missed himself. The pair of them could set up a pretty fair garden of Eden—serpents and apple-trees being excluded."

They were happy. Even when disappointments befell them and prospects were unpromising they were happy. They could look into each other's eyes and take comfort. Rupert's dark moods had melted away. He sometimes forgot they had ever ruled him. His old boyish craving for love and home was fed. The bare little rooms in the poor little house were home. Sheba and Tom were love and affection. When they sat at the table and calculated how much longer their diminishing store would last, even as it grew smaller and smaller, they could laugh over the sums they worked out on slips of paper. So long as the weather was warm enough they strolled about together in the fragrant darkness or sat in the creeper-hung porch, in the light of summer moons; when the cold nights came they sat about the store or the table and talked, while Sheba sewed buttons on or worked assiduously at the repairing of her small wardrobe. Whatsoever she did, the two men sat and admired, and there was love and laughter.

The strenuous life which went on in the busier part of the town—the politics, the struggles, the plots and schemes, the worldly pleasures—seemed entirely apart from them.

Sometimes, after a day in which Judge Rutherford had been encouraged or Tom had had a talk with a friendly member who had listened to the story of the claim with signs of interest, they felt their star of hope rising; it never sinks far below the horizon when one's teens are scarcely of the past—and Sheba and Rupert spent a wonderful evening making plans for a future of ease and fortune.

At Judge Rutherford's suggestion, Tom had long sought an interview with a certain member of the Senate whose good word would be a carrying weight in any question under debate. He was a shrewd, honest, business-like man, and a personal friend of the President's. He was much pursued by honest and dishonest alike, and, as a result of experience, had become difficult to reach. On the day Tom was admitted to see him, he had been more than usually badgered. Just as Tom approached his door a little man opened it cautiously and slid out, with the air of one leaving within the apartment things not exhilarating on retrospect. He was an undersized country man, the cut of whose jeans wore a familiar air to Tom's eye even at a distance and before he lifted the countenance which revealed him as Mr. Stamps.

" We ain't a-gwine to do your job no good to-day, Tom,"

he said, benignly. "He'd 'a' kicked me out ef I hadn't 'a' bin small—jest same es you was gwine ter that time I come to talk to ye about Sheby. He's a smarter man than you be, an' he seed the argyment I hed to p'int out to you. Ye won't help your job none to-day!"

"I haven't got a 'job' in hand," Tom answered; "your herds of stock and the Judge's coal mines and cotton fields are different matters."

He passed on and saw that when his name was announced the Senator looked up from his work with a fretted movement of the head.

"Mr. De Willoughby of Talbot's Cross-roads?" he said. Tom bowed. He became conscious of appearing to occupy too much space in the room of a busy man who had plainly been irritated.

"I was told by Judge Rutherford that you had kindly consented to see me," he said.

The Senator tapped the table nervously with his pencil and pushed some papers aside.

"Well, I find I have no time to spare this morning," was his brutally frank response. "I have just been forced to give the time which might have been yours to a little hoosier who made his way in, heaven knows how, and refused to be ordered out. He had a claim, too, and came from your county and said he was an old friend of yours."

"He is not an old enemy," answered Tom. "There is that much foundation in the statement."

"Well, he has occupied the time I had meant to give you," said the Senator, "and I was not prepossessed either by himself or his claim."

"I think he's a man to gain a claim," said Tom; "I'm afraid I'm not."

In Connection with
The De Willoughby Claim

"It is fair to warn you that I am not friendly to claims made by the families of men who lived in a hot-bed of secession," said the Senator. He had been badgered too much this morning, and this big, rather convincing looking applicant worried him. "I have an appointment at the White House in ten minutes."

"Then this is no place for me," said Tom. "No man is likely to be friendly to a thing he has no time to talk of. I will bid you good-morning."

"Good-morning," returned the Senator, brusquely.

Tom went away feeling that he was a blunderer. The fact was that he was a neophyte and, it was true, did not possess the qualities which make a successful lobbyist. Mr. Stamps had wheedled or forced his way into the great man's apartment and had persisted in remaining to press his claim until he was figuratively turned out by the shoulders. Big Tom had used only such means to obtain the interview as a gentleman might; he had waited until he was called to take his turn, and so had lost his chance. When he had found the Senator hurried and unwilling to spend time on him he had withdrawn at once, not feeling Mr. Stamps's method to be possible.

"I suppose I ought to have stayed and buttonholed him in spite of himself," he thought, ruefully. "I'm a green-horn; I suppose a man in my place ought to stand his ground whether it's decent or indecent, and make people listen to what he has to say, and be quite willing to be kicked downstairs after he has said it. I'm a disgrace to my species—and I don't think much of the species."

As he was walking through one of the corridors he saw before him two men who were evidently visitors to the place. He gathered this from their leisurely movements and the interest with which they regarded the objects about them. They looked at pictures and remarked upon decorations. One was a man who was unusually well-built. He was tall and moved well and had lightly silvered hair; his companion was tall also, but badly hung together, and walked with a stoop of the shoulders.

Tom walked behind them for some yards before his attention was really arrested, but suddenly a movement of one man's head seemed to recall some memory of the past. He did not know what the memory was, but he knew vaguely that it was a memory. He followed a few yards further, wondering idly what had been recalled and why he should be reminded of the mountains and the pine-trees. Yes, it was the mountains and pine-trees—Hamlin County, but not the Hamlin County of to-day. Why not the Hamlin County of to-day? why something which seemed more remote? Confound the fellow; he had made that movement again. Tom wished he would turn his face that he might see it, and he hurried his footsteps somewhat that he might come within nearer range. The two men paused with their backs towards him, and Tom paused also. They were looking at a picture, and the taller of the two made a gesture with his hand. It was a long, bony hand, and as he extended it Tom slightly started. It all came back to him—the memory which had been recalled. He smelt the scent of the pines on the hillside; he saw the little crowd of mourners about the cabin door; inside, women sat with bent heads, upon two wooden chairs rested the ends of a slender coffin, and by it stood a man who lifted his hand and said to those about him: "Let us pray."

The years swept back as he stood there. He was face to face again with the tragic mystery which had seemed to end in utter silence. The man turned his face so that it was plainly to be seen—sallow, rugged, harsh in line. The same face, though older, and perhaps less tragic—the face of the man he had left alone in the awful, desolate stillness of the empty room.

The next moment he turned away again. He and his companion passed round a corner and were gone. Tom made no attempt to follow them.

"There is no reason why I should," was his thought, "either for Sheba's sake or his own. She is happy, and he feels his secret safe—whatsoever it may have been. Perhaps he has had time to outlive the misery of it, and it would all be brought to life again."

But the incident had been a shock. There was nothing to fear from it, he knew; but it had been a shock nevertheless. He did not know the man's name; he had never asked it. He was plainly one of the many strangers who, in passing through the Capital, went to visit the public buildings. The merest chance might have brought him to the place; the most ordinary course of events might take him away. Tom went back to Dupont Circle in a thoughtful mood. He forgot the claim and the Senator who had had no leisure to hear the statement of his case.

Rupert and Sheba were waiting for his return. Rupert had spent the afternoon searching for employment. He had spent many a long day in the same way and with the same result.

"They don't want me," he had said when he came home. "They don't want me anywhere, it seems—either in lawyers' offices or dry-goods stores. I have not been particular."

They had sat down and gazed at each other.

In Connection with
The De Willoughby Claim

"I sometimes wonder," said Sheba, "what we shall do when all our money is gone—every penny of it. It cannot last long now. We cannot stay here and we cannot pay our way back to the mountains. What shall we do?"

"I shall go out every day till I find something to do," said Rupert, with the undiscouraged fervour of youth. "I am not looking for employment for a gentleman, in these days; I am looking for work—just as Uncle Matt is."

"He chopped some wood yesterday and brought home two dollars," Sheba said. "He made me take it. He said he wanted to pay his 'bode.'"

She laughed a little, but her eyes were wet and shining.

Rupert took her face between his hands and looked into it adoringly.

"Don't be frightened, Sheba," he said; "don't be unhappy. Lovely darling, I will take care of you."

She pressed her soft cheek against his hand.

"I know you will," she said, "and of Uncle Tom, too. I couldn't be unhappy—we all three love each other so. I do not believe we shall be unhappy, even if we are poor enough to be hungry."

So their moment of dismay ended in smiles. They were passing through a phase of life in which it is not easy to be unhappy. Somehow things always brightened when they drew near each other. His observation of this truth was one of Tom's pleasures. He knew the year of waiting had managed to fill itself with sweetness for them. Their hopes had been alternately raised and dashed to earth; one day it seemed not improbable that they were to be millionaires, the next that beggary awaited them after the dwindling of their small stock of money; but they had shared their emotions and borne their vicissitudes together.

In Connection with
The De Willoughby Claim

When Tom entered the room they rose and met him with questioning faces.

"Was it good fortune?" they cried. "Did you see him, Uncle Tom? What did he say?"

He told his story as lightly as possible, but it could not be transformed, by any lightness of touch, into an encouraging episode. He made a picture of Stamps sidling through the barely opened door, and was terse and witty at the expense of his own discomfiture and consciousness of incompetence. He laughed at himself and made them laugh, but when he sat down in his accustomed seat there was a shade upon his face.

The children exchanged glances, the eyes of each prompting the other. They must be at their brightest. They knew the sight of their happiness warmed and lightened his heart always.

"He is tired and hungry," Sheba said. "We must give him a beautiful hot supper. Rupert, we must set the table."

They had grown used to waiting upon themselves, and their domestic services wore more or less the air of festivities. Sheba ran downstairs to Miss Burford's kitchen, where Uncle Matt had prepared the evening meal in his best manner. As the repasts grew more and more simple, Matt seemed to display greater accomplishments.

"It's all very well, Miss Sheba," he had said once, when she praised the skill with which he employed his scant resources. "It's mighty easy to be a good cook when you'se got everythin' right to han'. The giftness is to git up a fine table when you ain't got nuffin'. Dat's whar dish yer niggah likes to show out. De Lard knows I'se got too much yere dis ve'y minnit—to be a-doin' credit to my 'sperience—too much, Miss Sheba."

In Connection with
The De Willoughby Claim

He was frying hoe-cake and talking to Miss Burford when Sheba came into the kitchen. He was a great comfort and aid to Miss Burford, and in a genteel way the old lady found him a resource in the matters of companionship and conversation. Her life was too pinched and narrow to allow her even the simpler pleasure of social intercourse, and Matt's journeys into the world, and his small adventures, and his comments upon politics and social events were a solace and a source of entertainment to her.

Just now he was describing to her the stories he had heard of a celebrated lecturer who had just arrived in the city.

"Whether he's a 'vivalist or jes' a plain preacher what folks is runnin' after, I cayn't quite make out, ma'am," he was saying. "I ain't quite thinkin' he's a 'vivalist, but de peoples is a-runnin' after him shore—an' seems like dey doin' it in ev'y city he goes to. Ev'ybody want to heah him—ev'ybody—rich en pore—young en ole. De Rev'end John Baird's his name, an' he's got a fren' travellin' with him as they say is like Jonathan was to David in dese yere ole Bible times. An' I heern tell ev when he rise in de pulpit de people's jest gets so worked up at what he preach to 'em—dey jest cries an' rocks de benches. Dat's what make me think he might be a 'vivalist—cos we all knows dat cryin' an' rockin' an' clappin' hands is what makes a 'vival." He was full of anecdotes concerning the new arrival whose reputation had plainly preceded him.

"He gwine ter preach nex' Sat'day on ' 'Pentance,' " he said to Sheba, with a chuckle. "Dat's his big lecture ev'ybody want to hear. De hall shore to be pack full. What I'm a-hopin' is dat it'll be pack full er Senators an' members er Congrest, an' he'll set some of 'em a-'pentin', dey ain't 'tend to dere business an' git people's claims through. Ef

I know'd de gen'leman, I'd ax him to menshun dat special an' pertickler."

As they sat at supper, Sheba repeated his stories and comments. All the comments were worthy of repetition, and most of the anecdotes were suggestively interesting, illustrating, as they did, the power of a single man over many.

"I should like to go and hear him myself," she said. "Uncle Tom, have you anything to repent? Rupert, have you? Uncle Tom, you have not forgotten the Senator. You look at me as if you were thinking of something that was not happy."

"The Senator was not particularly happy," remarked Tom. "He had just had an interview with Stamps, and he certainly was not happy at the sight of me. He thought he had another on his hands. He's in better spirits by this time."

Sheba got up and went to his side of the table. She put her arms round his neck and pressed her cheek against his.

"Forget about him," she said.

"I am not remembering him particularly," said Tom, the shade passing from his eyes; I am remembering you— as you were nineteen years ago."

"Nineteen years ago!" said Sheba. "I was a baby!"

"Yes," answered Tom, folding a big arm round her, and speaking slowly. "I saw a man to-day who reminded me of the day you were born. Are you glad you were born, Sheba? that's what I want to be sure of."

The two pairs of young eyes met glowing. Tom knew they had met, by the warmth of the soft cheek touching him.

"Yes, I am glad—I am glad—I am glad!" with grateful sweetness.

"And I—and I," cried Rupert. He sprung up and held

out an impetuous boyish hand to Tom. "You know how glad, Uncle Tom—look at her—look at me—see how glad we both are; and it is you—you who have made it so."

"It's a pretty big thing," said Tom, "that two people should be glad they are alive." And he grasped the ardent hand as affectionately as it was offered.

CHAPTER XXXII

THE Reverend John Baird and his friend the Reverend
Lucien Latimer were lodged in a quiet house in a quiet
street. The lecturing tour had been fatiguing, and Baird
was glad of such repose as he could secure. In truth, the
excitement and strain of his work, the journeying from
place to place, the hospitalities from which he could not
escape, had worn upon him. He had grown thinner, and
often did not sleep well at night. He used to find himself
lying awake repeating to himself mechanically words from
his own lecture. "Repentance is too late," his voice would
whisper to the darkness. "Repentance cannot undo."

His audiences found him an irresistible force. He had
become more than the fashion of the hour; he was its passion. People liked to look at as well as to hear him. He
was besieged by lion-hunters, overwhelmed with attentions
in each town or city he visited. Reporters followed him,
interviewers besought appointments, agreeable people invited him to their houses, intrusive people dogged him. Latimer stood between him and as many fatigues as he could.
He transacted business for him, and interviewed interviewers; and he went to tiring functions.

"When I enter a room without you, and make your ex-
cuses, they must make the most of my black face; and they
make the most of it, but they don't love me," he said. "Still
it is a thing to be borne if it saves you when you need all
your forces. What does it matter? I have never expected
to be smiled at for my own sake as they smile at me for
yours."

In Connection with
The De Willoughby Claim

In these days of close companionship each found in each new qualities increasing the tie between them. Latimer felt himself fed by the public affection surrounding the man who was his friend. He was thrilled by the applause which thundered forth at his words; he was moved by the mere sense of his success, and the power he saw him unknowingly exercise through mere physical charm.

"I am nearer being a happy, or at least a peaceful, man than I had ever thought to be," he said to Baird; "your life seems to fill mine, and I am less lonely." Which was indeed a truth.

On the evening of the day on which big Tom had caught his glimpse of the two strangers in the corridor of the Capitol, Baird dined at the house of the Senator, whose adverse mood had promised such small encouragement to the De Willoughby claim. And in the course of the meal the host spoke of both claim and claimants.

"The man is a sort of Colossus," he said, "and he looked all the heavier and bigger because my last visitor had been the smallest and most insignificant of the hoosier type."

"Is this man a hoosier?" was asked.

"No. He has lived among the most primitive, and Rutherford tells me is a sort of county institution; but he is not a hoosier. He has a large, humane, humorous face, and a big, humorous, mellow voice. I should rather have liked the fellow, confound him, if I hadn't lost my patience before he came into the room."

"Did he tell you the story of the claim?" enquired his married daughter.

"No, I didn't let him. I was feeling pretty sick of claims, and I had no time."

"Oh, father, I wish you had let him tell it," exclaimed

the pretty young woman. " The truth is, I am beginning to be interested in that claim myself. I am in love with Judge Rutherford and his stories of Jenny and Tom Scott. His whole soul is bound up in ' pushing this thing through ' —that's what he calls it. He is the most delightful lobbyist I ever met. He is like a bull in a china shop—though I don't believe anyone ever saw a bull in a china shop."

" He does not know enough to give his friends a rest," said the Senator. "If he was not such a good fellow he would bore a man to death. He bores many a man as it is, and people in office won't stand being bored. He's too ingenuous. The shrewd ones say his ingenuousness is too good to be true. He can't keep De Willoughby's virtues out of his stories of him—and a man's virtues have nothing much to do with his claim."

" I met him in one of the squares yesterday," said Mrs. Meredith, " and he almost cried when he spoke of the claim. He told me that everything was going wrong—that it was being pushed aside by all sorts of things, and he had lost heart. His eyes and nose got quite red, and he had to wink hard to keep back the tears."

" The fellow believes in it, at any rate," said the Senator; " he has that to support him."

" He believes in everything," said Mrs. Meredith, " and it would have touched your heart to hear him talk about the claimants. There is a young nephew and a beautiful girl creature, who is big Mr. De Willoughby's adopted daughter. She is not a claimant, it is true, but they all adore each other, and the nephew is in love with her; and if the claim goes through they will be happy forever afterwards. I saw the nephew once, and he was a beautiful boy with Southern eyes and a charming expression. Upon the whole, I think I am in love with the young couple, too. Their story sounded like a pastoral poem when Judge Rutherford told it."

"Suppose you tell it to us, Marion," said the Senator, with a laugh, and a glance round the table. "It may appeal to our feelings and advance the interests of the claim."

"Pray, tell it, Mrs. Meredith," Baird put in; "the mere mention of it has appealed to my emotions. Perhaps Senator Harburton and Mr. Lewis will be moved also, and that will be two votes to the good—perhaps more."

"The charm of it is that it is a story without a plot," Mrs. Meredith said. "There is nothing in it but youth and love and innocence and beauty. It is Romeo and Juliet without the tragedy. Romeo appeared on a moonlight night in a garden, and Juliet stood upon a balcony among roses— and their young souls cried out to each other. It is all so young and innocent—they only want to spend their lives together, like flowers growing side by side. They want nothing but each other."

"And the claim," added the Senator.

"They cannot have each other if the claim fails. They will have to starve to death in each other's arms like the 'Babes in the Wood'; I am sure the robins will come and cover them with leaves."

"But the big uncle," her father asked.

"Poor fellow," Mrs. Meredith said. "Judge Rutherford is finest when he enlarges on him. He says, over and over again, as if it were a kind of argument, 'Tom, now—Tom, he wants those two young ones to be happy. He says nature fixed it all for them, so that they could be happy—and he doesn't want to see it spoiled. He says love ain't treated fair, as a rule, and he wants to see it given a show—a real show."

At least one pair of deeply interested listener's eyes were fixed upon her. They were the Reverend John Baird's.

" It might be a beautiful thing to see," he said. " One does not see it. There seems a fate against it. The wrong people meet, or the right ones do not until it is too late."

" I should like to see it myself," said the host, " but I am afraid that the argument—as an argument—would not support a claim on the Government."

" I am going to see the claimants and hear all the arguments they can bring forward," was Mrs. Meredith's conclusion. " I want to see Romeo and Juliet together."

" May I go with you? " asked Baird.

Latimer had not come in when he returned to their lodgings. He also had been out to spend the evening. But it was not many minutes before Baird heard his latch-key and the opening of the front door. He came upstairs rather slowly.

" You are either ill," Baird said, when he entered, " or you have met with some shock."

" Yes; it was a shock," was the answer. " I have been dragged back into the black pit of twenty years ago."

" Twenty years? " said Baird.

" I have seen the man who—was with us in the hillside cabin, through that night she died. He passed me in the street."

Baird stood still and looked at him without speaking. What was there to be said?

" He is such a noticeable looking fellow," Latimer went on, " that I felt sure I could find out who he was. In the mountains they called him ' Big Tom D'Willerby.' His real name is De Willoughby, and he has been here for some months in pursuit of a claim, which is a great deal talked about."

"The great De Willoughby claim?" said Baird. "They talked of it to-night at dinner."

Latimer tapped the table nervously with the fingers of an unsteady hand.

"He may be living within a hundred yards of us—within a hundred yards," he said. "We may cross each other's path at any moment. I can at least know—since fate has brought us together again—I should never have sought him out—but one can know whether—whether *it* lived or died."

"He has with him," said Baird, "a girl of nineteen who is his adopted daughter. I heard it to-night. She is said to be a lovely girl who is in love with a lovely boy who is De Willoughby's nephew. She is happy."

"She is happy," murmured Latimer, biting his livid lips. He could not bring himself back to the hour he was living in. He could only see again the bare little room—he could hear the cries of terrified anguish. "It seems strange," he murmured, "that Margery's child should be happy."

CHAPTER XXXIII

It was not difficult to discover the abiding place of the De Willoughby claimants. The time had come when there were few who did not know who occupied the upper floor of Miss Burford's house near the Circle. Miss Burford herself had gradually become rather proud of her boarders, and, as the interest in the case increased, felt herself becoming a prominent person.

"If the claim goes through, the De Willoughby family will be very wealthy," she said, genteelly. "They will return to their Southern home, no doubt, and restore it to its fawmah magnificence. Mr. Rupert De Willoughby will be lawd of the mannah."

She spent many hours—which she felt to be very aristocratic—in listening to Uncle Matt's stories of the "old De Willoughby place," the rice-fields in "South Ca'llina," and the "thousands of acres of gol' mines" in the mountains. There was a rich consolation in mere conversation on the subject of glories which had once had veritable substance, and whose magnitude might absolutely increase if fortune was kind. But it was not through inquiry that Latimer discovered the whereabouts of the man who shared his secret. In two days' time they met face to face on the steps of the Capitol.

Latimer was going down them; big Tom was coming up. The latter was lost in thought on his affairs, and was not looking at such of his fellow-men as passed him. Suddenly he found himself one or two steps below someone who held out a hand and spoke in a low voice.

In Connection with
The De Willoughby Claim

"De Willoughby!" the stranger exclaimed, and Tom lifted his eyes and looked straight into those of the man he had seen last nineteen years before in the cabin at Blair's Hollow.

"Do you know me again?" the man asked. "It's a good many years since we met, and I am not as easy to recognise as you."

"Yes, I know you," answered big Tom, grasping the out-stretched hand kindly. "I saw you a few days ago and knew you."

"I did not see you," said Latimer. "And you did not speak to me?"

"No," answered Tom, slowly; "I thought it over while I walked behind you, and I made up my mind that it might do you no good—and to hold back would do none of us any harm."

"None of us?" questioned Latimer.

Big Tom put a hand on his shoulder.

"Since you spoke to me of your own free will," he said, "let's go and have a talk. There are plenty of quiet corners in this place."

There were seats which were secluded enough, though people passed and repassed within sight of them. People often chose such spots to sit and talk together. One saw pairs of lovers, pairs of politicians, couples of sight-seers.

They found such a seat and sat down. Latimer could not well control the expression his face wore.

"None of us?" he said again.

Tom still kept a friendly hand on his shoulder.

"She is a beautiful young woman, though she will always seem more or less of a child to me," he said. "I have kept

her safe and I've made her happy. That was what I meant
to do. I don't believe she has had a sad hour in her life.
What I'm sick of is seeing people unhappy. I've kept unhappiness from her. We've loved each other—that's what
we've done. She's known nothing but having people about
who were fond of her. They were a simple, ignorant lot
of mountain hoosiers, but, Lord! they loved her and she
loved them. She's enjoyed the spring, and she's enjoyed
the summer, and she's enjoyed the autumn and the winter.
The rainy days haven't made her feel dull, and the cold
ones haven't made her shiver. That's the way she has grown
up—just like a pretty fawn or a forest tree. Now her young
mate has come, and the pair of them fell deep in love at
sight. They met at the right time and they were the right
pair. It was all so natural that she didn't know she was
in love at first. She only knew she was happier every
day. I knew what was the matter, and it made me happy
just to look on. Good lord! *how* they love each other—
those children. How they look at each other every minute
without knowing they are doing it; and how they smile
when their eyes meet—without knowing why. I know why.
It's because they are in paradise—and God knows if it's
to be done I'm going to keep them there."

"My God!" broke from Latimer. "What a heart you
have, man!" He turned his face to look at him almost
as if in reverent awe. "Margery's child! Margery's child!"
he repeated to himself. "Is she like her mother?" he
asked.

"I never saw her mother—when she was happy," Tom
answered. "She is taller than her mother and has eyes
like a summer morning sky. It's a wonderful face. I
sometimes think she must be like—the other."

In Connection with
The De Willoughby Claim

" I want to see her," said Latimer. " She need know nothing about me. I want to see her. May I? "

" Yes. We are staying here to push our claim, and we are living near Dupont Circle, and doing it as cheaply as we can. We haven't a cent to spare, but that hasn't hurt us so far. If we win our claim we shall be bloated bondholders; if we lose it, we shall have to tramp back to the mountains and build a log hut, and live on nuts and berries until we can raise a crop. The two young ones will set up a nest of their own and live like Adam and Eve—and I swear they won't mind it. They'd be happy rich, but they'll be happy poor. When would you like to come and see her? "

" May I come to-morrow? " asked Latimer. " And may I bring a friend with me? He is the human being who is nearest to me on earth. He is the only living soul who knows—what we know. He is the Reverend John Baird."

" What! " said Tom. " The man who is setting the world on fire with his lectures—the ' Repentance ' man? "

" Yes."

" She'll like to see him. No one better. We shall all like to see him. We have heard a great deal of him."

They did not part for half an hour. When they did Latimer knew a great deal of the past. He knew the story of the child's up-growing, with the sun rising from behind one mountain and setting behind another; he seemed to know the people who had loved and been familiar with her throughout her childish and girlish years; he knew of the fanciful name given her in infancy, and of the more fanciful one her primitive friends and playmates had adopted. He knew the story of Rupert, and guessed vaguely at the far past in which Delia Vanuxem had lived and died.

" Thank God I saw you that day! " he said. " Thank

God I went to you that night!" And they grasped hands again and went their separate ways.

. . . .

Latimer went home and told Baird of the meeting and of the appointment for the following day.

"I felt that you would like to see the man," he said. "He is the finest, simple being in the world. Soul and body are on a like scale."

"You were right in thinking I should like to see him," answered Baird. "I have thought of him often." He regarded his friend with some anxiety.

"To meet her face to face will be a strange thing," he added. "Do you think you can hide what you must feel? It will not be easy—even for me."

"It will not be easy for either of us—if she looks at us with Margery's eyes. You will know them. Margery was happy, too, when the picture you have seen was made."

That—to see her stand before them in her youth and beauty, all unknowing—would be a strange thing, was the thought in the mind of each as they walked through the streets together, the next evening. The flare of an occasional street-lamp falling on Latimer's face revealed all its story to his companion, though it might not have so revealed itself to another. Baird himself was wondering how they should each bear themselves throughout the meeting. She would be so wholly unconscious—this girl who had always been happy and knew nothing of the past. To her they would be but a middle-aged popular lecturer and his unattractive-looking friend—while each to himself was a man concealing from her a secret. They must eliminate it from their looks, their voices, their air. They must be frank and courteous and conventional. Baird turned it all over

363

in his mind. When they reached the house the second-story windows were lighted as if to welcome them. Matt opened the door for them, attired in his best and bowing low. To receive such guests he felt to be an important social event, which seemed to increase the chances of the claim and point to a future when distinguished visitors would throng to a much more imposing front door. He announced, with an air of state, that his master and young mistress were "receivin'," and took ceremonious charge of the callers. He had brushed his threadbare coat and polished each brass button singly until it shone. An African imagination aided him to feel the dignity of hospitality.

The sound of a girl's voice reached them as they went upstairs. They glanced at each other involuntarily, and Latimer's breath was sharply drawn. It was not the best preparation for calmness.

A glowing small fire was burning in the stove, and, plain and bare as the room was, it was filled with the effect of brightness. Two beautiful young people were laughing together over a book, and both rose and turned eager faces towards the door. Big Tom rose, too, and, advancing to meet the visitors, brought the girl with him.

She was built on long and supple lines, and had happy eyes and lovely bloom. The happy eyes were Margery's, though they were brown instead of harebell blue, and looked out from a face which was not quite Margery's, though its smile was hers. Latimer asked himself if it was possible that his manner wore the aspect of ordinary calm as he stood before her.

Sheba wondered at the coldness of his hand as she took it. She was not attracted by his anxious face, and it must be confessed that his personality produced on her the effect it frequently produced on those meeting him for the first time. It was not he who was the great man, but she felt timid before him when he spoke to her.

No one was shy of Baird. He produced his inevitable effect also. In a few minutes he had become the centre of the small company. He had made friends with Rupert, and launched Tom in conversation. Sheba was listening to him with a brightness of look charming to behold.

They sat about the table and talked, and he led them all back to the mountains which had been seeming so far away. He wanted to hear of the atmosphere, the life, the people; and yet, as they answered his queries and related anecdotes, he was learning from each one something bearing on the story of the claim. When Tom spoke of Barnesville and Judge Rutherford, or Rupert of Delisleville and Matt, their conversation was guided in such manner that business details of the claim were part of what was said. It was Tom who realised this first and spoke of it.

"We are talking of our own business as if it was the one subject on earth," he said. "That's the worst of people with a claim. I've seen a good many of them since I've been in Washington—and we are all alike."

"I have been asking questions because the subject interests me, too," said Baird. "More people than yourselves discuss it. It formed a chief topic of conversation when I dined with Senator Milner, two nights ago."

"Milner!" said Tom. "He was the man who had not time to hear me in the morning."

"His daughter, Mrs. Meredith, was inquiring about you. She wanted to hear the story. I shall tell it to her."

"Ah!" exclaimed Tom; "if *you* tell it, it will have a chance."

"Perhaps," Baird laughed. "I may be able to help you. A man who is used to audiences might be of some practical value."

He met Sheba's eyes by accident. A warm light leaped into them.

"They care a great deal more than they will admit to me," she said to him, when chance left them together a few minutes later, as Tom and Rupert were showing Latimer some books. "They are afraid of making me unhappy by letting me know how serious it will be if everything is lost. They care too much for me—but I care for them, and if I could do anything—or go to anyone——"

He looked into her eyes through a curious moment of silence.

"It was not all jest," he said after it, "what I said just now. I am a man who has words, and words sometimes are of use. I am going to give you my words—for what they are worth."

"We shall feel very rich," she answered, and her simple directness might have been addressed to a friend of years' standing. It was a great charm, this sweet acceptance of any kindness. "But I thought you were going away in a few days?"

"Yes. But I shall come back, and I shall try to set the ball rolling before I go."

She glanced at Latimer across the room.

"Mr. Latimer—" she hesitated; "do you think he does not mind that—that the claim means so much for us? I was afraid. He looked at me so seriously——"

"He looked at you a great deal," interposed Baird, quickly. "He could not help it. I am glad to have this opportunity to tell you—something. You are very like—

366

very like—someone he loved deeply—someone who died years ago. You must forgive him. It was almost a shock to him to come face to face with you."

"Ah!" softly. "Someone who died years ago!" She lifted Margery's eyes and let them rest upon Baird's face. "It must be very strange—it must be almost awful—to find yourself near a person very like someone you have loved— who died years ago."

"Yes," he answered. "Yes—awful. That is the word."

When the two men walked home together through the streets, the same thought was expressed again, and it was Latimer who expressed it.

"And when she looked at me," he said, "I almost cried out to her, 'Margery, Margery!' The cry leaped up from the depths of me. I don't know how I stopped it. Margery was smaller and more childlike—her eyes are darker, her face is her own, not Margery's—but she looks at one as Margery did. It is the simple clearness of her look, the sweet belief, which does not know life holds a creature who could betray it."

"Yes, yes," broke from Baird. The exclamation seemed involuntary.

"Yet there was one who could betray it," Latimer said.

"You *cannot* forget," said Baird. "No wonder."

Latimer shook his head.

"The passing of years," he said, "almost inevitably wipes out or dims all things; but sometimes—not often, thank Fate—there comes a phase of suffering in some man or woman's life which will not go. I once knew a woman— she was the kind of woman people envy, and whose life seems brilliant and full; it was full of the things most people want, but the things she wanted were not for her, and there was a black wound in her soul. She had had a child who had come near to healing her, and suddenly he was torn out of her being by death. She said afterwards that she knew she had been mad for months after it happened, though no one suspected her. In the years that followed she dared not allow herself to speak or think of that time of death. ' I must not let myself—I must not.' She said this to me, and shuddered, clenching her hands when she spoke. ' Never, never, never, will it be better. If a thousand years had passed it would always be the same. One thought or word of it drags me back—and plunges me deep into the old, awful woe. Old—it is not old— it never can be old. It is as if it had happened yesterday— as if it were happening to-day.' I know this is not often so. But it is so with me when a thing drags Margery back to me—drags me back to Margery. To-night, Baird; think what it is to-night! "

He put a shaking hand on Baird's hand, hurrying him by the unconscious rapidity of his own pace.

" Think what it is to-night," he repeated. " She seems part of my being. I cannot free myself. I can see her as she was when she last looked at me, as her child looked at me to-night—with joyful bright eyes and lips. It was one day when I went to see her at Boston. She was doing a little picture, and it had been praised at the studio. She was so happy—so happy. That was the last time."

" Don't, don't," cried Baird; " you must not call it back."

" I am not calling it back. It comes, it comes! You must let me go on. You can't stop me. That was the last time. The next time I saw her she had changed. I scarcely knew how—it was so little. The brightness was blurred. Then —then comes all the rest. Her growing illness—the anxiousness—the long days—the girl at the mills—the talk of those women—the first ghastly, damnable fear—the nights—the lying awake! " His breath came short and fast. He could not stop himself, it was plain. His words tumbled over each other as if he were a man telling a story in delirium.

" I can see her," he said. " I can see her—as I went into her room. I can see her shaking hands and lips and childish, terrified eyes. I can feel her convulsive little fingers clutching my feet, and her face—her face—lying upon them when she fell down."

" I cannot bear it," cried Baird; " I cannot bear it." He had uttered the same cry once before. He had received the same answer.

" She bore it," said Latimer, fiercely. " That last night —in the cabin on the hillside—her cries—they were not human—no, they did not sound human——"

He was checked. It was Baird's hand which clutched his arm now—it seemed as if for support. The man was swaying a little, and in the light of a street-lamp near them he looked up in a ghastly appeal.

" Latimer," he said. " Don't go on; you see I can't bear it. I am not so strong as I was—before I began this work. I have lost my nerve. You bring it before me as it is brought before yourself. I am living the thing. I can't bear it."

Latimer came back from the past. He made an effort to understand and control himself.

" Yes," he said, quite dull; " that was what the woman I spoke of told me—that she lived the thing again. It is not sane to let one's self go back. I beg your pardon, Baird."

CHAPTER XXXIV

" It's a curious job, that De Willoughby claim," was said in a committee-room of the House, one day. " It's beginning to attract attention because it has such an innocent air. The sharp ones say that may be the worst feature of it, because ingenuousness is more dangerous than anything else if a job is thoroughly rotten. The claimants are the most straightforward pair the place has ever seen—a big, humourous, well-mannered country man, and a boy of twenty-three. Rutherford, of Hamlin County, who is a monument of simplicity in himself, is heart and soul in the thing—and Farquhar feels convinced by it. Farquhar is one of the men who are not mixed up with jobs. Milner himself is beginning to give the matter a glance now and then, though he has not committed himself; and now the Reverend John Baird, the hero of the platform, is taking it up."

Baird had proved his incidental offer of aid to have been by no means an idle one. He had been obliged to absent himself from Washington for a period, but he had returned when his lecture tour had ended, and had shown himself able in a new way. He was the kind of man whose conversation people wish to hear. He chose the right people and talked to them about the De Willoughby claim. He was interesting and picturesque in connection with it, and lent the topic attractions. Tom had been shrewdly right in saying that his talk of it would give it a chance.

He went often to the house near the Circle. Latimer

did not go with him, and had himself explained his reasons
to big Tom.

"I have seen her," he said. "It is better that I should
not see her often. She is too much like her mother."

But Baird seemed to become by degrees one of the household. Gradually—and it did not take long—Tom and he
were familiar friends. They had long talks together, they
walked side by side through the streets, they went in company to see the men it was necessary to hold interviews
with. Their acquaintance became an intimacy which established itself with curious naturalness. It was as if they had
been men of the same blood, who, having spent their lives
apart, on meeting, found pleasure in the discovery of their
relationship. The truth was that for the first time in his
life big Tom enjoyed a friendship with a man who was
educated and, in a measure, of the world into which he
himself had been born. Baird's world had been that of New
England, his own, the world of the South; but they could
comprehend each other's parallels and precedents, and argue
from somewhat similar planes. In the Delisleville days Tom
had formed no intimacies, and had been a sort of Colossus
set apart; in the mountains of North Carolina he had con-
sorted with the primitive and uneducated in good-humoured,
even grateful, friendliness; but he had mentally lived like
a hermit. To have talked to Jabe Doty or Nath Hayes
on any other subjects than those of crops and mountain
politics or sermons would have been to bewilder them hopelessly. To find himself in mental contact with a man who
had lived and thought through all the years during which
he himself had vegetated at the Cross-roads, was a wonderful
thing to him. He realised that he had long ago given up
expecting anything approaching such companionship, and

that to indulge in it was to live in a new world. Baird's voice, his choice of words, his readiness and tact, the very carriage of his fine, silvering head, produced on him the effect of belonging to a new species of human being.

"You are all the things I have been missing for half a lifetime," he said. "I didn't know what it was I was making up my mind to going without—but it was such men as you."

On his own part, Baird felt he had made a rich discovery also. The large humour and sweetness, the straightforward unworldliness which was still level-headed and observing, the broad kindliness and belief in humanity which were so far from unintelligent or injudicious, were more attractive to him than any collected characteristics he had met before. They seemed to meet some strained needs in him. To leave his own rooms, and find his way to the house whose atmosphere was of such curious, homely brightness, to be greeted by Sheba's welcoming eyes, to sit and chat with Tom in the twilight or to saunter out with him with an arm through his, were things he soon began to look forward to. He began also to realise that this life of home and the affections was a thing he had lived without. During his brief and wholly unemotional married life he had known nothing like it. His years of widowerhood had been presided over by Mrs. Stornaway, who had assumed the supervision of his child as a duty. Annie had been a properly behaved, rather uninteresting and unresponsive little person. She had neat features and a realisation of the importance of respectability and the proprieties which was a credit to Willowfield and her training. She was never gay or inconsequent or young. She had gone to school, she had had her frocks lengthened and been introduced at tea-parties, exactly as had been planned for her. She never committed a breach of discretion and she never formed in any degree an element of special interest. She greatly respected her father's position as a successful man, and left it to be vaguely due to the approbation of Willowfield.

Big Tom De Willoughby, in two wooden rooms behind a cross-roads store, in a small frame house kept in order by a negro woman, and in the genteel poverty of Miss Burford's second floor, had surrounded himself with the comforts and pleasures of the affections. It was not possible to enter the place without feeling their warmth, and Baird found himself nourished by it. He saw that Rupert, too, was nourished by it. His young good looks and manhood were developing under its influence day by day. He seemed to grow taller and stronger. Baird had made friends with him, too, and was with them the night he came in to announce that at last he had got work to do.

"It is to sell things from behind a counter," he said, and he went to Sheba and lifted her hand to his lips, kissing it before them all. "We know a better man who has done it."

"You know a bigger man who has done it," said Tom. "He did it because he was cut out for a failure. You are doing it because you are cut out for a success. It will be a good story for the reporters when the claim goes through, my boy."

Baird perceived at once that it was a good story, even at this particular period—a story which might be likely to arouse curiosity and interest at a time when the awakening of such emotions was of the greatest value. He told it at the house of a magnate of the Supreme Court, the next night. He had a varied and useful audience of important

politicians and their wives and daughters, the latter specially fitted to act as mediums of transmission to other audiences. He told the anecdote well. It was a good picture,
that of the room on Miss Burford's upper floor, the large
claimant smiling like a benign Jove, and the handsome
youngster bending his head to kiss the girlish hand as if
he were doing homage to a queen.

"I think his feeling was that his failure to get a better
thing was a kind of indignity done her," Baird explained.
"He comes of a race of men who have worshipped women
and beauty in a romantic, troubadour fashion; only the
higher professions, and those treated in a patrician, amateur
style, were possible to them as work. And yet, as he said,
a better man than himself had done this same thing. What
moves one is that he has gone out to find work as if he had
been born a bricklayer. He tells me they are reaching the
end of all they depend on."

"I'll tell you what it is," said Senator Milner to his daughter, a few days afterwards; "this is going to be a feminine
claim. There was a time when I swore I wouldn't touch it,
but I foresee what is going to happen. I'm going to give
in, and the other opposers are going to give in, and in the
end the Government will give in. And it will be principally
because a force of wives and daughters has marshalled itself
to march to the rescue. No one ever realises what a power
the American woman is, and how much she is equal to ac-
complishing. If she took as much interest in politics as
English women do, she would elect every president and
control every party. We are a good-natured lot, and we
are fond of our womenkind and believe in them much more
than other nations do. They're pretty clever and straight,
you know, as well as being attractive, and we can't help

realising that they are often worth listening to. So we listen, and when they drive a truth home we are willing to believe in it. If the feminine halves of the two Houses decide that the De Willoughby claim is all right, they'll prove it to us, and there you are."

"I believe we can prove it to you," answered Mrs. Meredith. "I went to see the people, and you could prove anything straightforward by merely showing them to the Houses in session. They could not conceal a disingenuous thought among them—the delightful giant, the boy with the eyelashes, the radiant girl, and the old black man put together."

In the meantime Judge Rutherford did his honest best. He had been too sanguine not to do it with some ruefulness after the first few months. During the passage of these few months many of his ingenuous ideals had been overthrown. It had been borne in upon him that honest virtue was not so powerful a factor as he had believed. The obstacles continually arising in his pathway were not such as honest virtue could remove. The facts that the claim was "as straight as a string," and that big Tom De Willoughby was the best fellow in Hamlin were bewilderingly ineffective. When prospects seemed to shine they might be suddenly overshadowed by the fact that a man whose influence was needed, required it to use for himself in other quarters; when all promised well some apparently unexplainable obstacle brought things to a standstill.

"Now you see it and now you don't," said Tom, resignedly. "That's the position. This sort of thing might go on for twenty years."

He was not aware that he spoke prophetically; yet claims resting on as solid a basis as his own passed through the same dragging processes for thirty years before they were finally settled. But such did not possess the elements of unprofessional picturesqueness this particular one presented told to its upholders and opposers.

Uncle Matt himself was to be counted among these elements. He had made himself as familiar and popular a figure in the public places of the Capital as he had been in Delisleville. He made friends in the market-house and on the steps of the Capitol and the Treasury and the Pension Office; he hung about official buildings and obtained odd jobs of work, his grey wool, his polished air of respectfulness, his readiness and amiability attracted attention and pleased those who came in contact with him. People talked to him and asked him friendly questions, and when they did so the reason for his presence in Washington and the importance of the matter which had brought his young master to the seat of government were fully explained.

"I belongs to de gen'elmen dat's here tendin' to de De Willoughby claim, sah," he would say. "Co'se, sah, you've heern 'bout it up to de Capitol. I'se yere waitin' on Marse Rupert De Willoughby, but co'se he don' live yere—till ye gets his claim through—like he do in de ole family mansh'n at Delisleville—an' my time hangs heavy on my han's, cos I got so much ledger—so I comes out like dish yer—an' takes a odd job now an' agen."

It was not long before he was known as the De Willoughby claimant, and loiterers were fond of drawing him out on the subject of the " gol' mines." He gathered a large amount of information on the subjects of claims and the rapid methods of working them. He used to come to Tom sometimes, hot and excited with his struggles to comprehend detail. "What all dish yer 'bout Marse Rupert's granpa'n' bein' destructively disloyal? Dar warn't no disloyal 'bout it. Ef dar was a fault to be foun' with the old Judge it was dat he was mos' too loyal. He couldn' hol' in, an' he qu'ol with mos' ev'y gen'elman he talk to. He pass shots with one or two he had a disagreement with. He pass shots with 'em. How's de Guv'ment gwine call a gen'elman 'destructively disloyal' when he ready any minit to pass shots with his bes' fren's, ef dey don' 'gree with his pol'tics—an' his pol'tics is on de side er Marse Ab'am Lincoln an' de Yankees?"

The phrase "constructively disloyal" rankled in his soul. He argued about it upon every possible occasion, and felt that if the accusation could be disproved the De Willoughby case would be triumphantly concluded, which was in a large measure true.

"I steddies 'bout dat thing day an' night," he said to Sheba. "Seems like dar oughter be someone to tes'ify. Ef I had de money to travel back to Delisleville, I'd go an' try to hunt someone up."

He was seated upon the steps of a Government building one afternoon, discussing his favourite subject with some of his coloured friends. He had been unusually eloquent, and had worked himself up to a peroration, when he suddenly ceased speaking and stared straight across the street to the opposite side of the pavement, in such absorption that he forgot to close his mouth.

He was gazing at an elderly gentleman with a hook nose and the dashing hat of the broad brim, which was regarded as being almost as much an insignia of the South as the bonnie blue flag itself.

Uncle Matt got up and shuffled across the street. He

had become unconsciously apish with excitement. His old
black face worked and his hands twitched.

He was so far out of breath when he reached the stranger's side that he could scarcely make himself heard, as, pull-
ing his hat off, he cried, agitatedly:

"Doctah! Doctah Atkinson, sah! Doctah Williams Atkinson!"

The stranger did not hear him distinctly, and waved him
off, evidently taking him for a beggar.

"I've nothing for you, uncle," he said, with condescending good-nature.

Uncle Matt found some of his breath, though not enough
to steady his voice. But his strenuousness was almost passionate. "Doctah Williams Atkinson," he said, "I ain't
beggin', Doctah Atkinson, sah; on'y axin' if I might speak
a few words to you, sah!" His shrewd insistance on the
name was effective.

The elderly gentleman turned and looked at him in surprised questioning.

"How do you know me?" he said. "This is the first
time I have been in Washington—and I've not been here
an hour."

"I knowed you, Doctah Atkinson, sah, in Delisleville,
Delisle County. Ev'ybody knowed you, Doctah! I was
dar endurin' er de war. I was dar de time you—you an'
Judge De Willoughby passed shots 'bout dat Confed'ate
flag."

"What do you want?" said Dr. Atkinson, somewhat un-
smilingly. These were days when stories of the Confederate
flag were generally avoided. Northerners called it the rebel
flag.

Matt had had the discretion to avoid this mistake. He

was wild with anxious excitement. Suddenly here had appeared a man who could give all the evidence desired, if he would do so. He had left Delisleville immediately on the close of the war and had not been heard of. He might, like so many, be passing on to some unknown point, and remain in the city only between trains. There was no time to find any better qualified person than himself to attend to this matter. It must be attended to upon the spot and at this moment. Uncle Matt knew all the incongruities of the situation. No one could have known them better. But a sort of hysteric courage grew out of his desperation.

"Doctah Williams Atkinson, sah!" he said. "May I take de liberty of walking jes' behin' you an' axin' you a question. I mustn't keep you standin'. I beg you to 'scuse me, sah. I kin talk an' walk at de same time."

Dr. Williams Atkinson was an amenable person, and Matt's imploring old darky countenance was not without its pathos. He was so evidently racked by his emotions.

"What is it all about?" he enquired.

Matt stood uncovered and spoke fast. The hand holding his hat was shaking, as also was his voice.

"I'm nothin' but a ole niggah man, Doctah Atkinson, sah," he said. "It ain't for myself I'se intrudin' on ye; it's cos dar wasn't time to go fer Marse De Willoughby that could talk it like it oughter be. I jes' had to push my ole niggah self in, fear you'd be gone an' we'd nevah set eyes on you agin."

"Walk along by me," said the Doctor. "What about the De Willoughbys; I thought they were all dead."

"All but Marse Thomas and Marse Rupert. Dey's yere 'tendin' to de claim. Has you done heern 'bout de claim, Doctah Atkinson?"

"No," the Doctor answered. "I have been in too far out West."

Whereupon Matt plunged into the story of the "gol' mines," and the difficulties which had presented themselves in the pathway of the claimant, and the necessity for the production of testimony which would disprove the charge of disloyalty. The detail was not very clear, but it had the effect of carrying Dr. Williams Atkinson back to certain good old days in Delisleville, before his beloved South had been laid low and he had been driven far afield to live among strangers, an alien. For that reason he found himself moved by the recital and listened to it to its end.

"But what has this to do with me?" he asked. "What do you want of me?"

"When I seed you, sah," Uncle Matt explained, "it all come back to me in a minnit, how you an' de Judge pass shots 'bout dat flag; how you axed him to a dinner-party, an' dar was a Confed'ate officer dar—an' a Confed'ate flag hung up over de table, an' de Judge when he seed it he 'fused p'int blank to set down to de table, an' it ended in you goin' out in de gyardin' an' changin' shots."

"Yes, damn it all," cried Dr. Atkinson, but melted the next moment. "The poor old fellow is dead," he said, "an' he died in disgrace and without friends."

"Yes," Uncle Matt protested, eagerly; "without a single friend, an' all 'lone 'ceptin' of Marse Rupert—all 'lone. An' it was 'cos he was so strong for de Union—an' now de Guv'ment won't let his fambly have his money 'cos dey's tryin' to prove him destructively disloyal—when he changed shots with his bes' friend 'cos he wouldn't set under de Confed'ate flag."

A grim smile wakened in Dr. Atkinson's face.

"What!" he said; "do you want me to explain to the Government that the old scamp would have blown my brains out if he could?"

"Doctah Atkinson, sah," said Uncle Matt, with shrewd gravity, "things is diff'rent dese days, an' de Guv'ment don't call dem gen'elmen scamps as was called dat in de Souf."

He looked up under the broad brim of his companion's hat with impassioned appealing.

"I jes' 'member one thing, sah," he said; "dat you was a Southern gen'elman, and when a enemy's dead a Southern gen'elman don't cherish no harm agin him, an' you straight from Delisleville, an' you deed an' heerd it all, an' de Guv'-ment ken see plain enough you's no carpet-bag jobber, an' ef a gen'elman like you tes'ify, an' say you was enemies—an' you did pass shots count er dat flag, how's dey gwine talk any more about dis destructive disloyal business? How dey gwine ter do it?"

"And I am to be the means of enriching his family—the family of an obstinate old fool, who abused me like a pickpocket and spoiled a dress-coat for me when dress-coats were scarce."

"He's dead, Doctah Williams Atkinson, sah, he's dead," said Matt. "It was mighty lonesome the way he died, too, in dat big house, dat was stripped by de soldiers, an' ev'y-body dead belonging to him—Miss De Willoughby, an' de young ladies, an' Marse Romaine, an' Marse De Courcy—no one lef' but dat boy. It was mighty lonesome, sah."

"Yes, that's so," said Dr. Atkinson, reflectively. After a few moments' silence, he added, "Whom do you want me to tell this to? It may be very little use, but it may serve as evidence."

Uncle Matt stopped upon the pavement.

In Connection with
The De Willoughby Claim

"Would you let me 'scort you to Senator Milner, sah?"
he said, in absolute terror at his own daring. "Would you
'low me to 'tend you to Senator Grove? I knows what a
favior I'se axin'. I knows it doun to de groun'. I scarcely
dars't to ax it, but if I loses you, sah, Marse Thomas De
Willoughby an' Marse Rupert may lose de claim. Ef I lose
you, sah, seems mos' like I gwine to lose my mind."

.   .   .   .

There were a thousand chances to one that Senator Milner might not be where Uncle Matt hoped to find him;
there were ten thousand chances to one that he might be
absorbingly engaged; there were uncountable chances
against them obtaining an interview with either man, and
yet it so happened they had the curious good luck to come
upon Senator Milner absolutely without searching for him.
It was rather he who came upon them at one of the entrances
of the Capitol itself, before which stood his daughter's carriage. Mrs. Meredith had spent the morning in the Senate,
being interested in the subject under debate. She was going
to take her father home to lunch, and as she was about to
enter her carriage her glance fell upon the approaching figures of Uncle Matt and his companion.

"Father," she said, "there is the faithful retainer of
the De Willoughby claimants, and there is not a shadow of
a doubt that he is in search of you. I am convinced that
he wishes to present that tall Southerner under the big hat."

In a moment's space Uncle Matt was before them. The
deprecatory respect implied by his genuflections could
scarcely be computed.

"Senator Milner, sah," he said, "Doctah Williams Atkinson of Delisleville has had de kindness to say he do me
de favior to come yeah, sah, to tes'ify, sah——"

In Connection with
The De Willoughby Claim

The large hat was removed by its owner with a fine sweep. "The old fellow thinks I can do his people a service, Senator," explained Dr. Atkinson. "He is the servant of the De Willoughby claimants, and it seems there has been some question of Judge De Willoughby's loyalty. During the war, sir, he was called *dis*loyal by his neighbours, and was a much hated man."

Uncle Matt's lips were trembling. He broke forth, forgetting the careful training of his youth.

"Dar wasn't a gen'elman in de county," he cried, "dar wasn't a gen'elman in de State, mo' hated an' 'spised an' mo' looked down on."

The lean Southerner nodded acquiescently. "That's true," he said. "It's quite true. He was a copperhead and a firebrand. We detested him. He insulted me at my own table by refusing to sit down under the Southern flag, and the matter ended with pistols."

"This is interesting, by Jove," said the Senator, and he looked from Uncle Matt to his capture. "I should like to hear more of it."

"Will you confer a pleasure on me by coming home to lunch with us?" said Mrs. Meredith, who had begun to look radiant. "I am interested in the De Willoughby claim; I would give a great deal to see my father entirely convinced. He has been on the verge of conviction for some time. I want him to hear the story with all the details. I beg you will let us take you home with us, Dr. Atkinson."

"Madame," replied Dr. Williams Atkinson, with an eighteenth century obeisance, "Judge De Willoughby and I lived in open feud, but I am becoming interested in the De Willoughby claim also. I accept your invitation with pleasure." And they drove away together.

CHAPTER XXXV.

"THERE is a man who seems to have begun to haunt my pathway," Baird said to Tom; "or perhaps it is Latimer's pathway, for it is when Latimer is with me that I meet him. He is small and sharp-featured and unwholesome."

"It sounds like Stamps," laughed big Tom.

He related the story of Stamps and his herds. The herds had not gained the congressional ear as Mr. Stamps had hoped. He had described their value and the gravity of his loss to everyone who would listen to his eloquence, but the result had been painfully discouraging. His boarding-house had become a cheaper one week by week, and his blue jeans had grown shabbier. He had fallen into the habit of hanging about the entrances of public buildings and the street corners in the hope of finding hearers and sympathisers. His sharp little face had become haggard and more weasel-like than before. Baird recognised big Tom's description of him at once.

"Yes, it must be Stamps," he said. "What is the meaning of his interest in us? Does he think we can provide evidence to prove the value of the herds? What are you thinking of, De Willoughby?"

In fact, there had suddenly recurred to Tom's mind a recollection of Sheba's fifth birthday and the visit Mr. Stamps had made him. With something of a shock he recalled the shrewd meekness of his voice as he made his exit.

In Connection with
The De Willoughby Claim

"It begins with a 'L,' Tom; it begins with a 'L.'"

The need of money was merely the natural expression of Mr. Stamps's nature. He had needed money when he was born, and had laid infant schemes to secure cents from his relatives and their neighbours before he was four years old. But he had never needed it as he did now. The claim for governmental restitution of the value of the daily increasing herds had become the centre of his being. His belief in their existence and destruction was in these days profound; his belief that he should finally be remunerated in the name and by the hand of national justice was the breath of life to him. He had at last found a claim agent whose characteristics were similar to his own, and, so long as he was able to supply small sums with regularity, this gentleman was willing to encourage him and direct him to fresh effort. Mr. Abner Linthicum, of Vermont, had enjoyed several successes in connection with two or three singular claims which he had "put through" with the aid of genius combined with a peculiar order of executive ability. They had not been large claims, but he had "put them through" when other agents had declined to touch them. In fact, each one had been a claim which had been fought shy of, and one whose final settlement had been commented upon with open derision or raised eyebrows.

"Yours is the kind of claim I like to take up," he had said to his client in their first interview; "but it's the kind that's got to be engineered carefully, and money is needed to grease the wheels. But it'll pay to grease them."

It had needed money. Stamps had no large sums to give, but he could be bled by drops. He had changed his cheap boarding-place for a cheaper one, that he might be able to save a few dollars a week; he had left the cheaper one for one cheaper still for the same reason, and had at last camped in a bare room over a store, and lived on shreds of food costing a few cents a day, that he might still grease the wheels. Abner Linthicum was hard upon him, and was not in the least touched by seeing his meagre little face grow sharper and his garments hang looser upon his small frame.

"You'll fat on the herds," he would say, with practical jocularity, and Mr. Stamps grinned feebly, his thin lips stretching themselves over hungry teeth.

The little man burned with the fever of his chase. He sat in his bare room on the edge of his mattress—having neither bedstead nor chairs nor tables—and his fingers clutched each other as he worked out plans and invented arguments likely to be convincing to an ungrateful Government. He used to grow hot and cold over them.

"Ef Tom 'd hev gone in with me an' helped me to work out that thar thing about Sheby, we mought hev made suthin' as would hev carried me through this," he said to himself more than once. He owed Tom a bitter grudge in a mild way. His bitterness was the bitterness of a little rat baulked of cheese.

He had kept safely what he had found in the deserted cabin, but, as the years passed, he lost something of the hopes he had at first cherished. When he had seen Sheba growing into a tall beauty he had calculated that her market value was increasing. A handsome young woman who might marry well, might be willing to pay something to keep a secret quiet—if any practical person knew the secret and it was unpleasant. Well-to-do husbands did not want to hear their wives talked about. When Rupert De Willoughby had arrived, Mr. Stamps had had a moment of discouragement.

In Connection with
The De Willoughby Claim

"He's gwine to fall in love with her," he said, "but he'd oughter bin wealthier. Ef the De Willoughbys was what they'd usedter be he'd be the very feller as 'ud pay for things to be kept quiet. The De Willoughbys was allers proud an' 'ristycratic, an' mighty high-falutin' 'bout their women folk."

When the subject of the De Willoughby claim was broached he fell into feverish excitement. The De Willoughbys had a chance in a hundred of becoming richer than they had ever been. He took his treasure from its hiding-place—sat turning it over, gnawing his finger-nails and breathing fast. But treasure though he counted it, he gained no clue from it but the one he had spoken of to Tom when he had cast his farewell remark to him as he closed the door.

"Ef there'd hev been more," he said. "A name ain't much when there ain't nothin' to tack on to it. It was curi's enough, but it'd hev to be follered up an' found out. Ef he was only what he 'lowed to be—'tain't nothin' to hide that a man's wife dies an' leaves a child. I don't b'lieve thar wasn't nothin' to hide—but it'd hev to be *proved* —an' proved plain. It's mighty aggravatin'."

One night, seeing a crowd pouring into a hall where a lecture was to be delivered, he had lingered about the entrance until the carriage containing the lecturer drove up. Here was something to be had for nothing, at all events— he could have a look at the man who was making such a name for himself. There must be something in a man who could demand so much a night for talking to people. He managed to get a place well to the front of the loitering crowd on the pavement.

The carriage-door was opened and a man got out.

In Connection with
The De Willoughby Claim

"That ain't him," said a bystander. "That's Latimer. He's always with him."

The lecturer descended immediately after his companion, but Stamps, who was pushing past a man who had got in front of him, was displaying this eagerness, not that he might see the hero of the hour, but that he might look squarely at the friend who had slightly turned his face.

"Gosh!" ejaculated the little hoosier, a minute later. "I'd most swear to him."

He was exasperatedly conscious that he could not quite have sworn to him. The man he had seen nineteen years before had been dressed in clumsily made homespun; he had worn his black hair long and his beard had been unshaven. Nineteen years were nineteen years, and the garb and bearing of civilisation would make a baffling change in any man previously seen attired in homespun, and carrying himself as an unsociable hoosier.

"But I'd most sw'ar to him—most." Stamps went through the streets muttering, "I'd most *swar!*"

It was but a few days later that Latimer saw him standing on a street corner staring at him as he himself approached. It was his curious intentness which attracted Latimer. He did not recognise his face. He had not seen him more than once in the days so long gone by, and had then cast a mere abstracted glance at him. He did not know him again— though his garments vaguely recalled months when he had only seen men clothed in jeans of blue, or copperas brown. He saw him again the next day, and again the next, and after that he seemed to chance upon him so often that he could not help observing and reflecting upon the eager scrutiny in his wrinkled countenance.

In Connection with
The De Willoughby Claim

"Do you see that man?" he remarked to Baird. "I come upon him everywhere. Do you know him?"

"No. I thought it possible you did—or that he recognised one of us—or wanted to ask some question."

After his conversation with big Tom De Willoughby, Latimer heard from Baird the story of the herds and their indefatigable claimant.

"He comes from the Cross-roads?" said Latimer. "I don't remember his face."

"Do you think," said Baird, rather slowly, "that he thinks he remembers yours?"

A week passed before Latimer encountered him again. On this occasion he was alone. Baird had gone South to Delisleville in the interests of the claim. He had unexpectedly heard rumours of some valuable evidence which might be gathered in a special quarter at this particular moment, and had set out upon the journey at a few hours' notice.

Stamps had passed two days and nights in torment. He had learned from Mr. Linthicum that his claim had reached one of the critical points all claims must pass. More money was needed to grease the wheels that they might carry it past the crisis safely. Stamps had been starving himself for days and had gone without fire for weeks, but the wheels had refused to budge for the sum he managed to produce. He was weak, and so feverish with anxiety and hunger that his lips were cracked and his tongue dry to rasping.

"It's all I kin scrape, Linthicum," he said to that gentleman. "I kin get a few dollars more if Minty kin sell her crop o' corn an' send me the money—but this is every cent I kin give ye now. Won't it do *nothin'*?"

"No, it won't," answered the claim agent, with a final

389

sort of shrug. "We're dealing with a business that's got to be handled well or it'll all end in smoke. *I* can't work on the driblets you've been bringing me—and, what's more, I should be a fool to try."

"But ye wouldn't give it up!" cried Stamps, in a panic. "Ye couldn't throw me over, Linthicum!"

"There's no throwing over about it," Linthicum said. "I shall have to give the thing up if I can't keep it going. Money's *got* to be used over a claim like this. I have had to ask men for a thousand dollars at a time—and the thing they were working was easier to be done than this is."

"A thousand dollars!" cried Stamps. He grew livid and a lump worked in his throat, as if he was going to cry. "A thousand dollars 'ud buy me and sell me twice over, Mr. Linthicum."

"I'm not asking you for a thousand dollars yet," said Linthicum. "I may have to ask you for five hundred before long—but I'm not doing it now."

"Five hundred!" gasped Stamps, and he sat down in a heap and dropped his damp forehead on his hands.

That night, as Latimer entered the house of an acquaintance with whom he was going to spend the evening, he caught sight of the, by this time, familiar figure on the opposite side of the street.

The night was cold and damp, and rain was falling when the door closed behind him. He heard it descending steadily throughout the evening, and more than once the continuance of the downpour was commented upon by some member of the company. When the guests separated for the night and Latimer turned into the street again, he had scarcely walked five yards before hearing a cough; he cast a glance over his shoulder and saw the small man in blue jeans. The jeans were wet and water was dropping from the brim of the old felt hat. The idea which at once possessed his mind was that for some mysterious reason best known to himself the wearer had been waiting for and was following him. What was it for? He turned about suddenly and faced the person who seemed so unduly interested in his actions.

" Do you want to speak to me? " he demanded.

This movement, being abrupt, rather upset Mr. Stamps's calculations. He came to a standstill, looking surprised and nervous.

" Thar ain't no harm done," he said. " I aimed to find out whar ye lived."

" Have you been waiting for me to come out of the house? " asked Latimer, feeling some curiosity.

Stamps admitted that he had, the admission being somewhat reluctant, as if he felt it might commit him to something. Having so far betrayed himself, however, he drew something nearer, with a suggestion of stealthiness.

" Ye're mighty like a man I once knowed," he said. " Yer powerful like him. I never seed two men more liker each other."

" Where did he live when you knew him? " Latimer enquired, the wretched, dank little figure suddenly assuming the haunting air of something his eye must have rested on before.

" I seen him in North Ca'llina. He did not live thar— in the way other folks did. He was jest stayin'. I won't keep ye standin' in the rain," insinuatingly. " I'll jest walk along by ye."

Latimer walked on. This dragged him back again, as other things had done once or twice. He did not speak, but strode on almost too rapidly for Stamps's short legs. The short legs began to trot, and their owner to continue his explanations rather breathlessly.

"He warn't livin' thar same as other folks," he said. "Thar was suthin' curi's about him. Nobody knowed nothin' about him, an' nobody knew nothin' about his wife. Now I come to think of it, nobody ever knowed his name —but me."

"Did he tell it to you?" said Latimer, rigidly.

"No," with something verging on a chuckle, discreetly strangled at its birth. "Neither him nor his wife was tellin' things just then. They was layin' mighty low. She died when her child was borned, an' he lit out right away an' ain't never been heern tell of since."

Latimer said nothing. The rain began to fall more heavily, and Mr. Stamps trotted on.

"'Lowin' for store clothes an' agein'," he continued, "I never seen two fellers favour each other as you two do. An' his name bein' the same as yourn, makes it curi'ser still."

"You are getting very wet," was Latimer's sole comment.

"I got wet to the skin long afore you come out that house where ye was," said Mr. Stamps; "but I 'low to find out whar ye live."

"I live about a quarter of a mile from here," said Latimer. "The brick house with the bay windows, opposite the square. Number 89."

"I'd rather see ye in," replied Stamps, cautiously.

"I might go into a house I do not live in," returned Latimer.

"Ye won't. It's too late. Ain't ye gwine to say nothin', Mr. Latimer?"

"What do you want me to say?"

"Sheby's good-lookin' gal," Stamps said. "Tom's done well by her. Ef they get their claim through they'll be powerful rich. Young D'Willerby he's mightily in love with her—an' he wouldn't want no talk."

"There is the house I live in at present," said Latimer, pointing with his umbrella. "We shall be there directly."

"Ministers don't want no talk neither," proceeded Stamps. "Ef a minister had made a slip an' tried hard to hide it an' then hed it proved on him he wouldn't like it—an' his church members wouldn't like it—an' his high class friends. There'd be a heap er trouble."

"Number 89," said Latimer. "You see I was speaking the truth. This is the gate; I am going in."

His tone and method were so unsatisfactory and unmoved that—remembering Abner Linthicum—Stamps became desperate. He clutched Latimer's arm and held it.

"It'd be worth money fur him to git safe hold of them letters. Thar was two on 'em. I didn't let on to Tom. I wasn't gwine to let on to him till I found out he'd go in with me. Them as knowed the man they was writ by 'ud be able to see a heap in 'em. They'd give him away. Ye'd better get hold of 'em. They're worth five hundred. They're yourn—ye wrote 'em yourself. Ye ain't jest like him—ye're *him*—I'll sw'ar to ye!"

Latimer suddenly saw his mother's mild New England countenance, with its faded blue eyes. He remembered the hours he had spent telling her the details of the sunny days in Italy, where Margery had lain smiling in the sunset. He looked down the long wet street, the lamps gleaming on its shining surface. He thought of Baird, who would not return until the day on which he was to deliver a farewell lecture before leaving Washington. He recalled his promptness of resource and readiness for action. If Baird were but in the room above in which the light burned he would tell him! His mind seemed to vault over all else at this instant —to realise the thing which it had not reached at the first shock. He turned on Stamps.

"You say there were letters?" he exclaimed, forgetting his previous unresponsiveness.

"Two. Not long 'uns, an' wrote keerful—without no name. But they say a heap. They was wrote when he had to leave her."

Latimer's heart seemed physically to turn over in his side. He had never known she had had a line of handwriting in her possession. This must be some scrap of paper, some last, last words she clung to with such anguish of desperation that she could not tear herself from them, and so had died leaving them in their secret hiding-place. The thought was a shock. The effort it cost him to regain his self-control was gigantic. But he recovered his outward calm.

"You had better go home and change your clothing," he said, as coldly as he had spoken before. "You are not a young man or a strong one, and you may kill yourself. You are making a mistake about me; but if you will give me your address I will see you again."

"I thort ye would—mebbe," said Stamps. "I thort mebbe ye would. They're worth it."

And he scribbled a few words on a scrap of paper with a stump of a pencil—producing both rapidly from his pocket—and thrusting it into Latimer's hand, trotted away contentedly down the long wet street.

CHAPTER XXXVI

As he entered his rooms, Latimer glanced round at Baird's empty chair and wished he had found him sitting in it. He walked over to it and sat down himself—simply because it was Baird's chair and suggested his presence. Latimer knew how he would have turned to look at him as he came in, and that he would at once have known by instinct that the old abyss had been re-opened.

" If he were here," he thought, " he would tell me what to do."

But he knew what he was going to do. He must buy the little hoosier's silence if it was to be bought. He should see the letters. Through all those months she had hidden them. He could imagine with what terror. She could not bear to destroy them, and yet he knew there must have been weeks she did not dare to go near their hiding-place. They must have been concealed in some cranny of the cabin. How she must have shuddered with dread when he had accidentally approached the spot where they lay concealed. He recalled now that several times he had been wakened from his sleep in the middle of the night by hearing her moving about her room and sobbing. She had perhaps crept out of her bed in the darkness to find these scraps of paper, to hold them in her hands, to crush them against her heart, to cover them with piteous kisses, salt with scalding tears.

On one such night he had risen, and, going to the closed door, had spoken to her through it, asking her if she was ill.

"No, no, Lucien," she had cried out, "but—but I am so lonely—so lonely."

She had told him the next day that the sound of the wind soughing in the pines had kept her from sleep, and she had got up because she could not bear to be still and listen.

He had known well what she meant by her desolate little answer to him. She had been a beloved thing always. As a child her playmates had loved her, as a school-girl she had won the hearts of companions and teachers alike. Nature had endowed her with the brightness and sweetness which win affection. The smile in her eyes wakened an answer even in the look of passing strangers. Suddenly all had changed. She was hidden in the darkness, crushed and shamed, an outcast and a pariah—a thing only to be kept out of sight. Sometimes, after she had been sitting lost in thought, Latimer had seen her look up bewildered, glance at her little, deformed body, and sit white and trembling.

"Everything is different," she panted out once. "It is as if all the world was black. It is—because—because I am black!"

Latimer had made no effort to wring from her the name she had prayed to be allowed to hide; yet he had often wondered that in some hysteric moment it had not escaped her—that mere helpless anguish did not betray her into uttering some word or phrase which might have served as a clue. But this she had never done, and between them there had been built a stone wall of silence. Yet, in spite of it, he had known that her young heart was broken with love for this nameless traitor—a love which would not die. He had seen it in the woe of her eyes, in the childlike longing of her look when she sat and gazed out over the wild beauty of the land, thinking she was unobserved. In his own soul there had been black, bitter hate, but in hers only loneliness and pain.

There came back to him—and he sprang up and ground his teeth, pacing the floor as he remembered it—a night when she had wandered out alone in the starlight, and at last he had followed her and found her—though she did not know he was near—standing where the roof of pine-trees made a darkness, and as he stood within four feet of her he had heard her cry to the desolate stillness:

" If I could see you once! If I could see you once—if I could touch you—if I could hear you speak—just once—just once! "

And she had wailed it low—but as a starving child might cry for bread. And he had turned and gone away, sick of soul, leaving her.

He had told this to Baird, and had seen the muscles of his face twitch and his eyes suddenly fill with tears. He had left his seat and crossed the room to conceal his emotion, and Latimer had known that he did not speak because he could not.

The letters were written with caution, Stamps had said, and the mention of names had been avoided in them; and, though he ground his teeth again as he thought of this, he realised that the knowledge brought by a name would be of no value to him. Long ago he had said to big Tom in the cabin on the hillside: " If ever we meet face to face knowing each other, I swear I will not spare him." Spare him? Spare him what? What vengeance could he work which would wipe out one hour of that past woe? None. He had grown sick to death in dwelling with the memories he could not bury. He had been born cursed by the temperament which cannot outlive. There are such. And it was the temperament to which vengeance brings no relief. No; if they two met face to face, what words could be said—what deeds could be done? His forehead and hands grew damp with cold sweat as he confronted the despair of it.

"Better that I should not know his name," he cried. "Better that we should never meet. Pray God that he is dead; pray God the earth does not hold him."

The man who had followed him had plainly but one purpose, which was the obtaining of money. He looked as if he needed it directly. He would go to him and pay him what he asked and get the papers. They must be in no other hands than his own. When he had them, Baird and himself would destroy them together, and that would be the end.

He encountered no difficulties when he went in search of the address Stamps had given him. The room he had directed him to was over a small store on the south side of Pennsylvania Avenue. When he entered it he saw at once that the man whose circumstances reduced him to living in it must be one whose need of money was great indeed. It was entirely unfurnished, except for a mattress lying on the floor, and Stamps was stretched upon it, coughing and feverish.

"Come in," he said. "I knowed ye'd be here purty soon. Thar ain't no chair to ax ye to set down in."

"I do not want to sit," said Latimer. "You are ill. You caught cold last night."

"I s'pose I did, durn it," answered Stamps. "I got drenched to the skin, an' I hadn't nothin' dry to put on when I got home. But I'd seen ye—an' told ye what I'd 'lowed to tell ye."

"Where are the papers you spoke of?" Latimer asked.

Stamps's feverish lips stretched themselves in an agreeable smile.

"They ain't yere," he answered; "an' they won't be yere till I've got the pay fur 'em. Ef thar was names in 'em they'd cost ye a heap more than five hundred dollars—an' they'd cost ye more anyhow ef I hadn't a use for that five hundred jest this particular time."

"Where are they?" enquired Latimer. He meant to waste no words.

"They're in North Ca'lliny," answered the little mountaineer, cheerfully. "An' I've got a woman thar es'll send 'em when I want 'em."

"She may send them when you wish."

Stamps fell into a paroxysm of coughing, clutching his side.

"Will ye give five hundred?" he panted when it was over.

"Yes."

"Ye want 'em pretty bad, do ye?" said Stamps, looking at him with a curiosity not untinged with dubiousness. He was sharp enough to realise that, upon the whole, his case was not a strong one.

"I don't want them for the reason you think I want them for," Latimer replied; his voice was cold and hard, and his manner unpromisingly free from emotion or eagerness. "I want them for a reason of my own. As for your pretence of recognising me as a man you have seen before, go out into the street corners and say what you choose. My friends know how and where my life has been spent, and you are shrewd enough to know how far your word will stand against mine. If you need the money now, you had better produce what you have to sell."

"I could get ye mightily talked about," said Stamps, restlessly.

"Try it," answered Latimer, and turned as if to walk out of the room. He knew what he was dealing with, and saw the fevered cupidity and fear in the little, shifting eyes.

Stamps struggled up into a sitting posture on his mattress and broke forth into coughs again.

"Come back yere," he cried between gasps; "ye needn't ter go."

Latimer paused where he stood and waited until the fit of coughing was over; and Stamps threw himself back exhausted. His shifty eyes burned uncannily, his physical and mental fever were too much for him. Linthicum had just left him before Latimer arrived, and upon the production of five hundred dollars rested the fate of the claim for the herds.

"Ef ye'll bring the money—cash down—next Saturday," he said, "I'll give ye the papers. I'll hev 'em yere by then. When ye've got 'em," with the agreeable grin again, "ye kin go to yer friend's far'well lecture easy in ye mind. Ye wouldn't be likely to go to many of 'em ef he knowed what I could tell him. He's powerful thick with Tom D'Willeby and Sheby. They think a heap of him. Tom must hev guessed what I've guessed, but he don't want no talk on accounts o' Sheby. Tom knows which side his bread's buttered—he ain't nigh as big a fool as he looks."

Latimer stood still.

"Next Saturday?" was his sole response. "In the meantime, I should advise you to send for the doctor."

He left him coughing and catching at his side.

CHAPTER XXXVII

DURING this week Judge Rutherford's every hour was filled with action and excitement. He had not a friend or acquaintance in either House whom he did not seek out and labour with. He was to be seen in the lobby, in the corridors, in committee-rooms, arguing and explaining, with sheafs of papers in his hands and bundles of documents bulging out of his pockets. He walked down the avenue holding the arm of his latest capture, his trustworthy countenance heated by his interest and anxiety, his hat thrust on the back of his head. "There's got to be justice done," he would protest. "You see, justice has got to be done. There's no other way out of it. And I'd swear there ain't a man among you who doesn't own up that it is justice, now all this evidence has been brought together. The country couldn't be responsible for throwing the thing over—even till another session. Everything's in black and white and sworn to and proved—and the papers Baird has sent in clinch the whole thing. Now just look here—" And he would repeat his story and refer to his documents, until even the indifferent succumbed through exhaustion, if not conviction.

He appeared at Dupont Circle two or three times a day, always fevered with delighted hope, always with some anecdote to relate which prognosticated ultimate triumph. If he could not find anyone else to talk to he seized upon Miss Burford or Uncle Matt and poured forth his news to them. He wrote exultant letters to Jenny, the contents of which, being given to Barnesville, travelled at once to Talbot's

401

Cross-roads and wakened it to exhilarated joyfulness, drawing crowds to the Post-office and perceptibly increasing the traffic on the roads from the mountains to that centre of civilised social intercourse.

"Tom's agwine to win his claim," it was said. "Judge Rutherford's walkin' it right through for him. Tom'll be way ahead of the richest man in Hamlin. Sheby 'll be a hairest. Lordy! what a sight it'll be to see 'em come back. Wonder whar they'll build!"

In Washington it had begun to be admitted even by the reluctant that the fortunes of the De Willoughby claim seemed to have taken a turn. Members of substantial position discussed it among themselves. It was a large claim, and therefore a serious one, but it had finally presented itself upon an apparently solid foundation.

"And it is the member from the mountain districts, and the old negro, and the popular minister who will have carried it through if it passes," said Senator Milner to his daughter. "It is a monumental thing at this crisis of affairs—a huge, unpopular claim on a resenting government carried through by persons impelled solely by the most purely primitive and disinterested of motives. An ingenuous county politician, fresh from his native wilds, works for it through sheer prehistoric affection and neighbourliness; an old black man —out of a story-book—forges a powerful link of evidence for mere faithful love's sake; a man who is a minister of the gospel, a gentleman and above reproach, gives to its service all his interest, solely because he cherishes an affectionate admiration for the claimants. Nobody has laboured with any desire for return. Nobody has bargained for anything. Nobody would accept anything if it was offered to them. The whole affair has been Arcadian."

In Connection with
The De Willoughby Claim

" Will it be decided for the De Willoughbys—will it? "
said Mrs. Meredith.

" Yes," answered the Senator; " I think it will. And
I confess I shall not advance any objections."

Meeting big Tom on the avenue, Ezra Stamps stopped
him.

" Tom," he wheezed, hoarsely, " I heern tell you was
likely ter git yer claim through."

" There are times when you can hear that about almost
any claim," answered Tom. " What I'm waiting for is to
hear that I've got it through."

Stamps gnawed his finger-nails restlessly.

" Ye're lucky," he said; " ye allus was lucky."

" How about the herds? " said Tom.

Stamps gave him an agonised look.

" Hev ye ever said anything agen me, Tom—to any man
with inflooence? Hev ye, now? 'Twouldn't be neighbourly of ye if ye hed—an' we both come from the Cross-
roads—an' I allus give ye my custom. Ye won't never go
agen me, will ye, Tom? "

" I've never been asked any questions about you," Tom
said. " Look here, you had better go to some hospital and
ask to be taken in. What are you walking about the street
for in that fix? You can scarcely breathe."

" I'm a-gwine to walk about until Saturday," answered
Stamps, with a grin. " I'm lookin' arter my own claim—
an' Abner Linthicum. Arter Saturday I'll lie up for a
spell."

" You'd better do it before Saturday," Tom remarked
as he left him.

Stamps stood and watched him walk away, and then
turned into a drug-store and bought a cheap bottle of cough

mixture. He was passing through the early stages of pneumonia, and was almost too weak to walk, but he had gone from place to place that morning like a machine. Linthicum had driven him. So long as he was employed in badgering other men he was not hanging about the agent's office. Linthicum was not anxious that he should be seen there too frequently. After the payment of the five hundred dollars there would be no more to be wrung from him, and he could be dropped. He could be told that it was useless to push the claim further. Until the five hundred was secured, however, he must be kept busy. Consequently, he went from one man to the other until he could walk no more. Then he crawled back to his room and sent a note to Latimer.

"I cayn't git the papers tel Saturday afternoon. Ef ye bring the money about seven ye ken hev them. 'Tain't no use comin' no earlier."

Latimer found the communication when he returned to his rooms in the evening. He had been out on business connected with Baird's final lecture. It was to be a special event, and was delivered in response to a general request. A building of larger dimensions than the hall previously used had been engaged. The demand for seats had been continuously increasing. The newspaper and social discussion of the prospects of the De Willoughby claim had added to the interest in Baird. This brilliant and popular man, this charming and gifted fellow, had felt such a generous desire to assist the claimants that he had gone South in the interest of their fortunes. He had been detained in Delisleville and could barely return in time to appear before his audience.

The enthusiasm and eagerness were immense. Every

man who had not heard him felt he must hear him now;
everyone who had heard him was moved by the wish to
be of his audience again. Latimer had been besieged on
all sides, and, after a hard day, had come home fagged and
worn. But he was not worn only by business interviews,
newspaper people, and applicants for seats which could not
be obtained. He was worn by his thoughts of the past days,
by his lack of Baird's presence and his desire for his return.
His influence was always a controlling and supporting one.
Latimer felt less morbid and more sane when they were
together.

This same night Senator Milner and Judge Rutherford
called in company at the house near the Circle. When
Uncle Matt opened the door for them Judge Rutherford
seized his hand and shook it vigorously. The Judge was in
the mood to shake hands with everybody.

" Uncle Matt," he said, " we're going to get it through,
and in a week's time you'll be a rich man's servant."

Matt fled back to Miss Burford trembling with joy and
excitement.

" Do ye think we is gwine t'rough, ma'am? " he said.
" D'ye think we is? Seems like we was the Isrilites a-cross-
in' the Red Sea, an' the fust of us is jest steppin' on de sho'.
Lordy, Miss Burford, ma'am, I don't know how I'se gwine
to stan' dat great day when we *is* th'ough, shore enuff.
Wash'n'ton city ain't gwine be big enuff to hol' me."

" It will be a great day, Uncle Matthew," replied Miss
Burford, with elated decorum of manner. " The De Willoughby mansion restored to its former elegance. Mr.
Thomas De Willoughby the possessor of wealth, and the
two young people—" She bridled a little, gently, and
touched her eyes with her handkerchief with a slight cough.

In Connection with
The De Willoughby Claim

"When Marse De Courcy an' Miss Delia Vanuxem was married, dar was people from fo' counties at de infar," said Matt. "De fust woman what I was married to, she done de cookin'."

Senator Milner was shaking hands with big Tom upstairs. He regarded him with interest, remembering the morning he had evaded an interview with him. The little room was interesting; the two beautiful young people suggested the atmosphere of a fairy story.

"You are on the verge of huge good fortune, I think, Mr. De Willoughby," he said. "I felt that I should like to come with Rutherford to tell you that all is going very well with your claim. Members favour it whose expression of opinion is an enormous weight in the balance. Judge Rutherford is going to speak for you—and so am I."

Judge Rutherford shook Tom's hand rather more vig-orously than he had shaken Matt's. "I wish to the Lord I was an orator, Tom," he said. "If I can't make them listen to me this time I believe I shall blow my brains out. But, what with Williams, Atkinson, and Baird, we've got things that are pretty convincing, and somehow I swear the claim has begun to be popular."

When the two men had gone the little room was for a few moments very still. Each person in it was under the influence of curiously strong emotion. Anxious waiting cannot find itself upon the brink of great fortune and re-main unmoved. Some papers with calculations worked out in them lay upon the table, and big Tom sat looking at them silently. Sheba stood a few feet away from him, her cheeks flushed, light breaths coming quickly through her parted lips. Rupert looked at her as youth and love must look at love and youth.

"Uncle Tom," he said, at last, "are you thinking of what we shall do if we find ourselves millionaires?"

"No," answered Tom.

His eyes rested on the boy in thoughtful questioning.

"No; I'll own I'm not thinking of that."

"Neither am I," said Rupert. He drew nearer to Sheba. "It would be a strange thing to waken and find ourselves owners of a fortune," he said. "We may waken to find it so—in a few days. But there is always a chance that things may fail one. I was thinking of what we should do if—we lose everything."

Sheba put out her slim hand. She smiled with trembling lips.

"We have been across the mountain," she said. "We came together—and we will go back together. Will you go back with us, Rupert?"

He took her in his strong young arms and kissed her, while Tom looked on.

"That is what I was thinking," he cried; "that it does not matter whether we win the claim or lose it. The house is gone and the store is gone, but we can add a room to the cabin in Blair's Hollow—we can do it ourselves—and I will learn to plough."

He dropped on one knee like a young knight and kissed her little, warm, soft palm.

"If I can take care of you and Uncle Tom, Sheba," he said, "will you marry me?"

"Yes, I will marry you," she answered. "We three can be happy together—and there will always be the spring and the summer and the winter."

"May she marry me, Uncle Tom," Rupert asked, "even though we begin life like Adam and Eve?"

" She shall marry you the day we go back to the mountains," said Tom. " I always thought Adam and Eve would have had a pretty fair show—if they had not left the Garden of Eden behind them when they began the world for themselves. You won't have left it behind you. You'll find it in the immediate vicinity of Talbot's Cross-roads."

CHAPTER XXXVIII

THE facts in detail which the Reverend John Baird had journeyed to Delisle County in the hope of being able to gather, he had been successful in gaining practical possession of. Having personal charm, grace in stating a case, and many resources both of ability and manner, he had the power to attract even the prejudiced, and finally to win their interest and sympathies. He had seen and conversed with people who could have been reached in no ordinary way, and having met them had been capable of managing even their prejudices and bitterness of spirit. The result had been the accumulation of useful and convincing evidence in favour of the De Willoughbys, though he had in more than one instance gained it from persons who had been firm in their intention to give no evidence at all. This evidence had been forwarded to Washington as it had been collected, and when Baird returned to the Capital it was with the knowledge that his efforts had more than probably put the final touches to the work which would gain the day for the claimants.

His train was rather late, and as it drew up before the platform he glanced at his watch in some anxiety. His audience for the lecture must already have begun to turn their faces toward the hall in which the evening's entertainment was to be held. He had hoped to reach his journey's end half an hour earlier. He had wanted a few minutes with Latimer, whose presence near him had become so much a part of his existence, that after an absence he felt he had lacked him. He took a carriage at the depot and drove quickly to their rooms. They were to leave them in a day or two and return to Willowfield. Already some of their possessions had been packed up. The sitting-room struck him as looking a little bare as he entered it.

" Is Mr. Latimer out," he asked the mulatto who brought up his valise.

" Yes, sir. He was called out by a message. He left a note for you on the desk."

Baird went to the desk and found it. It contained only a few lines.

" Everything is prepared for you. The audience will be the best you have had at any time. I have been sent for by the man Stamps. He is ill of pneumonia and wishes to deliver some letters to me. I will be with you before you go on the platform."

Since he had left Washington, Baird had heard from Latimer but once and then but briefly. He had felt that his dark mood was upon him, and this reference to letters recalled the fact.

" Stamps is the little man with the cattle claim," he commented to himself. " He comes from the neighbourhood of the Cross-roads. What letters could he have to hand over? "

And he began to dress, wondering vaguely.

. . . .

Stamps had spent a sleepless night. He could not sleep because his last interview with Linthicum had driven him hard, even though he had been able to promise him the required five hundred dollars; he also could not sleep because the air of the city had been full of talk about the promising outlook of the De Willoughby claim. Over the reports he had heard, he had raged almost with tears.

"The Dwillerbys is ristycrats," he had said. "They're ristycrats, an' it gives 'em a pull even if they was rebels an' Southerners. A pore man ez works hard an' ain't nothin' but a honest farmer, an' a sound Union man ain't got no show. Ef I'd been a ristycrat I could hev got inflooence ez hed hev pulled wires fur me. But I hain't nothin' but my loyal Union principles. I ain't no ristycrat, an' I never aimed to be none."

The bitterness of his nervous envy would have kept him awake if he had had no other reason for being disturbed, but most of all he was sleepless, because he was desperately ill and in danger he knew nothing of. Cold and weeks of semi-starvation, anxiety, excitement, and drenched garments had done the little man to death, and he lay raging with fever and stabbed with pain at each indrawn breath, tossing and gasping and burning, but thinking only of Linthicum and the herds and the scraps of paper which were to bring him five hundred dollars. He was physically wretched, but even while he was racked with agonised fits of coughing and prostrated with pain it did not occur to him to think that he was in danger. He was too wholly absorbed in other thoughts. The only danger he recognised was the danger that there might be some failure in his plans—that Linthicum might give him up—that the parson might back out of his bargain, realising that after all letters unsigned save by a man's Christian name were not substantial evidence. Perhaps he would not come at all; perhaps he would leave the city; perhaps if he came he would refuse to give more than half or quarter the sum asked. Then Linthicum would throw him over—he knew

Linthicum would throw him over. He uttered a small cry like a tortured cat.

"I know he'll do it," he said. "I seen it in his eye yesterday, when he let out on me an' said he was a-gettin' sick of the business. I shed hev kept my mouth shut. I'd said too much an' it made him mad. He'll throw me over Monday mornin' ef I don't take him the money on Sunday."

He ate nothing all through the day but lay waiting for the passing of the hours. He had calculated as to which post would bring the letter from Minty. He had written to tell her of the hiding-place in which he had kept the bits of paper safe and dry through all the years. She was to enclose them in a stout envelope and send them to him.

Through the long, dragging day he lay alone burning, gasping, fighting for his breath in the attacks of coughing which seemed to tear his lungs asunder. There was a clock in a room below whose striking he could hear each hour. Between each time it struck he felt as if weeks elapsed. Sometimes it was months. He had begun to be light-headed and to think queer things. Once or twice he heard a man talking in a croaking wail, and after a few minutes realised that it was himself, and that he did not know what he had said, though he knew he had been arguing with Linthicum, who was proving to him that his claim was too rotten to have a ghost of a chance. By the time the afternoon post arrived he was semi-delirious and did not know how it happened that he at last found himself holding Minty's letter in his hand. He laughed hysterically when he opened it. It was all right. There were the two yellowed sheets of paper—small sheets, written close, and in a peculiar hand. He had often studied the handwriting, and believed if he had seen it again he should know it. It was small but strong and characteristic, though that was not what he had called it.

"Ef I'd hed more time an' could hev worked it out more—an' got him to write suthin' down—I could hev hed more of a hold," he said, plaintively, "but Linthicum wouldn't give me no time."

The post arrived earlier than he had expected it, and this gave him time to lie and fret and listen again for the striking of the clock in the room downstairs. The waiting became too long, and as his fever increased he became insanely impatient and could not restrain himself. To lie and listen for his visitor's footsteps upon the stairs—to lie until seven o'clock—if he did not come till then, would be more than he could endure. That would give him too long to think over what Linthicum would do if the whole sum were not forthcoming—to think of the reasons why the parson might make up his mind to treat the letters as if they were worthless. He lay and gnawed his finger-nails anew.

"I wouldn't give nothin' for 'em ef I was in his place," he muttered. "Ef thar'd been anythin' in 'em that proved anythin' I should hev used 'em long sence. But then I'm a business man an' he's a parson, an' doesn't know nothin' about the laws. But he might go to some man—say a man like Linthicum—who could put him up to things. Good Lord!" in a new panic, "he mayn't come at all. He might jest stay away."

He became so overwrought by this agonising possibility that instead of listening for the striking of the clock, he began to listen for the sound of some passing footstep—the footstep of someone passing by chance who might be sent to the parson with a note. With intolerable effort and suf-

fering he managed to drag himself up and get hold of a
piece of paper and a pencil to write the following lines:

"The letters hes come. You'd as well come an' get 'em.
Others will pay for 'em ef ye don't want 'em yerself."

His writing of the last sentence cheered his spirits. It
was a support to his small, ignorant cunning. "He'll
think someone else is biddin' agen him," he said. "Ef
there was two of 'em biddin', I could get most anythin' I
axed."

After he had put the communication in an envelope he
dragged himself to the door almost bent double by the
stabbing pain in his side. Once there he sat down on the
floor to listen for footsteps.

"It's hard work this yere," he panted, shivering with
cold in spite of his fever, "but it's better than a-lyin' thar
doin' nothin'."

At length he heard steps. They were the running,
stamping feet of a boy who whistled as he came.

Stamps opened the door and whistled himself—a whistle
of summons and appeal. The boy, who was on his way
with a message to another room, hesitated a minute and
then came forward, staring at the sight of the little, un-
dressed, shivering man with his head thrust into the passage.

"Hallo!" he said, "what d'yer want?"

"Want ye to carry this yere letter to a man," Stamps got
out hoarsely. "I'll give ye a quarter. Will ye do it?"

"Yes." And he took both note and money, still staring
at the abnormal object before him.

When the messenger arrived Latimer was reading the
letters which had arrived by the last delivery. One of them
was from Baird, announcing the hour of his return to the

city. Latimer held it in his hand when Stamps's communication was brought to him.

"Tell the messenger that I will come," he said.

. . . .

It was not long before Stamps heard his slow approach sounding upon the bare wooden stairs. He mounted the steps deliberately because he was thinking. He was thinking as he had thought on his way through the streets. In a few minutes he should be holding in his hand letters written by the man who had been Margery's murderer—the letters she had hidden and clung to and sobbed over in the blackness of her nights. And they had been written twenty years ago, and Margery had changed to dust on the hillside under the pines. And nothing could be undone and nothing softened. But for the sake of the little old woman ending her days quietly in Willowfield—and for the sake of Margery's memory—yes, he wanted to save the child's memory—but for these things there would be no use in making any effort to secure the papers. Yet he was conscious of a dread of the moment when he should take them into his hand.

Stamps turned eager, miserable eyes upon him as he came in.

"I thought mebbe ye'd made up yer mind to let the other feller hev them," he said. "Hev ye brought the money in bills?"

Latimer stood and looked down at him. "Do you know how ill you are?" he said.

"Wal, I guess I kin feel a right smart—but I don't keer so's things comes my way. Hev ye got the moncy with ye?"

"Yes. Where are the papers?"

In Connection with
The De Willoughby Claim

" Whar's the money? "

Latimer took out a pocket-book and opened it that he might see.

Stamps's countenance relaxed. The tension was relieved.

" Thet's far an' squar," he said. " D'ye wanter know whar I found 'em? Tom Dwillerby never knowed I hed more than a envelope—an' I tuk care not to tell him the name that was writ on it. Ye was mighty smart never to let no one know yer name; I don't know how you done it, 'ceptin' that ye kept so much to yerselves."

Latimer remained silent, merely standing and letting him talk, as he seemed to have a feverish, half-delirious tendency to do. He lay plucking at the scanty bed-covering and chuckling.

" 'Twas five years arter the child was born," he went on. " I was ridin' through Blair's Holler an' it come to me sudden to go in an' hev a look round keerful. I looked keerful—mighty keerful—an' at last I went on my hands an' knees an' crawled round, an' there was a hole between the logs, an' I seen a bit of white—I couldn't hev seen it ef I hadn't been crawlin' an' looked up. An' I dug it out. It hed been hid mighty secret." He put his hand under his wretched pillow. " Give me the money," he wheezed. " When ye lay it in my hand I'll pass the envelope over to ye. Count it out first."

Latimer counted the bills. This was the moment. Twenty years gone by—and nothing could be changed. He put the money on the bed.

Stamps withdrew his hand from under the pillow. A stout, ill-directed envelope was in its grasp and he passed it over to Latimer. He was shivering and beginning to choke a little, but he grinned.

" I reckin' it's all right," he said. " D'ye want to read 'em now? "

" No," Latimer answered, and putting them in his breast-pocket walked out of the room.

He passed down the stairs and into the avenue where the lamps were lighted and which wore its usual somewhat deserted evening air. He walked along quietly for some minutes. He did not quite know where he was going. Having left a line for Baird explaining his absence, he had time to spare. If he wished to be alone, he could be so until the hour of the beginning of the lecture. For certain reasons it would be necessary that he should see Baird before he went upon the platform. Yes, he must be alone. His mood required it. He would go somewhere and look at the two yellowed letters written twenty years ago. He did not know why it was that he felt he must look at them, but he knew he must. They would satisfy no curiosity if he felt it, and he had none. Perhaps it was the old tragic tender feeling for Margery which impelled him. Perhaps he unconsciously longed to read that this man had loved her—that she had not given her life for nothing—that the story had not been one of common caprice and common treachery. As he walked his varied thoughts surged through his brain disconnectedly. Every now and then he involuntarily put his hand to his breast-pocket to feel the envelope. Once there crossed his mind a memory of the woman whose boy had died and who dare not let herself recall him, and so be swept back into the black maelstrom of woe. To-night, with these things on his breast, it was not twenty years since he had heard Margery's dying cries—it was last night—last night—and the odour of the pine-trees was in his nostrils —the sough of their boughs in his ears.

In Connection with
The De Willoughby Claim

He stopped near the entrance to the grounds of the Smithsonian Institute. They were as secluded as a private park at this time, but here and there was a seat and a light. He turned in and found his way to the most retired part where he could find these things—a bench to sit down on, a light to aid him to read. He heard his own breathing as he sat down; he felt the heavy, rapid pulsations of his heart, as he took the papers from his breast his hand was shaking, he could not hold it still. He took out more papers than the envelope Stamps had given him. He drew forth with this the letter which had arrived from Baird, and which he had been reading when the messenger arrived. He had abstractedly put it in his pocket. It fell from his shaking hand upon the ground at his feet, and he let it lie there, forgetful of its existence.

Then he withdrew the two letters from the large envelope and opened one of them.

．　．　．　．　．　．　．　．　．　．　．

He read them through once—twice—three times—four. Then he began again. He had read them a dozen times before he closed them. He had read them word by word, poring over each character, each turn of phrase, as a man might pore over an enigma or a document written in a foreign language of which he only knew stray words. If his hands had shaken at first, he had not turned a page before his whole body was shaking and his palms, his forehead, his hair were damp with cold dew. He had uttered one sharp, convulsed exclamation like a suffocated cry— then he went on reading—reading—reading—and shuddering as he read. They were not long letters, but after he had read them once he understood them, and each time he read them again he understood them better. Yes, he could

418

translate them. They were the farewells of a man tossed by
a whirlwind of passionate remorseful grief. The child had
been loved—her very purity had been loved while she had
been destroyed and deceived. The writer poured forth
heart-sick longing and heart-sick remorse. He had not at
first meant to conceal from her that he was not a free man
—then he had lost control over his very being—and he had
lost his soul. When she had discovered the truth and had
not even reproached him but had stood silent—without a
word—and gazed at him with her childish, agonised, blue-
flower eyes—he had known that if men had souls his was
damned. There was no pardon—he could ask none—pardon would not undo—death itself would not undo what he
had done. "Margery! Margery! Oh! child—God hear me
if there is God to hear—I loved you—I love you—Death
will not undo that either."

He was going abroad to join his wife. He spoke of the
ship he sailed on. Latimer knew its name and who had
sailed in it. In the second letter he besought her to let
him see and speak one word to her—but knew she would
not grant his prayer. He had seen her in the street, and
had not dared to approach. "I did not fear what a man
might fear from other women," he wrote. "I felt that it
might kill you, suddenly to see me near when you could
not escape."

And after he had read it a third time Latimer realised a
ghastly truth. The man who wrote had gone away unknowing of the blackness of the tragedy he had left behind. He plainly had not known the secret Death itself
had helped to hide. Perhaps when he had gone Margery
herself had not known the worst.

Latimer, having finished his reading, rested his head on

his hand for a dull moment and stared down at the letter lying upon the ground at his feet—the letter he had dropped as he took out the others. He felt as if he had not strength or inclination to pick it up—he had passed through a black storm which had swept away from him the power to feel more than a dull, heavy, physical prostration.

But after a few minutes he stooped and picked the letter up. He laid it on his knee by the other two and sat gazing again.

"He did not know," he said, in a colourless voice. "I told him. He heard it first from me when I told him how she died."

The handwriting of the letters was Baird's—every character and word and phrase were his—Baird was the man who had written them.

CHAPTER XXXIX

THE street in which the lecture hall stood began to wear the air of being a centre of interest some time before the doors of the building were opened. People who had not been able to obtain reserved seats wished to arrive early. The lectures which had begun by being popular had ended by being fashionable. At the outset an audience of sober, religious tendencies had attended them, but after the first one had been delivered other elements had presented themselves. There had been a sprinkling of serious scientific men, a prominent politician or so, some society women whose faces and toilettes were well-known and lavishly described in the newspapers. On this last night the audience was largely of the fashionable political world. Carriages drove up one after another and deposited well-dressed persons who might have been expected that night to appear at certain brilliant social functions, and who had come to hear " Repentance " instead.

" He has always had good audiences," said a member of the Committee of Arrangement, " but he has never had one like this—in Washington at least. There is the Secretary of State with his wife and daughter. I believe the President is to be here. He has awakened an enormous interest. The house will be literally crammed. They are filling the aisle with seats already."

Baird was in the small retiring-room which had been arranged for his convenience. His journey had somewhat fatigued him, and he was in the physical and mental condition to feel glad that this lecture was to be the last of the series. He was going back to Willowfield, though he was not to remain there. He had received a call from an important church in New York and had accepted it. He was endeavouring to make arrangements that Latimer could be near him. On his return this evening he had found a letter he had been expecting. It referred to Latimer, and he was anxious to talk it over with him. He wished he would come in, and felt a little restless over his delay, though he knew they would have time to say but few words to each other before it was time for the lecture to begin. He walked up and down the room looking down at the green carpet and thinking, his thoughts wandering vaguely to the little pursuant of the herd claim and the letters he had wanted to deliver. He smiled faintly, remembering the small frame in the over-large clothes and the bucolic countenance with its over-sharpness of expression.

The member of the committee looked into the room.

"They are beginning to turn people away from the doors," he said. "Half the Cabinet is here—I never saw such an audience."

As he went away smiling, someone passed him in entering the room. Baird, who was smiling also, changed his expression of courteous appreciation to a smile of greeting, for the man who had entered was Latimer.

He advanced, holding out his hand.

"I am glad you have come," he began to say. "I wanted at least a word with you before I went on."

Then his smile died out, leaving blank amazement which a breath's space later was alarmed questioning. He recalled later how for a second he stood and stared. Latimer's face was white and damp with sweat. Its lines were drawn and sunken deep. His eyes were fixed on the man before him with something which had a ghastly resemblance to an unsteady smile which was not a smile at all. He looked as if illness—or death—or madness had struck him. He did not seem a sane man, and yet a stillness so deadly was expressed by his whole being that it seemed to fill the small, neat, business-like green-room.

Baird strode towards him and seized him by the shoulder.

" What is it? What is it? What is it? " he cried out.

Latimer's face did not alter in a line. He fumbled stiffly in his breast-pocket and held out some pieces of yellowed letter-paper—this being done stiffly, too. He spoke in a hoarse whisper. It seemed to search every corner of the room and echo there.

" See! " he said. " These are two letters. A man wrote them to a poor, half-mad child twenty years ago."

The door opened, and the member of the committee looked in again, radiant with exultation.

" The audience waiting in such breathless silence that you might hear a pin drop. Two thousand of them, if there's one. Ten minutes to eight."

" Thank you," answered Baird.

The door closed again and he stood looking at Latimer's rigid hand and the papers.

" They were written to Margery," went on Latimer. " Stamps found them in a chink in the logs. She had hidden them there that she might take them out and sob over and kiss them. I used to hear her in the middle of the night."

Baird snatched them from his hand. He fell into a chair near the table and dropped his face upon the yellowed fragments, pressing them against his lips with awful sobbing sounds, as if he would wrest from them the kisses the long-dead girl had left there.

"I, too!" he cried. "I, too! Oh! my God! Margery!"

"Don't say 'God!'" said Latimer. "When she was dying, in an agony of fear, she said it. Not that word! Another!"

He said no other—and Latimer drew nearer to him.

"You wrote them," he said. "They are written in your hand—in your words—I should know them anywhere. You may deny it. I could prove nothing. I do not want to prove anything. Deny it if you will."

Baird rose unsteadily. The papers were clutched in his hand. His face was marred by the unnaturalness of a man's tears.

"Do you think I shall deny it?" he answered. "It is true. I have sat and listened to your talk of her and thought I should go quite mad. You have told me of her tortures, and I have listened. I did not know—surely she did not know herself—of the child—when I went away. It is no use saying to you—how should it be?—that I loved her—that I was frenzied by my love of her innocent sweetness!"

"No, there is no use," answered Latimer, in a voice actually void of emotion, "but I daresay it is true."

"There is no use in calling myself by any of the names invented for the men who bring about such tragedies. They are true of some men perhaps, but they were not true of me. I don't know what was true of me. Something worse than has ever been put into words perhaps, for I loved her and I have loved her for twenty years. I would have given up my career—my life, anything she had asked!"

"But when she found you had acted a lie to her——"

"It seemed to fill her with the frantic terror of a child. I dare not approach her. I think she thought she would be struck dead by Heaven. Great God! how I understood your story of her prayers. And it was I—it was I!"

He turned on Latimer with a kind of ferocity.

"You have crucified me!" he cried out. "Let that comfort you. You have crucified me by her side, that I might see her die—that I might hear her low little piteous voice—that I might see her throes and terrors. And I love her—and remember every look of her loving child's eyes—every curve and quiver of her mouth. Through all the years I have been crucified, knowing I had earned all that I felt."

Latimer moved across the room, putting the table between them. He went and stood by the mantel. A murmur of impatient applause from the audience came through the door.

"You loved her," he said, standing with his hand holding something in his breast. "And I loved you. She was the one brightness of my life when I was a boy and you were its one brightness when I was a man. You gave me a reason for living. I am not the kind of man to be my own reason. I needn't tell you what you have been to me. You were the one man on earth I dared to confess to. I knew you would understand and that you knew what pity was."

Baird groaned aloud. He wiped the sweat from his forehead with his handkerchief as he listened.

"I knew you were the one man I could trust. I could *trust* you. I could confide in you, and talk to you about Margery. One day you said to me that you had learned to love her and that we might have been brothers."

"When I was left free I had but one thought," Baird said, "to return to her—to atone, so far as atonement could be—to pray of her upon my knees. But she was dead—she was dead!"

"Yes, she was dead, and I had no one left to talk to about her. You were my one comfort and support and friend."

He drew his hand out of his breast. Baird started and then stood quite quiet. The hand held a pistol.

"Are you going to kill me?" he said. "You know I asked you that once before."

"No," said Latimer, "I am not going to kill you. I am going to kill the man who loved you, and found you his reason for living. It's all done with!"

"No! no!" shrieked Baird, and he hurled himself across the table like a madman. "No! You are not! No, Latimer! No! God! No!"

They were struggling together—Baird hung to his arm and tried to drag the pistol from his grasp. But it was no use; Latimer's long, ill-hung limbs were the stronger. His fixed face did not change, but he wrenched himself free and flung Baird across the room. He set the pistol against his heart and pulled the trigger. He gave something like a leap and fell down.

The door opened for the returning member of the committee and the impatient applause of the audience came through it almost a roar.

Baird was struggling to rise as if his fall had stunned him. Latimer was stretched at full length, quite dead.

CHAPTER XL

Tom walked up the staircase pondering deeply. The De Willoughby claim was before the House. Judge Rutherford was making his great speech, and the chief claimant might have been expected to be sitting breathless in one of the galleries. But he was not. He was going to Baird, who had sent for him, and Baird was sitting in the room in which Latimer lay dead with a bullet in his heart. He had been sitting there for hours, and when Tom had arrived at the house he had been told that Baird had asked that he should be taken to him in the death-chamber. He was sitting on a chair by the bed on which Latimer was stretched, rigid with a still face, which looked like a mask of yellow wax, appearing above the exceeding freshness of the turned-down linen sheet. Baird did not move as Tom entered, but continued to gaze at the dread thing with dull, drooping eyes. Tom went to him and laid his hand on his shoulder. He saw the man was stupefied.

" There's nothing to say, Baird," he said after a silence, " when it comes to this."

" There is something for me to say," Baird answered, very quietly. " I want to say it before him, while he lies there. I wonder if he will hear? "

" He may."

" It would not do any good to anyone if he did," Baird said. " The blackness of it all lies in that—that he would not be helped, she would not be helped—I should not."

" She? " said Tom.

Baird got up at once, stiffly and unsteadily. He stood upright, the lithe-limbed slender form, which was so much admired upon the platform, held rigidly. His face looked lined and haggard.

"No other man shall feel an affection for me—I think you are beginning to feel an affection for me—under a false impression. That man loved me for long years, and I loved him. I think I helped him to something that was as near happiness as his nature would allow him to feel. God knows I owed it to him. I was one of those who repented too late. That is why I have preached of repentance. I have done it with a secret, frenzied hope."

"Did he know your reason?" asked Tom.

"Not until last night. When he knew it, he killed himself."

"Because—?" began Tom.

"Because he had loved and trusted me for half a lifetime—because I was the one human creature to whom he had confided the tragedy of his life—knowing he would be sure of comprehension and sympathy. It was to me he poured forth the story of that poor child. You saw her die. She was his sister. And I——"

Tom turned and looked at the face of the dead man and then, slowly, to the face of the living one, who stood before him.

"You—were the man?" he said.

"Yes."

Tom turned to the dead man again. He put his big, warm hand with a curiously suggestive movement—a movement somehow suggesting protection—upon the stiff, clasped fingers.

"No, poor fellow!" he said, as if speaking to him. "You

—no, no, there was nothing but this—for you. God have mercy on us."

"No," said Baird, "there was nothing else for him. I know that. Everything was whirled away. I had hours last night thinking there is nothing else for me. Perhaps there is not. But first I shall take his body back to his mother. I must tell her lies. This is the result of an accident. That is what I shall tell her. She is a little old woman who will not live long. I must take care of her— and let her talk to me about her son who loved me—and her daughter."

He began to walk up and down the room.

"A man does not live—for fifteen years—side by side with another—that other loving him wholly—and see the blackness of his own deed laid bare—and hear again and again of the woe he has wrought—he does not live so in peace."

"No," answered Tom.

"I tell you—" wildly—"I tell you there have been hours —as he has talked to me of her—when the cold sweat has stood upon my flesh."

He came back to Tom. He was frantic with agonised restlessness.

"In all the cruelty of it," he cried, "there seems to have been one human pitying soul. It was yours. You were tender to her in those last hours. You were merciful— you held her hand when she died."

"Yes," said Tom, in a somewhat husky voice, since he remembered it so well, "she was frightened. Her little hand was cold. I took it in mine and told her not to be afraid."

Baird flung out his own hand with a movement of passionate feeling—then let it fall at his side.

"We shall not meet again," he said, "you will not want to see me."

Big Tom gave him a long, steady look.

"Good Lord, man!" he said, after it, "am I the man to judge another? I've made nothing of life."

"You have done no creature a wrong," Baird said. "And you have helped some to happiness."

"Well," admitted Big Tom, "perhaps that's true. But I've been a lumbering failure myself. I've just judgment enough now to know that there's nothing a man can say about a thing like this—nothing—and just sense enough not to try to say it."

"If you go back to North Carolina," asked Baird, "may I come to see you—and to see her? She need never know."

"I shouldn't want her to know," Tom answered, "but you may come. We shall go back, and I intend to let those two young ones set up a Garden of Eden of their own. It will be a good thing to look on at. Yes, you may come."

"That is mercifulness," said Baird, and this time when he put out his hand he did not withdraw it, and Tom gave it a strong, sober clasp which expressed more than one emotion.

.   .   .   .

When Tom returned to the little house near Dupont Circle, Uncle Matt wore a rigidly repressed air as he opened the door, and Miss Burford stood in the hall as if waiting for something. Her ringlets were shaken by a light tremor.

"We have either won the claim this afternoon or lost it," Tom said to himself, having glanced at both of them and exchanged the usual greeting.

They had won it.

In Connection with
The De Willoughby Claim

Judge Rutherford was striding up and down the sitting-room, but it was Sheba who was deputed to tell the news.

She did it in a little scene which reminded him of her childhood. She drew him to a chair and sat down on his knee, clasping both slim, tender arms round his neck, tears suddenly rushing into her eyes.

"You and Rupert are rich men, Uncle Tom, darling," she said. "The claim has passed. You are rich. You need never be troubled about mortgages again."

He was conscious of a tremendous shock of relief. He folded her in his arms as if she had been a baby.

"Thank the Lord!" he said. "I didn't know I should be so glad of it."

CHAPTER XLI

THE unobtrusive funeral cortége had turned the corner of Bank Street and disappeared from view almost an hour ago. In the front room of the house in which had lived the man just carried to his grave, the gentle old woman who had been his mother sat and looked with pathetic patience at Miss Amory Starkweather as the rough winds of the New England early spring rushed up the empty thoroughfare and whirled through the yet unleafed trees. Miss Amory had remained after the other people had gone away, and she was listening to the wind, too.

"We are both old women," she had said. "We have both lived long enough to have passed through afternoons like this more than once before. Howsoever bad other hours may be, it seems to me that these are always the worst."

"Just after—everything—has been taken away," Mrs. Latimer said now; "the house seems so empty. Faith," tremulously, "even Faith can't help you not to feel that everything has gone—such a long, long way off."

She did not wipe away the tear that fell on her cheek. She looked very small and meek in her deep mourning. She presented to Miss Amory's imagination the figure of a lovable child grown old without having lost its child temperament.

"But I must not complain," she went on, with an effort to smile at Miss Amory's ugly old intelligently sympathetic countenance. "It must have been all over in a second, and he could have felt no pain at all. Death by accident

is always an awful shock to those left behind; but it must
scarcely be like death to—those who go. He was quite
well; he had just bought the pistol and took it out to
show to Mr. Baird. Mr. Baird himself did not understand
how it happened."

"It is nearly always so—that no one quite sees how
it is done," Miss Amory answered. "Do not let yourself
think of it."

She was sitting quite near to Mrs. Latimer, and she leaned
forward and put her hand over the cold, little, shrivelled
one lying on the lap of the mourning-dress.

"Though it was so sudden," she said, "it was an end
not unlike Margery's—the slipping out of life without realising that the last hour had come."

"Yes; I have thought that, too."

She looked up at the portrait on the wall—the portrait
of the bright girl-face. Her own face lighted into a smile.

"It is so strange to think that they are together again,"
she said. "They will have so much to tell each other."

"Yes," said Miss Amory; "yes."

She got up herself and went and stood before the picture.
Mrs. Latimer rose and came and stood beside her.

"Mr. Baird has been with me every day," she said. "He
has been like a son to me."

A carriage drew up before the house, and, as the occupant got out, both women turned to look.

Mrs. Latimer turned a shade paler.

"They have got back from the funeral," she said. "It
is Mr. Baird."

Then came the ring at the front door, the footsteps in
the passage, and Baird came into the room. He was haggard and looked broken and old, but his manner was very

gentle when he went to the little old woman and took her hands.

"I think he scarcely knew he had so many friends at Janney's Mills," he said. "A great many of them came. When I turned away the earth was covered with flowers."

He drew her to a chair and sat by her. She put her white head on his arm and cried.

"He was always so sad," she said. "He thought people never cared for him. But he was good—he was good. I felt sure they must love him a little. It will be better for him—*now*."

Miss Amory spoke from her place before the fire, where she stood rigidly, with a baffled look on her face. Her voice was low and hoarse.

"Yes," she said, with eager pitifulness. "It will be better now."

The little mother lifted her wet face, still clinging to Baird's arm as she looked up at him.

"And I have it to remember," she sobbed, "that you—*you* were his friend, and that for years you made him happier than he had ever been. He said you gave him a reason for living."

Baird was ashen pale. She stooped and softly kissed the back of his hand.

"Somehow," she said, "you seemed even to comfort him for Margery. He seemed to bear it better after he knew you. I shall not feel as if they were quite gone away from me while I can talk to you about them. You will spare an hour now and then to come and sit with me?" She looked round the plain, respectable little room with a quiet finality. "I am too old and tired to live long," she added.

It was Baird who kissed her hand now, with a fervour

almost passion. Miss Amory started at sight of his action, and at the sound of the voice in which he spoke.

" Talk to me as you would have talked to him," he said. " Think of me as you would have thought of him. Let me—in God's name, let me do what there is left me! "

. . . .

Miss Amory's carriage had waited before the gate, and when she went out to it Baird went with her.

After he had put her into it he stood a moment on the pavement and looked at her.

" I want to come with you," he said. " May I? "

" Yes," she answered, and made room for him at her side.

But he took the seat opposite to her and leaned back, shutting his eyes while Miss Amory's rested upon him. The life and beauty which had been such ever-present characteristics of his personality seemed to have left him never to return. Miss Amory's old nerves were strung taut. She had passed through many phases of feeling with regard to him as the years had gone by. During those years she had believed that she knew a hidden thing of him known by no other person. She had felt herself a sort of silent detective in the form of an astute old New England gentlewoman. She had abhorred and horribly pitied him. She had the clear judicial mind which must inevitably see the tragic pitifulness of things. She had thought too much to be able to indulge in the primitive luxury of unqualified condemnation. As she watched him to-day during their drive through the streets, she realised that she beheld a kind of suffering not coming under the head of any ordinary classification. It was a hopeless, ghastly thing, a

breaking up of life, a tearing loose of all the cords to which
a man might anchor his existence.

When they reached the house and entered the parlour,
she went to her chair and sat down—and waited. She
knew she was waiting, and believed she knew what for.
In a vague way she had always felt that an hour like this
would come to them. They were somehow curiously akin.
Baird began to walk to and fro. His lips were trembling.
Presently he turned towards the rigid figure in the chair
and stood still.

"It was not an accident," he said. "He killed himself."

"That I felt sure of," Miss Amory answered. "Tell
me why he did it."

Baird began to tremble a little himself.

"Yes, I will," he said. "I must. I suppose—there is
a sort of hysteric luxury in—confession. He did it because
there was nothing else left. The foundations of his world
had been torn from under his feet. Everything was gone."
His voice broke into a savage cry. "Oh! in one short lifetime—the black misery a man can bring about!"

"Yes," said Miss Amory.

He threw himself into a chair near her.

"For years—years," he said, "he hid a secret."
Miss Amory bent forward. She felt she must help him
a little—for pity's sake.

"Was it the secret of Margery?" she half whispered.
"Did you know it?"

"When a woman has spent a long life alone, thinking—
thinking," she answered, "she has had time to learn to
observe and to work at problems. The day she fainted in
the street and I took her home in my carriage, I began
to fear—to guess. She was not only a girl who was ill—

she was a child who was being *killed* with some horror; she was heart-breaking. I used to go and see her. In the end I knew."

" I—did not," he said, looking at her with haggard eyes.

There was a long pause. She knew he had told her all in the one sentence—all she had guessed.

" She did not know I knew," she went on, presently. " She believed no one knew. Oh, I tell you again, she was heart-breaking! She did not know that there were wild moments when she dropped words that could be linked into facts and formed into a chain."

" Had you formed it," he asked, " when you wrote and told me she had died? "

" Yes. It had led me to you—to nothing more. I felt death had saved her from what would have been worse. It seemed as if—the blackest devil—would be glad to know."

" I am the blackest devil, perhaps," he said, with stony helplessness, " but when I received your letter I was grovelling on my knees praying that I might get back to her —and atone—as far as a black devil could."

" And she was *dead*," said Miss Amory, wringing her hands together on her lap; " dead—dead."

She stopped suddenly and turned on him. " He killed himself," she cried, " because he found out that it was *you!* "

" Yes. I was the one man he loved—he had told his secret to me—to *me!*—the black devil. Now—now I must go to his mother, day after day, and be her son—because I was his friend—and knew his love for Margery—and of her sweetness—and her happy, peaceful death. He used to talk to me for hours; she—poor, tender soul—will talk to me again—of Margery—Margery—Margery—and of Lucien, whose one happiness I was."

"It will — almost — be — enough," said Miss Amory, slowly.

"Yes," he answered; "it will almost be enough—even for a black devil."

And he turned on his chair and laid his face on his folded arms and sobbed like a woman.

CHAPTER XLII

THE springtime sunshine had been smiling upon Talbot's Cross-roads all the day. It was not hot, but warm, and its beauty was added to by the little soft winds which passed through the branches of the blossoming apple and pear trees and shook the fragrance from them. The brown earth was sweet and odorous, as it had been on the Sunday morning Sheba had knelt and kissed it, and the garden had covered itself, as then, with hyacinths and daffodils and white narcissus.

During the last weeks the Cross-roads had existed in something like a state of delirium. People rode in from the mountains and returned to their homes after hours of conversation, semi-stupefied with enjoyment. Tom D'Willerby had won his claims. After months of mystified discouragement, in which the Cross-roads seemed to have lost him in a vague and distant darkness, life had seemed to begin again. Nobody was sufficiently analytical of mind to realise in what measure big Tom D'Willerby had been the centre of the community, which was scattered over miles of mountain road and wood and clearing. But when he had disappeared many things seemed to melt away with him. In fact, a large, shrewd humanity was missing.

"I'll be doggered," had been a remark of Mr. Doty's in the autumn, "ef crops hes done es well sence he went."

There had been endless talk of the villanous tendencies of Government officials, and of the tricks played whose end was to defraud honest and long-suffering claimants of their rights. There had even been dark hours when it had seemed possible that the vitiating effect of Washington life might cause deterioration in the character of even the most upright. Could Tom himself stand it, and what would be its effect on Sheba?

But when the outlook was the most inauspicious, Fortune's wheel had swept round once and all was changed.

A letter brought the news—a simple enough letter from Tom himself. The claim was won. They were coming back to Hamlin County, he and Sheba and Rupert De Willoughby. Sheba and Rupert were to be married and spend the first weeks of their honeymoon on the side of the mountain which had enclosed the world the child Sheba had first known.

On this particular day every man and woman who had known and played with her appeared at the Cross-roads. There had not been a large number of them perhaps, but gathered together at and about the Post-office and about the house and garden, they formed a crowd, as crowds are counted in scattered communities. They embodied excitement enough to have exhilarated a much larger body of people. Half a dozen women had been helping Aunt Mornin for days. The house wore a gala air, and the cellar was stored with offerings of cake and home-made luxuries. The garden was a mass of radiant scented bloom of spring. Mis' Doty sat at the open window of the kitchen and, looking out on nodding daffodils, apple-blossom, and pink peach-flower warmed in the sun, actually chuckled as she joyfully sniffed the air.

" The way them things smells," she said, " an' the hum-

min' o' them bees goin' about as ef the world hadn't nothin'
but flowers an' honey in it, seems like it was all jest got
up for them two young uns. Lordy, I do declar', it's a
plum sight."

" That bin a heap got up for 'em, seems like," said
Molly Hollister, smiling at the nearest apple-tree as if it
were a particular friend. " Fust off, they're dead in love
with each other, an' we uns all knows how that makes
people feel—even in the dead o' winter, an' when they
ain't a penny in their pockets; they're as good-hearted
as they kin be—an' es hansum'—an' they're rich, an' they
was married this mornin', an' they're comin' home with
Tom D'Willerby to a place an' folks that loves 'em—an'
the very country an' the things that grows seems as if
they was dressed out for a weddin'. An' it's Sheba as
Tom took me to look at lyin' in her little old wooden
cradle in the room behind the store."

She laughed, as she said it, a little hysteric laugh, with
suddenly moist eyes. She was an emotional creature.

The road had been watched steadily for many hours before any arrival could have been legitimately expected. It
gave restless interest—something to do. At noon one of
Molly Hollister's boys came running breathlessly up the
road, waving his hat.

" They're a-comin'! " he shouted. " They're a-comin'!
They're in a fine carriage."

" Let Tom D'Willerby alone for havin' the finest team
in Hamlin," said Mr. Doty, with a neighbourly grin.

Almost immediately the carriage was to be seen. The
horses lifted their feet high, and stepped at a pace which
was felt worthy of the occasion. Uncle Matt drove. Rupert and Sheba sat side by side. They looked very young

and beautiful, and rather shy. They had only been married a few hours, and were bewildered by the new radiance of things. Big Tom humanely endeavoured not to look at them, but found it difficult to avert his eyes for any length of time. There was that about them which drew his gaze back in spite of himself.

"That's old Tom!" he heard familiar voices proclaim, as they drew near the Post-office. "Howdy, Tom! Howdy, Sheby! Wish ye much joy! Wish ye much joy!"

Then the horses stopped, and the crowd of long-known faces surged near and were all about the carriage. The clamour of the greeting voices, the grasping of one hand after another seemed to Sheba and Rupert like something happening in a dream. They were too far away from earth to feel it real just now, though it was part of the happiness of things—like the sunshine and the soft wind and the look in Tom's eyes, when, amid hand-shakes and congratulations, and welcoming laughter, he himself laughed back in his old way.

"Ye look jest like ye used ter, Tom—jest like ye used ter," cried Jake Doty. "Ye hain't changed a durned bit!"

•   •   •   •   •   •   •

How did the day pass? Who knows? What does it matter? It was full of strange beauty, and strange happiness, and strange life for two young souls at least. People came and went, congratulating, wondering, rejoicing. Talbot's Cross-roads felt that it had vicariously come into the possession of wealth and dignity of position. Among the many visitors, Mrs. Stamps rode up on a clay-bank mare. She was attired in the black calico riding-skirt and sunbonnet which represented the mourning garb of the mountain relict.

"I'm a widder," she said to big Tom, in a tone not unresigned. "Ye got yer claim through, but Stamps hadn't no influence, an' he was took off by pneumony. Ketched cold runnin' to Linthicum, I guess. His landlady was a honest enough critter. She found a roll o' five hundred dollars hid in his bed when she went to lay him out, an' she sent it back to me. Lord knows whar he got it from— I don't. But it come in mighty handy."

By sunset the welcoming crowd had broken up and melted away into the mountains. Horses and ox-waggons had been mounted and ridden or driven homeward. The Post-office was closed; no one was to be seen in the porch. No one was to be seen anywhere except in the garden among the blossoms where Rupert and Sheba walked under the fragrance of the trees, talking to each other in low, softly broken words.

Tom sat in the porch and watched the moon rise in a sea of silver. The scents the wind wafted to him, the occasional sound of a far-off night-bird, the rustle of the leaves brought things back to him—things he had felt in his youth. There had been nights like this in the days when he had been a big, clumsy young fellow, wild with hopeless love for Delia Vanuxem. On such nights the air had been full of this night breath of flowers, the birds had stirred in their nests with just such sounds, the moon had mounted, as it did to-night, higher and higher in a sky it thrilled a man's soul to lift his face to.

"Yes, it was all like this," he said, leaning back and clasping his big hands behind his head. "Just like this! And those two out there are living it over again, only they've been fairly treated, and they are trembling with the joy of it. They're pretty safe," he ended. "They're pretty safe. They've had a fair show."

Rupert and Sheba walked slowly side by side. They saw and felt everything. If a bird stirred with a sleepy sound, they stopped to listen and smiled tremulously at each other. More than once Sheba knelt down and hid her face among the flowers, kissing them. Her arms were full of white blossoms. She and Rupert had made white garlands for her hair and waist, such as she had worn the night he had first seen her standing on her little balcony. When Rupert held her to his side, the scent from their crushed petals filled the air they breathed. The early night was at its stillest and fairest, and the moonlight seemed to flood all the world, when Sheba stopped and looked up, speaking softly:

"Shall we go now?" she said. "The moon will be shining down between the pines. It will be so quiet."

"Yes," he answered. "Let us go now."

They had planned weeks ago the things they were going to do. They were going to say good-night to the small mound at Blair's Hollow.

When they left their horses at the foot of the hill even the pines could not look darkly under the fair light. The balmy air passing through their branches made a sound as if it was hushing a child to sleep.

The little mound lay in the soft brightness of clear moon-beams. Sheba knelt beside it and began to lay her bridal blossoms on the grass-covered earth. Rupert stood and watched her. His heart beat with a reverent, rapturous tremor. She looked like a young angel.

She bent down and laid her cheek upon the grass; her

arm was thrown out as if she clasped something to her girl's breast. She spoke in a whisper—thrilled with love. "I am happy," she said. "I am happy. Oh, do you hear? Do you hear?"

THE END.

In Connection with
The De Willoughby Claim

12mo. $1.50

MRS. BURNETT'S new novel is a literary event of the highest importance. From first to last one reads on with breathless interest of the winning of the great claim which was to reinstate good-natured "Big Tom" De Willoughby in his birthright. Interwoven with it is the story of a woman deceived by the man of whom the world would have least expected it, his identity being effectually concealed till the terrible revelation of the dramatic final chapters. The fate of the heartless fanatic who stood nearest the loving couple, brutal in his loyalty to his idea of the right, has a dramatic significance which is intensified in the light of his past conduct.

As if to compensate, however, for the mother's grief, her child survives her; and in this beautiful child-life Mrs. Burnett has added another charming portrait to her gallery of juvenile characters. How Tom De Willoughby's life was saved from blackness and desolation and made to overflow with happiness—this the reader will learn for himself.

The tragedy of the story, intensified by the contrast of the fanatical New England temper with Southern chivalry and kindness, is not its only side. The love between a beautiful, romantic child and a strong man who is her protector fills the book with a sweetness that matches its dramatic fire.

Uniform Edition of Novels and Stories

❧ ❧ ❧

" Mrs. Burnett discovers gracious secrets in rough and forbidding natures — the sweetness that often underlies their bitterness — the soul of goodness in things evil. She seems to have an intuitive perception of character. If we apprehend her personages, and I think we do clearly, it is not because she describes them to us, but because they reveal themselves in their actions. Mrs. Burnett's characters are as veritable as Thackeray's."—R. H. STODDARD

❧ ❧ ❧

That Lass o' Lowrie's

12mo. $1.25

" No character in modern fiction is drawn with a surer hand than Jean Lowrie. The interest of the book is intense, and the skill and delicacy with which the leading incidents of the story are managed compel the admiration of the critical reader. . . . We know of no more powerful work from a woman's hand in the English language, not even excepting the best of George Eliot's."
—*Boston Transcript.*

❧ ❧ ❧

Haworth's

Illustrated. 12mo. $1.25

" One of the few great American novels."—*Hartford Courant.*
" A product of genius of a very high order."—*The Nation.*

❧ ❧ ❧

Through One Administration

12mo. $1.50

" As a study of Washington life, dealing largely with what might be called social politics, it is certainly a success. As a society novel it is indeed quite perfect."—*The Critic.*

" Mrs. Frances Hodgson Burnett never wrote a dull story in her life."—LONDON TRUTH

* * *

A Lady of Quality

Being a most curious, hitherto unknown history, related by Mr. Isaac Bickerstaff, but not presented to the World of Fashion through the pages of the *Tatler*, and now for the first time written down.

12mo. $1.50

"A story which may safely be counted on to interest a wide circle of readers. It has the charm of romance, of an ingenious plot, and it is composed with skill in the language of the period described."—*New York Tribune.*

" Mistress Clorinda Wildairs is a heroine of whom any author might be proud. It is something to have written ' Through One Administration' and ' That Lass o' Lowrie's,' but it is a greater thing than all, in an age in which the dispassionate historical student begins to wonder whether woman has abandoned all her old privileges in order to compete on equal terms with man, to come across such a lady as appears in the ' Lady of Quality,' a heroine wrought out of all those indefinable qualities of conquering womanhood with which we were more familiar in the earlier ages than we are now."—*London Telegraph.*

" Clorinda is a character that will live, for she is of real flesh and blood. The story is one of the most original and vigorous that we have read in many a long day."—*Chicago Tribune.*

" It appears to me the most interesting and remarkable thing Mrs. Burnett has done. Clorinda as vixen, mistress, and murderess, yet remaining withal the matchless Clorinda, and finding her soul and her womanhood through all this stress and storm, is indeed a bold conception, . . . always radiant, beautiful, witty, triumphant, rose-crowned, the toast of the beaux, and the envy of the belles, inimitable whether in conversation or equitation, half angel, and half demon, and all a wonder and a wild desire. . . . Few lady novelists among her contemporaries have excelled Mrs. Burnett, either in virility or in femininity, and ' A Lady of Quality' will add a new field to her already ample province."—*I. Zangwill.*

❧ ❧ ❧

The Pretty Sister of José

With 12 illustrations by C. S. Reinhart

12mo. $1.00

" ' The Pretty Sister of José ' is delightfully written ; and the bull-fight scenes, especially the last, are pieces of genuinely graphic description."—*The Academy*.

" Simple and unassuming as the little story is, it is as artistic as anything which its distinguished author has written."—*The Congregationalist*.

" It is altogether a vivid, bewitching, tropical little story, and one which leaves in one's memory a fragrance as of the flowers of the far South.   It shines among modern stories like a scarlet-plumed tanager among sober sparrows and linnets.   Too many such tales might dazzle and weary, but an occasional one brightens the day."—*Boston Transcript*.

❧ ❧ ❧

The One I Knew the Best of All
A Memory of the Mind of a Child

Richly and abundantly illustrated by R. B. Birch

12mo. $2.00

" This ' Memory of the Mind of a Child ' has the engaging candor and transparency of all sincere autobiography, yet it is revealed with such exquisite delicacy and absence of self-consciousness that we forget that the child heroine is Mrs. Burnett *in petto*.   .   .   .   As a foreshadowing of the career of the future author, the chapter on Literature and the Doll is significant. The dramatized stories through which she 'talked to herself' are marvellously real, and related with such dash and fire and *abandon* that the reader is carried breathlessly along in the wake of the thrilling adventures befalling the unconquerable Doll and the Green Arm-Chair."—Mrs. KATE DOUGLAS WIGGIN.

" With all its blending of simple pathos and childish humor, with the innumerable delicately sympathetic touches, with the quaint terms of expression and the genial reflection of the fancy of a gifted child, the book will please many people."—*London Times*.

"She is undoubtedly one of the foremost writers of the day, any one of whose works carries with it delight, power, and artistic skill."—PHILADELPHIA TIMES

* * *

Louisiana

12mo. $1.25

" A delightful little story, original and piquant in design, and carried out with great artistic skill."—*Boston Saturday Evening Gazette.*

* * *

A Fair Barbarian

12mo. $1.25

" To store 'infinite riches in a little room' seems to be, among modern novelists, the gift pre-eminently of Mrs. Burnett. And as a song will haunt when a symphony is forgotten, so while 'One Administration' may win its author hundreds of friends, thousands will be won to her by 'The Fair Barbarian.'"—*Boston Transcript.*

* * *

Surly Tim

And Other Stories

12mo. $1.25

" Uncommonly vigorous and truthful stories of human nature."—*Chicago Tribune.*

* * *

Vagabondia

A Love Story

12mo. $1.25

" One of the sweetest love-stories ever written."—*Brooklyn Eagle.*

* * *

Earlier Stories

FIRST SERIES—Theo—Miss Crespigny—Lindsay's Luck
SECOND SERIES—Pretty Polly Pemberton—Kathleen

2 vols. 12mo. Each, $1.25

" These are love stories pure and simple, told with the dramatic power and sympathetic touch which make her works so fascinating."—*Public Opinion.*

"It is a story to linger over in the reading, it is so brightly, frankly, sweetly, and tenderly written, and to remember and return to. In creating her little gentlewoman, 'Sara Crewe,' so fresh, so simple, so natural, so genuine, and so indomitable, Mrs. Burnett has added another child to English fiction. No one who reads this story can read it without feeling or can doubt the loving genius of Mrs. Burnett."—R. H. STODDARD.

"'Little Saint Elizabeth' is one of the most winning and pathetic of Mrs. Burnett's child heroines. The fairy tales which follow her history, retold from a lost fairy book, are quite charming."—*The Athenæum.*

❈ ❈ ❈

Piccino
And Other Child Stories
Illustrated by R. B. Birch

"The history of Piccino's 'two days' is as delicate as one of the anemones that spring in the rock walls facing Piccino's Mediterranean—a study rather than a story of child life. . . . It is indeed a tribute to Mrs. Burnett's faculty to inspire sympathy for her creations, that Piccino, like every other wee creature she has devised, tempts one to stoop and caress him. . . . The other stories in the book have the charm of their predecessor in material and manner."—Mrs. BURTON HARRISON.

❈ ❈ ❈

Giovanni and the Other
Children Who have Made Stories
Illustrated by R. B. Birch

"There is a tender pathos in these simple tales and a gentle, loving spirit that gives the book a peculiar charm."—*Philadelphia Times.*

"Beyond all doubt Mrs. Burnett is a born story-teller, and that she has the artist's temperament and power we see on every page."—*The Critic.*

"Stories beautiful in tone, and style, and color."—KATE DOUGLAS WIGGIN.

CHARLES SCRIBNER'S SONS, Publishers
153–157 FIFTH AVENUE, NEW YORK